WHEN THE DEVIL DRIVES

Chris Brookmyre

**WINDSOR
PARAGON**

First published 2012
by Little, Brown
This Large Print edition published 2012
by AudioGO Ltd
by arrangement with
Little, Brown Book Group

Hardcover   ISBN: 978 1 445 84673 6
Softcover   ISBN: 978 1 445 84674 3

British Library Cataloguing in Publication Data available

Printed and bound in Great Britain by
MPG Books Group Limited

For Greg Dulli

PART I

PART I

This Filthy Witness

I took her life.

I cannot deny it, never have done, at least not to myself. Beneath a vast, black, star-spattered Highland sky, with our colleagues, our friends oblivious in the great house near by, I took her life.

I took her life, and my life was the better for her death. That is undeniable also; unpalatable, perhaps, an ugly truth but a truth just the same.

I have lived with this for three decades. I will not lie and claim not a day goes by that I don't see her face; that may have been true once, during those first months, even first years, but in time the intervals between my recollections became greater, the fear incrementally diminished, the guilt more dilute. I can still see her now though, as vividly as on that night. I can still picture her face vibrantly alive, filled with colour and expression; and I can picture it blank and empty and drained, like a reflection of the full moon above. My memory of her is not faded, only stored away like the scene paintings from a struck set. Every so often something inside me calls for a revival.

No stage illusion, no theatrical artifice, no trick blood would ever look convincing enough to me again. That night I learned what death truly looked like.

I can still see the pale skin of her arms and legs in that short-sleeved dress, her limbs folded awkwardly about her where she lay, like a ventriloquist's dummy or a marionette, a doll's eyes locked forever in a glassy stare. It was not a stare that accused. It stared past me, focused on a place no longer in the same world as the one I inhabited.

She lay in the soft earth, the moon shining down to dimly light her funeral procession, trees her pall-bearers, the eyes of timid, fearful creatures blinking unseen as they bore witness (and one of those timid, fearful, unseen creatures would turn out to be human).

No words were spoken over her grave, no tributes and no tears. It was solemn, however, and silent.

I could hear music coming from the house. It sounded distant, disconnected from this place I was standing, an island in time where no one yet knew what had happened. And yet it was so close. All it would take was someone to come looking for me, for her, and that island would be engulfed. I had the chance to maintain that disconnection, but as it carried on the night air, the music reminded me that I had to act fast and remain resolute.

They say that justice, like love, is blind. I knew that I must deny both. She would not have justice. I would not have love. But for all that, I would live free. I would not spend my best years in prison as the price of one moment of desperation.

I knew the decision I was making, and I'll tell you now that I would make it again. For all my guilt, from which I have never been free, I know that my life—and more importantly, my future family's lives—were served better by my actions than any notion of 'justice' would have been served by the truth.

Each death changes the world. Not so much as each birth, true, but certain deaths change the world more than others. This death changed so many worlds, so many lives. At the time I saw only

4

how it would change my own, but the roots and tendrils already intertwined between so many of us—though some of us had known each other mere weeks—meant that we would all be in some way transformed.

Ibsen said that 'to be oneself is to kill oneself'. He meant that in order to truly become who you are, you must first kill off all the other possible selves you might be. If you don't you become as Peer Gynt, like an onion, each layer peeling away to reveal another, but with ultimately nothing at its centre. None of us finds who we really are without sacrificing those other selves and cauterising the stumps where we severed the dreams that held them in place.

Sometimes we kill off those other selves, and sometimes they are killed for us.

A young woman's life ended that night: *all* the selves she would ever be, and that is something I have never allowed myself to lose sight of. But so many other lives ended too: lives we might all have led, different people we might all have become, had that night played out differently. How many of us would go back and change it, though? There's a question.

We were all transformed, for better or worse. Some of those transformations took time, but the greatest of them were instantaneous. Life into death; human into animal; morality into sheer instinct: how much can change irrevocably in a twinkling. Hers was the worst change, of course, the most horrifying, not only to the hands that wrought it and the eyes that saw, but to anybody. How could she, how could any of us, be in one moment a human being—animate, warm, alert, responsive,

5

infinite entities impossibly contained within a single form—and then in the next merely a discarded vessel, all those things it carried irretrievably lost?

And what is changed in the person who did this? Is he made something different by the act, or first made something different before he can commit it? Perhaps it is both. Either way, I knew that in killing I had been altered by the deed, but on that night saw a chance to prevent myself becoming the deed's creature.

I took her life, covered up her murder and left everyone else to live their transformed lives beneath the slowly corrosive drip of unanswered questions. I left suspicion and bitterness, anger and blame, the hollow ache of absence and the gnawing agony of not knowing. For doing that, I feel regret and I feel remorse, but I feel no guilt. My guilt I reserve only for her.

I don't like to consider how much the others would hate me if they learned the truth, but deep down they must all know that the blame is not for me alone to carry.

I was not the only sinner among us, and far from the worst.

Predator and Prey

Good things come to those who wait, Jasmine thought to herself. It had been a long time coming, and the road had been neither straight nor smooth, but after all these years she finally had an acting job in theatre.

Jasmine had wanted to be an actress since she

6

was six years old. She knew the age exactly because she could pinpoint the precise moment—or at least the precise evening—when this ambition had taken hold. Her mum had taken her to the theatre from the age of roughly three and a half, from Christmas pantomimes at the King's to children's plays at the Traverse, some of which were interactive to the point of almost functioning as crèches. She preferred the pantos inasmuch as she preferred anything that took place under a proscenium arch, before circles and balconies, an orchestra pit and ladies selling ice cream. Even when Mum took her to a kids' matinee performance of *The Very Hungry Caterpillar* featuring a cast of three and providing an early introduction to minimalism in terms of costume and production design, the fact that it took place at the Festival Theatre on Nicholson Street made it a spectacle in itself. Though the steeply towering layers of seating were spookily empty and the actors all but lost upon such a great wide stage, it felt more like a proper show than anything she had been sat in front of at any of the city's more intimate venues.

She preferred it to her early experiences of the cinema too, which had been divided between the plasticky sterility of the multiplex at Newcraighall and the sticky-carpeted gloomy auditoria to be found in the city centre. At that tender age, however, these theatrical spectacles didn't make her dream of treading the boards any more than the films she saw made her imagine life as a movie star.

Her epiphany came when she was taken to see a production of *Juno and the Paycock* at the Lyceum. It would be redundant to state that this was not really a production aimed at six-year-olds, but in a way that itself was the catalyst. Her mum was supposed to be going to see it alone, before meeting up with some friends she had in the cast and crew for a late supper. For a single mother with a full-time job, it was a rare and relished opportunity for an adult night out, but unfortunately the babysitter phoned to cancel less than an hour before she was due to turn up.

Her mum instantly accepted that her late supper was now a write-off, but dearly wanted to see the play. She elicited from her daughter sincere vows of good behaviour, balancing her solemn homilies about the importance of sitting quietly in her seat with promised rewards of ice cream at the interval and chips on the way home. Jasmine, in her ignorance, didn't understand why her mum had such anxious reservations, never having sat through anything that wasn't punctuated by singalong musical numbers and the tossing of bags of sweets into the audience.

In the event, Jasmine's vows were never put to the test, as Mum bumped into her friend Kirsten front of house as she queued at the box office, intending to return her single seat in the stalls for two together wherever might be left. Railroading through Mum's typical reluctance to inconvenience anybody or accept unearned favours, Kirsten escorted them backstage, where she said Mum could watch the performance from the wings, and where Jasmine might be found various things to amuse herself, to say nothing of being relieved of the requirement to sit still for the best part of three hours.

Jasmine thought Kirsten must be the head of

the ushers, as not only was she allowed to go anywhere in the theatre, but she evidently had the power to grant Jasmine and her mum any seat they liked, even special ones to the side of the scenery. Jasmine learned later that Kirsten was actually 'the director' of the play, though it was several more years still before she had any understanding of what this meant.

Jasmine was brought a drink with a straw, a bag of sweets and a pad and pencils for drawing and colouring, and told she could play on the floor by her mum's feet as long as she remained quiet and didn't stray past a line on the floor marked out in yellow tape.

Her drawing efforts did not last beyond the gunshot that rang out at the beginning of the production. It gave her quite literally the fright of her life, calling her attention not only to the action on the stage, but the action all around her. Jolted away from the cosy little bubble of her sweets, her drink and the comfort of her mum's legs, she suddenly noticed how the scenery and backdrops looked up close. She became aware of the platforms, ramps and stairways the actors were using to access different areas of the set, as well as the slides, pulleys and counterweights that were making elements zip in and out of place. And if the gunshot had initially summoned her attention, what held it thereafter was the actors themselves.

Prior to this, people she had watched on stage had seemed little different to the people she watched on TV. They inhabited this unreachable otherworld, barely more real or tangible than cartoon characters. That night, she saw not only that they were real people, brushing past in a waft of heat and smells, but she witnessed them each become something altogether different from themselves. They stood in the wings or behind the backdrop in their costumes, faces painted vividly with make-up so thick that close up they were like circus clowns. Some would chatter quietly to one another, some remained alone and withdrawn, but when they stepped on to the stage they instantly became other people. Their accents changed, their posture and manner changed; they even seemed taller or shorter than mere seconds before. Women in tears made their exits and then traded little smiles and jokes once they had cleared the sightlines. An actor stood alone: reflective, shy and even a little sullen, then stepped before the audience and was instantly a cheerfully drunken and voluble braggart.

Having been taken to all those pantomimes and other shows, six-year-old Jasmine was already familiar with spectacle. This, however, was magic. She knew that night that theatre was no longer something she merely wanted to watch. It was something she wanted to be part of.

When she played with her dolls thereafter, it wasn't make-believe. Some of them were the cast, others the audience, and whatever the former were about—whether it be tea parties or hair dressing—it was all part of a play. She recalled gluing together kitchen-roll tubes and panels cut from cardboard boxes, placing them either side of her doll's house, its front hinged open where it sat on her bedroom floor. It was no longer a doll's house. It was a stage set.

She took part in children's drama clubs, youth theatre groups, school musicals; and with her mum being a drama teacher whose time and duties

10

were divided between two separate secondaries, when Jasmine wasn't acting she was helping sew costumes, paint backdrops and fashion props.

When it came to her vocation, there was no question of Jasmine having a Plan B.

She recalled her mum's pride, delight and no little relief when Jasmine got accepted into the Scottish Academy of Theatre and Dance, even though it would involve her daughter flying the nest and taking up residence through in Glasgow. Any fears Mum might have for Jasmine being on her own away from her vigilant eyes in a different city (and one whose darker side Beth Sharp was warily familiar with) would prove unfounded. She certainly didn't have to worry about her little girl being seduced by the temptations of her student lifestyle. Jasmine had been seduced by a jealous suitor way back at the Lyceum and remained monogamously single-minded to the point of anti-social where it came to the study of her chosen craft. She relaxed and began letting her hair down a bit more during her second year, but admittedly even that had a vocational element to it, as she began to appreciate how important it was to be making contacts and getting her face known in certain circles. Whatever it took, she was going to do it.

Then Mum got sick.

It was around the start of Jasmine's final year that Mum was diagnosed with pancreatic cancer and given her unmerciful, unthinkable, *impossible* prognosis. Jasmine dropped out of college and moved back in with her in Corstorphine, to be with her as much as possible during the time they had left. Mum only had months, and Jasmine only had months left to spend with the person who had raised her, alone, the person she was closest to in the world, the person she could not possibly do without. But eventually, inescapably, Jasmine *would* have to do without.

People talk about picking up the pieces, getting back on with your life, but the pieces scattered around Jasmine looked like grains of sand on a beach, and she spent a lot of time in her mum's empty house contemplating them, unable to assemble them into any pattern that made sense. She didn't feel like she had a life to get back on with. She had no job, no career, no studies any more, and barely an echo of her previously consuming aspirations.

Eventually, she decided to move back to Glasgow and the little flat she still rented, as a means of forcing herself to push forward, of making some attempt to re-gather the threads of her ambitions. And they were ambitions now, at best, not dreams. Dreams were what little girls had as they squatted in the wings at their mother's feet.

All she had left were pragmatic necessities, amid the rather unsettling realisation that she had, as the phrase goes, her whole life ahead of her. This sounded to her a daunting and arduous prospect rather than a rallying cry for the passions of youth. Suddenly it didn't seem so visionary to have spent her whole life in pursuit of a profession with an unemployment rate comparable with dinosaur obedience trainers and banking-sector humility advisers. To make matters worse, in a game where visibility was the key to opportunity, she had completely fallen off the grid. Nobody knew who she was, and among her former peers, those who hadn't forgotten about her completely seemed to have assumed that she hadn't merely dropped out of her course, but abandoned acting altogether.

Auditions were a struggle to come by. Sure, there were occasionally parts you could turn up and read for, but there were auditions and there were auditions. There was a difference between being asked to try out for something because the director thought you might be what they were looking for, and simply making up the numbers because protocol dictated that the audition at least *appear* to be open.

The only real nibble she got was a call-back from Fire Curtain, a touring company founded by the prodigiously talented, formidably connected and more than a little capricious Charlotte Queen, who had been a year above Jasmine at the SATD. Charlotte claimed to have found the academy 'a path too well-trodden' in terms of a route into theatre, and cited 'itchy feet' as a further spur to setting up her own company at the precocious age of twenty-two. (To talented and connected should also be added 'a bit posh', which in Jasmine's eyes made Charlotte's bold move somewhat less of a gamble, as well as that bit easier to fund.)

Jasmine didn't get the part, but was nonetheless tantalised by Charlotte's suggestion that she'd be great as Miranda in a planned production of *The Tempest* she had pencilled in as their Edinburgh Fringe project a year hence. In the meantime, with bills to pay, she reluctantly and very much half-heartedly accepted an offer of work from Uncle Jim, an ex-cop who ran his own private investigation firm. Jim sold it to her on the premise that in a business replete with ex-cops, he could really use someone whom his subjects wouldn't recognise as such from a mile off, and further sugared the pill by claiming that it would require a degree of acting. Jasmine strongly suspected that Jim's true motivation was a sense of familial duty towards his late cousin's daughter, particularly given the patience he showed in the face of her serial incompetence.

Perhaps ironically, it was a reciprocal sense of duty towards Jim that made her stick it out, though admittedly it helped that it paid considerably better than bar work or a job in a call-centre. She didn't feel entirely comfortable taking money for something she was rubbish at, but Jim seemed sincere in both his intentions and his faith that she would come good. Jasmine gradually began to dig in, despite the actor's whispering angst that commitment to another job was a gentle way of letting go your dreams.

She was barely ready for the water wings to come off when she was hurled in at the deep end by Jim going missing, forcing her to play detective for real in attempting to track him down. She did so in the end, but Jim's own end had preceded that, leaving her not only bereft once more, but technically unemployed.

Amazing what can change in a year; or nine months anyway. As she stood by Jim's grave at the end of last summer, she'd never have thought that by the following spring she'd be acting in theatre. Unfortunately the theatre in question was one of seven in the surgical suite at St Mungo's General Hospital, where Jasmine was currently working as a clinical support worker, and the acting part was largely about concealing from the rest of the staff that, much as was the case in her fledgling PI days, she didn't really know what she was doing.

Her present task was straightforward enough, at least now that she was beginning to get a handle on where various items of equipment were kept. She was wheeling in a stack for a laparoscopy. It looked very much like the kind of set-up they had at her secondary school for whenever the teacher wanted to show them a film or television programme: an aluminium trolley bearing a large monitor atop a short column of electronic equipment with cables spilling untidily out on all sides. The patient wasn't even in the anaesthetic room yet, and once he or she was under it could still be ten or fifteen minutes before the surgeon showed up, so they were a long way off 'knife to skin'.

There were two theatre nurses setting up as Jasmine entered: Sandra was unwrapping the sterile seals from a tray of surgical instruments, while Doreen was filling in some paperwork for an audit. They paid her little heed as she rolled the stack steadily through the double doors, but her arrival invited greater notice from Liam, the operating department assistant, who cast an interested eye over her as he chatted to a young and slightly nervy orderly named David.

Mr Assan was the surgeon performing the procedure, while Dr Hagan would be anaesthetising the patient. The power relationship there was as complex as it was delicate, but beneath that level there was less ambiguity. Among the theatre staff, Liam wanted everyone else to understand that he was the man in charge.

Liam was in his early forties, and had worked in the hospital for more than twenty years. Doreen and her three decades' service could trump him in the 'in with the bricks' stakes, but he had arrogated a seniority in the pecking order that took little cognisance of rank and that he did not wear lightly. Even Geraldine, the theatre manager, seemed wary to the point of deference when she was addressing him.

With Jasmine being the new arrival, he had wasted little time in impressing upon her that he was the theatre suite's alpha male, picking her up on every mis-step in what struck her as a rather transparent bid to undermine her confidence, albeit it wasn't her position to judge, and she was certainly ensuring he didn't want for opportunities to criticise. However, this didn't represent the full repertoire of his territorial pissing.

'Here, have you seen that new bird they've got doing the weather on *Reporting Scotland*?' he asked David.

Jasmine had caught the tail end of his last remarks, something about an ongoing dispute between two of the surgeons. It had been gossipy and guarded, a little snide but carefully circumspect. This was a sudden change in subject and register, and though she wasn't the one being addressed she knew it was for her benefit.

'Naw, I usually watch the news on Scotia,' David replied uncertainly, clearly regretful that he couldn't give the desired answer. He needn't have worried. Liam wasn't asking with a view to soliciting his thoughts. It was simply a pretext.

'Aw, man, she looks pure filth. You can just tell. Serious, if I got hold of her, I'd leave her fanny like a ripped-oot fireplace. I'd be on her until the neighbours phoned the council aboot the smell.'

16

Jasmine knew this was for her ears, but though it was Liam who was talking, it was David who looked her way, a fleeting, uncomfortable glance.

Jasmine could feel her cheeks flush but she knew she mustn't respond.

Sandra let out a tut followed by a disapproving sigh, while Doreen simply shook her head.

'Whit?' Liam snapped, looking round sharply at Sandra. It was hard to tell if he was more annoyed by her impertinence or by the fact that it wasn't her response that was being sought. 'Christ's sake, just a wee bit of banter. Figure of speech, like.'

'There's ladies present,' Doreen sallied in support, part complaint, part appeal.

'It's just youse old miseries that are making a fuss.'

Then, inevitably, he looked towards Jasmine, having found a way to return the focus to his original target. 'You're no' bothered, are you, wee yin?'

There was laughter in his voice and a smile on his lips, but steel in his gaze as he eyed her across the operating table. To disagree was to get her card well and truly marked, while to accede was to betray Doreen and Sandra while inviting further such remarks.

'I'm sorry, I was in a bit of a dwam. I wasn't paying attention,' she lied, offering all parties a way out.

Liam wasn't for taking it.

'I'm just saying you're open-minded. Lassies your age aren't all buttoned-up and prudish about sex, not like the older generations. A healthier attitude. That's why the young lassies these days take an interest in how they look down below. Go into

17

Boots and it's full of wax strips and depilatories and all sorts. See, this pair here won't even know what I'm talking about. Women their age, it must look like Terry Waite's garden inside their kickers.'

He was giggling to himself as though this was just some benign frivolity, but nobody else was laughing. The two nurses were simmering silently while poor David stared at the floor, afraid to meet anyone's eyes, least of all Liam's. Jasmine knew that this was precisely the type of situation he'd been trying to effect. An atmosphere of tension and poison was a result for him: if everyone else was feeling on edge he had nothing to fear from any of them.

He was looking at her again, checking how she was taking it, waiting eagerly for her response now that she couldn't play the same get-out card.

How on earth did I end up here, Jasmine asked herself, putting up with shit like this? Honestly. The things you had to do for money.

'I'm sorry, I don't quite follow,' she told him. 'Was there something in particular you wanted to ask me?'

'Aye. I was trying to tell them you're not bothered by us talking about this kinda stuff, so they shouldnae be stopping us just because they don't like it. That's right, isn't it?'

Jasmine knew she had to eschew a response ostensibly agreeing with him and adding, in this spirit of sexual candour that permitted speculation about colleagues' genitals, how she imagined he probably had a cock like a budgie's tongue. Instead her words had to be measured and carefully chosen.

'I don't think you should be saying anything that makes the people you're working with uncomfortable, and what you just said was grossly

18

disrespectful to all of us as colleagues and as women. I think you'd have to consider yourself very lucky if neither Doreen nor Sandra put in a complaint.'

Liam looked towards her with a glare that told her they probably weren't going to be BFFs.

'Oh, sorry, were you wanting my actual opinion, or just a wee bit of "banter"?' she asked.

The atmosphere did not improve, but at least everybody was equally uncomfortable and Liam wasn't getting to enjoy himself. What disappointed Jasmine, however, was that Sandra and Doreen thereafter seemed almost as pissed off at her as they were at Liam. Evidently, she shouldn't have poked the tiger.

Once the operation was over, the patient was wheeled into recovery by Dr Hagan and Sandra, while Liam went off on a break, having said very little throughout. Jasmine was helping clear up, though she had learned not to touch anything until directed to do so by one of the nurses.

'You'd better watch yourself now,' Doreen told her quietly. 'You're new, so you weren't to know, but you're better just ignoring him. Get on his bad side and it's more trouble than it's worth.'

'But he clearly thinks that's acceptable, and it isn't. You should put in a complaint.'

Doreen gave a sour laugh.

'You think nobody ever has? Also more trouble than it's worth. Behind his back, his nickname round here is Eliot.'

'I don't get it.'

'As in Ness?'

'Still don't get it,' Jasmine confessed.

'What age are you?'

19

'Twenty-one.'

'Before your time, right enough. *The Untouchables*.'

'I see.'

'No, you don't know the half. He's a law unto himself, knows the system inside out. He's well in with Brian Anderson, the Unison FoC, and he's got Brian believing that all the complaints are trumped-up charges because management have it in for him. Well, technically that's true: management would love to get rid of him, but they can never make anything stick.'

'Why not? His behaviour today was in front of several witnesses.'

'Nobody ever feels like talking by the time the grievance proceedings are heard. That's why I'm warning you to watch out. He's very intimidating. Christ, Sharon Murphy's been off five months long-term sick with stress; Julie Philips was off the best part of a year and then put in for a transfer. He's not daft either. There was a porter saw him moving boxes of drugs out the back door, which there's been rumours about for years. Liam knew this porter was in a flute band, so he claimed the guy had made it up to get him sacked because he was a Catholic. Don't think Liam's darkened the door of a chapel in twenty years, but management panicked soon as he'd played that card. It was his word against the porter's, same as it was his word against Sharon's over the sexual harassment. As I say, it's not worth it. Keep your head down. Stay out his way.'

Jasmine knew it was too late for that. She could try not to antagonise him any further, but the damage was done. Even if she kept her head down, as Doreen suggested; even if she did her best to physically avoid him, she suspected Liam would be making a point of seeking her out.

* * *

He didn't wait long. It happened the next day.

Jasmine was wheeling a stack of equipment along the corridor following a colonoscopy list when Liam appeared at her side and began pushing the trolley too. His left arm was stretched across her shoulders, not quite touching, but enclosing her between him and the stack nonetheless.

'Many hands make light work,' he said.

'I've got it,' she said. 'I'm fine myself.'

'Don't be daft. Between us we can have this back where it belongs in no time.'

His tone was polite and matter-of-fact, lacking any trace of grudge or aggression. It sounded like an olive branch, or at least as if it was supposed to.

Oh, you're good, she thought. But not as good as you think.

'I said I'm fine. I'd prefer it if you took your hand away. You're crowding me and it makes me feel uncomfortable.'

His hand seemed to grip the steel a little tighter for a moment, probably an indicator of suppressed rage, then he let go, holding both hands up in an exaggerated gesture, giggling a little, as though mocking what an unnecessary fuss she was making.

'Wouldn't want that,' he said. 'Just trying to help out. I'm heading this way anyway. I'm going to orthopaedic theatre. Mr Williams has his usual over-long list this afternoon. Be lucky if we're finished by seven.'

He kept walking alongside her, talking. Talking

21

too much. Explaining himself when he didn't need to. Jasmine felt a dull dread in her stomach. She wasn't liking this.

They passed two nurses dawdling in the other direction, probably pacing themselves so that they'd have time to finish the packet of biscuits they were eating between them before they got back to their ward.

'You know, nobody's going to think you can't manage by yourself just because you've accepted a bit of help,' he said, still polite, still cheerful, still walking way too close alongside.

The room where the stacks were stored was just up ahead.

'I *can* manage by myself and I'd rather you left me alone.'

Liam glanced forward and gave a dismissive shake of the head, a hollow smile remaining on his lips.

'Just trying to help, hen.'

He skipped ahead a couple of paces and pulled open the door to the equipment room.

'At least let me get this for you.'

Jasmine would have preferred he didn't, but she didn't really have a choice. He was already holding it. She looked up and down the corridor, disappointed to see nobody coming.

Liam looked at his watch, partly to mock her hesitation but possibly also to check how long before he was due in theatre.

Jasmine wheeled the stack through the open door and into the narrow storage room, where several similar trolleys were ranged against the walls. She heard the door close behind her and turned to see that Liam was standing in front of it. He put an arm across her shoulders again and began pushing the stack towards an empty slot.

'Tricky parking these things,' he said, his arm now resting across her neck.

The stack bumped the back wall and Jasmine turned around. Liam had both hands on the stack, either side of her arms, trapping her.

'Let me past,' she said. 'You shouldn't have followed me in here. I find what you're doing extremely intimidating.'

'What? You that can manage by herself? You that doesn't need anybody's help? You're saying you're intimidated now?'

'You're a man twice my age and twice my size and you've got me pinned up close inside an enclosed space where nobody can see us. Yes, I'm intimidated. Let me past.'

Liam lifted his right hand from the stack and held it in front of her, but he didn't move out of the way. Instead he waited until she made to move, then he placed it upon her shoulder. He focused a steely stare into Jasmine's eyes and slowly slid his hand downwards.

Jasmine took a breath and swallowed, both to fight back tears and to steady her voice to speak.

'Your hand is on my breast,' she said, just managing to keep the timbre of her voice above a whisper. It sounded like a cruel parody of words spoken in a lover's clinch. 'That is considered sexual assault.'

'Not if it never happened,' he replied, moving his face closer to hers, the sour smell of cigarettes on his breath. 'Like you said, nobody can see us. Your word against mine, hen.'

'Is that how it was with Sharon Murphy? Your

23

word against hers?'

'If you heard about Sharon, you'll know what I'm trying to say here.'

Jasmine did: loud and clear. This wasn't about sexual harassment: sexual harassment was merely the weapon he used. This was about power.

'I don't take shite from anybody,' he said, almost nose to nose, his right hand lightly squeezing her left breast. 'Not from torn-faced boots like her and not from snobby wee cows like you. See I clocked your type right away. Student summer job is it? Just passing through so you think you're better than the likes of me. Talking all proper, like you're giving a commentary. "Your hand is on my tit,"' he mimicked. 'Think you'll be buying and selling me one day, don't you. Well I've got news for you, bitch. In here, I'm the one that owns you.'

Jasmine reached to his hand and pulled it away from her.

'I think that's enough,' she said.

'*I'll* decide what's enough,' he growled, throwing off her grip and replacing his hand on her breast.

'Actually, I think you'll find it's a third party who'll decide it's enough. More than enough.'

She had spoken clearly but he didn't hear what she was telling him.

'Third party? You still arenae listening, are you, hen? Your word against mine, remember, and who are they gaunny believe? I'm an ODA, been here twenty-odd years. You're in the door five minutes and you're just a clinical support worker.'

Jasmine allowed herself a smile.

'That's where you're really quite disastrously wrong,' she told him brightly.

She could see the change of tone provoke first

24

surprise, then confusion and then, as she went on, true, exquisite horror.

'I'm not a clinical support worker, I'm a private investigator, and the reason I'm giving a running commentary is for the benefit of your employers who are listening in. Hence you're profoundly mistaken about your own job status too: trust me on this, maggot, you *were* an ODA.'

King of Shadows

The tallest trees stand like Greek columns, making a proscenium of a Highland glade, grass lush and soft beneath bare feet. A felled trunk lies at the centre like some minimalist modern sculpture, an ancient thing of indeterminate purpose: climbing frame, picnic table, bench and even bower. There are human figures curled before it, feigning sleep. The moon hangs impossibly above like a glitterball, a globe rather than a mere disc of light, shadows and contours rendering it perceptibly spherical. It looks mere miles away, and thus too solid to simply sit there unsupported, not like some wispy cloud that can plausibly drift upon the air. It appears thus because though it is evening, the sky is not yet dark. All above the trees there is clear blue, minute by minute more tinged with the magenta promise of another summer's day.

It may seem an incongruous setting for a malign conspiracy, but the hour is later than the light would indicate, and even the prettiest arbour hides secrets in its shadows.

A demon and a god stand either side of the

felled trunk, malice in their souls, but neither is the darkest spirit lurking amid the woods this midsummer's night.

'Captain of our fairy band,' the demon addresses the god. 'Helena is here at hand, And the youth, mistook by me, Pleading for a lover's fee. Shall we their fond pageant see? Lord, what fools these mortals be!'

'Stand aside,' his lord replies. 'The noise they make Will cause Demetrius to awake.'

'Then will two at once woo one; That must needs be sport alone; And those things do best please me that befal preposterously.'

The audience observes from three rows of tiered seating atop an articulated trailer, one end of which is hitched to a tractor. There is no need of a curtain nor of slides or backdrops, as each change of scene is effected by the audience being relocated to another part of the castle grounds, where their champagne flutes are replenished silently and solicitously by waiting staff in black tie and cocktail dresses. A susurrus of fizzing greets each new act like quiet applause, giving way to occasional whispers, a resultant modicum of shushing, the low buzz of phones on vibrate and, as the performance draws on, in one instance light snoring.

The sleeper apart, most of the audience are enjoying the play; or at least telling themselves that they are enjoying the play, for not to would be to admit to lacking in culture. Some would have preferred seats for Murrayfield, or even seats for *Mamma Mia* if theatre was the theme, but they know that this is a privilege. The greater part of its worth is in simply being able to say that you were there, that you were invited, as this trip is regarded as a cut far above the corporate hospitality the bank ordinarily proffers. It says something about your standing if you are taken to Cragruthes Castle: not merely your worth as a client, but the class of individual the bank perceives you to stand among. This is no mere dramatic spectacle either: the play is bracketed by dinner in the grand hall and overnight accommodation in rooms fit for (and in some cases previously used by) royalty.

Among the audience there are those whose appreciation of the evening is less equivocal, and they are as distinct in this as they are in their dress.

One is the man in trews. He is as relaxed and content as he has been since this time last year, though there is just a tiny shade of melancholy running through his reverie: of regret at a different life never led. His pleasure is twofold. He is the Laird of Ruthes, owner of the castle that has been in his family for four centuries, but none of his forebears were so challenged by the burden of its upkeep. Even before the predations of the credit crunch upon his portfolio, he had been forced to look for ways in which the castle and its policies could pay for itself, and corporate entertaining has proven its saviour. Cragruthes was not big enough, not of sufficient historical importance nor stuffed with the requisite treasures to attract the level of what the consultant called 'footfall' required to make it worth opening its doors to tourism. However, as a venue for select events it had what he was told was 'high-end niche value'. Thus businesses could hire it to conduct top-level meetings amid aristocratic luxury, or to reward their executives—or perhaps their clients— with a few days' private and exclusive hunting

27

and fishing. These activities proved lucrative, but by their nature they tended to be sporadic and unpredictable. For eight years now, the most reliably consistent revenue stream on the calendar has been the midsummer plays staged in the grounds. The troupe are, strictly speaking, amateurs, but their company does get paid, and handsomely. This engagement goes a long way towards funding whatever else they choose to produce throughout the year.

The plays run for two weeks, accommodating twelve performances, weather permitting. This traditionally includes a 'dress preview' for guests of the cast and the castle staff, but thereafter each night is sold as a package to a different corporate sponsor, minus a few house seats for the laird and his guests. The laird attends most nights. This year he has taken in five of the eight performances so far, but this one is particularly savoured, for falling on the twenty-first of June itself.

The second and greater part of his pleasure is in simply watching the actors work. He is their host and their patron, so it gives him a glow to feel part of their enterprise. The first couple of nights he will allow himself to become lost in the story, but after that the thrill for him is almost Brechtian in appreciating the artifice. It takes him back decades, to his student days: lets him revisit a time that was far from responsibilities, a time when he got to be somebody else.

He only gets to watch now. It is enough, but there still burns inside him an unquenched desire to participate. He knows he couldn't, though. It wouldn't do, for one thing, and besides, he'd be too self-conscious. The rehearsal schedule might also be a problem, and he'd hate to let anybody down.

He knows they would accommodate him if he asked: they wouldn't turn him away even if he was rubbish, and he knows that would be wrong. This is *not* rubbish. It never is. It's not the RSC either, but these corporate packages wouldn't be selling out if the plays were not beautifully staged.

He smiles at the weaver's words:

'First, good Peter Quince, say what the play treats on, then read the names of the actors, and so grow to a point.'

They are school teachers and GPs, housewives and IT consultants. They are the rude mechanicals of their day, but they are not shambling fools here to be patronised and indulged. He'd call them accomplished amateurs, but they're raised above that by a certain guiding hand. There's a touch of genius in there, and no matter what base stuff dilutes it, the essence remains.

Alongside the laird is a man in a kilt. He has frequently watched the finest of actors, their performances shaped by brilliant directors, framed amid the craft of visionary designers, and yet he is transported too. He loves the setting, loves not just the staging of theatre outdoors, as it was first performed, but of this beautiful outdoors *as* a theatre. He senses the pure joy of performing from the cast, knows they'll live off this thrill for months to come. They don't know and wouldn't care whether the audience is half cut, half asleep or half engaged with texting their friends.

He notes with approval that the actor playing Theseus is also playing Oberon; and how Hippolyta is similarly doubled with Titania. He thinks of Peter Brook's production at Stratford in 1970, though

29

surely Brook was far from the first. So many small companies of players down the centuries must have done likewise as they calculated which characters must be on stage at the same time. Few, however, could have anticipated the sexual resonance this casting gave in Brook's production, amid its trapezes, scaffolds, ramps and metal trees.

At his present age, it is the sexuality between these older pairs that the man in the kilt finds himself relating to, far more than the four young lovers being tormented by Robin Goodfellow.

'Then will two at once woo one.'

As the demon spoke these words, the man in the kilt would have to admit he thought not of Helena, but of Titania.

The actress playing Titania and Hippolyta is in her fifties, like him, which some might say is a little old to be counting down the days and nights as her nuptial hour draws on apace. She looks younger than that, though, and not just because of the dimming light, the make-up or the distance. It's stage presence. It's grace. In the vulgar modern coinage, she might be described as a MILF. To the man in the kilt, who has a more elegant frame of reference to draw upon, she is an heir of Madame Vestris. He knows Vestris understood that neither sex appeal nor sex itself was the preserve of the young. She went from opera to burlesque before taking to the popular stage and ultimately ruling the roost at the Lyceum. Men paid for plaster casts of her famous legs, and she always made sure her costumes showed them off. When Vestris staged this play she cast herself as Oberon, and in playing a man paradoxically accentuated her femininity, invoking the ambiguous, fetishistic sexuality that

30

is now familiar to every young male who sits wondering why he feels strange stirrings watching the pantomime's principal boy.

Mostly, however, Vestris understood the power of spectacle: that the audience wanted to be transported, to see before them a different world. That is what the laird's guest is enjoying most tonight. He is far from cares, from work, from worry, from the stress, the angst, the fears and the disputes of recent times. Like the laird, he is elevated in reverie: times past, different selves he once was, and reminded of different selves he might have been.

* * *

There is another observer who is similarly qualified to appreciate the play on a level far higher than the corporate visitors. He does not sit among them, however, for he is no one's guest. Instead, both spectacle and audience are magnified for his vision courtesy of Carl Zeiss optronics.

Like the man in the kilt, his thoughts alight on various stagings of this play that he has witnessed personally or read about in books and, coincidentally, one of those is Peter Brook's. In his case, though, he is thinking with regard to tonight's audience rather than its players. To them, Ben Kingsley is at best Gandhi, at worst a Hollywood villain, while Patrick Stewart is the captain of the Starship Enterprise or the leader of the X-Men; not, respectively, Demetrius and Snout.

Pearls before swine. They are treated as though they are cultured because they are in the higher echelons of finance and commerce, two areas

31

whose denizens, in his experience, have consistently proven more synonymous with philistinism.

Despite his distaste for the audience, this uninvited observer is transported too: taken back in time to another highland estate and another Shakespeare play.

A thin smile makes its way across his lips as he recalls it. Act One, Scene One. A desert place.

When shall we three meet again.

Tonight, as fate would have it.

We three: one who authored a fell deed, one who was witness, and one who remains protected by ignorance of the truth.

But the hurly-burly's not yet done.

The tractor moves thrice more, finally returning to its starting point before the grand avenue leading to the front of castle, which, as at the play's opening, comes to represent Athens. The floodlights are on now, the moon merely one more shining disc, and the theatre space in front of the audience more truly resembles a stage for being picked out against the gathering dusk.

The young lovers have resolved into their rightful couples, meaning Theseus and Hippolyta can look forward to their wedding in a spirit of harmony, reflected in the reconciliation of their shadow-selves, Oberon and Titania.

It is time for the demon of the woods to have his final say.

'Give me your hands, if we be friends, And Robin shall restore amends.'

There is enthusiastic, if champagne-fuelled, applause as the players enjoy their many bows. Then the laird steps down from the trailer and bids his guest to join the gathering beneath the lights, announcing him with great fanfare, which makes the man in the kilt blush just a little, embarrassed that he might steal any of the limelight, for this is not his moment but theirs.

He is handed a fresh flute of champagne as he steps down on to the ground and picks his steps carefully on the soft grass.

'Give me your hands, if we be friends,' he says, and the cast move to greet him. They seem giddy, almost over-excited, and predictable jokes are made about this being their big break due to the influence he wields in the world of the arts. He knows this excitement is not about him; he is merely its outlet. They are still buzzing and jangling from their performance.

The actress playing Titania gives the laird a warm hug and a kiss on the cheek as she accepts his congratulations. The laird wonders at her accent, that trace of the Antipodes detectable in the odd word, despite her having lived the majority of her life here in Scotland. Some things shape you for the long haul, he reflects, no matter what twists and turns your life may take. Certain events, certain decisions, the marks of certain experiences are simply indelible.

A man with a camera moves to the centre in front of the trailer and a picture is called for. The man in the kilt makes to step clear, but both the laird and the actress playing Titania insist he remain. He and the laird stand where they are while the cast assemble themselves into a practised tableau: Titania and Theseus pose on one knee, hands outstretched to touch each other's shoulders, like they are about to embrace. They are flanked by Puck and Bottom, the four lovers lying at their feet,

33

heads resting on palms above pivoted elbows.

The photographer asks them all to smile.

The man in the kilt has been photographed many times, though he has always been the man behind the scenes, the facilitator for more talented others. He knows to suck in his cheeks and close his eyes for a moment, which will help him hold his expression. He raises his champagne flute in a gesture of salute. The camera flickers, the red-eye-reducing pre-flash. The man with the kilt blinks in reflexive response, then his head bursts open and he jolts sharply backwards, as though reeling from a slap.

He slumps down, the power gone from his legs, half his face torn away, liquid and matter spread around him on the grass.

As the screams ring out, the demon of the woods spirits himself deeper into the darkness from whence he was summoned thirty years before.

Easy Money

Jasmine knew what she was looking at the moment the client walked through her office door. She was conscious that, at twenty-one and barely a year into working as a private investigator, she was probably a little young to be sounding hardboiled, but it wasn't that she had become experienced and cynical enough to recognise a wide taxonomy of clients on sight: just this particular sub-genus, as she had seen a lot of specimens since last September.

Jesus, had it really been that long she'd been doing this? The calendar said yes, though the date didn't really resonate, mainly because the weather of late had felt nothing like late spring. It *had* been that long, though: it was almost June. Wimbledon would be starting in three weeks, and that did resonate, because all through her school years the sight of tennis whites on the telly had meant the summer holidays were almost upon her.

It had been at Jim's funeral that his eldest daughter, Angela, took Jasmine aside and told her about the will. Jim had left Sharp Investigations to his family, not as a specific bequest but simply under a general directive covering a variety of things. The family had discussed it and decided it would be fitting to offer the business to Jasmine, not least because they were sure it was what Jim would have wanted. It was a kind gesture but not one so munificent as to make her feel duty-bound to accept. By Angela's admission, the business was almost worthless except as a going concern and, having been a one-man operation prior to Jasmine's brief recruitment, it wasn't going to be going at all without her. The office was rented, so there was no property tied into it, and other than a van that might be worth two or three grand at trade in, the only material assets were barely worth liquidating. There was an ageing PC that most third-world charities would turn up their noses at, particularly given that it lacked an operating system due to the hard disc having been completely erased by the conspirators responsible for Jim's death. There was a range of surveillance equipment and covert recording devices that had probably cost a few grand to amass, but for which the second-hand market was extremely limited. Like the business itself, they were only worth something if they were being put to use.

Angela didn't put her on the spot. She gave Jasmine a few weeks to consider the offer, aware of her truncated dramatic training and how heavily those years weighed in the vocational stakes against her brief few months as Jim's barely—or rarely—competent assistant. Jasmine was equally decorous in saying she would take those weeks to mull it over, when her instinctive response was to tell Angela to terminate the lease on the office and stick all its contents on eBay.

However, something quite unexpected beset Jasmine at Jim's funeral, as it had also done at the commemorative services held in the wake of the Ramsay case. People were saying thank you to her. Grown-up people, people generations older than her, were taking her hands in theirs and offering often tearful gratitude in acknowledgment of what she had done for them. Since her mother's death—and throughout the months preceding its inevitability—Jasmine had spent so much time feeling afraid, vulnerable, abandoned: a lost and scared little girl.

When she was eight years old, one Saturday afternoon she came back from playing at a friend's house to find her mum's front door locked and no answer to the bell, no matter how many times she tried it in her growing, tear-streaked desperation. What she most recalled was the feeling of rising panic giving way to cold dread as she realised that she didn't know where her mum had gone, it never having occurred to her that her mum could be anywhere other than at home in the flat waiting to welcome her inside. It didn't—simply wouldn't—cross her mind that Mum might have nipped out to the shops, nor did it strike her that Mum had been expecting her back at five as usual, when in fact Jasmine had returned closer to quarter-past four, cutting her visit short because Rachel's annoying younger cousin had turned up and ruined their game.

All she knew was that her mum wasn't there, and it utterly terrified her. She had stood at the door in a tearful blur, feeling helpless. Theirs was a basement flat with its entrance down a short flight of steps beneath street level, so she was enclosed in her own isolated little courtyard of fear and misery, no neighbours noticing and coming down to offer help. Eventually she pulled herself together enough to come up with a plan of action, which was to return to Rachel's house, where there were other trusted adults. She felt reluctant to implement this plan, however, as it seemed to cement the idea that her mum had gone away and left her; as though by embarking on the journey back to Rachel's house she was taking her first steps into a world without her mum.

After Mum's death, that combination of rising panic and cold dread was something she felt almost every day, burned into her emotional memory and anchored to that specific incident. She became that terrified eight-year-old over and over again as she stared beyond the precipice into this world of isolation and responsibilities. At her best, at her most together and controlled, she felt like she was doing nothing more than walking back to Rachel's house in search of other adults to look after her.

At those services following the Ramsay case, she was made to feel that she had—without trying to, without even realising it—been the one doing the

37

looking after; that she had given all of these people something that made them feel less scared and confused. She held outstretched hands and looked into earnest, solemn faces, and in their moist eyes glimpsed this young woman they were all looking at, someone very different to the lost and scared little girl she imagined herself to be. Perhaps for the first time in her life it gave her a genuine sense of what it felt like to be an autonomous, functioning grown-up.

She could still feel like a lost child inside, but maybe everyone else did too, and it was in the reflection of her deeds that she got to see the person the rest of the world saw when they looked at her. So maybe, just maybe, against all instinct and expectation, this was something she could do, and do well; something that might make her feel she had a purpose, and therefore less abandoned, lost and afraid.

What ultimately tipped the scales was the answering machine at the office, when she went back there after taking a couple of weeks to get her head straight. The phone rang when she was barely in the door so she let the machine take the call, at this point remaining unsure whether it was—or was at least going to be—her business. It was still Jim's voice on the outgoing message, which was all the more unsettling for the time that had passed since his death. He sounded affable without being inappropriately breezy, encouraging without promising the Earth. But none of the messages—and there were plenty—were for him. Without exception, it was her name they asked for, because to each of the callers the Sharp in Sharp Investigations meant Jasmine.

She was aware that the story had been all over the media, but although she gave a few quotes to reporters she had been too caught up in the aftermath to pay the coverage any heed. She didn't want to read about it because she didn't want to think about it. She just wanted to be past it. In her mind it had been a frightening and frequently traumatic few weeks, just something awful that had happened to her, and something far worse that had happened to Jim. She forgot that, to the outside world looking in, the story was about a multiple murder case that had remained a mystery for twenty-seven years until she became involved; and that as a result this little business that was hers to take or leave had recently enjoyed the publicity equivalent of a multi-million-pound national ad-spend.

Jasmine discerned immediately that many of the callers were under the misapprehension that Sharp Investigations was something a great deal grander than a one-woman show, with enquiries covering a spectrum from missing moggies to private bodyguard hire. This was why the most significant call was not from someone who had never heard of Sharp Investigations until a fortnight before, but from someone who had been doing business with Jim for years: Harry Deacon at Galt Linklater.

Harry had worked with Jim on the force, and when Jim first retired Harry had tried to recruit him for the big investigation firm. Jim preferred to go it alone, having felt compromised too often by the tangled and conflicting loyalties that complicated his police work. Their relationship did prove mutually beneficial, however, as from Sharp Investigations' inception a great deal of Jim's work comprised sub-contracts from Galt Linklater, often supplementing their manpower on major jobs or taking stand-alone cases the larger outfit couldn't cover.

Harry had introduced himself briefly at Jim's funeral but had made no overtures towards talking shop. His message simply asked Jasmine to call back regarding 'the resolution of outstanding contracts'. She had assumed this meant the formalities associated with whatever loose ends would be left hanging at Galt Linklater by Sharp Investigations ceasing to operate. Instead, Harry laid out an offer to keep the firm on a retainer, which would pay a minimum even on months that she wasn't sub-contracted. He added that he expected this would prove moot, stating blankly that if Jasmine could clone herself he could keep both versions busy most months. This was for precisely the reasons Jim had laid out when he recruited her: they could always use somebody who didn't look like an ex-cop, somebody their subjects would never see coming.

Jasmine asked if it mattered whether this somebody actually knew what she was doing, a corrosive little voice in her head seizing upon a sense of déjà vu. She recalled her scepticism when she had heard the same rationalisation from Jim, whom she had believed simply to be acting out of duty towards a relative recently deceased.

Harry had responded by acknowledging that he knew she still had plenty to learn, and that Galt Linklater's guys would help her out, as Jim had, with on-the-job training. She was about to ask— with pronounced dubiety—whether Jim had ever mentioned how that on-the-job training had been

40

going, when it hit her with some surprise that he must have, and that his accounts may not have comprised what she assumed.

This guy owed Jasmine nothing, even if he had been close to Jim both personally and professionally. This offer wasn't charity, and what was really a jolt was that it proved Jim's hadn't been either. It struck her that not only did Harry's offer indicate that he believed she could do the job, but that Jim must indeed have spoken to him about how she was shaping up—and the implication was that Jim hadn't been lying out of kindness all those times he'd reassured her she was doing better than she thought.

Some of those times, undoubtedly, but not all.

'Didn't Jim tell you about my screw-ups?' she asked uncertainly.

'Aye. But you should hear other people's screw-ups.'

Jasmine forced herself to admit she'd never been handed so much on a plate before, between what Jim's family and Galt Linklater were laying in front of her. Her discomfort at door-stepping people under false pretences, or covertly following them around, not to mention her discomfort at catastrophically screwing up the basic fundamentals of both, died hard in the memory, and she knew that, soon enough, she'd be tasting both flavours again if she signed up for more. However, she had to acknowledge that it also felt pretty good when she got something right, especially when bringing her acting abilities to bear had been beneficial. Actors talked about live performance being high-stakes, but for all it could feel like life and death when you were out on that stage, in reality the most

41

they were risking was embarrassment. Jasmine knew what it felt like to be acting at gunpoint, and while she was in no hurry to play those odds again, it had all but erased her trepidation about ringing some personal-injury fraudster's doorbell and pretending to be someone she was not.

She told Angela her decision, which seemed to mean a lot more to Jim's daughter than Jasmine could have anticipated. She said it was a comfort to know that an important part of her father's life was enduring, acknowledging the irony that while he was alive his over-dedication to his work had been the cause of much hurt to all of them.

Thus Sharp Investigations re-opened for business, under new management.

Galt Linklater kept her in the back seat for the first couple of weeks, often literally, but when she was finally deployed into the field she quickly began to understand why Harry, like Jim before him, was prepared to be so patient and encouraging. With a little bit of confidence in her armoury, she really was the secret weapon. She was their ninja, the one operative that even the most hardbitten subjects never saw coming.

Serving papers was a particular speciality. Jasmine was able to get an instant result with guys who wouldn't answer their front door to a middle-aged male but were eager enough when a fresh-faced young woman came striding up their garden path.

'It's okay, I'm not selling anything, I promise,' was her standard opening, accompanied by a friendly, slightly self-conscious and therefore all-the-more innocent smile. It was Harry's suggestion, a cute little piece of misdirection because it made the

42

subject think that the worst he ought to be worried about was being asked to make a donation or sign up for something.

'Do you get a lot of junk mail?' she'd ask, almost unvaryingly receiving a response in the affirmative. 'We're offering a free opt-out service that will get your details removed from mailing lists. It doesn't cost anything: we're funded by Royal Mail to try to cut down on unnecessary carriage. Would you be interested, or are you content to keep receiving mail shots?'

That was when the mark was only too happy to give his name, which she would then ask him to confirm, whereupon she would flip over the top sheet on her clipboard and hand him the papers that had been tucked underneath.

In the early days her nervousness accounted for a few dismally faltering performances at front doors, but even her worst efforts yielded results. It had long been a source of grief to Jasmine that she looked younger than her years, sufficiently so that she anticipated being carded in pubs and clubs until she was pushing thirty. On the job, however, it worked like a force-field, deflecting all suspicion.

As well as donning a suit to look like a particularly earnest (and crucially guileless) young professional woman in order to serve papers, she could dress up or dress down according to the circumstances. She could play the student, the clubber, the jogger, the teenage daughter: just whatever it took to blend into the background for surveillance or allay suspicion when someone had to be made to identify themselves. Hell, she could pass for a schoolgirl if she needed to, though she had resisted doing so. She felt a little iffy about the ethics of it, but rather than rule it out completely she decided she'd keep it in her locker for just in case.

And, of course, she could play a newly recruited clinical support worker when Galt Linklater needed someone to go undercover at St Mungo's General. This was precisely the kind of job they'd have struggled with or even had to pass up altogether before Jasmine became an available resource.

The South Glasgow NHS Hospitals Trust approached Galt Linklater with a view to gathering evidence against Liam O'Hara ahead of their planned sacking of him, reckoning that if they amassed enough damning material it would preclude an industrial tribunal. It wasn't just theatre staff who referred to him as Eliot: hospital management were aware that he had worked long and resourcefully to make himself virtually unsackable. There was never any evidence against him other than individual testimony, which, as well as being uncorroborated, had a habit of being recanted the closer it came to a grievance hearing. Large institutions generally ended up simply having to tolerate individuals like Liam, having learned that attempting to get rid of them was more trouble than it was worth, particularly when it was doomed to failure.

What forced the South Glasgow Trust's hand was the impact on manpower. It wasn't just the nurses who had made complaints against him who ended up going off on long-term sick leave. Those who had incurred his bullying and intimidation for whatever other reason often decided that the best way of avoiding further harassment was to get their GP to sign them off with stress. The Trust was

44

shelling out a lot of sick pay to people who would be perfectly fit for work if Liam O'Hara could be removed from the equation.

Without Jasmine, the most Galt Linklater could have done was place one of their middle-aged males in the hospital as a porter or orderly. He'd have been wired for sound and vision to observe and record Liam's general conduct around his colleagues, in particular the way he used sexually inappropriate talk as a form of both intimidation and harassment.

That had been Jasmine's basic remit too, but they expected they'd get a lot more of the real Liam on tape when the new element was a shy-looking young girl. Had it been a burly middle-aged man Liam might well have been more circumspect, in case the new guy decided to clean his clock on behalf of an offended female colleague.

In the event, Jasmine's involvement went a lot further than observe-and-record, though she had been very careful to avoid possible entrapment. That was why her responses consisted of spelling out explicitly how she or her colleagues might be feeling, her words sometimes almost verbatim from the Trust's written policies. However, by standing up to Liam at all she had made it imperative that he put her in her place, and that was how she ended up serving him to his bosses on a golden platter.

It was almost worth getting her tit groped just to see the look on the sweaty creep's face as he began to realise who was the predator and who was the prey.

But though Jasmine and Galt Linklater were proving very good for each other, sub-contracting wasn't Sharp Investigations' only revenue stream.

As well as Jim's own long-standing roster of legal firms, there was a new sub-set of individual clients who came specifically to seek out Jasmine, and that was what she instantly understood she was dealing with on this particular May morning.

She had no jobs booked that day, and Jasmine was anticipating—she wouldn't use the phrase 'looking forward to'—a strictly office-bound shift, tackling a backlog of admin chores: from writing up surveillance reports to invoicing and, gulp, updating the company's tax files. Harry Deacon kept telling her to hire an accountant, as she was too busy with practical work to be dealing with things like that. She was in complete agreement, and fully intended to do so, but the problem was that she was also too busy to have gotten around to finding one.

She didn't mind writing up case-work, and would often catch up with that side of the job at home of an evening. Among the many lessons she had learned from observing Jim's practices was the importance of logging every minor detail, no matter how apparently insignificant, no matter how strong the temptation to skip to the highlights. When a trail went dead you had to be able to re-trace your steps, and the detail you were missing might well be found along the path less travelled.

The accounts, however, she could neglect for weeks at a time, content to procrastinate in order to defer that horrible feeling she got whenever she opened up the books. It wasn't that the accounts were particularly labyrinthine, or that she had no head for numbers; indeed, once she got going she was diligent and methodical about filling in every transaction. It was just that she spent the whole exercise worried that she was doing it all completely

46

wrong, so that when the time finally came to submit a company tax return, none of what she had recorded would make any sense. Her resultant garbled filing would precipitate an HMRC investigation and she'd find herself in a Kafkaesque hell of endlessly resubmitting her figures until she went insane or to jail.

Thus the distraction of an unexpected inquiry was most welcome, doubly so given what Jasmine had come to recognise this particular type of client as representing:

Easy money.

She felt guilty admitting it to herself, guiltier still taking the jobs given that invariably she was getting paid to deliver bad news to sad old punters, but as she had learned on the Ramsay case, the not knowing is worse.

The woman looked late sixties or early seventies, her slim build but one aspect of a neat and precise appearance, from the tailored fit of her navy-blue three-piece suit to her beret above a full head of dark brown hair, not a strand of which was either astray or chromatically out of kilter with its neighbours. Her dress was neither that of a wee pensioner nor a woman in denial of her years, but soberly appropriate, the choices of someone who had always known what to wear—and been able to afford it. She was not merely slim, however, but noticeably drawn and rather gaunt, her face thickly made-up though certainly not gaudily so. A year ago Jasmine would have guessed she was looking at a chronic heavy-smoker's face, and in fact if she'd met the woman anywhere else she'd have made the same deduction. But that she was standing inside Sharp Investigations, unannounced, offered a different perspective, and it wasn't the office light that told Jasmine her full head of hair was not a full head of hair.

'Hello, I'm looking for . . .' she started uncertainly. 'Would you be Jasmine Sharp?'

'Yes, I am,' Jasmine replied, pitching her tone at solicitous. 'Why don't you take a seat?'

Jasmine beckoned her further into the office and pulled a swivel chair across on its castors, positioning it in front of her desk. It struck her, as it always did, that she really ought to get hold of something more grand or at least formal-looking for seating clients, but it remained on the growing list of things she hadn't got around to yet.

The woman settled herself gingerly into the chair, as though concerned the wheels might cause it to skite out from under her, while Jasmine went to put the kettle on. The kettle, the sink and a small fridge were in a partitioned area that formed a box within one corner, creating an L-shaped layout in the rest of the office. Jasmine found that if she just went off and filled the kettle before asking these older clients were more likely to accept the offer of a cup of tea or coffee as it looked like she was making one anyway. She wanted them to settle in and feel unhurried, as she knew they were probably feeling nervous, awkward and a bit dubious about even saying why they were here.

Jasmine already knew why this woman was here.

They always turned up in person, they didn't phone ahead. Was it a generational thing, she wondered: you don't go online, you don't call up, you just go round to the local optician, local travel agent, local private investigator? Was it that they didn't quite believe anything would be initiated

48

if they merely spoke over the phone, even if—perhaps especially if—they were paying for it? Was it that they feared they'd be told she couldn't help and they believed they'd have less chance of being turned down if she met them personally and saw their angst? On the other hand, it could be that they all wanted a look at Jasmine before deciding to engage her services. In that case, she was surprised they never recoiled at what they saw. Perhaps when you got to a certain age everyone below a particular threshold looked equally young, but most likely her appearance simply wasn't a surprise because they'd remembered her age from the newspapers.

That, after all, was why they were here.

'I'm trying to track down somebody I lost touch with a long time ago,' the woman said, offering a nervous smile that was all about seeking approval and nothing about happiness or warmth. 'Would that be, you know, something you could . . .' she tailed off, visibly retreating into herself in the chair.

Jasmine nodded sincerely and solemnly. Yes, this would be something she could . . .

'What's your name?' Jasmine asked, getting out her notepad.

'It's Alice. Alice Petrie. Mrs,' she added, as though it was a point of honour.

That was definitely a generational thing. Women of a certain age could stress their married status in a way that made it sound like an OBE. Right enough: given Jasmine's relationship history, or abject lack thereof, if she ever did manage to get married, she'd regard it as an achievement too.

'And who is it that you're trying to get in contact with?'

Jasmine liked to phrase it this way. Partly this

49

was because terms such as 'track down' and 'get hold of' carried the rather stalkerish implication that the subject didn't wish to be found, but mainly because to 'get in contact with' was something one did to people who were still alive. It was polite and reassuring to make the client think that their quest was one commenced in hope, even if its resolution was almost invariably the confirmation that the person they sought was long-since deceased.

This was the mixed blessing bestowed upon Jasmine in the wake of the Ramsay case: part dividend and part curse, like a two-headed spirit set loose by her disturbing the earth covering a long-buried past. A lot of people had played their part in finding out the truth of what happened to Jim, but the media had to frame the narrative in a way that simplified the story. In trying to find her missing uncle, Jasmine had played her part in uncovering the fates of three people whose disappearance had haunted and baffled police and press alike for twenty-seven years. Thus Jasmine became, in many people's minds, someone who could find the missing relative they hadn't heard from in decades.

They weren't wrong, either. She had a one hundred per cent record so far. Unfortunately, they were one hundred per cent dead.

It was never people who had been missing for a month or a year, because people who were genuinely worried about someone wouldn't go to a novice. They would go to the police, and if they had no evidence of foul play they'd go to an outfit like Galt Linklater, which was full of salty ex-cops. Whereas the people coming to Jasmine had probably never considered hiring a PI until they read about her in the paper. They were always

50

in search of the long-lost, usually relationships severed in anger and bitterness that took too many years to transmute into regret.

At first she thought the law of averages ought to start pitching her a few happy endings to shape the bell curve, but Harry explained what was skewing it. If people are coming to a private investigator to find someone they lost touch with decades ago, it's because all their own channels have proven fruitless. Most of the time—not all, he stressed, but most of the time—this will be because the subject died years ago, way before the client thought to start looking.

Jasmine now had contacts that allowed her to access information by means not immediately open to her clients. Through these she was able to establish, usually with very little effort and no greater time, where and when the subject had died. Sometimes she was even able to furnish them with the address of the cemetery where they were buried or commemorated.

It brought in money, but it was very depressing. Despite answering their uncertainty, it seldom brought closure, other than that of the door to their last hope of healing a wound that had been seeping for years. She saw it in their eyes when she showed them her findings. Inside, they had known this was the most likely explanation, but there was always that last ember still burning and she was not only extinguishing it, but charging for the service.

It always felt a little wrong, but she knew the alternatives were worse. Either they would go on, possibly to their graves, haunted by never finding out, and by never having tried hard enough to do so, or they could go to a less scrupulous investigator who might bleed them slowly of as much as he could squeeze, drip-feeding hints of progress to keep the money coming before ultimately giving them the same news.

'Her name was Tessa Garrion.'

That was common too, the use of the past tense. They spoke like they were talking about someone they used to know, but the other implications hung in the air like ghosts.

Jasmine wrote the name down.

'And how did you know her?'

Mrs Petrie's mouth quivered a little, which told Jasmine the answer wasn't going to be 'childhood friend'. Anger and bitterness transmuted into regret, and throw in not a little shame at how long the process took. This was family.

'She was my sister.'

Mrs Petrie's speech threatened to falter as she began, but she recovered.

'My younger sister,' she added. She sounded guilty, as though these simple words were an admission of her fault in the estrangement.

'When did you last speak to her?'

'It was at our mother's funeral.'

'I see. And when was this?'

'February 1981.'

Jasmine paused for a beat, letting the significance have its moment.

'That's a long time,' she said, pitching her tone as neutral as possible; too heavy might sound judgmental, too light potentially flippant.

Mrs Petrie nodded sombrely, eyes down.

'Were there words?' Jasmine asked.

Mrs Petrie gave a sad little shake of her head.

'No. Not harsh ones, if that's what you mean. But

not many words of any kind.'

There was the rub. Whatever was wrong had been wrong before this funeral.

'We weren't very close. Not as close as we should have been, certainly, but the circumstances were . . .'

She dried for a moment, looking out of the window behind Jasmine, her face strained. She was trying to find a simple way of expressing something almost infinitely complex.

'What you have to understand is that Tessa was a lot younger than me. I was fifteen when she . . . no, sixteen, in fact, when she was born. I left home to get married when she was six.'

'And what age would she be now?'

'Fifty-three. She was twenty-two when my mother died.'

'And your father? Is he . . .?'

'No, he died when Tessa was twelve. He was a good bit older than my mother. Seventeen years, give or take a few months. He had been married before but his wife died in childbirth. Lost the baby too.'

'Tessa would have been very close to your mother, then,' Jasmine observed, knowing a lot about growing up in such circumstances.

'Close to both of them. She was their wee pet.'

'Late additions get spoiled rotten,' Jasmine suggested, nudging Mrs Petrie towards where she thought she needed to go.

'Yes,' she agreed regretfully, contritely even. 'Looking back, I wouldn't say she was spoiled; definitely not compared to kids these days. But at the time, I certainly thought so. I was resentful of the things she was allowed to do—and to get away

53

with—because my parents had never been like that with me. I always felt I was on a tight leash, whereas Tessa was allowed to get away with murder. She wrapped them round her pinkie. Always knew how to grab the limelight.'

Mrs Petrie gave a bittersweet smile, some pleasure in the memory tinged perhaps with regret about how it had made her feel at the time.

'I wasn't the most tolerant big sister, I'd have to admit.'

'I guess when you're in your late teens and adolescence you don't want a toddler cramping your style,' Jasmine offered.

'No, you don't,' she replied, once again looking towards the window, as though it was a widescreen TV and scenes from her life were playing on it.

'So after you got married and moved out, did you stay in touch? I mean, did you move far away? Where are you from?'

'Dumfries,' she replied, causing Jasmine to repress a self-reproaching tut. She normally had a very precise ear for locating accents, but there was a certain middle-class Scottish neutrality to this one that had flummoxed her. Most times when she found herself unable to place this accent it had hailed from the western side of the Borders—Wigtonshire or Dumfries and Galloway—yet whenever she encountered it again, it failed to pop into her head as an option.

'I grew up in Dumfries, I should say. When I got married I moved to Cornwall, where my husband is from.'

'Not handy for an afternoon visit,' Jasmine noted.

'No, I didn't see a lot of my family. The odd weekend, Christmas, that sort of thing. So by the

54

time my mother died, Tessa and I really didn't have a lot in common. I barely recognised her, to be honest. Hadn't seen her in a few years as she'd been away at college any time I came back to Dumfries, then moved out altogether after that. At the funeral, I was in my late thirties with two children and a job teaching at a local primary school, while she was this rather bohemian young creature from a completely different world. We just didn't find much to say to each other, and after that, with both my mum and dad gone, we lost touch.'

'And neither of you made an attempt to get in contact before now? A letter, a phone call, a Christmas card? Facebook?' Jasmine added, then wished she hadn't, given Mrs Petrie's expression. It was an ill-judged note of levity, prompted by a desire not to sound too accusatory, but the joke fell flat and the note of accusation had clearly been struck.

'You're young,' she stated, not retaliatory, just matter-of-fact, even accompanied by a dry chuckle. 'Right now you probably think six months ago was another era. You'll be amazed how fast time passes as you get older. And the things you mean to do, the things you know you ought to do, it becomes so much harder to do them the longer you leave it. Plus you always think you'll have time.'

Which, Jasmine knew, obviated the need for her to ask 'why now?'.

Mrs Petrie had been sipping politely at her tea, but now she pushed it away with a grimace, as though it had turned cold.

'I don't have time,' she said, working very hard to keep her voice steady. 'Do you understand?'

Jasmine nodded.

'My mother died of pancreatic cancer. It was very late-presenting. Months. I'm hoping for a little longer than that. It's my colon. I could have three years, five, seven. I could live longer than you, for all we both know, but even at my age you never accept life is finite until you get something like this. It changes everything, when you no longer have forever. Once the doctor has shown you your best-before date, the world never looks the same. Drastic change in priorities, in what's important. In what *matters*. Family matters. Nothing matters more.'

Mrs Petrie began filling up.

'Years I've wasted,' she went on. 'Thinking my own wee world was complete. Thinking she ought to be the one to get in touch: I've never moved house. Decades. She could have kids of her own, kids I've never met.'

Now she broke down, the composure of her neatly made-up face cracking in a contortion of grief.

Jasmine got up from her chair and moved around the desk, tissues proffered in her fingers.

Mrs Petrie waved her away, cradling her head in her right hand but holding up her left, her index finger aloft. A teacher's gesture.

'I'll be okay. I just need a moment.'

Mrs Petrie produced a hanky of her own and dabbed delicately at her nose and eyes. True enough, in a short while she was composed enough to speak steadily once again.

'I realise there's a possibility that I'm starting this too late,' she admitted, before betraying that she wasn't *really* admitting it. 'But I have to assume that if she'd died, then I'd have heard. We drifted apart, but it's not like we had some feud that meant I'd be barred from her funeral. Someone would have been in touch.'

Not necessarily, Jasmine thought but didn't say. Instead she moved Mrs Petrie on to practical matters, the 'can do' part. She wasn't in the business of selling false hope, but she understood that in these cases all hope was sacrosanct until it was gone.

'The more you can tell me about her, the more I'll have to work with. What was the last address you had for her?'

'I'm sorry. That's long gone from the memory. I very much doubt I'd have it written down anywhere after all this time.'

'That's okay. I really just want to know where she went after she left home.'

'Glasgow,' Mrs Petrie replied. 'That's why I came here to hire somebody. That and . . .'

She looked sheepish, clearly feeling a little stupid and slightly embarrassed by this, which was far more self-conscious than most of Jasmine's previous clients.

'That and the fact that I'd read about you. Well, rather, a friend of mine did. When I mentioned I was thinking of hiring an investigator she told me about what you'd done.'

'Cornwall is a long way to travel on spec. You could have rung ahead.'

'Oh no, it's not like that. I'm staying here for a few days. My son lives in Paisley. I was visiting my friend there at the weekend. I think the cowardly part of me was hoping you wouldn't be in, so that I could dismiss the idea, but now that I'm here I realise I should have done this years ago, done

57

everything in my power.'

'Well, you're here now,' Jasmine said, trying to head off any further self-recrimination. 'And you were telling me Tessa was living in Glasgow.'

'Yes. She went to college there, and stayed on when she got a job.'

'What did she do for a living?'

'She was an actress.'

Jasmine skipped a beat, hoping her moment of mild gaping passed unnoticed. It was a daft reflex she couldn't quite shake. Whenever she heard about someone being an actress, she felt this unsettling mix of envy and curiosity: what kind of work, how did she get there, where did she train?

Mrs Petrie could have read her thoughts.

'She studied drama in Glasgow, at the SATD. Sorry, that's the Scottish Academy of Theatre and Dance,' she explained, assuming Jasmine would never have heard of it. 'Then, after that, she got a job in the Pantechnicon. I remember when my mother told me, I thought she meant a part, but it turned out the theatre was something called a rep, which means they put on several plays a year and so the same people act in each show.'

Jasmine said nothing, nodding politely as Mrs Petrie so helpfully explained the practice of a repertory company.

Straight out of the academy and into a job in rep. It was a dream as common as it was unlikely, such that a friend from the Academy once referred to harbouring such a fantasy as being like masturbation: nobody would admit to it, but everybody did it. It was so improbable as to be a joke, yet for this Tessa Garrion it had apparently been a reality; not just any old rep either, but the

58

Pantechnicon, which begged a number of questions, most of them deeply unworthy.

Catch a grip, girl, Jasmine warned herself. Here she was, impugning the three-decades-past sexual integrity of an actress she'd never even heard of just because she'd got a part in a company. It told her that, for all she was starting to settle into her new career, she still wasn't quite ready to admit to herself that she'd given up on her first choice. It happened every so often, something that would precipitate a glimpse of her old dreams, enough both to keep the flame burning and to torture her a little over whether she was making the right choice by sticking with Sharp Investigations.

Most recently, the cause had been a chance meeting with Charlotte Queen, whom she bumped into in the Tron Theatre bar when they were both there to see a revival of *Swing Hammer Swing!* Jasmine had feared it would be an uncomfortable encounter: that at best Charlotte would make play of ignoring her, or that she would be subject to much faux-polite sneering with regard to their respective career trajectories. The last time their paths had crossed, just before Jim disappeared, Jasmine was eyeball on a foot-follow of a surveillance subject when she passed Charlotte having coffee at a pavement table outside a West End café. Even though they had seen each other and Charlotte called out to her by name, Jasmine could neither stop nor take her eyes off the subject. Effectively, she had completely rubbered the notoriously egotistical Ms Queen in front of her friends. It had come as no surprise when Charlotte never got back in touch about that mooted production of *The Tempest*.

Instead, Charlotte had been all over her in the bar: hugs and kisses and oh-my-Gods.

'I read all about you in the papers. God, how amazingly exciting. I mean, dangerous, of course, sure, you must be so brave. I couldn't believe it, though. I was, like, *so* telling everybody I knew you. And then I remembered I saw you one time and you walked right past and I thought you maybe had headphones on or were in a daydream, but I realised you must have been actually tailing somebody, like in a film. I mean, wow. That is so cool.'

'I was on a foot-follow,' Jasmine was relieved to be able to explain at last.

'God, that is so amazing. It's, like, being in character, except you're really, really *deeply* in character. That's major.'

'Not really,' Jasmine corrected, but only by way of taking the opportunity to tell Charlotte about the aspects of the job that truly did require acting. She had surely never sounded so enthusiastic about her job, but she couldn't help it. Charlotte was lapping it up, and Jasmine was basking in the light of her enthusiasm. Impressing Charlotte was like a drug: you just wanted more and more and more. It was why she got so much out of people, on stage and off.

'So you're, like, a real detective?'

Jasmine could hear those commas, but knew that if she edited them out it would still be an unearned accolade. *Like* a real detective? No. Not even close.

As it turned out, Charlotte's production of *The Tempest* wasn't going to happen anyway. She had dropped the idea in favour of a revival of Liz Lochead's Scots-dialect translation of *Tartuffe*

60

by Molière, having heard through the grapevine that the Scottish government were planning a series of events aimed at both celebrating and cementing artistic ties with France. In her ability to combine vision, ambition, networking and sheer opportunism, it showed just why Charlotte had come a long way in a short time and was destined to go a great deal further. The play was scheduled to run both in Edinburgh and Paris, under the imprimatur of the Scottish government and therefore financially assisted by Arts Council Scotland.

This had predictably rankled with a lot of people; more so than even the usual grumbling that followed the awarding of grants to anybody other than oneself. Fire Curtain was perceived to be well down the list of companies in need of public funding: it was believed that, as the daughter of Hamish Queen, Charlotte had been the beneficiary of more hand-outs and hand-ups than anybody else in Scottish theatre.

The roots of this resentment lay in artistic snobbery as much as financial jealousy. Hamish Queen had made millions putting on big, flashy musicals in London's West End. To a certain constituency, it wasn't 'proper' theatre, just ultra-commercial flummery aimed at fleecing tourists and philistines, so it stung all the more that his money and influence were facilitating his daughter's rise to prominence—ignoring, of course, the fact that Charlotte was very much about putting on 'proper' theatre.

'I'd still love to work with you some time,' she told Jasmine in the Tron bar. 'I think if the part was right, with your real-life experience, it would be

61

electric.'

If the part was right. A hypothetical among hypotheticals, a throwaway remark, one fleeting thought amid millions that must pass through a capricious mind such as Charlotte's, always looking for the next idea. But to Jasmine, it was enough to tantalise and to torment, keeping that door open just enough to let in a chink of light that kept distracting her from the here and now.

'Tessa was a born performer,' Mrs Petrie went on. 'I don't think she was out of nappies before she'd learned that she could get attention from Mum and Dad by putting on a show. She was a prodigious mimic. She would impersonate the voices she heard on the radio, and of course that would get the praise raining down upon her about how clever she was. I don't mean that it made her conceited, because she wasn't. Precocious, certainly, but not self-centred. I just mean that she took a lot of encouragement from it. A lot of confidence. She wasn't egotistical, but she knew what she was worth, so it didn't surprise me when I learned she was actually on the stage.'

'And when she was at the Pantechnicon,' Jasmine said. 'What years would she have been there? What did you see her in?'

At this, Mrs Petrie's face darkened somewhat. Jasmine feared she had said the wrong thing, but she soon saw that it was more self-reproach.

'I never saw her on stage,' she confessed, and clearly a confession it was.

'Well, of course, if you were down in Cornwall . . .' Jasmine suggested.

'That didn't make it easy, true, but I should have made the effort. To be honest, I didn't want to.'

'Why not?'

Mrs Petrie swallowed and her mouth went thin, pinched.

'I was jealous.'

'You wanted to be an actress too?' Jasmine asked, hoping she wasn't being granted a glimpse of herself fifty years into the future, eaten away by bitterness and regret.

'No. It would never even have occurred to me. But that's the point. I could just imagine my parents' faces if I'd said I wanted to be an actress. The same way they instilled in Tessa a confidence that she could do anything and the desire to spread her wings, they instilled in me a sense of responsibility and a need to keep my feet on the ground. If by some whim I had decided that I wanted to be an actress, or a dancer, or whatever, I'd simply never have had the confidence, the nerve, to go out there and try.

'Tessa did, though. She was all passion and impulse. She didn't look before she leapt, and I used to think she'd end up in trouble because what if something goes wrong? I forgot to ask myself: what if it goes right? Tessa didn't let worrying about what might go wrong hold her back, and I think that's what I was jealous of most. I felt I had lived a life of cause and effect, of always being mindful of consequences.'

'I'm informed it's a common complaint of the oldest child in most families,' Jasmine told her. 'They need to be the responsible one, while their wee brothers and sisters get to have their heads in the clouds.'

'That's as may be, but it doesn't make it any easier to sit here knowing I never saw Tessa act, and now I never will.'

She began choking up again, her voice failing her.

'You don't know that,' Jasmine stated, going for matter-of-fact rather than consolatory, as though reining in self-pity. She realised it sounded a little harsh, so followed it up with something a little more ameliorative. 'She could be in some wee provincial rep in British Columbia for all we know.'

Mrs Petrie had staunched her tears, but she was shaking her head with grave certainty.

'No. She gave up the stage a long time ago.'

'How do you know?'

'When I decided I should try to find Tessa, one of the first things I thought to do was to contact Equity. I spoke to a very helpful man there who checked into the archives for me. He could only access files going back twenty-five years, but he had no record of her in all that time. He told me her membership must have lapsed prior to 1986.'

Mrs Petrie sighed reflectively, as though trying to see a good side to this.

'I suppose it's possible she met some rich admirer who saw her on stage and whisked her away to a life of luxury,' she said, not sounding like she believed it. 'To be honest, I'm not sure that any amount of luxury would have made Tessa quit the stage, but I can't think of any other reason why she would give up on what had been her dream for so long. Can you?'

'No,' lied Jasmine, who could think of one or two.

Trail of the Sniper

Detective Superintendent Catherine McLeod didn't think her husband would have made much of a criminal, or a card player for that matter. All it had taken was for her to make her overture—not even to broach the subject—and he was already wearing his 'Oh God, do we have to?' face.

It was generally one of the things she loved about him: that what you saw was what you got. He had the emotional honesty of a Labrador puppy and a reluctance to put on masks out of deference or decorum. It once amused her to observe that the only thing that could be more out of place than Drew in a Merchant Ivory movie or a Henry James novel would be a spaceship. On the downside, this boyish openness could make him seem terribly vulnerable and cause Catherine to feel every one of the nine years between them, and a good few more besides.

The look he wore now suggested he was afraid of being scolded. She already knew that she would get her way, but also that the outcome was not the most important aspect of the discussion. Actually having it would be more of a result.

She had chosen her moment carefully: not just bringing it up when he was trying to watch the Wimbledon highlights earlier, or the moment she was in the door from work, but during a late dinner, with both the boys long since tucked up in bed.

'I need to talk to you about something,' she had said.

That wasn't when he made the face, but it had

probably put him on alert.

'It's about Duncan, and that money we gave him for his report card.'

Duncan was the older of their two sons, his brother Fraser two years his junior. Duncan's interim report back in November had indicated he was falling behind in maths; his teacher suggested he wasn't paying as much attention as he should, perhaps because he was finding the subject a struggle. Mindful of this becoming a vicious circle, Duncan had been encouraged by his parents to do a little extra maths at home until he was more comfortable with the day-to-day classwork and therefore better able to keep pace. It had been a grind at first, for child and parents alike, but all three of them had stuck it out. It had borne results, with his teacher singling out his improvement for special comment ahead of parents' evening.

In order to reward this they had given Duncan money to spend on 'something for the summer holidays', having listened to him prattle on with promiscuously fickle enthusiasm about everything from goalie gloves to NERF guns.

(Fraser got money for his report too, following a philosophical discussion around the breakfast table over whether his consistent high standards should merit any less recognition than Duncan's fall and recovery. No firm consensus was agreed, but Duncan was privately given twenty pounds more than Fraser on the understanding that he kept the information to himself.)

'Has he blown it all on hookers and ice-lollies?' Drew asked, trying, and perhaps just hoping, to keep the tone light.

'He wants to buy a new game for his Xbox.'

Drew had rolled his eyes, but that wasn't when he got the look. He laughed a little.

'I'll have a word,' he said. 'Remind him about all the stuff he was planning to do when he couldn't get outside for the rain. Mind you, this does mean I've officially turned into my mum. I remember her wanting to shunt me outdoors all the time during the summer holidays when all I wanted was to watch videos and play computer games. I could never understand why she did it, but now I'm a parent I'm exactly the same.'

'I've already tried. He said he would still be outdoors plenty, but reminded me that we had said he could spend the money on whatever he liked.'

'Apart from hookers, obviously. It's true, though. We did say it was his money, and choosing what to spend it on was part of the reward. We can't really go back on that. To be fair, it'll probably rain all summer anyway.'

'I agree. It's not buying another computer game that's the issue. The problem is, the game he wants is *Trail of the Sniper*. It's got a fifteen certificate, but he says all his friends have got it.'

That was when Drew made the face.

Drew worked for a games development firm, so was several times bitten and consequently very shy of finding himself being held accountable for the evils and excesses of the entire industry, but this was only part of the reason for his wincing expression.

'He's starting Primary Five,' she added. 'He's ten, and as far as I can ascertain this game revolves entirely around shooting people in the head with graphically realistic consequences.'

Drew let out a very quiet sigh, one he was perhaps

67

hoping she wouldn't hear.

'If it's a fifteen, then he can't have it,' he said. 'He'll just have to accept that. His pals are probably lying anyway.'

'So you'll tell him?' she asked. 'It's just, you let him have that wrestling game that's a fifteen.'

'Yeah, but on those WWE games the certificate is actually an upper limit on who should be playing it,' he replied with a smile. Catherine wasn't in the mood for joking.

'I'm just saying, he's got his heart set on this and I don't want it to always be me that gets painted as the killjoy.'

'That's fair enough,' he said. 'It should come from me. He'll not be happy, but the fact that I did let him play the wrestling game should mean he understands this isn't capricious. I'll explain to him that there's content that's inappropriate. It's a fifteen and he's ten.'

And there it was, the moment Catherine had predicted. Drew was ostensibly agreeing with her, but in reality he was merely acquiescing. She could tell from his choice of words: he sounded like he was quoting rather than thinking out loud, and his rationale that 'it's a fifteen and he's ten' was in complete contrast to his previously stated opinions about each child's comprehension and maturity being too complex and individual to categorise by age bands. He was agreeing with her to keep the peace, in the short term possibly because it might improve his chances of the evening ending with a shag, and in the long term because . . . well, that was complex.

For one thing, Drew was sensitive about ever being considered irresponsible as a father, primarily because he was a lot younger than her, but partly also because he worked in an industry largely built on exploiting the more emotionally retarded aspects of the male psyche.

Catherine, in turn, was sensitive about being the one who always said no, who was risk-averse, disapproving, a killjoy.

The bad cop.

She didn't like to admit it to herself, but sometimes Catherine suspected Drew was a little scared of her. It could allow her to get her own way, as in this case, but prevailing because her husband was too cowed to stand up to her was a long way from what she wanted.

She knew she was on shaky ground complaining that Drew didn't want to discuss how he really felt about something, as he had frequent cause to lament how there was so much that his wife wouldn't reveal about herself. Partly it was derived from determination not to bring the job home; her resolve that her family should not live under a shadow of gloom cast by a wife and mother who often spent her working hours mired in the detritus of the worst things that human beings could do to one another. But Drew's complaint was not born of ingratitude at being spared regular, vivid and graphic insights into her caseload. It was something more, something other, something she wouldn't, couldn't share.

'There's this dark place you go,' he once put it. 'You're angry on the road to that place and you're unreachable when you get there. But what's hardest is you're numb for days afterwards.'

Drew refilled her wine glass and topped up his own. She could tell he was trying to think of something else to talk about: something light, that would indicate the previous matter was closed and there were no lingering issues about it, which only served to underline how the opposite was true.

They had to be adults about this. She wanted to know how he really felt, and why.

'You disagree, though, don't you,' she said. 'You don't have to pretend, Drew. In fact, you can't, not to me. There's very few can lie to me across a short table and get away with it. If it was up to you, you'd let him play it, wouldn't you?'

Drew looked flustered and defensive, and not a little put-upon, like he was resentful at receiving precisely the scolding he had feared.

'I haven't seen the game in question, so I couldn't say.'

'Yes, but in general you don't think playing these games is inappropriate for Duncan. You just go along with me because you know I don't like them.'

'That's not fair,' he replied. 'There are plenty of games I wouldn't want the boys seeing, let alone playing. I've never shown them anything from our *Hostile* series, despite the added curiosity of them being the games Daddy makes.'

'But you let them play other violent games, not just the wrestling one. Even Fraser gets to play that *Serious Sam* thing.'

Fraser was the factor that upped the stakes for Catherine on this issue, because she knew that any game Duncan got, he would be watching over his shoulder and asking for a shot. She knew it was not fair on Duncan that everything he played or watched should be acceptable for his wee brother, at an age when two years of maturity was practically a generation. But equally she didn't want Fraser

70

growing up too fast, and certainly didn't want him exposed to anything so disturbing that it had been given a fifteen certificate.

'It's set so that the monsters spray flowers instead of blood when you shoot them. It's the equivalent of shooting wooden ducks at the fairground.'

'But don't you think the violence itself is the issue?'

Drew sighed more loudly this time, looking all the more like he didn't want to get into this, because he was aware it was a fight he couldn't win.

'I just think that clicking on a cursor is a long way distant from pulling a trigger. Nobody's worried about *Gran Turismo* making people go out and drive their cars at a hundred and fifty miles an hour, or *SimCity* making people want to be town planners.'

'But those are representations of racing, or managing resources and designing landscapes. This *Trail of the Sniper* game is about shooting people in the head, Drew. All these games are about shooting people. I don't want my sons getting desensitised to the idea of that.'

'That's your prerogative as their mother, and that's why I'm content to back you up all the way. I'll tell Duncan he's not on, and I'll make it plain that it's my judgment, not yours. I'm not arguing with you about this.'

'But you don't agree,' she re-stated, not quite sure why this bothered her so much.

For some reason, Catherine had always assumed she'd have girls. There was no rationale behind this, just the vision she had always enjoyed of being a mother. Instead, she had got two boys, and was frequently dismayed by the insights they provided

71

into their gender.

She had nonetheless been of the opinion that boys didn't have to turn out to be feral, hyper-masculine monsters obsessed with the brutal and the disgusting. To that end, theirs was a house that didn't tolerate violence, raised voices or displays of excessive temper. Duncan and Fraser's gender role models were progressive, enlightened and far from conventional. Their dad was home more than their mum and did more than his share of the cooking, shopping and other domestic chores; their mum was a police officer, out fighting crime and catching bad guys. Yet none of this had prevented them becoming, well, feral, hyper-masculine monsters obsessed with the brutal and the disgusting. Something in them sought out the horrible, no matter how much you tried to guide them otherwise. They really were made of frogs and snails and puppy-dog tails, and Catherine worried constantly about what was in their heads, and about what might *get* in their heads.

'I agree partly. I just don't feel so strongly about it. It clearly means more to you that the boys shouldn't play certain games than it does to me, so I'm happy to go along with that. It's no biggy.'

'But I don't want you just to go along with it. I want you to see what I see here. I want you to understand what's wrong with the idea of our children learning to kill via a simulator.'

Drew reeled a little at this, and she thought for a moment she had really struck a telling blow, one that truly altered his perspective. He took a moment then sighed again, which informed her that this was not in fact the case.

'With respect, Cath,' he began, then paused,

considering and perhaps carefully revising what he was going to say. 'You're a long way off your patch here. I don't want to fight about this, but what I will say is that, in my experience, people who disapprove of violent video games have usually never played one.'

Catherine felt the surge of quite disproportionate anger that came whenever she sensed somebody was trying to put her in her place. So when her mobile rang, interrupting a post-prandial conversation for the several hundredth time in their marriage, it was probably a mercy upon both of them.

'I have to take this,' she said, given the name that was flashing on her screen.

Drew gave a resigned and slightly huffy shrug.

He was generally very tolerant and understanding of these interruptions, acknowledging that he had long since accepted they were part of the package that came with Catherine, but on occasion the timing could test his patience to the limit. This was one of those times, largely because she could tell he was already a little pissed off at her for the evening not going how he'd hoped.

Catherine, for her part, was usually just as frustrated and resentful when the calls came out of hours, but in this instance some spiteful part of her welcomed it, perhaps because she didn't have a come-back for Drew's last gambit.

It was Sunderland, the Almighty: calling when she was, nominally at least, off duty. This usually meant he was handing her a whole bundle of grief, the true extent and ungodly nature of which would only reveal itself over time.

'There's been a shooting in Cragruthes, up near

73

Alnabruich,' Sunderland told her, his voice weary with portent. She could tell there was a fire starting to catch and he wanted her to douse it before somebody got very badly burned. 'I need you up there first thing in the morning to take charge.'

Alnabruich, though: that was up in the Highlands, so she didn't get the angle. Was it related to something else she was working on?

'And DI McSheepshagger of Highland can't deal with this because . . .?' she inquired.

'Because it's not on his manor. Alnabruich is a long way from Govan, but it's still Strathclyde's patch. It's Argyllshire.'

Bugger, she thought.

'What's the script?' she asked. 'Murder?'

'Fatal shooting is the line at this stage. Took half his face off. Possibility that it was accidental still to be ruled out.'

This wasn't exactly blowing her skirt up so far. A shooting in the back of beyond that might not even be a murder wasn't the kind of thing you gave to a copper of her rank, especially not when she was off duty.

'Okay, all very unfortunate, but you want to tell me why you're punting it to me?'

'Because the shooting took place in the grounds of Cragruthes Castle, and the vic was standing two feet from Sir Angus McCready, the laird of Ruthes, when it happened.'

'Ah,' she replied as all became clear. Everyone was equal in the eyes of the law, and the police treated everybody the same. Apart from the people they treated completely different. 'So we're talking major media scrutiny, political interference, connected individuals stomping their footprints

74

all over our investigation, your maxi-zoom deluxe nightmare?'

Sunderland chuckled darkly.

'Oh, you don't know the half, McLeod. I haven't told you who the victim is yet.'

A few minutes later Catherine disconnected the call, then walked to the sink and poured her wine away.

'I'll have to call it a night,' she announced. 'I'm looking at an early start in the morning and I'll need a clear head.'

'Why? What's so important *this* time?' Drew asked, not attempting to hide his resentment at how the evening had panned out, and inadvertently inviting a knockout blow.

'Because somebody's been shot in the head. In *real life*, Drew. Here in real life.'

Bad Debts

Jasmine had already decided that Mrs Petrie's inquiry might not prove such easy money even before anything started to go awry.

This sort of case was normally a matter of making a few phone calls and setting certain processes in motion, then profitably getting on with other jobs while she waited for the information to start coming in. Out of sight, out of mind. The biggest source of angst and self-examination was usually over what she considered fair to charge, considering it generally didn't gobble up a lot of man hours.

She wasn't sure whether time spent lying awake thinking about the case was billable, but that hadn't been a consideration until now.

If there was a checklist for this genus of client, Mrs Petrie would have ticked most of the boxes, right down to the abruptly altered perspective upon mortality having precipitated a need to forgive and not forget. There was one anomaly, however, and it was major. The subject would be fifty-three years old, which was at least two decades younger than anybody Jasmine had been asked to look for since re-opening Sharp Investigations. It changed the game entirely when there was a far greater possibility that the person being sought might actually be alive.

Tessa Garrion had been in her head all day and a blearily uncomfortable portion of the night. It had pushed a few buttons to learn that she had been an actress, but not as many as learning that she had suddenly *ceased* to be an actress some time in her mid-twenties, despite a promising career ahead of her. This bothered Jasmine because she could have been talking about her mother.

Mum had seldom talked about her brief acting career, except in the most oblique terms, as though afraid of leaving behind any clues Jasmine might follow that could unlock the secrets of her past. Jasmine had grown up without a father, and been told that he had died between her mum falling pregnant and Jasmine's birth. Mum never told her anything else about him. From an early age she understood it to be a closed subject and learned not to ask. She got the sense that her mother's reticence was as much about protecting Jasmine as it was about her reluctance to revisit certain memories and thought that, one day, when she had proven that she was all grown up and demonstrably stable of mind and body, she might encourage Mum to reveal just a little.

One day.

What little she did know she picked up largely from chat between Mum's friends and relatives. Their words were guarded, even when they didn't know Jasmine was in earshot, as though they were as wary of being caught in such discussions by Beth Sharp as being overheard by her daughter. Through these disparate fragments she learned that Mum had been brought up in a violent area of Glasgow and had made some dangerous friends by way of a desperate survival strategy. It wasn't a matter of falling in with a bad crowd and being led astray, as it seemed she had been as single-minded and passionate about her vocation as Jasmine would be years later. Rather it was that when her career should have allowed her to move on and move up, she couldn't extricate herself from certain entanglements of her past. The greatest of those entanglements, Jasmine had to assume, must have been her father.

She knew nothing about him. The only descriptions she had were individual words, scattered like snowflakes over the years, leaving merely a blurred outline of where this man had been. What was unmistakable was that it was not the outline of a good person.

Dangerous. Brutal. Ruthless. Terrifying.

And, of course, deceased.

Jasmine never heard any details, only allusions to living by the sword and dying by the sword.

She knew that, following his death but before Jasmine's birth, her mum had moved to Edinburgh to start again, to create a new life away from the influences of the people she had become involved with. It was only forty miles along the M8, but apparently that was far enough. These were people who didn't see a broad horizon and wonder what was beyond it. They were busy inside their own little goldfish bowl and Mum knew that she and her daughter would be safe enough as long as they remained outside it. That was why Mum seldom went back to Glasgow, not if there was something she wanted to see at one of its theatres and not even to visit Jasmine at her student digs. It was as though she was afraid even a chance encounter might be enough to corrupt her new life.

She gave up her acting career to raise Jasmine, working initially with a theatre-in-the-community group until qualifying as a drama teacher. Jasmine knew she had left a job with a rep company based in Glasgow, but it was only recently that she had given much thought to the sacrifice her mum had made and considered how she had given up just as many dreams as her daughter. When she was growing up, Jasmine had heard how her mother used to be an actress, but it meant nothing to a child: Mum was just Mum, a drama teacher who had friends in theatre.

It was only since making the leap to take on Sharp Investigations and accepting that she was slowly closing the door on acting that Jasmine had begun to appreciate how her mum had gone through the same thing before her. Worse, in fact, because unlike Jasmine her mum had been walking the walk, doing it for real, not merely training in hope. Did she keep the guttering flame alight for a few years, telling herself a second chance might come once her daughter was off to school, perhaps? Did it hurt a little every time she went to the theatre, seeing the art she used to practise and the life she could have had? Did it hurt especially on that unforgettable night backstage at the Lyceum? Was the same perspective that brought forth Jasmine's epiphany for her merely a cruel reminder of all she had lost?

If so, she was indeed one hell of an actress, because she had covered it up all Jasmine's life. She never spoke of regrets, never gave Jasmine the impression she was off roaming in the realms of what if. Presumably, one of the possible answers to what if had been made vividly apparent and she was very grateful for what she had now. Her life as an actress was inextricable from a life in the orbit of dangerous, violent people, one of whom had been Jasmine's father. Knowing this, Jasmine guessed, difficult as it was, her mother would make the same choice every time.

But there are always other what ifs, and sometimes hidden layers of complexity within the first.

When her mum was suddenly forced to confront her own mortality, she had done the same thing as Mrs Petrie and so many others before her: she had gone to a private investigator to find someone she wanted to talk to, one last time, before it was too late. And unlike all the clients Jasmine had worked for, her mother had gotten her wish.

Jasmine, however, had known nothing about this.

Then, in the course of the hunt for her missing uncle, Jasmine had come across the name Glen Fallan in Jim's files.

She heard him described by a senior police officer.

Dangerous. Brutal. Ruthless. Terrifying.

These all applied, but there were others too. Torturer. Debt-collector. Enforcer. Hit-man.

'Ice-cold killer,' the policeman had told her. 'And when I say that, I mean like the ice doesn't feel anything when it freezes you to death.'

Despite being thus forewarned, Fallan's name was the only clue Jasmine had to go on at that stage, so she located and confronted him. He was indeed dangerous, brutal, ruthless and terrifying. He also saved her life—twice—and put himself to considerable pains in order to help her get to the bottom of Jim's disappearance. Nothing she witnessed of him suggested the cop's descriptions were exactly libellous, but they didn't show the whole picture either. For one thing, he was a lot less dead than the police believed him to be.

Following Jim's funeral, Jasmine learned that despite Fallan reputedly having died two decades back, her mother had requested that her cousin track him down. Jim had done so successfully, and Fallan had subsequently visited Mum shortly before her death.

Jasmine then discovered that Fallan had been sending money to her mother, every three or four months for twenty years. It wasn't a fiver a time, either. Looking back, it explained how they had got by at certain times, at ages when Jasmine was oblivious of all financial considerations. Even when she was a student it would never have occurred to her to try to balance the books in terms of what a drama teacher earned and how much she was able to give Jasmine to help with her rent and other expenses.

All her life this man, Glen Fallan, had been

secretly, invisibly supporting her.

She confronted him once more, driving down to Northumberland to the women's refuge where he served as a volunteer: gardener, handyman, courier, bodyguard. He was working in the grounds of the house, wielding a leaf-blower in one hand like it was a dust-buster. When he saw her approach there was warmth in his face but he didn't smile. It was as though he was pleased to see her but not glad that she was there, because he had already deduced why.

There was a fresh breeze blowing and he was wearing only a sleeveless top above his camo trousers, but she could feel heat coming from him as he stood a few feet away, the smell of the outdoors, fresh sweat and recent ablutions in her nose. His presence was almost overwhelming. He made her feel so small, so weak by comparison.

She thought her voice would fail her and part of her wanted to turn and run, but she couldn't run from this. It had already found her. She knew she had no choice but to find it in herself to speak the most difficult four words of her life, a question she only had the strength to ask because she was already certain of the answer.

'Are you my father?'

She recalled that she ceased to feel the breeze, that though they were outdoors in the rolling grounds of that spooky big house she could have been in a stark white room or a bare stage, nothing else in the world but her and this man.

He looked at her with a sadness born of pity and regret, though she remained unsure who it was for.

'I always feared that one day I'd have to answer this question,' he said. 'I thought I'd got away with it. Your mum told me to stop the payments once she had gone. Safe to say she didn't want us to meet. I guess fate took a few decisions for us.'

He looked away towards the hills, pained, but not as much as she was. Then he turned to her again, that mix of sadness and concern all the more pronounced.

'I'm not your father, Jasmine,' he said, his normally steady voice faltering like the words were ashes in his mouth. 'I'm sorry. Nothing here is as it seems.'

The problem with only asking a question because you're certain of the answer is that you are blown wide open when that answer is not the one you receive. Jasmine felt like she had been beamed off the planet momentarily, then teleported back to a replica world that looked the same but was strangely, minutely different. She remembered being acutely aware of her surroundings once again, of the wind about her ears, the leaves that were blowing around, more green than brown, the first falls of autumn. It was no longer a white room, an empty stage. She was still standing with this man but he was somebody else, not the man she thought he was, and she felt so very lonely.

'You're lying,' she protested. 'Why are you lying? Some old promise to my mum? She's not here any more. I've got nobody and I need to know the truth.'

'That is the truth.'

'How can it be? Why would you be sending money for twenty years? Why would she send Jim to find you?'

There were tears starting to run from the corners of her eyes. She was managing to keep her voice steady but there was a desperation to her tone, like she was starting to realise there would be an explanation she hadn't anticipated, her blockbuster pieces of evidence crumbling in her hands.

Fallan looked solemnly into her eyes, pain etched deep in his own, pain for both of them.

'Do you remember I once mentioned how, in some cultures, if you kill a man, as your penance you are made responsible for those he left behind?'

Jasmine spent a moment trying to place when he had said this; it was at a time when she had been a little too distracted to give his words her full attention, as they hadn't really been aimed at her. This time they were, and as she discarded the memory of the old surveillance van where she first heard them, their true meaning came to the fore.

'You *killed* my father?'

But even as she said the words she couldn't accept them.

'That's why you kept sending the money? That doesn't add up. This is Glasgow we're talking about, not some remote valley in the Amazon. Why would you do that? And why would my mum want to see you before the end?'

Fallan took a breath, gathering his thoughts, choosing his words.

'Your mum and I were very close. We were good friends in very bad times. We both knew what kind of a world we'd become mired in, and when she became pregnant it made it all the more stark that she had to get out. I wanted her to be able to escape, make a clean break, start a new life.'

'So you killed the man she was involved with, my father?'

'No, that's not why I killed him. But his death

83

made it easier for your mum to leave.'

'That doesn't answer why you would keep sending the money. She made that clean break, started up a new life in Edinburgh.'

'It was the price of redemption. Or the price of believing in redemption. I needed to get out of that world too, but I couldn't just physically leave without taking my past with me. I needed to pay for my sins. I needed to make amends, to help somebody in order to believe that I could be something better. It was important to me that something good came out of that time, and it did. The life you've had, compared to the lives you and your mum might have had . . . . That's why I kept sending the money.'

Jasmine could feel the tears streaming now. She didn't know what to feel, what to think of Fallan. She just knew that it hurt.

Fallan reached into a pocket and offered her a tissue. Jasmine refused, wiping her eyes and her nose on her sleeve like a snottery little toddler. Then she swallowed, gathering her forces for a defiant charge.

'What was his name?'

Fallan shook his head. She wanted to scream.

'Please. What was his name?'

'I can't tell you. You were right: I did make certain promises to your mum. Two promises. She didn't want you knowing about me: there's nothing we can do about that now. But she seriously didn't want you knowing about him, and that's a promise I *can* keep.'

'You don't have to tell me anything else. Just his name would be enough.'

'His name *would* be enough,' he agreed. 'That's

84

why I can't tell you it. We both know you'll do precisely what your mum was afraid of. You'll try to find out who he was, and that would expose you to everything she spent her life protecting you from.'

'Can't you tell me anything? You can stay off specifics,' she bargained. 'Anything at all.'

'There's nothing I could tell you that would make you feel better.'

Fallan had a look about him that she had come to recognise: impermeable. This was not a man who could be prevailed upon. But she had spent enough time around him to recognise when he was being pulled apart. Maybe it was just desperation, but something inside her still wouldn't accept that what he was saying was true.

'I still don't believe you. I believe you made only one promise to my mum: a promise never to tell me who my father was, because my father was you.'

Fallan looked away to the hills again, and when he looked back at Jasmine his face was etched once more with that mixture of pity and regret. He knew that what he had to say would hurt her, but he knew he had to say it.

'Okay. I'll tell you his name, just his first name, because that will be enough. That will make everything clear. His name was James.'

Jasmine stared back uncomprehendingly, wondering for a moment whether he was being facetious, to teach her a harsh lesson. James. What the hell would that make clear?

'But James is not what anybody called him,' Fallan went on. 'He was known to your mum, as he was known to everybody else, as Jazz.'

It took her a moment, but then she heard it, and Fallan was right. It was enough. It rang true, devastatingly true.

'She didn't love him and she didn't mourn him, but for whatever reason, she still named you for him.'

Records

The next day, Jasmine didn't get the opportunity to chase up any of her contacts as she was on the road for Galt Linklater: a possible insurance fraud up on the Black Isle. The request had come in at the last minute, another of their investigations having escalated in terms of manpower, leaving them short-handed. As the job was a good three hours' drive from Glasgow it would require an overnight stay—and possibly two—up in Inverness. The upside of such trips was that they clocked up plenty of billable overtime, but the big variable was who she might be teamed with.

She had got to know most of Galt Linklater's roster, enough to have composed a mental list of the best and worst men to be working with on any particular job. Some were friendlier than others, more patient, more tolerant, while there were those who scored poorly in the above categories but were nonetheless smart operators from whom she knew she could learn a lot.

Her great fear, the moment she told Harry Deacon she was available, was that he would then inform her she was going on this road trip with Johnny Gibson—known as Grumpy Gibby—the most miserable ex-cop in the world. Gibby was always friendly to Jasmine and scored high on patience and tolerance, never getting frustrated with her when she got into difficulties. The problem was that she was the only thing he didn't complain about. He could moan for Scotland, but all of his minor grizzling was a mere support act to the main event, which was for him to go on about his divorce until you were toying with blowing the surveillance just so that you wouldn't have to listen any more. It usually took him about half an hour to get on to the subject, then it was all divorce, all the time, we never close.

She lucked out, though. It transpired that she'd be with Rab Forrest, which indicated just how swamped Galt Linklater must be if old Rab was getting into a car with an overnight bag. One of the firm's elder statesmen, he mostly worked on the management side under Harry, but wasn't daunted by the prospect of a bit of field work when it was required. He wasn't daunted by anything, in fact, because in his decades as a cop and a PI there really wasn't much he hadn't seen before.

He was easy company, with the added benefit that she didn't have to worry so much about uncomfortably flirty behaviour from a man in his seventies. That was always a nagging concern whenever she pulled an overnighter. All of Galt Linklater's investigators were old enough to be her father, but there was no accounting for how deluded some men could become, especially if you were being pleasant to them and they'd had a few drinks. So far there had been nothing inappropriate, but her mental list contained a subsection for the guys she'd least like to be sharing a hotel with. Rab Forrest, being old enough to be her grandfather, wasn't in it.

They had an early start, requiring eyes on the subject's house and car for seven o'clock. His name was Roddy Harris, a former joiner recently relocated from Perth, and it was the veracity of the 'former' part that they were there to establish. He was receiving income-protection payouts from an insurance firm, having been diagnosed with multiple sclerosis, which had, he claimed, caused him to give up his work. Rab further informed Jasmine that Harris had sold up a four-bedroom house in Perth, he and his wife downsizing to a two-bedroom flat in Beauly now that their kids had grown up and left home.

As a self-employed joiner, he had taken out an income-protection policy with Steadfast Insurance twelve years back. This had followed a two-month lay-off from work due to a back injury, the resultant lack of income causing him to realise his vulnerability given that he had no employer to rely on for sick pay. His first claim on this policy was for something a bit more than a slipped disc, however. He was diagnosed with MS, which, among its other privations, at times could leave him incapable of gripping his tools. Unable to guarantee his ability to take on jobs, he was forced to close his business. Steadfast's policy required that they pay him roughly thirty grand a year until retirement age, which meant they were looking at a total dispensation of more than a quarter of a million pounds. However, the insurance firm had suspicions that Mr Harris was more capable than his diagnosis was making out, and hired Galt Linklater to gather evidence.

'How do you get a fake diagnosis of MS?' Jasmine asked Rab.

'You don't,' was his stark answer.

They followed Harris from Beauly to Inverness, where they promisingly observed him going into B&Q. He emerged with some timber and a roll of chicken wire, which he put into the back of his Volvo estate.

He stopped off for some groceries at a supermarket, then headed back across the Kessock Bridge. However, instead of proceeding home to his flat in Beauly he stopped about a mile outside, at an isolated cottage in expansive but rather unkempt grounds.

They watched him take the timber and chicken wire from his car and approach the front door, which was answered by an elderly woman with white hair below a black headscarf. He disappeared inside the cottage, then emerged again a few minutes later, this time producing a toolbox and a saw from the rear of the Volvo.

On a hunch, Rab sent Jasmine out on foot, down a farm track that afforded a view of the land at the cottage's rear. She took up position using the cover of a hedge and focused her video camera to capture Harris carrying out repairs on a chicken coop while the old woman hovered near by, and at one point brought him a cup of tea and a roll.

As she relayed quietly to Rab over the radio, it was painful to watch. Harris kept dropping his tools, dropping nails, dropping timber, and adopted a repertoire of awkward postures while sawing and hammering in order to compensate for his inability to grip properly. Crucially, however, he did ultimately get the job done, which pleased the old woman, but not as much as it would please Steadfast Insurance.

Jasmine kept her head down and her gait stooped as she made her way back along the farm track, but she felt that her posture could not be low enough to match her conduct. She got back in the car, then Rab drove a hundred yards back down the Inverness road and turned, pulling into a layby from where they could follow Harris upon his exit. Rab had mounted the video camera on the dashboard again, so that they could resume recording their pursuit of Harris's car.

She watched him put his tools into the Volvo, followed by the rotted boards and rusted wire he'd replaced. Rab watched too, all the while talking on the phone to Harry Deacon, recounting what they'd just seen and recorded. She didn't follow all of what was being said; hearing one side of a conversation could be hard enough to follow, but much of this exchange seemed to be conducted in an arcane code. Further confusing her was Rab's reference to Harris's moonlighting as 'an arson job'.

Rab terminated the call just as Harris was making his final exit, wiping his hands on a rag. The old woman appeared again, hurrying from the front door like she was afraid he'd already left. They watched her present him with a bottle of whisky, then the familiar pantomime of refusal and insistence. Jasmine remembered her mum telling her there was a grace to receiving that was hard to learn, and the memory briefly delayed her realisation that Harris hadn't been looking to be paid. He was just helping out some old crofter woman who needed her chicken coop repaired.

'Aye,' Rab said with a sigh. 'Puts me in mind of a pal of mine who was doing a favour for his upstairs neighbour in a tenement close. Old woman's pulley was jiggered, so she couldnae dry her washing. He went up and fixed it. I think the cord had snapped, so he replaced it. When he was finished he says tae her: "Right Mrs McGlumphur, you can get your clothes up noo." The wee woman says: "Aw, son, if it's all right with you, I was just gaunny give you a bottle of whisky."'

Jasmine didn't feel like laughing, though.

'What's up?' Rab asked. 'You not like that one?'

'No, it's . . .'

'Never mind. You'll like this.'

And with that he pressed rewind on the camera, cueing the tape back to before she got out of the car. He then resumed filming, recording over Jasmine's footage.

'What are you doing?' she asked, though it was staringly self-evident. She hoped she managed to sound professionally shocked rather than personally delighted.

She must have done. He told her not to worry, assuring her he'd cleared it with Harry, and reiterated his curious reference of before.

'How is it arson?' she asked. 'Are you going to tell Steadfast the tape got burnt?'

Rab laughed.

'Naw, not arson. Arsène. As in Wenger. It means "I did not see ze incident",' he explained, putting on a cod French accent.

'See, screwing chancers is our bread and butter. Some fly-man claiming compo for his gammy leg then going out and playing five-a-sides, I'll nail him seven days a week. But sometimes these insurance firms can be like the world's worst bookie. They're happy enough to rake in money on long-odds bets,

91

but they cannae accept that the laws of probability dictate that sometimes they'll be unlucky. So they cry foul and look for any way they might be able to invalidate the claim: welshing on the bet.'

'So we're going to report that we saw nothing untoward?'

'No, we're going to report exactly what we witnessed: that Mr Harris is so debilitated by multiple sclerosis that he couldn't possibly make a living as a joiner.'

'Roger that,' said Jasmine.

'He who pays the piper calls the tune, but this isn't a job without its moral choices. I did not see ze incident,' he repeated. 'And we didn't have this conversation either, you understand?'

'What conversation?'

*   *   *

Jasmine got a call as they passed through Aviemore on the drive back down the A9. Her phone didn't associate the number with any of her listed contacts, but Jasmine recognised it as the main switchboard at the tax office: outgoing calls from internal extensions weren't identified. It was her contact, Polly Seaton, which meant progress on Mrs Petrie's case. Polly had been in Jasmine's class throughout secondary school, and now worked at Centre One in East Kilbride. Tax records were the most reliable means of tracing anybody, and though there were strict limits on what details Polly could divulge, it was usually enough.

She always felt a little guilty at how obliging Polly was, as they hadn't been bosom buddies or anything back in the day. Truth be told, she'd always found

Polly a bit dull and literal-minded, so she felt a little hypocritical about coming across so friendly when it was really only a means of securing a favour. Jasmine didn't feel comfortable using people and she kept telling herself she ought to take Polly out for a few drinks some night by way of gratitude, but thus far that sentiment was in the same pending tray as buying new office furniture, finding an accountant and acquiring a social life.

'You're in luck,' Polly reported. 'There's only one Tessa Garrion on record, so no worries about whether I've retrieved files on the right person.'

This was always good to know. The experience of spending two days sifting through piles of information in order to find the right Jean Clark was still fresh in Jasmine's memory.

'I had to go back a long way, as you warned me. Got her P60 filings starting from October 1980: her payee was the Pan . . . technician Theatre. Does that sound right?'

Jasmine smiled at Polly's misreading but considered it impolite to correct her.

'That's definitely her. She worked as an actress, but gave that up some time around the mid-eighties. I'm trying to find out what she did next.'

'Early eighties, by the look of it. Her last wages from this Pantechnithingy Theatre were paid April 1981. After that, looks like she moved briefly into retail footwear. The Glass Shoe Company. She was only with them one month, though.'

'And where did she go next?'

'After that, I've got nothing. No further filings.'

'So she moved away. Do you have a record of what district would have her tax records after that?'

'No, I'm saying she had no tax records after that:

not here, not anywhere. She didn't pay tax after August 1981.'

* * *

Jasmine thanked Polly and hung up, realising as soon as she'd done so that she'd forgotten to suggest a drink. Then she accepted that maybe she hadn't really forgotten.

There's a grace to receiving, she remembered. She had to remind herself that people weren't always playing an angle, only giving in order to get. There was a grace to not being a using cow as well, though.

'You look a bit dischuffed,' Rab observed. 'Dead end?'

'Missing person. Trying to follow her tax trail. Turns out it ends in 1981. Doesn't sound like the first step towards a happy ending.'

'Ah, but maybe it was,' Rab countered. 'Mr Right comes along and sweeps her off her feet. Lassie never has to work another day.'

'Her sister did moot that possibility, but if she got married she never invited anybody to the wedding.'

'Had they fallen out?'

'More drifted apart.'

'Aye,' Rab considered, narrowing his eyes. 'You'd get a card at least. And if there was no big melodramas you'd have to think she'd let her sister know if she had any weans. Could have been living over the brush with some fancy man, maybe somebody the family wouldn't have approved of. You said she was an actress? Rich, older admirer. Rich, *married* admirer?'

'Plausible enough,' she agreed. 'But not easy

94

to trace.'

Rab reached down and disconnected his mobile from the hands-free cradle, offering it to Jasmine.

'Go into contacts and call Annabel Downie,' he told her.

Jasmine complied and replaced the handset in its cradle as it began to ring. Switched to speaker, the tone pulsed loud inside the car for a few rings, before being answered by a female voice.

'DC Downie,' he addressed her. 'You got five minutes?'

'Only for you,' she replied warmly.

'Can you run a name through STORM for me, and give us a call back?'

'No bother. Just grabbing a pen here. What's the name?'

Her eyes on the road, it took Jasmine a moment to realise that the growing pause was awaiting her to fill it.

'Oh. Tessa Garrion,' she said.

'Tessa—' Rab began to relay.

'Garrion. I'm on it. Call you right back.'

Rab hung up.

'Thanks,' Jasmine said. 'What's STORM?'

'Systems for Tasking and Operational Resource Management. It's a police database.'

'So we'll find her if she's ever been in bother?'

'No. We'll find her if she's had any dealings with the polis whatsoever. If she ever phoned the emergency services, or even handed in a dropped purse at the local nick, they'll have her number and address at the time.'

Jasmine's eyes widened. This might be easy money after all. She could have a result by the time they reached Kingussie.

95

Rab's phone rang again shortly.

'That's a big zero, I'm afraid,' DC Downie reported.

'Nothing?' Rab asked.

'Absolutely nothing. Not so much as a call to complain about a car alarm going off.'

'Ach well, worth a try. Thanks, Annabel.'

'Any time, Dad.'

Rab gave Jasmine a warm wee smile, both proud and conspiratorial. It was an invitation for her to share a moment recognising the special bond between father and daughter. Rab having just tried to do her a favour, Jasmine considered it polite to fake it.

'How accurate is STORM?' she asked. 'I mean, how far back?'

'Last twenty years, everything is logged and backed up. If you gave a witness statement, gave your details to an officer after a wee car prang, it's there. Before that, it's a bit more sketchy, variable from force to force depending on what records they kept and what they got around to computerising.'

'Twenty years, though. How many people go that long without paying any tax and having any recorded contact with the police?'

'Well, it matches two kinds of profile,' Rab suggested. 'One being the extremely rich.'

'And what's the other?'

'The extremely dead.'

*   *   *

Upon reflection, the possibilities weren't quite as stark as Rab had painted them.

Jasmine considered that Tessa Garrion could

have got married a few years down the line and felt sufficiently estranged from her sister by that time as to feel no need to inform her. If she took her husband's surname she wouldn't appear on the STORM system under her maiden name. In fact, she could have got married in July 1981 and not bothered telling anyone, because the two sisters might not have been on quite such neutral terms as Alice Petrie was making out.

She might also have gone overseas, though Jasmine wasn't sure whether that would have been noted on her tax records. If she was domiciled elsewhere she wouldn't be eligible to pay tax, but if she hadn't been earning anything anyway, maybe that aspect of her status wouldn't be updated.

The one thing Jasmine was still intrigued by, however, was the seemingly abrupt end to Tessa's theatrical career. Did she get dropped? Depressingly plausible, but surely she wouldn't give up just like that. Working in a shoe shop was also a plausible stop-gap, something she'd do to pay the bills while she was waiting for a part to come up elsewhere. The name Glass Shoe Company rang a bell, but Jasmine couldn't place why. As far as she could think, there was no such shop in Glasgow, but it sounded familiar nonetheless. It had slightly uncomfortable subconscious associations too: something out of reach, unattainable, perhaps prohibitively expensive. She was talking the eighties, so maybe it was a now-defunct chain that had been around when she was a little girl or even before: somewhere her mum talked about but couldn't afford.

First thing the next morning, Jasmine got busy chasing up her inquiries, finding that the two-day gap had been long enough to yield results, though she could hardly call them fruitful. She was informed that Tessa Garrion had not received any kind of welfare payments in thirty years: no unemployment claims, no child benefit, no disability allowance, nothing.

A further call to Polly established that neither Tessa nor any husband had claimed or transferred a married person's allowance, and there was nothing in her records to indicate that she had left the country either.

The investigation was starting to take on a familiar feel. Tessa wouldn't be the first subject who turned out to have died whole decades before the client tried to re-establish contact, but she would certainly be the youngest, a tragedy Jasmine was feeling more acutely given the ways Tessa's life had echoed both her own and, to a greater extent, her mother's.

Jasmine felt a sense of duty-bound resignation as she reluctantly called Archie Cairnduff, her contact at New Register House in Edinburgh. This would put a lid on the whole thing, after which it would be a matter of finding out the location of the cemetery and as much information as could be gleaned about what Tessa had done with her brief life in the few years since her mother's funeral.

As she dialled the General Register Office, Jasmine realised she was assuming Mrs Petrie hadn't done so herself. She certainly didn't mention it, only remarking her presumption that someone would have got in touch if Tessa had died. It was weird how many clients neglected to do this. Several of Jasmine's investigations had been resolved through a simple inquiry to the GRO,

Archie calling back in a day or so with the missing subject's date and place of death. At first Jasmine wondered whether the clients simply didn't realise this was a line of inquiry freely open to themselves, but when she pointed it out they always preferred that she do it 'as part of her investigations', even though it would cost them money.

It took her a while to understand what they were really paying her for. They didn't go to the Registrar themselves because they didn't want to hear their fears confirmed, a fait accompli mouldering in a file for years, even decades. It was important to them to make some kind of effort—not to mention a small financial sacrifice—while the possibility still existed, a gesture of penitence and regret, perhaps, before ultimately making peace with their loss.

Upon the advice of Harry Deacon, the first couple of times she got in touch with the GRO she had gone to West Register Street in person. Harry said it was important that she strike up a rapport with somebody there, so that they could put a face to her name when she called up in future. 'It'll help you skip the queue now and again,' he said.

On her first visit she had utterly failed to strike up anything beyond the most functionary conversation with some bleakly humourless female apparatchik who looked like she hated her job. More happily, upon her return she got talking to Archie, who had worked for the GRO forever, had a thousand stories to tell and was delighted to have someone who wanted to hear them.

That morning he began by expounding upon the office's address, telling her how West Register Street was the phrase neurologists got patients to repeat in order to check for symptoms of stroke

Jasmine was happy for him to procrastinate. She always felt a little sad when it was confirmed that a subject was deceased, but this was one she had really come to hope was alive. Eventually, though, they had to get down to business. Archie confirmed that the date and place of birth checked out, so that they could be sure there was indeed only one Tessa Garrion. There was, as anticipated, no record of her ever marrying or having any children.

'She hasn't troubled the scorers, as the cricket commentators like to say.'

'Hasn't? You mean she's still alive?'

'Well if she isn't, then the Register's Office knows nothing about it. Have you any evidence indicating otherwise?'

'No. Just a complete absence of evidence of this woman having existed after summer 1981.'

Fell Purpose

It was when he spoke to the girl, Jasmine, that he realised with a hollow dread what would have to be done.

She wasn't much to look at: freckle-faced, slight; one might even say scrawny, wearing a suit that didn't make her look businesslike so much as resembling a school-leaver dressed up for her first job interview. She was softly spoken, far from strident in her manner; the girl's body language under-confident, almost apologetic.

Yet he knew she had already uncovered the secrets of the Ramsay family's disappearance. This

100

was a worrying enough precedent, but far worse was the passion he recognised in her. She had trained as an actress. Her dead mother had been an actress. Now she was looking for an actress who had gone missing at around the same age as she was now; probably the same age her mother had been when she gave it up to raise the girl.

He could see it in her eyes: this was not a pay-packet to her, it was a quest. A crusade.

Everyone he loved, everything he was, everything he'd done, it would all be taken away. Everything he was working towards and everything he had ever achieved: all of his work would be erased from history. He would be remembered only as the monster who had killed that girl, one more squalid murderer rotting in jail.

The truth would destroy not only him. He could barely bring himself to imagine the pain and the shame that would rain down upon those he loved, those who relied upon him. What had any of them ever done to deserve this? Everything he had ever stood for would be burnt to ashes, all his family's reputations tarnished by the flames. Each of their lives would be ruined.

There was no other path now, he knew. It was his duty as a husband, as a father.

She would have to die.

Circus Games

Catherine could seldom remember seeing so many police in one place without any civilians in the picture. Given the auspiciousness of her surroundings, it looked like a convention, one that would have riots on the streets if the tax-payers found out the polis were having a mass jolly at Cragruthes Castle. The lawns, the paths, the avenues and the woods were swarming with officers. She could imagine the groundskeeper and the head gardener considering a suicide pact at the prospect of the damage.

It was about as far removed from the standard crime scene as she had ever encountered. Some castles just looked like very grand houses, a turret, a flag and an ancient family name all that distinguished them from other large country properties near by. The larger ones, such as Stirling and Edinburgh, comprised groups of grey buildings atop hills and volcanoes, fortified compounds rather than remarkable individual structures. This place, however, was the full fairy tale, precisely what every little girl and boy thought a castle ought to look like.

'It's beautiful, isn't it,' observed Beano Thomson, one of her young DCs. Beano had a fairly dry sense of humour, but could also be boyishly enthusiastic and almost annoyingly positive. Consequently, it wasn't easy to be sure when he was joking.

'Yes,' Catherine replied. 'If I'm ever going to get shot dead, I want it to be in a place just like this.'

Beano and DI Laura Geddes reported to Catherine as soon as she had stepped out of DC Zoe Vernon's car. They had been among the first of the Glasgow contingent to arrive, getting there at around two in the morning.

'What's the script?' Catherine asked them.

Laura had already given her the breakdown over the phone while Zoe drove them north, but she liked a recap whenever she was on site, and not just to keep abreast of updates. The memory could play strange tricks, and the way Catherine visualised things when she was first told them could linger confusingly in the mind if she didn't hear the same points made when she was actually looking at the scene.

'Incident happened at around nine-fifty last night,' Laura said, her soft Edinburgh accent rising towards the end of each sentence, as though framing it as a question. 'The laird and thirty-five corporate guests were watching an outdoor performance of, ironically enough, *A Midsummer Night's Dream* by a local amateur dramatics company.'

'What's ironic about it?' asked Beano.

'It was the twenty-first of June, bawheid,' Zoe told him. 'And it was nobody's idea of a dream evening.'

'The play was staged at several different settings around the castle grounds,' Laura went on, 'and the audience taken around on a seated gantry mounted on a trailer. Catering staff were following on foot, serving champagne between each scene change. At the end of the performance the victim and the laird came down from the audience and joined the cast to pose for a group photo. That was when it happened. Ambulance got here ten thirty-two, and the victim was pronounced dead ten thirty-five, but there wasn't exactly any doubt about his condition. His brains were on the lawn.'

'Ouch. Corporate, you said?'

'Yes,' Laura replied. 'A delegation of senior bods from the Royal Scottish Bank, plus their very select guests. Seems it was a very high-class corpie, with

103

the RSB paying the laird five hundred quid a skull. Wee bit more upscale than lunch and a soft seat at the football, so we're not talking about a group of small businessmen,' she added pointedly.

Christ, Catherine thought. A wankerfest. This just got better and better. 'Where are they now?'

'They're all in the castle. The theatre company people as well, plus the catering staff.'

'Have you got everybody's details?'

Laura held up a list.

'There are six detectives in there, questioning them all in turn. The lateness of the hour and the booze meant they'd no option but to stay the night as planned. There was one or two of the corporate guests talking about calling drivers up from Edinburgh and Glasgow, but I put the kibosh on that. I asked them all to remain here to assist in our inquiries, but now that the shock is starting to recede, the goodwill and sense of civic duty are wearing off too. They all want to go home and back to their terribly important jobs, and I get the distinct impression that lawyers are going to start being called any minute.'

'If they haven't been already,' Catherine suggested. 'Okay, make sure we've got everybody's details and then let them go. We're not going to get much out of them just now anyway. Now, the victim, was he a guest of the bank too?'

'I don't think so. I'm sure somebody said he was the special guest of the laird, but I haven't spoken to him. Not sure anybody has, in any depth. He was being handled by one of the local officers, a familiar face for a bit of reassurance. He was practically catatonic with shock. One minute you're standing there with a photographer going "Say 'cheese!'", and the next . . .'

'Your guest suffers a permanent loss of face,' said Catherine. 'What about the photo? Do we have it? Who took it?'

'We've got the camera. It was one of the castle staff, an amateur enthusiast taking the snap, but it was for the laird. He always poses with the cast, apparently, and keeps a framed pic as a souvenir.'

'Well, let's make sure it's the only souvenir. Thirty-five guests means thirty-five phones, means thirty-five other cameras. Find out who else snapped anything. Get hold of those phones and sequester every image that was taken over the past twenty-four hours; I don't care if that includes pictures of their dicks that they've been texting to their bit on the side.'

'We're already doing that,' Laura assured her.

'Some of them had their cameras set to automatically upload photos to online albums,' warned Beano.

'In that case, before you let them leave, make sure all of them know that if a "tragic last moments" photo—or something worse—finds its way on to the pages of any newspaper or website, then whoever leaked it will very soon be left wishing his father had just cracked one off.'

'You got it, boss,' said Laura.

Her debrief complete, Laura went back inside the castle to relay Catherine's order, while Beano accompanied her around the grounds to the locus on the far side of the building.

Because of the distance she had travelled and the unsettlingly picturesque surroundings, it felt weird to see so many familiar faces wandering around out of their normal context. She knew it

105

was Strathclyde's jurisdiction, and she had made various calls last night to ensure she had her own people on the ground this morning, but some subconscious part of her must have expected to feel like an interloper parachuted in to commandeer a whole load of strangers, not to mention anticipating all the grief that went with that. Instead it was like a school trip, and she was teacher.

There had been a time when Catherine would find herself standing among a mass of detectives and feel grateful that she wasn't the ringmaster of such a circus. The more bodies you had at your disposal, the more the politics and the pressure to get results must be hellish, she thought. Now that she was the one in charge, she looked at the manpower milling about the place and just felt grateful that she could deploy such resources without any questions being asked. In fact, the only questions would have come had she chosen to deploy less. As anticipated, the political machinations had already begun; not so much a matter of certain people wanting results so much as making sure nobody would be able to say the authorities hadn't done everything they could.

The question was, was it the victim or the venue that was loosening the purse strings? Probably a bit of each. Both the host and the headshot were of aristocratic background, as well-connected as they were well-heeled, and the tragic loss of the latter had to be multiplied by the embarrassment to the former when it came to calculating the score on the official priority index.

It really didn't do to have people shot dead in the grounds of fairy-tale castles. Not with the tourist season just heating up; to say nothing of the

106

ramifications of such a tragedy striking somebody more commonly to be found on broadsheet arts pages than tabloid front pages. In this instance the term 'victim profile' had altogether different connotations. He knew everybody and everybody knew him. The news feeds were already buzzing with tributes not just from all corners of the arts world but charities too, calling him a miracle-worker, fêting his tireless endeavour, his generosity and his vision.

'Hard to imagine we're going to find a motive when nobody had anything bad to say about him,' Zoe had observed wryly on the drive north. But it was always like that when the body was still warm. Once the victim was colder, so would be the opinions.

View from the Stage

Jasmine took a short drive from her office in Arden on the south side to Eglinton Street, still south of the river, on the edge of the Gorbals. The Civic was starting to make a slightly worrying noise, half gurgle, half rattle, and she had to really rev it a few times going round corners in low gear. She resorted to the standard technical remedy for such automotive issues, which was to turn up the stereo until she couldn't hear it any more.

She wasn't sure this was going to cut it for much longer. Jimmy Eat World filled the air, covering the gurgle/rattle noise, but she could still feel the vibrations against the pedals and the occasional surge of complaint from the engine. At least it was her own choice of music that was covering the problem these days, since she'd purchased a cassette-shaped adapter for her mp3 player. Prior to that, she'd been reliant on the radio, the cassette deck having chewed up and spat out its last tape many years ago. She had been meaning to buy a CD player for it, but that had always been a low priority behind the constant replacement of parts that the car actually needed in order to keep running. In fact, she had sent it into the garage so often that, at this rate, she'd soon have assembled an entire new vehicle, but at far more expense than if she just went into a dealership and bought one.

She knew that was the more economical option, as well as the more sensible one. She even had the money these days to be able to afford it. The problem was, she just couldn't give up this car.

It had been her mum's car and as such a part of Jasmine's life since she was seven. It was the car Jasmine sat in the back of while her mum drove her to school on rainy mornings, to the theatre on excitingly dark nights, or just to the supermarket at Canonmills a couple of times a week. It was the car Jasmine practised in while she was trying to get her licence. And it was the car in which she drove her mum to the hospital: for tests, for checks, for treatments and then for the last time.

It still smelled of her; or at least the smell of the car still made Jasmine feel like her mum was near by.

The little red Civic had meant so much to Mum, as it had been the first new car she'd ever owned; or nearly new, anyway. It was a special deal because although it had barely two hundred miles on the clock it was still second-hand. It had been owned by some well-off academic who normally treated himself to a new car each year with his book royalties, but who had decided to bring his purchase forward when Honda brought out a new model of the Civic.

Jasmine couldn't understand why he'd want the updated version, as it seemed plain and fuddy-duddy compared to its predecessor: sleek and low-slung like a sports car. But sporty and sleek as it was, as well as being pre-owned, the professor's Civic was now officially last year's model, which meant Beth Sharp got a bargain.

Looking back, Jasmine wondered whether Mum felt able to splash the cash because Glen Fallan had been particularly generous with his guilt money that year.

God, was this the start of him corrupting her happiest memories? She could hear his voice in her head right then, saying: 'See? This is why your mum was adamant that you shouldn't find out about these things.'

She parked in front of a row of railway arches accommodating tiling and carpet showrooms, then got out and walked the short distance to her destination.

The Pantechnicon Theatre was the smallest of four auditoria either side of a quarter-mile stretch around where Eglinton Street became Pollokshaws Road. None of the four were serving the purposes they were built for, but the Pantechnicon could claim to be closest. It had begun life as a music hall before being converted into a cinema in the 1920s, functioning as such for four decades until the spread of television led to its closure in 1962. Three years later, it was reopened by Peter and Francis

109

Winter, two brothers with the vision—and crucially the finance—to start a small repertory theatre.

Of its three near neighbours, one had been a Victorian theatre called The Colosseum, once notorious for being the first Scottish venue to stage Ibsen's *A Doll's House*. This came a full seven years after its London debut, the outraged response to which left many people under the mistaken impression that the play had in fact been banned. Jasmine considered it an unworthy fate that the walls once echoing to the 'door-slam heard around the world' now heard no more dramatic cry than 'house!'

There were also two purpose-built picture houses: both huge, sprawling venues whose grandeur was testament to the popularity of cinema during its heyday. Neither had shown a film since the seventies, and both had served time as bingo halls. One was now enjoying a new lease of life as a music venue, while the other was a 'development opportunity'.

All four venues stood out like the last surviving teeth in an aged boxer's mouth, their size emphasised by the absence of any construction around them. They were surrounded by waste ground, car parks and tree-dotted open space, like abandoned cathedrals to a religion with no remaining followers. It seemed strange that the landscape should be dominated by these places of popular entertainment when there was no evidence of a populace to be entertained. This was because all the tenements that used to stand in between them had been torn down in the sixties. It was, after all, the Gorbals.

Jasmine had found that if you mentioned

Glasgow to English people they would often respond by solemnly intoning the words 'oh yes, the Gorbals', even though that place didn't exist any more. The area that carried the name was a strange mishmash of light industrial units, isolated high-rise blocks, the aforementioned open spaces and these grand remnants. It was almost apocalyptic the way they stood so massive against a flat and largely barren landscape. It made Jasmine think of the movie *Delicatessen*, a favourite of her mum's.

It was too early for the box office to be open, so she was surprised to see the lights on inside. She had thought she'd need to knock at the doors or even phone the office, but Jasmine found one of the sets of swing doors unlocked and entered the Pantechnicon's modest little foyer. It seemed even smaller when it was empty, difficult to imagine how quite so many people could throng there just before a show. She heard the wheezy hum of a vacuum cleaner from upstairs, in the lobby to the rear of the dress circle, and was about to make her way up when a young guy in a shirt and tie emerged from the entrance to the stalls. Jasmine vaguely recognised him from previous visits: he was the front-of-house manager, she was sure.

'Can I help you?' he asked, sounding like he would if he could, and scrutinising her in a way that suggested he knew her face but couldn't quite place her.

'My name is Jasmine Sharp,' she replied, handing him a business card. She still found it easier to do that than to actually say 'I'm a private investigator', because it still didn't sound right coming out of her mouth, and the card at least looked in some way official.

111

He looked at it with surprise, but at least it was a surprise that indicated this was a more interesting visit than he was expecting, rather than surprise at the mismatch between what was stated on the card and the person who had handed it to him.

'Robert Newsome, assistant manager,' he said.

'I was wondering if you would be able to give me a number or an address where I could reach Dorothy Prowis.'

His eyes widened and a smile began to form. He seemed both relieved and amused, like a problem had presented itself and then instantly been resolved.

'I can do better than that. She's through there, up on the stage, but she's got a group of students with her. I'm sure she'll be able to spare a moment when she's finished. I take it she's not in any kind of trouble?' he added as an afterthought, his expression indicating how unlikely he considered this.

'Dot?' Jasmine responded. Her incredulous tone was intended to communicate not only that her answer was in the negative, but that she knew more than he might assume about the subject of her inquiry.

She made her way into the stalls, where she could hear the familiar sound of Dot Prowis's voice, but the woman herself was obscured by a raggle-taggle gathering of drama students standing on the apron. Even more than the foyer, the stalls and the circle looked so much smaller when there was no one sitting in them. She remembered being taken here by her mum's friend Judith to see a production of *Peter Pan*, and from her position near the back downstairs it had seemed every bit as big and grand

112

as the King's in Edinburgh, or the Lyceum or the Festival Theatre. Standing behind the last row now, it seemed so neat and compact, such a short distance to the stage. And as she knew, the view from the stage looking out at an empty house made it seem smaller still.

She had stood on that same apron, listening to the same talk, just a few years previously. Dot Prowis was retired from theatre now, but she still taught SATD students about theatrical design, and when possible preferred to do so not in a lecture hall or rehearsal studio but on the very stage where she had done most of her work. Dot had been Francis Winter's protégée, assisting him since the early seventies and eventually taking over from him in 1986 as the Pantechnicon's designer, a post she held until her own retirement in 2005. Jasmine knew that she would have worked with Tessa Garrion and, given Dot's memory for detail, was hoping that thirty years wasn't too long a stretch for her recall.

The Winter brothers were born in Durham, where their father owned and managed a theatre, so they had grown up helping with everything from repairing ripped seats to painting scenery. They renovated the Pantechnicon—largely with their own hands—and rapidly built up a successful repertory theatre established upon aesthetic principles that Dot still evangelised. Frustrated by what Peter Winter described as 'the tyrannous geometry' of the proscenium arch, Francis frequently designed sets that brought the action into the auditorium, appropriating the boxes and constructing catwalks, all at the nightly expense of seats that could not therefore be sold.

113

Dot had taken this concept of 'exploding the space' to its apotheosis in 1988 with her design for *Ubu Roi*. She built two gangways from the stage to either side of the dress circle, allowing the actors to run in a great Escher-esque loop during the play's chase and battle scenes. She strung a flying-fox zip line from the highest of the stage's many platforms all the way down the aisle to the back of the stalls, and she had a trampoline in the orchestra pit. Jasmine had studied this production in depth, staring longingly at photographs and wishing she'd been around to see it. Even now she felt a pang of regret amid the fascination as Dot talked the students through how it was done.

'Of course, health and safety would never allow it nowadays, but it was magnificent. The audiences adored it . . . almost as much as the cast.'

Jasmine let go a little sigh even as the students laughed. That was when she knew the pang wasn't about never having had the chance to see the Pantechnicon's famous *Ubu*. It was about the chance she still did have, the last time she was standing in this room listening to the same lecture, the first week of June only a short few years ago. The students were next year's intake, participating in the annual induction course designed to prime their summer reading before they started in earnest in the autumn.

Dorothy spoke for a few more minutes, still obscured by her audience, then she finally came into view as the students dispersed. Jasmine remembered the drill: the students would now be encouraged to physically explore the set, to do what the audience could not. She could hear Dorothy tell them not to just wander around like it was

114

sculpture, but to 'truly inhabit it, treat it like one of those . . . *soft-play* facilities for children'.

In that respect it was a good set to have the run of, particularly considering it was the end of the theatre's spring programme. The final play in each season tended to be the most minimalist in terms of production values due to the budget having largely been spent by that time, but the present designer, Keith Farrel, had made inventive use of stock equipment and made a cheap set look expensive. The stage was fitted with a panoply of scaffolds and platforms, bedecked in sweeping red and blue drapes, flags and banners. It looked both lush and kinetic, faintly reminding Jasmine of the cover of the last Biffy Clyro album.

The play was *Iphigénie* by Racine, a quintessential example of seventeenth-century French neoclassicism. Directors of a naturalist bent were drawn to the psychological realism of Racine's characters, often opting for modern dress or seventeenth-century costume to emphasise a timelessness to the characters. This being the Pantechnicon, however, and the director being Peter Winter's son Daniel, they were most definitely back in ancient Greece, the banners and flags indicating a war footing in preparation for the assault on Troy.

Jasmine made her way up on to the stage at the right-hand side of the apron by means of the short black steps that were all but invisible from just a few rows back in the stalls. As she climbed, a male student went flying past her, leaping from the stage with Dorothy's encouragement.

'That's it,' she was saying. 'Explode the space.'

Dorothy was facing stage left, her back to

Jasmine. She was dressed in a black trouser suit, her silver hair swept back on to her collar.

'Ms Prowis?' Jasmine asked, prompting Dorothy to turn delicately on her heel.

Jasmine couldn't help but smile as she took in her gold earrings and red silk scarf. Black, red and gold. They were the Pantechnicon's unofficial colours, emphasised in all of Francis Winter's early sets. Dorothy wore them like a priest or disciple. They spoke of spectacle, opulence, grandeur and just a hint of the bawdy.

Dorothy stared at her for a moment, as though trying to piece together why she didn't quite fit the picture. Then a curious little smile told Jasmine she'd worked it out.

'Goodness gracious. Jasmine Sharp. Goodness gracious.'

Dorothy's tone was always as precise as it was polite, almost accentless but with just a whisper of Welsh if you knew what to listen for. Jasmine reckoned you could write down much of what Dorothy said and insert it seamlessly into a play from just about any period since the eighteenth century. Conspicuously modern coinages, when she had no choice but to use them, seemed almost quarantined within her sentences, like she didn't quite trust them or didn't know what to do with them; hence her hesitation over the term soft-play.

'How are you? I was most sorry to hear about your mother.'

Jasmine never knew how to respond to such sentiments—should you say thank you?—so she simply nodded.

'I saw her act, you know, back at the Tron. More than once, I'm sure, but I particularly remember

116

her from a John Byrne play, the second of the *Slab Boys* trilogy, the name of which I can never recall. She had just the right quality of what the locals refer to as "gallusness". I'm sorry I never said as much to you before, but I was unaware that you were her daughter until quite recently.'

'That's okay,' Jasmine managed, reeling somewhat from the clarity of this reminiscence. She was aware of secreting it away in her mind, a precious and most unexpected treasure to be unwrapped and appreciated later. She'd love to press Dorothy on what else she might tell her about Mum back in the eighties, but they both had business to attend.

'I heard you had to drop out. What are you doing with yourself nowadays?'

Jasmine knew that on this occasion she couldn't just whip out a card, so she took a breath and gathered herself before answering.

'I'm working as a private investigator.'

Working as. That was the qualification that helped her say it without sounding foolish. It was like a disclaimer that stated she wasn't laying claim to anything. You didn't say you were 'working as' something you had trained for years to do, like a doctor or an archaeologist.

Dorothy blinked and said nothing for just a little longer than was normal during small talk.

'I quite don't know what to say to that,' she eventually replied.

'That's okay,' said Jasmine with an apologetic laugh, as though she was responsible for Dorothy's discomfiture.

'No, sincerely. I'm seldom astonished by the answer when I make that inquiry of former

117

students. I would ordinarily be able to respond with "well done" or "how interesting" or a usefully noncommittal "oh, yes?" but you've left me with no frame of reference whatsoever. Goodness gracious. And are you here . . . on business?'

'I am indeed. I was hoping you might be able to offer some insight into a case I'm working on. Do you have a few minutes?'

'Certainly, certainly.'

Dorothy stepped off into the wings, while the students continued to wander, climb, jump and occasionally tumble from the platforms. The Pantechnicon's stage had a surprisingly steep rake, so that moving downstage was also moving downhill, and this was going to do for someone's ankle if they didn't learn quickly.

'I'm looking for information about an actress who worked here back in the early eighties. Her name was Tessa Garrion.'

Dorothy looked down at the floor for a moment, searching her thoughts, then stared back at Jasmine with genuine surprise.

'Tessa Garrion? My goodness, isn't that extraordinary? I'd quite forgotten that name.'

'Well, it has been a very long time.'

'No, you misunderstand. I have total recall when it comes to actors, and she's no different. I can see her right there, beneath the fly gallery, as Katherina to Morgan Spark's Petruchio in *The Taming of the Shrew*. But it just struck me that I hadn't heard her name in all this time. Theatre can be a small world, but people move on and you don't hear what happened to them unless they become terribly famous, or perhaps you're talking to someone and they happen to mention working with a person you

118

used to know. Tessa Garrion. One moment she's standing on that stage. Boom. Thirty years pass and you're the first person to say her name.'

'What do you remember of her?'

'I remember thinking we had unearthed a gem. Quite simply, the woman could act. I know that sounds rather trite, but it was as true then as it is now that a young girl with a pretty face can have a lot of stage presence, often concealing a lack of true talent. The same goes for beautiful young men. Tessa was not classically good looking. She was far from *un*attractive, but it wasn't her face that drew so much notice. She had real craft. As a result, she was incomparably adept at playing women older than herself.'

Dorothy smiled wryly at a memory, casting her eyes to the apron as though Tessa Garrion was standing there.

'She was Lysistrata. Quite brilliant. She could convey the sense of a young woman wise beyond her years, and she could truly convince as an older woman; which is not to say she couldn't play a giddy young thing when required. But you have to understand that the wisdom and maturity were all in the performance. In person, there was probably more of the giddy young thing about her than the wise old head on young shoulders; though perhaps my impression was skewed by the maturity of her work, which tended to make one forget she was only in her early twenties. I don't wish to imply that she was particularly giddy or impulsive; just that one noticed it more in contrast to her professional conduct.'

'And what about her personal life?' Jasmine asked. 'Do you remember anything about that?

119

Did she have anyone significant in her orbit at that time?'

'I'm afraid I have less of a facility for recalling such details, unless they impacted professionally. She didn't want for male attention, I remember that much, and she enjoyed it. Not in any kind of coquettish manner; she enjoyed male company. She held her own around men. She was the kind of young woman that men wished to impress, and by that I mean that first and foremost they wanted her to respect them, as opposed to merely wishing to possess her. What is your interest, incidentally?'

'I'm trying to locate her for a relative. They lost touch some time ago and I'm having difficulty tracking her down. In fact, the last time they spoke, Tessa was still working here, so I'm trying to work out what she did after that.'

'I regret to say I won't be able to assist. I haven't heard from her or indeed of her since she left us after the spring season in 1981. *The Merchant of Venice*,' she added with a troubled frown. 'She was Jessica. It wasn't the best use of her talents. Not a very memorable production, in fact. End of the season. We were potless, so we engaged the standard tactic: put on some Shakespeare and hope the audience interprets a Spartan set as minimalist *mise-en-scène* rather than an indication that there wasn't enough left in the budget to buy a tin of paint.'

'Or a few drapes,' Jasmine replied with a glance to the stage, eliciting a knowing smile.

'Quite.'

'So when Tessa left the company, what were the circumstances?'

Though it was thirty years ago, Jasmine found it

120

indelicate to ask Dorothy outright whether Tessa was dropped. Theatre folk could be enduringly sensitive about these things, no matter on which side of a decision they had found themselves. She was trying to understand why Tessa would give up, and Dorothy thus far hadn't painted a picture of an actress whose ability was in doubt. It certainly sounded like money had been tight, so the company might have been forced to contract. It could have been last in, first out, but surely Tessa would have understood the realpolitik.

'I mean, was there bad feeling?' Jasmine added.

'In theatre there's always bad feeling at a parting of the ways. Artists tend to feel a little more keenly than the average. Nobody likes being on the end of rejection, even when they understand that realistically it couldn't be another way.'

'So do you remember if Tessa reacted particularly badly to being let go?'

Dorothy looked at her so intently that Jasmine feared her question had been interpreted as an accusation. It was, in fact, a combination of confusion and incredulity, with a little remembered exasperation sprinkled on top.

'Good God, girl, we didn't "let her go". We couldn't hold on to her.'

'She left of her own volition?'

'Of course. She was too good to serve much more than an apprenticeship at a regional rep. She knew it . . . and we knew it. Didn't stop a few huffs and tantrums, but one could interpret those as back-handed compliments. She was always going to spread her wings. I think she had several auditions lined up in London. West End, I'm assuming, though I do recall someone mentioning film or

121

television.'

Dorothy must have read Jasmine's confounded expression.

'Is this at odds with whatever else you've learned?'

'More than a little. What would you say if I told you Tessa Garrion never acted again. Not professionally, anyway.'

'I'd be flabbergasted. And I'd ask you how you could know this.'

'I've investigated her tax records. She never had another job in the theatre. After leaving the Pantechnicon, her only work of any description was in a shoe shop.'

'A shoe shop? Are you quite sure?'

'I got it from HMRC. Death and taxes, nothing surer. She left the Pantechnicon, then there was a gap—presumably her London auditions—after which her only paycheque came from the Glass Shoe Company. That's from before my time, and I don't think they're trading any more.'

Dorothy fixed her with a strange look.

'*Glass* Shoe?' she asked.

'Yes.'

There was a twinkle of amused curiosity in Dorothy's eyes.

'I don't think it was a shoe shop, my dear.'

Jasmine was about to reply that her contact at HMRC categorised the job as being in 'retail footwear', when she remembered that her contact at HMRC was the rather dull and literal-minded Polly Seaton. When Polly said that, she may not have been quoting from records, merely drawing an inference.

'Actually . . .' she stumbled.

'Because this couldn't possibly be a coincidence.'

'What couldn't?'

'The fact that there was, around the time you're talking about, a rather ambitious young man with designs on starting a new theatre company. He had trod these very boards—he was with us for three seasons, in fact—but with the self-confidence bordering on delusion that only aristocratic lineage can inculcate, he fancied himself as actor-director of his own troupe. He wasn't good enough at either, to be honest; time proved that. A competent enough actor, for sure, but nothing more. He did, however, have one genuine gift in abundance, one that many people in this business tend to undervalue: he may not have been a great talent himself, but he had a fine eye for recognising it in others. He knew what elements might work together to produce something magical, but he only really succeeded once he had accepted that he needed to leave it to experts to fine-tune the chemistry. Fortunately he became as adept at recognising talent in directors as in cast and crew.'

'So would he have worked with Tessa?' Jasmine asked impatiently. She could tell Dorothy was holding something back, but the older woman had a rather mischievous look on her face that suggested Jasmine somehow deserved to be thus toyed with.

'Oh yes. Their times here overlapped. They both worked under Peter and Francis, and they both had the nous to appreciate that it was a privilege. Make no mistake, this young chap greatly admired what the Pantechnicon had achieved. It wasn't so much that he thought he could do better as simply that he'd like to do different. Specifically, he believed the Pantechnicon wasn't *Scottish* enough. He felt

123

the Winters, being from Durham, were rather shy of the theatre taking on too overtly Glaswegian an identity, and that this manifested itself in their choice of plays.

'I suspect a few harsh run-ins with reality adjusted his sensibilities. He runs a rather successful little theatrical enterprise these days but, most ironically, his company is London-based and wouldn't dream of staging anything so parochial as a Scottish play. Nonetheless, its name harks back to his earlier ambitions.'

'Glass Shoe?'

'Yes. It's a little joke, a play on the original Gaelic name from which Glasgow is derived: Glaschu. But what has me curious, and what cannot possibly be a coincidence, is that the aforementioned enterprise is named Glass Shoe *Productions*.'

And there it was. It had been staring her in the face for days, and it certainly wasn't the negligible distinction between Company and Productions that had foxed her: just a classic case of can't see it for looking at it.

She understood why Dorothy had been wearing that strange little smile: she couldn't believe Jasmine hadn't worked it out and she knew she would kick herself when the penny finally dropped. Jasmine also understood why the name had prompted slightly uncomfortable associations, and they were nothing to do with where she or her mother could afford to shop. It was an unattainable dream: the West End stage.

Glass Shoe Productions appeared on the posters, in a little strap at the top that nobody paid attention to. Even Jasmine would have had to think for a moment if she'd been asked it as a quiz question.

It was an incidental detail. People didn't associate these shows with the name of a company, but the name of one man.

The Phoenix and the Ashes

So. Another dream come true, thought Jasmine, trying not to gag on the irony. First her career had put her on stage at the Pantechnicon and now, a few days later, here she was, treading the boards professionally at the Edinburgh Playhouse and working with Hamish Queen no less.

It had stung a little, calling in a favour from Charlotte Queen that was in no way directly beneficial to improving her chances of an acting gig, though in the tiny shrine in her heart the keeper of the flame was whispering to her that any kind of face time with the West End's dream-weaver-in-chief had to count for something. It was a chance to make an impression, at the very least. Presence based on genuine character? Authenticity deriving from true life experience? Stanislavski Method emotional memory? Got it all in spades, darling.

She'd just have to hope he was philosophical with regard to the fine line between acting and deceit.

Jasmine had learned the hard way not to tell an interviewee in advance what she really wanted to talk about. Not only did forewarned mean forearmed, it sometimes meant the interview didn't happen at all. The downside was that people could become very huffy about extending their cooperation under what they retrospectively considered false pretences. The trick was making

125

it appear that the conversation had moved on to sensitive territory by happenstance, and if Jasmine didn't pull that off today she'd be burning two very big bridges.

It had taken three calls to Charlotte to secure a meeting with her father, but not because she needed convincing. Charlotte seemed excited that Jasmine was asking, still tripping on that 'how exciting your job is' vibe, and had agreed right away. The subsequent calls had been necessary reminders because Charlotte, even when her sentiments and intentions were genuine, was not good at following up on things that weren't germane to her immediate ambitions. She came through in the end, though Jasmine couldn't help wondering how many goodwill points she had used up through her persistence.

Hamish Queen's PA, Melanie Gilhaus, got in touch on his behalf and, after several more phone calls, they finalised a time and place for a meeting. Initially, Jasmine thought she was going to have to fly to London and had called Mrs Petrie for authorisation regarding the expenses this would incur. Mrs Petrie was back down in Cornwall by this time, which made Jasmine fear the impetus might have dissipated, but rather she was adamant that Jasmine persist. Jasmine was doubly relieved, not only because it was good for business but because she'd have found it very difficult to walk away from this now. She told Mrs Petrie that she was following up a solid lead, but decided to hold back on the fact that it was the only one left, everything else pointing to her sister having been dead for thirty years.

Before she could book a flight, Melanie called

with an update on Hamish's travel plans. He was flying back from New York a couple of days early because he had decided to personally oversee the arrangements for his new touring production's opening run in Edinburgh. If she was available, Hamish would be able to squeeze in a meeting at the theatre.

Melanie was waiting for her at the theatre's main entrance on Greenside Place, where Leith Street, Queen Street and Leith Walk all converged. She was late twenties, *terribly* trendy, sunglasses perched on the top of her head even though she was mostly going to be indoors, an affectation all the more pronounced given that the shades were infringing on a haircut that Jasmine suspected cost more than her own suit.

She had an iPhone clipped to the waistband of her jeans, an iPad clutched in her left hand, a sheaf of script pages and two different-coloured highlighter pens grasped in her right, yet she still looked breezy and calm. Jasmine would have wanted to kill her if her thoughts weren't largely occupied by pleasant reminiscences of standing on this very concourse with anticipation thrilling through her so intensely that she recalled literally bouncing up and down.

She loved coming here when she was a wee girl. It was always big, first-class shows at the Playhouse, usually imported from London's West End. More unashamedly glitzy and commercial than anything at the Lyceum, more polished and cosmopolitan than touring shows at the King's. Some people were very sniffy about that, and at drama school she remembered feeling it would be wise not to mention how many such productions she had attended here at the Playhouse. She wasn't confident enough to argue her case back then, but Jasmine didn't believe that an appreciation of commercial theatre precluded appreciation or enjoyment of work from the other end of the spectrum, or vice versa. There were occasions when you fancied something intimate and *avant garde*, just as there were occasions when you fancied a meal of intricately arranged, artistically presented, even experimental cooking. But there were other times when you were in the mood for an old-fashioned burger and you knew nothing else would do. Those big West End shows at the Playhouse, the Hamish Queen and the Cameron Mackintosh productions, those burgers came with all the trimmings: a guilty pleasure par excellence.

Melanie greeted her with a professional smile—'You must be Jasmine'—and led her briskly inside, thumbing something on her iPad as they passed through the foyer. The implication was clear: Melanie was *this* busy, so just imagine how busy Hamish is.

The interior of the Playhouse was so plush, so opulent, that it always piqued Jasmine's incredulity that it was once a regular rock venue. She had heard her mum and her friends reminisce about who had played here during the eighties: U2, Big Country, INXS, REM, The Alarm, Echo and the Bunnymen, Mötley Crüe and even Metallica. From what they said, the shows were as raucous as the roster would suggest, these groups playing Barrowlands one night and this place the next. It was small wonder they opted for a more upmarket repertoire after the Playhouse's early nineties renovation.

Jasmine followed Melanie down the side aisle to the right of the stalls. She could see Hamish Queen standing still amid the ferment of movement and activity on stage, talking in animated but seemingly humorous tones to a man in grey overalls. He was dressed casually in jeans and a blue T-shirt under a dark tailored jacket, albeit they were designer jeans, a designer T-shirt and the tailor was probably on Savile Row. His appearance was less flamboyant than his media profile normally suggested, but Jasmine realised this was probably him in his work clothes.

He noticed Melanie's ascent to the stage and gave her the most fleeting of gestures, two fingers briefly extended at his waist. Melanie responded with a nod and relayed the information.

'Hamish is just going to be a few minutes. Are you all right here, or would you like to come upstairs for a coffee?'

Jasmine was happy to wait where she was. It gave her time to take in the sheer scale of what was going on around her. On her way from the car park, she had looked down from a glass-walled footbridge and seen the convoy of Stage Truck juggernauts parked down on Greenside Row. It was very clear nobody at Glass Shoe Productions was wondering how to design a set to disguise the fact that the budget had all but run out.

It looked like some administrative glitch had caused the sets for four different productions to have been simultaneously delivered. Jasmine had never seen so many wagons and skids, platforms and parallels, doors and flats, revolves and stairs, while above her head a massive motorised winch system suspended enough battens, drops and

129

drapes for several seasons' worth of plays at the Pantechnicon. It was no glitch. This was all for one show.

Her head spun to think of how much money had been spent on this affair, but that was pocket change compared to how much it was likely to bring in. This was the first touring run for the show that had reportedly proven to be Hamish Queen's most profitable West End production to date. However, despite five years of runaway box-office results, this was one production that he would not be transferring to Broadway. It was a strictly British phenomenon: a stage musical based on the eighties schooldays drama series *Grange Hill*.

Satisfied with whatever he'd said to the guy in the overalls, Hamish Queen strode across the stage to where Jasmine was waiting, slaloming scenery and stage-hands with practised grace.

He greeted her with a grin and a handshake.

'Hello. You must be Yasmin.'

'Jasmine,' Melanie corrected, before Jasmine could.

'Sorry. Jasmine. Shall we go somewhere a little quieter? Maybe grab a coffee?'

'That would be great.'

For a guy named Hamish, his accent was as Scottish as cricket and warm beer, but his sense of nationality had evidently always been very pronounced.

He led her through a side door out of the stalls and up a back stair, from which they emerged into the dress circle. They made their way to the bar, which was deserted, but even as Hamish pulled a seat out for her a member of the theatre staff entered briskly and ducked beneath the bar-top.

Jasmine didn't know if Melanie had facilitated this or whether the Playhouse staff were simply on standby for such courtesies, but either way it communicated that this was a man used to things quietly being arranged for his convenience. She was almost embarrassed now to consider the absurdity of believing she could make a lasting impression that might one day serve her well if she was ever to audition. Once this meeting was over he was as likely to remember her as he was the bloke who had sped in to serve them cappuccinos.

'Charlotte told me you were at the Academy together.'

'That's right. She was a couple of years ahead of me. A couple of light-years, actually.'

Hamish liked this. A man of his success was probably inured to flattery, but Jasmine doubted he'd ever tire of hearing his daughter being praised.

'Forgive me, I've been travelling and the old memory is still on New York time. Charlotte said something about you researching the early days of Glass Shoe. Is that right?'

'That's right,' she confirmed. Jasmine had phrased it very precisely too, saying she wanted to ask about 'Glass Shoe': not Glass Shoe Productions or the Glass Shoe Company. The ambiguity was intended to protect her by Hamish being the one who misinterpreted rather than her being the one who misled. She was aware that the Glass Shoe Company must have been a failure: that somewhere back in the day Hamish Queen's attempt to create a stridently artistic and distinctly Scottish repertory company, his dreams of being an actor-director and his aesthetic idealism had all crashed and burned. Glass Shoe Productions had risen in its

131

place, but Jasmine was aware that rich, powerful and successful people preferred to talk about the phoenix rather than the flames.

Hamish demonstrated that he was no exception by quickly turning the subject of the early days into a conduit for discussing his present concerns.

'I'm going to need the caffeine then, if I'm rifling through the dustier reaches of the memory vaults,' he said, having a sip of cappuccino. Then it was back to the future. 'It's certainly been quite a journey, though I do have to ask myself whether I've come all that far when I'm putting on a musical based on an eighties TV show. It's taken me aback, though, truly. I was always very wary about whether I could make it fly. When I first came up with it, I remember thinking to myself that it was either the best idea I'd ever had or by far the worst, and I don't think I'd made my mind up until I saw the first month's receipts.'

He was being modest, in the way one can afford to be when discussing the origins of an enterprise that delivered vindication in such bounteous measure. The *Grange Hill* musical was typical of his alchemical touch. As Dot Prowis had said, he had the vision and sometimes outright audacity to gather elements that didn't make sense until he'd put them together, then in retrospect they seemed so obvious that every other producer was asking themselves why they never thought of it first.

Other commentators Jasmine had read suggested he had signed a deal with the devil whereby all his naff ideas somehow turned to hits. The implied price, of course, was his artistic soul.

Making a musical out of *Grange Hill* was a perfect example of an apparently base idea rendered gold,

132

but to appreciate Hamish Queen's true acumen you had to look at how he'd packaged it, paying particularly close attention to the soundtrack albums. Plural. Instead of cherrypicking all the best-known (and thus over-familiar) hits of the eighties, he had bucked the West End singalong trend in pursuit of evoking what he called 'genuine nostalgia'.

'You don't feel nostalgic when you hear the big hits of the eighties,' he explained to Jasmine, relaxing into his subject, 'because you've been hearing them throughout every decade since. You feel genuine nostalgia when you hear something you *haven't* heard since then, something in the background that you weren't aware you were noticing at the time.'

To this end, he had scoured old playlists to find songs that had been in high rotation on radio stations during the eighties, but which had not been hits: songs such as 'See That Glow' by This Island Earth, 'Day and Night' by Balaam and the Angel, 'Swallow Glass' by The Flaming Mussolinis and 'Glasshouse' by The Promise. Not only did this give him the 'overheard' nostalgia effect he was looking for, but he picked up the track licensing rights for next to (and in some cases precisely) nothing. Then the true sprinkling of fairy dust came in casting a host of beautiful young teens, each already known to the public by being TV talent show runners-up, and getting them to record modern versions of the songs.

The result was a stage musical that was a massive hit across two generations, each purchasing its own preferred flavour of the official soundtrack. Those raised on *The X-Factor* bought the 'original

133

stage cast' album, while their parents snapped up a compilation of revived subconscious memories, few of which had previously been available on CD, never mind iTunes.

Jasmine's mum had bought it. Jasmine thought it was ghastly, strong evidence for why these songs had merely lurked in the background, with two notable exceptions: 'Send My Heart' by The Adventures and a track called 'Stranger on Home Ground'.

'But there I go, babbling about today's show when you're here to talk about the past. I have to apologise. I have this "auto-promote" reflex and go into publicity mode whenever I start talking to a journalist. Is it the *Stage* you're with? I can't remember if Charlotte said. I'm sure she told me, but it was a few days ago and I'm a bit jet-lagged.'

'I'm not a journalist, Mr Queen,' she decided to make clear. 'I'm a private investigator.'

She surprised herself by how easy that was to say. It helped that she had briefly contemplated a worse alternative, that of allowing Hamish to persist in his misapprehension.

His eyes narrowed for a second, then his face lit up in recollection.

'No, of course. I warned you the memory wasn't firing on all cylinders this morning. Charlotte told me all about you, I'm sure. You're the girl who was involved in that business over the Ramsay disappearances.'

'That's me,' she said, trying to sound professional and conceal the buzz it gave her that he knew about this stuff.

'I remember it from at the time. Spooky business. And yet you got to the bottom of it all these years later. I suppose I should be worrying about what skeletons you might shake out of my closet, especially if you're talking about the early days. *Metropolis* at the Dominion, *Treasure Island* at the Aldwych: there were some corpses strewn around those, let me tell you.'

He said all this with a little chuckle, benignly patronising. As Dorothy had so frankly confessed, people generally didn't know what to say when you told them you were a PI, but in Hamish's case nor had he given any thought to the ramifications, otherwise he might not be sounding so glib.

'I'm actually looking to dig a little further back than that. It's to do with an actress named Tessa Garrion. I believe she worked with you under the auspices of the Glass Shoe Company, the precursor to Glass Shoe Productions.'

He stopped mid-sip. Those ramifications were impacting now. I'm a private investigator. That means I'm going to be sticking my nose into the very things you least want anyone to. Such as your failed theatre company.

'Tessa Garrion,' he said, his eyes widening as he repeated the words. 'There's a name I haven't heard in . . .' He did his mental arithmetic. 'Jesus, is it really thirty years? And the Glass Shoe Company: where did you unearth that little coffin?'

'Tax records,' Jasmine told him. 'The Glass Shoe Company paid her a month's salary.'

'And no more, unfortunately. If you're trying to find Tessa Garrion, then I'm afraid the history of the Glass Shoe Company is unlikely to constitute a rich seam of information. It was a stillborn venture, over almost as soon as it began. It's a testament to the fastidiousness of our tax collectors that they

135

own the only record of the company's existence. Blink and you'd have missed it. We certainly didn't do anything so eyecatching as stage a play.'

'But you paid Tessa a month's salary. What for?'

'She was paid in advance, as much as anything to convince her that the company was the real deal. She wasn't a person who needed to take some dodgy deferred-payment gig just to get work.'

'I'm told she was very talented.'

'God, yes. A true natural,' Hamish said, with genuine warmth. 'When she announced she was leaving the Pantechnicon, I pleaded with her to join my company, even if only for one play. It was like asking a budding superstar to come and play for Elgin City when you knew Manchester United, Barcelona and Bayern Munich were waiting with open chequebooks.'

'But she said yes.'

'No, actually, she didn't. She went to London in search of stages big enough both for her ambitions and her talent.'

'So how come . . .' Jasmine prompted needlessly. They both knew he was going to explain, but she could tell that a few oohs and ahs were expected of her in the role of his audience.

'She ended up with Glass Shoe? I'm not entirely sure. There were offers in London, certainly. To return to the footballer metaphor, I think it was like the budding young superstar found his head was spinning as he contemplated the career that lay ahead of him, so he opted to play out the remainder of the season with Elgin City, knowing he could hone his game away from the bright lights.'

'Hadn't she done that enough at the Pantechnicon?'

'Those lights were still pretty bright. What we were planning was a tour of small Highland venues: community centres, church halls and the like. A few weeks later she called me up at rather short notice and asked if the offer was still open. I couldn't believe my luck. Turned out it was the only luck that particular venture enjoyed. We barely made it *into* rehearsal, let alone out.'

'What went wrong?'

'Oh, just a mishmash of rookie mistakes, naiveté and a large dollop of hubris. Typified by the fact that our debut production was going to be the Scottish play. Height of arrogance, tempting the fates like that. Glass Shoe derives from the Gaelic for Glasgow; I was determined that we be a Scottish company committed to putting on Scottish plays. Thus it was my bold—older heads might say reckless—declaration of intent to start with *the* Scottish play.'

'You mean *Macbeth*?' said Jasmine, committing this small heresy partly for purposes of clarity and partly because she hated both the superstition and the posturing that went along with it.

Hamish gave her a sour look, like some bourgeois auntie who had just heard her swear. Then he sighed regretfully, his head shaking just a little.

'I used to call it that too,' he confessed. 'I thought saying "the Scottish play" was a dreadful affectation, people wearing it like a badge just to show they were fully paid-up luvvies. I've learned humility since. It *is* a dreadful affectation, but experience has taught me to tread lightly regarding its source. Let's just say there won't be any light-hearted musicals based on it coming soon from Glass Shoe Productions.'

'So what happened afterwards? Do you know where Tessa went next? When did you last speak to her?'

Hamish picked up his coffee, saw that the cup was all but empty, put it down and frowned.

'I'm afraid I've no idea. I didn't speak to her afterwards. We all abandoned the project, went our separate ways—in my case to lick my wounds. Sent homeward to think again, though in retrospect I was more the Bruce with his spider than proud Edward. I did try again.'

And back to the phoenix, Jasmine thought.

She caught him glancing to the side and spied Melanie hovering just outside the bar. She was waiting to haul him away on a made-up pretext if she got the nod, and she'd just received it. Jasmine had time for one last question, if she got it in before Melanie reached the table.

'Who else was in the company?' she asked, interrupting before he could saddle up to go into auto-promote mode, as he'd described it.

Hamish glanced to the side again, tracking Melanie's progress. He wanted to be rescued.

'It's been such a long time. I really wouldn't know where to find any of them,' he said apologetically.

'That's my area,' Jasmine replied. 'I just need names.'

Melanie made it into range, iPhone in hand.

'I'm sorry,' the PA began. She was looking at Jasmine, ostensibly in apology for the interruption, but it could equally have been addressed to Hamish for not reacting sooner. 'Hamish, you're needed downstairs. It's Jocelyn. She says it can't wait.'

'Duty calls,' Hamish said to Jasmine, getting up from his seat.

'You were going to give me some names.'

'I'm afraid Mr Queen is needed quite urgently,' said Melanie, running interference.

'The only name that leaps to mind is Adam Nolan,' Hamish said. It sounded familiar, possibly from TV, but Jasmine couldn't place him.

'Beyond that I'm struggling. It was another lifetime. I could tell you a couple of first names I'm barely half certain of, but the surnames are gone.'

'Surely you must be able to remember more than that,' Jasmine stated, drawing a warning glare from Melanie, who was clearly unused to anyone treating her boss with anything less than deference. Jasmine ignored her. Hamish looked uncomfortable, caught on the back foot, and she had to press while she still could. 'I realise it was a long time ago, but you worked with these people.'

'Well, that's just it,' Hamish said, slightly exasperated. 'I didn't; or at least, I only worked with them very briefly before it all imploded. Following something like that, the aftermath is like a really bad break-up. You're rather raw and you want nothing to do with anyone who was involved or who even reminds you of it. Before you know it, weeks have turned into months and you're all on new paths that may never cross again.'

Melanie chose this juncture to remind Hamish once more of the urgency of her made-up crisis, and they both withdrew. Jasmine thanked him for his help and was given a distracted 'sure' in return. Most definitely not 'you're welcome'.

She watched him disappear through the door towards the stairs and reflected that Dot was right: Hamish Queen was a competent actor, but he wasn't good enough. He was lying. He knew more

139

than he was saying; much more.

If you're trying to find Tessa Garrion, then I'm afraid the history of the Glass Shoe Company is unlikely to constitute a rich seam of information.

She'd be the judge of that. So far it was telling her plenty. For one thing, Jasmine never said she was *looking for* Tessa Garrion. Granted, Hamish could have made this association based on what he knew about Jasmine's involvement in the Ramsay case, but it was still quite a leap. Why would he assume Tessa couldn't be found when nobody had said she was missing?

As soon as they were out of sight, she got out her phone and Googled Adam Nolan. Like Hamish, he had survived the wreckage of their failed venture and built a good career for himself. He had joined the RSC in 1983, but the reason Jasmine remembered his name was that he had been in the regular cast of *First Do No Harm*, a medical drama series from the late eighties, a favourite of her mum's that Jasmine had watched with her on DVD box sets. The other reason his name had a certain significance was that there was an Aids charity named after him, Adam Nolan having died from the disease in 1993.

Tessa Garrion dropped out of existence shortly after working with Hamish Queen's fledgling theatre company and the only other name he could give her was someone who died eighteen years ago? Aye, right. That meant there were others, and Jasmine was going to find them.

140

A Shot in the Dark

Ideally, of course, this would turn out to be some kind of freak accident. That was the result everybody wanted. Sure, there would be ramifications for hunting safety and the fall-out would provide soundbite opportunities for those Barbour-clad mutants in the Countryside Alliance, but it was far preferable to a murder hunt. So preferable, in fact, and in so many ways, that Catherine doubted she would be so fortunate.

'What are the chances this was just bad luck?' she asked the groundskeeper, as they stood on a perfectly manicured but heavily bloodstained lawn before the mobile gantry that had given so many people a perfect view of the fatality.

The groundskeeper was named Roddy Frail. He was a short man in his fifties, someone she could picture stalking silently through the undergrowth, although the smell of loose tobacco would give him away if he didn't stay upwind. His hands were rough and callused, conditioned by and to the outdoors, and his fingers were stained by no end of roll-ups. He was used to handling thorny vegetation, but thorny coppers not so much. He looked rattled, the place he'd worked for years suddenly seeming altogether foreign. He had been dragged from sleep and dropped into a milieu far more unfamiliar than that which had confronted any of the Glesca Polis bussed in from the big city.

'It's a possibility,' he conceded with anxious reluctance, like he was going to have to answer for it personally if it turned out to be so. Here was one

141

person who was probably hoping it was murder.

'A substantial part of the estate's income is corporate shooting junkets,' he went on. 'They pay big money to have exclusive access.'

'Was there hunting taking place last night?' Catherine asked dubiously, thinking it really would be this guy's balls if the answer was yes.

He hit her with a look of apparent consternation that he was being questioned by someone either stupid or quite mad.

'At night? With a play going on?'

'Just wondering whether someone ended up somewhere they shouldn't have been.'

'Never happen,' he insisted animatedly. 'I have very strict safety protocols. There's no hunting at all during the theatre weeks, never mind by night. The whole place is given over to the plays, every room booked out, so you've got people wandering about, exploring, walking woodland trails. See, when people are here to hunt they have the place to themselves. It's fully escorted, well away from the castle. And I only allow night-time stalking for very experienced hunters, who are very few and far between in this place. Most of the corporate guests barely know one end of a gun from the other when they first get here.'

'So why is an accident a possibility?'

Frail gave a weary grimace, like some persistent back problem was playing up. He was on uncomfortable ground.

'The thing is, these corporate guests, they're not going to come back to the fair if they never win a goldfish, you know? We keep the stocks high, which makes sure they at least *see* a deer when you take them out, even if they cannae hit one. But it also

142

makes the estate a honeypot for poachers.'

'I see. And I take it poachers prefer to work under cover of darkness?'

'Some are as brazen as you like. They know it's a big estate, and we cannae be in ten places at once. But some folk get a buzz about hunting in the dark and they kit out for it too. Night-scopes and silencers aren't unheard of for going after deer without a permit.'

'Was this a silenced shot?' she asked Beano.

'No, ma'am. Everybody heard a bang from back there, in the woods.'

Catherine looked towards the tree line, which was about two hundred yards away, behind the trailer bearing the seats.

'How close are the game going to be on a night when there's all this going on?' she asked Frail. 'You've got a tractor hauling that tiered-seating gantry, music over a PA, dozens of people chattering and applauding, artificial lights flooding the place. I can't imagine any skittish woodland creatures straying close to the edge of cover with so much human activity going on, nor an experienced poacher taking aim when there was a gathering of people in his field of vision, never mind his field of fire.'

'I only said it was a possibility. Could have been a ricochet. Could also have been a shot from distance. Some of these rifles are built to take down their prey from a long way off. Some chancer deep in the woods, a kilometre up the slope, could have lined up a shot without realising what was behind it if he missed.'

'Aye,' said Catherine, 'such as a major figure in the world of the arts.'

'Makes no difference to me who he was,' said Frail, his eyes wide and bloodshot. 'I'd never heard of the guy myself. But if this was something I could have prevented . . .'

He bit his lip, glancing back and forth from the bloodstained turf to the tree line, looking fidgety and confessional.

'How could you have prevented anything?' Catherine asked, eyeing him neutrally: neither accusatory nor reassuring.

He sighed, regret and contrition etched as vividly on his face as the nicks and calluses on his fingers.

'There's a lot of blind eyes get turned,' he said. 'As long as folk don't kick the arse out of it, sometimes it's easier to write off a bit of poaching loss than to try and prevent it. People know each other out here, know each other's business. The point is, I can give you some names, but the local polis are already aware of them. They know which doors to knock. They've just never had reason to before.'

Just Because You're Paranoid

Jasmine made it back to the office late afternoon and set about transcribing Hamish Queen's interview, which she had secretly recorded. In keeping with Jim's practices, she liked to have a hard copy down in black and white as well as the audio file. Transcribing could be tedious, but it forced a closer examination of what was said, and the act of typing out the words helped commit them to memory. She then backed up both the text document and the recording, after compressing

144

it from wav to mp3 format. Having had the office broken into during the Ramsay case, she had learned not to keep all her eggs in one basket. This had forced her to overcome her assumptions regarding the complexities of using a computer for things other than word processing and web browsing, with the result that she was now au fait with audio and video editing software, and the letters FTP were no longer just something she saw scrawled on bus shelters.

Her work safely copied to two separate remote servers, she was able to clock off for the day, with the rare prospect of a good night out to look forward to. Jasmine's friend Michelle, who'd been at the SATD with her, had free tickets for Ballet Scotland's production of *The Sleeping Beauty* at the Theatre Royal. Michelle had been studying dance and now had a job with Ballet Scotland's community outreach programme Steps Forward. She described it as being 'where ballet meets social work', but it was a satin-slippered foot in the door of the company proper. They were planning to meet in town for a bite to eat before heading up to Cowcaddens for the show.

Jasmine never cared much for ballet growing up, and the appreciation she developed of it through her time at the SATD was largely on an intellectual rather than emotional level, but the last time she went with Michelle she had really enjoyed it. The absence of dialogue and the lack of narrative complexity meant she could switch off parts of her brain that were becoming overtaxed through work, allowing the music and the spectacle to wash over her for a couple of hours. It was almost like a state of meditation and her mind felt much the better for it afterwards.

She had checked the clock as she uploaded the last of the files. Sharp Investigations was based in a two-storey office building in Arden, on a light industrial estate midway between Rouken Glen and the M77. As long as the traffic wasn't too horrendous, she could make it back to her flat on Victoria Road in about fifteen minutes, leaving her time enough for a quick shower and change before heading into town.

Jasmine glanced in her mirror as she left the car park at the rear of the building and noticed a silver Passat pull away from the kerb just a short distance down the street. Something about it bothered her, though she couldn't say what. She pulled out on to the main drag of Nitshill Road, heading straight on at the roundabout instead of her normal left as there were temporary traffic lights on Thornliebank Road and she didn't want to be stuck in a queue for twenty minutes while a crew of workmen got on with the important task of sitting in a van reading the paper. She hung a left at the next roundabout, taking her on to Fenwick Road, which was when she noticed the same Passat two cars behind her.

Harry Deacon had warned her about the onset of paranoia that could come with this job. Spend days at a time following people's vehicles, becoming familiar with surveillance tactics and pursuit patterns and you could begin to see those tactics and patterns in the behaviour of the cars around you. See the same car behind you after a couple of turns and you could convince yourself you were being tailed, when in fact five out of the next ten cars might make the same turns because they were on the common route towards a particular destination. If the guy in the Passat was going from the industrial estate to the south side or the city centre, wouldn't he also take Fenwick Road if he knew there were temporary lights on the parallel Thornliebank Road?

Jasmine caught herself rationalising this, and rejected the reassurance her simple explanation was offering. She reminded herself that something had troubled her about that Passat from the moment she saw it, well before she noticed it was still behind her. Harry Deacon's advice was a useful bulwark against letting the job get too far inside your head, but Jasmine had learned a greater lesson from Glen Fallan: when your mind or your body are telling you to be afraid, you should listen.

Your brain takes in far more information about your environment than you are conscious of it processing, and we frequently ignore danger because we try to rationalise feelings that are not rational but instinctive. We look for explanations for why we feel an irrational anxiety, explanations that always seek to reassure us nothing is wrong, ignoring the fact that, as Fallan put it, 'the part of your brain that tells you to run because your early-warning system detected a predator or an avalanche was there a lot longer than language and responds a lot more immediately'.

For whatever reason, Jasmine had felt uneasy at the sight of that Passat pulling away behind her, and now it was still on her tail. Her conscious mind was busy looking for reasons why she shouldn't be worried, a seduction she had learned to resist.

She checked her rear-view again, trying to get a look at who was behind the wheel. It was difficult to see through the moving obstacle of the Mondeo directly behind her. She couldn't make out a face, just a baseball cap with the visor pulled down low. That alone might have been part of what spooked her.

She slowed down a little, checking her pace so that she would meet a gap in the oncoming traffic just as she reached the junction with Merrycrest Avenue on the right-hand side. She turned without indicating, nipping across the junction before a further convoy of cars barred the route to the Passat. He'd have to wait to turn, and if he did turn it was official: she was being tailed, albeit not by someone who knew how to keep it discreet. Merrycrest Avenue linked Fenwick Road to the parallel Langside Drive, but it was hardly a rat run. The likelihood that he would 'just happen' to be going up it was minuscule.

Jasmine accelerated gently, staying under twenty, glancing in the rear-view mirror every few seconds. The near-side traffic heading southbound on Fenwick Road blocked her view of whether the Passat had kept going past the junction, but so far he definitely hadn't turned into it.

Okay.

The other thing about irrational reactions, as Fallan had admitted, was that much of the time nothing precipitated from them and you'd seldom discover quite why you'd felt spooked. Nonetheless, these false alarms constituted a modest premium for such a vital insurance policy: when it paid out, the stakes could be very high indeed.

Jasmine hung a left at the end on to Langside Drive, figuring she could follow it all the way around Queen's Park to where it met Victoria Road, not far from her flat. It occurred to her that

148

this was actually a quite valuable alternative route to have in the bank, her Glasgow geography still very much a work in progress.

She glanced in her mirror as she approached the roundabout at Muirend Road, which was when she saw the silver Passat emerge from Merryburn Avenue two junctions behind her. He had taken a parallel road and reacquired her, waiting for her to pass and then pulling out with two cars' cover.

Shit.

She was definitely being tailed and it did look like he knew what he was doing. Now she wasn't merely a little spooked but genuinely rattled.

He had been waiting for her close to the office. That meant he knew where she worked. At this time of day, from his point of view, the greatest probability was that she was heading home, so that suggested he was trying to find out where she lived. This would double the number of pick-up points he could use for future surveillance, and that was only the most palatable of the reasons he might want to know this.

She had to lose him. She went through the roundabout and proceeded towards the junction with Merrylee Road, where she knew there were traffic lights. They were green as she came in sight. She was willing them to turn amber so that she could slow down on the approach then speed through as they changed, with at least one of the two cars between them preventing the Passat from following her. The lights did change, but she was thwarted by the Nissan Micra in front, its white-haired driver braking well before the amber turned to red.

The Micra was just as cautious about getting

under way again, showing no signs of movement until the signals were fully green. It was long enough to make most drivers consider a peep on the horn in case the old dear had failed to notice the lights had changed. In Jasmine's experience, this was often counterproductive as the inevitable fright tended to result in the driver stalling their vehicle in a panicked hurry to get going.

With this thought, she devised a new stratagem for losing her tail. As the Micra finally began to move she allowed the Civic to stall, then feigned an authentically flapping response, turning the ignition with the car in gear to eat up a few more seconds.

She gave an apologetic wave to the driver behind, pretending she was having trouble re-starting the Honda, then when the lights turned amber again she zipped through at speed. The car immediately behind her followed across the junction, but its successor didn't risk it, leaving the Passat stranded. She sped on, waiting until the junction was out of sight in her rear-view, then turned right on Newlands Road, followed by two lefts. This allowed her to double back along Earlspark Avenue and take a snaking route through a number of quiet residential streets.

As she reached Pollokshaws Road she took a long, careful look to her left before pulling out. There was no sign of the silver Passat, but her relief almost instantly gave way to a depressingly familiar feeling of failure.

She had panicked at the thought of being followed home and in her desperation to lose her tail urgency had triumphed over judgment. She should have pulled a reciprocal: gone all the way around the roundabout at Muirend Road and doubled back to eyeball the bastard. She'd have got his registration and maybe even a look at his face if he wasn't sharp enough to suss what was going on and get his head down. Either way, the tail would have ended then and there because he'd know he'd been burned.

Instead, she'd learned nothing about him, meaning she'd be looking over her shoulder from here on in, every glimpse of a silver car putting her on edge.

'Jasmine screws up,' she muttered to herself.

Collision Course

Not that Jasmine had any real doubt Hamish Queen was holding out on her, but two days later she received hard evidence that firmly resolved the issue, while at the same time posing a number of new questions concerning why he'd be so blatantly lying about this.

It came in the post, the black Companies House logo distinguishing the envelope from the usual pile of paperwork, junk mail and the occasional cheque. She had requested it almost a week ago, well before she'd firmed up a meeting with him, and she had been hoping to receive it before their interview, just in case he claimed to know nothing about the earlier company. At that point she had been reasonably expecting their meeting to yield at least a few more names, if nothing else. Instead, Hamish Queen was claiming that he couldn't remember the names of anybody involved in the original Glass Shoe, other than the one she had given him—

151

Tessa—and that of an actor who had died in 1993.

To be fair, thirty years was a very long time. How many people might such a successful theatrical producer have worked with over that period? Hundreds, from London to New York, Sydney to Moscow, Tokyo to Paris. It was perfectly conceivable that he couldn't remember the names of some actors he hired and just as quickly fired without a single play making it to the stage. It was also understandable that this was not an episode he cared to revisit, which would further consign its details to some oubliette of the mind, locked away so as not to rise to the surface unbidden. If those actors had never subsequently made anything of themselves, then it was all the more plausible that their surnames would fade from his memory. Could Jasmine remember the surnames of all the kids she had worked with in youth theatre, or even those of the students she'd performed with at the SATD a mere three years back?

But by the same measure, could Hamish Queen *forget* the name of his partner in setting up his first company, especially when that man had gone on to become head of Arts Council Scotland?

There it was, staring up at her from the desk: the official memorandum and articles of association:

The Glass Shoe Company.
Incorporated 18 May 1981.
Managing director: Hamish Queen
Company Secretary: Julian Sanquhar

Jasmine checked online to make sure the document was referring to the same man. There was, understandably, no reference to his being a

152

partner in the short-lived Glass Shoe Company, but Jasmine quickly learned that Julian Sanquhar had enough in common with Hamish Queen to leave no ambiguity. They were born in the same year into wealthy rural land-owning Scottish families—Queen in the Highlands, Sanquhar in Roxburghshire—and had both been educated at Gordonstoun. Queen had gone on to Cambridge to study history, Sanquhar to Oxford to read law, but upon graduation both initially sought careers in theatre. Queen, being of the more extrovert nature, had successfully established himself as a repertory actor, but the reputedly introspective Sanquhar, despite acquitting himself quite capably on stage as an undergraduate, had proven more drawn to meeting administrative rather than thespian challenges.

On paper, and particularly in retrospect, it seemed an ideal pooling of talents: Hamish Queen, the man of grand vision and flamboyant audacity, augmented by Julian Sanquhar, the quietly ambitious facilitator. To Jasmine, this all the more keenly begged the question of what went wrong and, just as pertinently, why Queen was so determinedly lying about it.

Whatever had happened, they didn't work together again and, in keeping with what Queen told Jasmine, their paths had so seldom crossed thereafter that nobody seemed aware they had once had a professional relationship. No journalist or blogger appeared to have picked up on their Gordonstoun link, but unless you were specifically looking for it you wouldn't think there was a connection. While Queen was raking in the millions putting on his glitzy musicals, Sanquhar was

153

proving adept at making far smaller sums stretch as far as they'd go in a series of positions with regional theatres, arts funding bodies and charities.

He wasn't always just the man behind the scenes, although he had more of a public voice than public face. Sanquhar was an accomplished radio broadcaster, contributing to coverage of the arts and humanities for both Radio Four and Radio Scotland, with his two documentary series from Afghanistan, *Voices of Camp Bastion* and *Voices Beyond Camp Bastion*, garnering particularly high accolades. He worked in television also, but didn't present any of the programmes he had written or produced.

His stock was high at the BBC, and since standing down from his position as head of ACS it was widely believed he was imminently going to be appointed to the BBC Trust. This would be in addition to the various committees, boards and advisory bodies he sat on, all of which made Jasmine less than optimistic about the chances of being granted an audience.

Nonetheless, she left messages with several offices and organisations, requesting an interview. She kept the details vague: she didn't lie outright and say she was a journalist, but she didn't say that she was a private investigator either. She received responses spanning a wide spectrum of sincerity, assuring her that her request would be passed on, and made a note to follow up after a reasonable interval of three working days.

To her great surprise Sanquhar got in touch the following morning. No secretaries, no PAs, just the man himself, saying he could talk that afternoon if she could make it to Alloway Kirk, where he'd have

154

some spare time while the crew were setting up shots for a new documentary he was making.

She said she'd be there, expressing her astonishment at both the swiftness of his response and the fact that he'd done so personally.

He laughed at this.

'Someone once gave me this invaluable piece of advice,' he said. 'Never let a piece of paper touch your hand twice. You get a message, you act on it right then or you bin it, because otherwise you'll waste time before you end up making the same decision anyway. Plus, when you're as busy as I like to be, you find that going through intermediaries constitutes an unnecessary doubling of effort.'

Jasmine looked at the pile of paperwork on her desk, wondering how much time she had wasted sifting through the same documents, humming and hawing about how to respond before deferring a decision and putting them back where they were. This was why Julian Sanquhar was head of this and on the board of that while she was struggling to run a one-woman operation.

Driving this point home, she remembered that she already had a job booked for that day, delivering a summons to a particularly elusive subject in Perth. What were the chances she could manage that in time to get down to Ayrshire before Sanquhar wrapped up filming?

It was a Galt Linklater gig; she couldn't let them down. Not only that, but the big firm were running out of time themselves, which was why they'd brought her in. The subject was an ex-cop who had thus far proven extremely successful at spotting and evading their personnel, and refusing to acknowledge his own identity on the rare occasions

155

they had managed to buttonhole him. He had returned all posted summons papers marked 'gone away', and if the client law firm's papers weren't served soon they would lose their slot in court.

It wasn't exactly justice hanging by a thread: the ex-cop was being sued in Sheriff Court by his local council over some dispute Jasmine could barely follow regarding access rights to a disputed thoroughfare abutting his property. However, the details didn't matter. Galt Linklater paid her a retainer to have first dibs on her services and right now they needed their ninja.

She drove to Perth, reaching the subject's address just after eleven. Galt Linklater's Martin Grady, parked further down the street in a surveillance van, had been watching the house since nine and confirmed over the radio that the subject, one Wilson Todd, was definitely home. This was good news: no hanging about waiting—and hoping—for him to show. Jasmine placed the papers under her clipboard and walked confidently up to the front door, ready to snare him with the junk-mail trap. This would be over in moments, then she could get herself down to Alloway by the tail-end of lunchtime.

She tried the doorbell twice, to no avail. Not even a hint of footsteps in the hall or a twitch of curtains to suggest the subject was getting a look at her, which was the usual precursor to the door opening once they had seen harmless young Jasmine and not some burly ex-polis.

Bugger.

She made her way back to the Honda, inquiring of Martin over the radio whether he was definitely sure the guy was home. He just laughed, a welcome-to-my-nightmare cackle.

'I hope you don't have dinner plans,' he added.

She drove around the corner and parked out of sight, then spent an excruciating age waiting for a development, all the time fighting the urge to go back and have a second go. He could have been in the toilet or the shower, she told herself, but these possibilities were being suggested by the part of her that desperately wanted to talk to Julian Sanquhar. The part of her that was on a retainer for Galt Linklater knew that a subject as fly as Todd had almost certainly watched her surreptitiously either as she approached the house or as she left it, and possibly both. At this stage, as far as he knew, she was just some canvasser he hadn't answered the door to, but if she made a second appearance she was burning herself.

It was after one o'clock when he finally made a move, emerging from the house and very quickly getting into his Freelander. Martin relayed Todd's position so that Jasmine could stay close, but she wasn't to join the follow in case she or her vehicle got spotted.

The pursuit lasted a good twenty minutes, Todd going in circles, needlessly back and forth along dual carriageways and around industrial estates before making his way into the car park of a large supermarket close to the football stadium.

'He's letting me know he's aware,' Martin moaned. 'He didn't pull a reciprocal or try to burn me outright: he's just dicking me about as a means of giving me the finger.'

Jasmine made her way into the car park and picked out the Freelander, reversing into a space where she could keep an eye on Todd's vehicle.

Time kept on trickling away. It was approaching two o'clock. Even if she left this minute she wouldn't make it to Alloway until around four.

She could hear Sanquhar's voice on the phone that morning, his words about letting a piece of paper touch his hand only once and the unnecessary doubling of tasks. A black-belt in time management who had spotted a tiny window and offered it to her. What were the chances of a guy like that giving her a second bite?

She saw Todd returning to his vehicle carrying a single shopping bag. In there half an hour and he only had one bag? Bastard. An ex-cop and he knew the score. He was wasting their time because he knew he could. They had no option but to watch and wait. She was going to be here all day, and what was worse was that they weren't going to get this guy. He returned all mail, never answered his door and never acknowledged his name. The papers had to be delivered in person, and he had to verify his identity.

She watched him close the hatchback of his vehicle and place his solitary bag inside. Then he'd probably sit there, milking it a bit longer before reversing out. She hated this gig, she hated this guy and she hated that ridiculous, oversized vehicle. How could he even see out the back of it with that spare wheel covering the window?

Which was when she saw how to end this. It would come at a cost, but it would get the job done. How much did she want to make it to Alloway, that was the question.

'Bollocks to it,' was her answer.

She put the Civic in first and nipped out of the space, then crawled along the lane until she was a car's width back from where the Freelander would emerge. Its driver was blocked by a solid-walled Escort van from her line of sight—as she was from his.

She kept her feet balanced between the accelerator and the clutch, then picked her moment as the rear of Todd's vehicle withdrew. The Honda lurched forward and the back of the Freelander crunched into it. Nothing drastic, but hard enough that some panel work was definitely going to be required. As were his insurance details, what with him being the one who had reversed out without spotting a bright red car coming down the lane at his back.

She got out of her car first and had a look, feigning shock and not a little anger as Todd emerged to assess the damage. It wasn't a bad bash, but as predicted it would take some work; from experience a couple of hundred quid's worth. For that reason she made damn sure she had his insurance details written down and confirmed before handing him the envelope.

Warlocks in the Mirk

Jasmine made it to Alloway for five past four, and as she approached the junction closest to where the kirk sat she was hugely relieved to see a van parked near by, bearing the legend of an independent production company: First Glance Films. She recalled the words of one of her teachers at the SATD, warning them that 'television filming always expands to fill the time available'. This thought had

159

been at the back of her mind since Perth, but it hadn't eased her foot from the accelerator.

The Honda had been making that clunking noise again, as well as losing power in low gear. She hoped the dunt from Todd's Freelander hadn't shaken something else loose, and she didn't imagine flooring it for the best part of two hours was doing much for the poor thing's recuperation. She was here now, though, and crucially so was Julian Sanquhar.

She could see him standing close to the iconic ruin, drinking coffee from a paper cup and chatting to a woman while the film crew worked on setting up a shot among the ancient headstones.

He was shorter than the impression she'd garnered from photographs. She'd imagined a wiry figure, toweringly professorial, but though he was indeed thin he was maybe only five-six or five-seven and slight with it. He had wispy white hair, which was blowing around in the breeze coming in from the Firth of Clyde.

He was dressed in a grey suit with a waistcoat, in a cut that had never been in or out of fashion. To Jasmine it said old money well spent, but not spent on clothes very often.

The woman he was talking to turned her head. Jasmine recognised her as Kirsteen Currie, a former BBC Scotland newsreader who had worked the arts beat in recent years. She was the voice and face of whatever was being filmed, Sanquhar presumably the writer or producer, possibly both.

Jasmine had done her homework on him since getting the Glass Shoe information from Companies House. He had said early in his tenure as head of ACS that 'if I'm not the most

160

complained-about person in Scottish arts circles, then I'm doing it wrong'. On the surface these sounded like the arrogant words of a man who was not afraid of making enemies, but in practice evidenced pragmatic sensibilities and good-humoured humility, two qualities that had served him well throughout his career. He knew he wasn't going to be able to please everybody when it was his hands on the purse strings, but he had been the one looking for—and often denied—a hand-out from the arts budget plenty of times in the past, so he understood the frustrations.

'Begging is good for the soul,' was one of his quotes on the matter.

For those less inclined to be as philosophical as he had been upon having a funding application turned down, his surname offered an obvious rhyming outlet for their frustrations, but the nickname that seemed to have stuck was 'Saint Julian'. Jasmine remembered hearing it from lecturers at the SATD, and had at first assumed it was in reference to his renowned but seldom stated religious beliefs. He was known to be deeply—but just as privately—devout in his Catholicism, his faith being a personal matter about which he was neither outspoken nor inclined to bring into his public life in any way.

However, upon researching his career in more detail Jasmine came to discover that the real origin of his moniker was in affectionate and grateful tribute to his 'working miracles' in sourcing and stretching funds for theatre companies and other arts projects. He was said to be selfless, dedicated and utterly committed wherever he had worked, so perhaps the large quantity of goodwill he had carried into his ACS chairmanship meant he didn't get complained about as much as some of his predecessors.

Naturally, he wasn't without his detractors, even among those acknowledging their gratitude. He was praised for his efficiency, his diligence and in particular his resoluteness: his ability to make a decision quickly and to stick by it. However, this last was something of a double-edged sword, as he was criticised for being both impulsive and reluctant to admit when he'd screwed up. Most of the time, his forward planning was his strength, but one former ACS colleague warned that he was 'highly skilled at retro-engineering his logic to justify decisions made on the spur of the moment'.

On the whole, though, his tenure at ACS had been uncontroversial, and that was arguably the greatest compliment that could be paid to whoever held his post.

Jasmine approached on quiet feet, walking briskly but not wishing to appear too hurried. Sanquhar noticed her at around the same time as one of the production crew, who was about to intercept her when he got a wave from the boss to acknowledge that her presence was expected. Jasmine felt a measure of relief that Sanquhar had remembered she was coming, as she imagined that by the end of a day's filming, arrangements made first thing that morning could have long since dropped off the call sheet. It certainly felt more than just a matter of hours since they'd spoken on the phone, her beloved Civic bearing the scars of a long day.

Sanquhar broke off with an apologetic gesture to Kirsteen Currie and turned to greet her. It didn't do a great deal for Jasmine's composure to witness this woman she had grown up seeing on television every evening not only in the flesh a few yards away but effectively being put on hold.

'You must be Jasmine Sharp,' Sanquhar said, offering a hand.

'That's me,' she responded self-consciously. 'I'm sorry to interrupt,' she added, addressing Currie.

'Not at all,' said the presenter. 'Kirsteen Currie. Nice to meet you.'

It was very disconcerting to have a Scottish household name introduce herself like everyone who saw her didn't already know. Jasmine was lost for a response that wouldn't have her still cringing in a decade and so opted for a handshake and a mumbled 'hi'.

'I'll keep out of the way until you've got five minutes,' Jasmine assured Sanquhar. 'Or, well, as long as you can spare.'

'Oh, I can spare plenty right now,' he responded. 'I was the one keeping Kirsteen company while they set up this next shot. We can take a wander along the road to the hotel there and grab a cuppa, if you like.'

Jasmine glanced at the cup already in his hand and he caught her looking.

'Don't worry about that. It's instant muck. Great excuse to pour it away.'

'If it's all the same, I'm all right out here. I've been driving and I could use the fresh air.'

Currie gave a chuckle.

'I think Julian was just looking for an excuse to take a walk. He could stand and talk Burns with me all day, but I'm sure he'd rather not be doing so in a graveyard, even this graveyard. Maybe especially this graveyard. We're all very grateful for his stoicism thus far. The poor dear won't be sleeping

163

tonight after this. Can't handle the "warlocks and witches in a dance", can you, Jules?'

'I'd prefer the banks and braes o' bonnie Doon, it would be fair to say,' he said with a thin smile, indicating that Currie's was not an idle observation but something of a barb.

It took Jasmine a moment to grasp what she was alluding to. She had read the single interview in which Sanquhar had been less circumspect about his religious beliefs, or rather one aspect in particular. He had never been known to wear his faith as a badge, to paint himself as pious or to indulge in moral pontificating, so it seemed unfair to Jasmine that these few remarks had occasionally been cast up out of context. Perhaps his more typical reticence with regard to his religion meant that there wasn't a deluge of more bland and mundane bread-and-butter Christian platitudes in which to dilute them, or perhaps it was just one of those issues that was always going to attract attention.

He had said he believed in the devil: not as a generic catch-all term for human wickedness, but as an entity.

'Catholic doctrine states that Satan exists as a person,' he told an interviewer for the *Sunday Times*. 'And I hold that to be true. I don't believe in some figure of medieval wood carvings with cloven hooves and horns, and not as what you or I would recognise as an individual, corporeal being, but a form of consciousness nonetheless. An agency. Something that moves within this world. It's not a fashionable thing to say, and that is why I suspect more people believe it than would own up to it, but you go and ask the soldiers who were in Bosnia, in Kosovo, in Rwanda. They'll tell you there are evils

164

in this world greater than man.'

It had been in the course of a broadly philosophical discussion about the nature of evil, but the background tended to be left out whenever someone brought it up by way of a cheap dig, trying to make Sanquhar look like a nutter. It struck Jasmine that it would be enormously bad form on Currie's part to be doing so in front of a stranger, even if she and Sanquhar happened to be old friends. Thus she reasoned that Currie's remarks were more likely in reference to the one genuine storm that had blown up during Sanquhar's time as ACS chair.

During her research Jasmine had browsed dozens of news stories and amid the usual exchanges about funding decisions and the predictable jousts arising from arts-world personality politics, the only controversy worth mentioning had arisen over the film body Screen Scotland.

There was always an ongoing debate about whether public money should assist more artistically adventurous films that otherwise wouldn't stand a chance of getting made, or whether the funding would be better spent investing in more commercially viable projects that would showcase Scottish talent, locations and facilities as well as earning its keep at the box office. Every so often this would come to a head, usually when a disproportionately large share was awarded to a single commercial movie (the complaint being that it would have got made anyway) or when it transpired that the cash had been spread thinly across a number of more worthy projects, none of which had subsequently made it out of development. On this occasion the issue blew up because of Screen Scotland's decision *not* to award any support to a particular project, and the subsequent leaked revelation that Sanquhar had brought personal pressure to bear in the decision-making process.

Making it all the more juicy, from a media point of view, was that the project concerned was a horror film, and therefore battle was joined with all the vehemence and over-statement that journalists seemed to reserve exclusively for things that didn't matter very much.

There was a broad debate about the morality of presenting violence—and in particular the horror genre—as entertainment, with the outcry from the right-wing tabloids against public money being spent on it rendered no less shrill by being utterly moot. More soberly, in the broadsheet arts pages the spotlight was focused upon Sanquhar's hand in the veto and whether his personal prejudice or even individual taste had played an inappropriate role. This largely derived from Sanquhar being on record regarding his profound dislike for horror cinema, amid reports that he had always been very squeamish about both violence and sex on screen.

'I am not so naïve, like Keats's Grecian urn, as to believe beauty is truth and truth beauty,' he had once said. 'If art is about truth, then art must necessarily reflect ugliness. But my problem with even the very idea of these films is that they trade *only* in ugliness. Ugly images, ugly emotions, ugly sentiments and, of course, very ugly acts. One can't help but conclude that such works can only inspire ugly thoughts and ultimately inculcate ugly attitudes.'

The film-maker whose application sparked

the controversy was Russell Darius, a famously reclusive horror director whose media shyness would not have been much ameliorated by this particular storm. He restricted his response to a few well-chosen remarks that struck Jasmine as being ostensibly magnanimous but disguised an incendiary intended to ignite a different debate.

'I do not believe Julian Sanquhar acted outwith his remit,' he said in a written statement, 'and I do not believe he was motivated by prudery, by religious belief or by the desire to avoid the political fall-out from publicly funding a horror film. I also do not believe he has ever actually watched a horror movie all the way through. This wasn't a decision based upon moral concerns, but based upon artistic elitism.'

And with that, the consensus was that Darius had truly hit the mark.

'Why don't we take a wee dawdle anyway,' Sanquhar suggested. 'So that our chit-chat doesn't pollute Kirsteen's delivery.'

Kirsteen put her hands up briefly in a gesture of benevolently taking her leave. It was only as she turned away that Jasmine realised the presenter was effectively being dismissed, and for the second time. Saint Julian was a well liked and gentle natured man, but it was a timely reminder that he was also a powerful one.

His voice was soft, his tones mellow: not one accustomed to oratory, but nonetheless accustomed to being listened to. She recalled the advice of a lecturer on the importance of dynamic range and the power that lay at both ends of the spectrum: 'In the words of the late, great Bill Shankly, if you want people to listen, speak softly.'

Jasmine had remained under the impression that Shankly had been an influential theatre director until catching ten minutes of a documentary a few months back.

Sanquhar's accent was very similar to Hamish Queen's. They had hailed from opposite ends of Scotland but neither was going to be taken for a Glaswegian or a Leither any time soon. Nonetheless, there was something charming about the way he tarried over the words 'wee dawdle', like they were a treat on his tongue, savoured like a sneaky bite of deep-fried Mars bar in a health-food restaurant.

As they walked through the ancient churchyard in the watery afternoon sunshine it struck Jasmine that he hadn't asked her what she wanted or whether she was with a particular paper or magazine. It made her appreciate that he was very used to interviews and consultations, and was perhaps ready with some one-size-fits-all answers. On the plus side, she had him to herself: no PA hovering around to pull him away if the going got tough.

'I'd like to ask you about the Glass Shoe Company,' she said, trying to disguise her scrutiny of his reaction.

He didn't miss a beat.

'In that case, it's a good thing you said no to coffee. I'd have covered all there is to know before we made it to the Brig o' Doon hotel.'

'I realise it was a short-lived venture, but that in itself poses some questions. You and Hamish Queen, that's quite a combined pedigree. Yes, you were both young and inexperienced, but on paper it must have looked a formidable prospect. What

168

brought you together? What was your shared goal? Why didn't it work out?'

Sanquhar gave a flustered but friendly sigh.

'That's a lot of questions. In response to the last I'll just say it's unanswerable, because even in retrospect it's impossible to pick apart what went wrong in theatrical ventures. I could just scream out: "It was everybody else's fault" and that would be authentically luvvie, wouldn't it?'

He gave a wry smile and cast an eye back towards the church ruin, where Kirsteen was now talking to the sound engineer.

'Hamish and I met at school, at Gordonstoun. It would sound terribly precious to say that our common love of theatre forged a bond between us, but I'm not sure that our common love bonded us as much as our common disdain. Unlike most of our peers, we didn't much care for rugby and nor did we fancy ourselves as chancellor of the exchequer, head of a multinational or dictator of a small republic.

'We went our separate ways after school: he to Cambridge, myself to Oxford, but we kept in touch. I acted a bit at college and didn't do too badly, I'm told, but frankly I was always terrified. It really is a lot scarier than it looks, which nobody can understand unless they've tried it. Have you ever . . .?'

'I trained at the SATD, but didn't finish.'

'Oh really? Why not?'

'My mother . . . she was ill, and she died.'

'Oh, I'm terribly sorry.'

'She was an actress too,' Jasmine added, hurrying past this. 'Before I came along.'

'So if it's in the family, you'll understand what

169

I'm talking about. Scary stuff, but I loved being part of the shows. In college productions I loved the mucking in, the business of everybody having a dozen different jobs.'

'Less so a dozen different parts,' Jasmine suggested.

'Quite. That was actually worse than a lead role. When you're five different spear-carriers as well as an old woman it's like juggling knives. But they were good times. Great times. That's why I was always drawn to working with smaller companies, regional theatres. There's a strong sense of shared purpose and the ever-present excitement of flying by the seat of your pants. One might also call it the ever-present threat of imminent disaster, but there's no thrill where there's no danger. That's why I was tempted by Hamish's proposal.'

'He came to you?'

'Yes. Hamish is originally from the Highlands, as you may know. The summer before he left for Cambridge he saw 7:84 touring John McGrath's play *The Cheviot, the Stag and the Black Black Oil* when it came to Balnavon, the village closest to his family's estate. They performed it in the church hall and it made an enormous impression on him.'

'Politically?' Jasmine asked, aware of the play's history.

'To some extent, yes. I think it taught him a perspective upon his native Highlands that he'd never got from the family hearth and certainly not at Gordonstoun. But its true impact on Hamish was theatrical: the way it engaged with audiences right there in the heart of their communities. It didn't just bring the play to them, it brought them into the play, joining in the songs, reminding them that as

170

Highlanders it was their story.'

'Did you see it too?' Jasmine asked.

'Only on television: *Play for Today*. I didn't experience what Hamish did, but at least it meant I understood what he was so enthused about. From then on he kept talking about these two elements that had stuck with him: making theatre come alive for an audience and producing plays that were about modern Scotland.'

'Hence the name Glass Shoe,' Jasmine said, allowing him to skip a few pages.

'Indeed,' he replied, fixing her with a scrutinising stare, seeming both impressed that she knew this and a little wary. They were at the eastern boundary of the graveyard, as far from the kirk as the grounds extended, and he really wouldn't have a quick rescue if the conversation took an awkward turn.

'The problem was that Hamish was not what one would describe as politically literate, never mind politically driven. He understood spectacle and emotion: that's what had truly grabbed him about seeing 7:84. But the ideological motivation that was so clear and passionate in someone like McGrath became really just a woolly mix of duty and good intention in Hamish's case.'

'A kind of liberal guilt?'

'A little, yes. All the agitprop gusto that had initially energised him soon became a rather nagging sense of obligation. When we talked about starting our own touring company, one of my first tasks was to make him accept that although he'd been inspired by 7:84, and might feel he owed certain debts, in truth he didn't want to *be* 7:84. Yes, he wanted to make theatre come alive for audiences in places like Balnavon church hall, but he was more aesthete than activist and I had to make him accept how that was okay.'

'Hence Shakespeare instead of agitprop. Albeit Scottish and Highland-set.'

'Well, the great thing about the Bard is that it always saves on paying a playwright. I think it was me who suggested it, just as a for-instance, to help re-focus Hamish's vision. He seized upon it and from there on in we fairly fired each other up.'

He leaned back against a headstone and gave a self-deprecatory grin.

'Oh, we set the theatre world to rights in a few pubs, let me tell you. Ranting to each other about how patronising it was to suggest that these village halls would only respond to leftist rabble-rousing. We firmly believed there was an audience there who would come out for fresh, lively, exciting theatre. Get the right players together, talented actors who could share our passion, and we'd play a different church hall or community centre each night for months, then on the back of that we'd have longer runs in the cities, garnering plaudits and filling the coffers to fund the next production.

'When I say we believed, I mean we really believed, and we put our money where our mouths were. I gave up a position with a company in Leeds, Hamish walked away from the Pantechnicon and we both put in a stake. I was happy to because it was that college thing again: everybody mucking in, doing everything from painting flats to selling tickets on the door.'

Sanquhar looked away, beyond the church to somewhere much further away. He had this strange look of remembered optimism and regret. Jasmine waited for him to resume, but his focus remained momentarily elsewhere.

'So what went wrong?' she prompted. 'It's my understanding that the company imploded during rehearsals for its first production. Was the chemistry wrong somehow? Clashes of personalities? Artistic incompatibilities?'

She was hoping to edge him towards discussion of the personnel but, mindful of Hamish Queen's lies and evasion, she was treading lightly lest the shutters come down.

'It wouldn't be healthy to apportion blame. It's all too far back and we've all lived long lives since. We were all culpable in our own different ways.'

'That sounds like a politician's answer.'

'As it should. I've been a politician of sorts my whole career. The only difference is that in the arts you have to be twice as delicate.'

'Yes, but when a politician says something like that it just makes it all the more obvious that there's something else he's not saying. What happened in rehearsals?'

He shrugged.

'All the things you said: the wrong chemistry, personality clashes, artistic incompatibilities.'

As Sanquhar spoke, he was gazing east towards the sea: looking to his right, where Uncle Jim said your eyes strayed when you were lying. She'd trod lightly and the shutters had come down anyway. Time to be more direct.

'When I asked Hamish Queen about this he claimed he could only remember the names of two of the people involved, and yours wasn't one of them. I only learned you were partners from Glass Shoe's official records at Companies House.'

She watched for a response and got it. He looked

173

back at her sharply: not exactly reeling, but there was a hardening of his expression.

'I think that level of obfuscation indicates we're talking about more than just a few luvvie tantrums. And your own reluctance to apportion blame suggests to me that there's someone you *would* apportion it to if you weren't being "delicate".'

He stood up straight, taking his weight from the headstone. Jasmine thought he might be about to storm off, and she wondered whether this would be the moment he demanded to know who she was with and what was her angle.

He stared past her, back towards the auld kirk, but he wasn't signalling for rescue. It was as though he could see something there other than the production crew, something that was making him very uncomfortable.

'I know why you're here, Miss Sharp,' he stated, his tone still soft but an underlying edge to it. 'You're looking for Tessa Garrion. Hamish told me. He was on the phone as soon as he'd finished talking to you.'

So that was why he hadn't inquired in any depth about who she was: he already knew.

'Well, I'm glad we've got our cards out on the table. Here's an odd thing though, Mr Sanquhar. I never told Hamish Queen that I was looking for Tessa Garrion. I only said I was delving into her past. Why would he think she was missing?'

He stared at the kirk again, then back at Jasmine. No glance to the right.

'The same reason as our little enterprise imploded. She walked out during rehearsals and none of us ever heard from her again.'

'And was she the individual you're delicately *not*

174

blaming?'

'No, most definitely not. None of us were blameless, though if anyone came closest to that distinction it was Tessa. But you're right: it wasn't arguments and tantrums that drove her away.'

'What did?'

'If I was going to give you another politician's answer, I'd say lack of professionalism, but as you're being paid to look into this in depth, you ought to know the true nature of what you're dealing with.'

He glanced again towards the ruin and the ancient graveyard before it. It was as though he was afraid of being jumped by an assailant hidden behind one of the headstones.

'I have a reputation—I would say an unfair reputation—in certain circles for being something of a prude. I'm no fool: I'm aware the Saint Julian nickname isn't always intended generously. I don't get on my soapbox, but there are things I disapprove of, and I do so because I've seen them in extremis. When we rehearsed our ill-starred first play we did so at Hamish's estate. His family were abroad for a month so we had the run of the place.'

A glowering darkness came over his face, mixing distaste with genuine anger.

'These were not teenagers overdosing on the unaccustomed freedom of their parents being gone for the weekend. We were all grown adults, twenty-four, twenty-three at the youngest. This wasn't letting your hair down. This was letting something else in.'

The anger in him seemed to choke his voice and he fell silent.

'What are we talking here,' Jasmine prompted.

'Booze, drugs . . . orgies?'

He shot her an impatient look: she really wasn't getting it.

'William Blake said the road of excess leads to the palace of wisdom, which is true if you're sixteen years old and have woken up with a chastening hangover the morning after raiding your father's drinks cabinet. On the road of excess this wretched company was walking, there may well have been a palace of wisdom at the end but there were many crossroads to be negotiated and we were always travelling at midnight. Do you know what is said to wait at the crossroads at midnight?'

'No,' Jasmine confessed.

'Do you know where you are, Miss Sharp?'

That edge to his voice was hardening, like he was aware of a threat and not from her.

'I mean, do you understand why we're filming Kirsteen here?'

She nodded, and realised she knew also what he was alluding to regarding the crossroads myth.

'"A winnock-bunker in the east,"' she quoted, casting her eyes to the very spot. '"There sat auld Nick, in shape o' beast."'

Sanquhar nodded approvingly, though his expression didn't brighten any.

'Are you suggesting there was some kind of ritualism going on?' she asked, trying to keep incredulity from sounding like outright scorn.

'I was once less circumspect than I ought to have been regarding certain of my views,' he replied, demonstrating that she'd failed. 'What I was trying to convey is not something that is easy for people to understand. It's far easier to caricature what I was alluding to, because then it can be more

176

easily dismissed: a cloven-hoofed devil with horns and a pitchfork is clearly absurd, so we don't need to be afraid of it. But it was what I witnessed at Kildrachan House that made me believe there is something that feeds off the worst in men and further emboldens them. When there is a wanton will in man to seek the darkness, then there is something out there that listens, and it whispers back.'

Sanquhar's voice was low and dry, his eyes unblinking in the intensity of their stare. She recalled the unsensational tone of the *Sunday Times* article, the interviewer not sharing Sanquhar's belief but in no doubt about his conviction. Then, as now, he was said to seem genuinely afraid of whatever had inspired it.

'Tessa left because she was disgusted—and not a little scared, I should imagine. It's small wonder she never got back in touch with any of us.'

'But what actually happened? What kind of things are you talking about?'

He shook his head once, the gesture all the more final for its brevity.

'These are not memories I care to revisit. And you should understand that nobody else will either.'

Jasmine let out a small, measured sigh of frustration, less than she felt but precisely as much as she wished to convey.

'Do you at least recall the names of the people you're talking about, or are you going to lie to me like Hamish Queen did?'

'No,' he replied, sounding slightly impugned. 'I won't lie. How could I forget? But the names wouldn't do you much good. Hamish didn't only phone me after your visit, he called the others too.

They know about you. They're not going to return your calls.'

'You did,' she pointed out.

'I considered it a matter of conscience.'

'I don't follow.'

'I have a daughter not much older than you, and the thought of her doing what you are right now made me shudder.'

'I'm just asking people questions, Mr Sanquhar.'

'People with lives and reputations. People who will not forgive you for opening Pandora's Box. I don't know where Tessa Garrion went after she bailed out, but trust me on this: you won't find her by raking through the rubble of the Glass Shoe Company. You will only succeed in disturbing a great deal of long-buried hurt and shame, but what worries me is that you might awaken something worse.'

'I don't believe in the devil, Mr Sanquhar.'

'Nor did I, before the summer of eighty-one.'

'I'll take my chances. Give me the names. Who was in the company, apart from Tessa, Hamish and Adam Nolan?'

Sanquhar sighed with bad grace.

'Finlay Weir. He didn't have much of an acting career after that. I think he's a schoolteacher now. Maybe even a headmaster.'

Sanquhar paused, as though hoping his silence might be misinterpreted as the end of a very short list.

'Who else?'

He frowned.

'Murray Maxwell.'

Jasmine's eyes widened involuntarily.

'Murray Maxwell? As in *Darroch Glen*? As in

178

Raintown Blue?'

'And as in currently head of drama at Scotia Television, yes.'

'Well, I can really see why that one slipped Hamish's mind. Any more?'

'Just one.'

Sanquhar swallowed, as if his mouth had gone dry. When he spoke, it was clear that if the words 'wee dawdle' had been savoured as a treat, then these were shrivelling his lips like gall.

'Russell Darius.'

Jasmine concealed her reaction behind a further, redundant inquiry.

'No other women?'

'There aren't many female parts in *Macbeth*, and Tessa was very versatile. We didn't need anyone else.'

'So you're not superstitious?' she asked, as he hadn't substituted the name of the play.

'I told you, I'm not some religious nutcase. In my experience, the supposed curse around *Macbeth* is largely a self-fulfilling prophecy. One I fear we fell victim to. People fixate upon it when they have a self-destructive wish, seeking out darkness within themselves, perhaps hoping to confront it, to defeat it. Instead, it consumes them.'

Requiem for a Saint

Sir Angus McCready, head of his clan and laird of Cragruthes Castle, didn't look to Catherine like a man big enough or right then strong enough to bear so much nomenclature. He was huddled in an armchair in his private study, looking for all the world like a lost wee boy. The chair itself seemed too big for him, his feet not touching the carpet, but that was because he was withdrawn into it as far as he would fit.

Catherine was unsure whether this body language indicated merely his state of shock or his revulsion from her as the head of the police investigation. He had looked like his mammy was leaving him with a cold stranger when Sergeant Jim Wheaton, the local officer Laura had mentioned, had withdrawn at Catherine's request.

He enjoyed the brief reassurance of a familiar face as his housekeeper brought them both tea and a couple of scones. She urged the laird to take one and chided him for not having eaten anything at all today, like he was just being stubborn. Catherine guessed he wouldn't be hungry for a good while yet.

The study was a rectangular space tucked away behind a more modest door than any of the big public rooms: definitely Sir Angus's personal hidey-hole, though still a good deal more grand than the average den. No dartboard, retro arcade games or pinball machines (and no need for a pool table when there was a slate-bed twelve-footer in a dedicated billiards room elsewhere in the castle). The only modern touch was a micro hi-fi system next to a stack of largely classical CDs. Other than that, his personal pleasures ran mostly to the literary. There were large walnut bookcases on two of the walls, and an antique writing desk tucked in a corner. The shelves were not lined with leather-bound reference tomes or collector's editions, but well-thumbed and spine-broken volumes: books read and re-read. Many of them, she noticed, were about theatre.

It looked like it ought to be cosy but Catherine felt cold, and there was a fusty smell about the place. There was only one tiny window in the room and just one little radiator which she guessed wasn't switched on. It was probably warmer outdoors, where the sun was burning through the morning's misty clouds. It made her think of the house where she grew up, her parents refusing to turn on the heating if the sun was in the sky, their decisions governed by the calendar rather than the thermostat. Sir Angus looked better dressed for it, swaddled in an ancient tweed jacket, its material so thick it probably bent the coat-hook if you hung it up wet.

Where the study's walls were not lined with books they were decorated with framed photographs, again a sign of this being the laird's retreat: these were mementos for personal regard, unlike the paintings adorning so many of the castle's other interior walls. A cluster to Catherine's left showed black-and-white images from plays: individuals captured in expressive postures that identified them as stage shots, as opposed to movie stills or family snaps. It took her a few seconds to realise that they all showed her host as a wiry adolescent, handsome and vivacious in youth, all limbs and energy.

A caption mentioned Oxford. It had been a long, long time ago.

Another row of far more recent frames bore colour images of Sir Angus posing with an assembled theatre cast, his tartan trews distinguishing him from their Shakespearean garb. Once she had scanned a few Catherine saw through the make-up and costumes to recognise that he was

181

standing with largely the same people, the same cast, and in most he was grinning alongside the same non-performer: the one whose final act had been to pose for just such a photo the night before.

She wondered what was the connection that would make someone from the highest echelons of the arts come back over and over to watch some group of teuchter am-drams.

'I gather he was your guest last night,' she said, indicating one of the colour stills. She reckoned it a delicate way to broach the subject: hark back to happier times, avoid mentioning the name too soon. 'As opposed to the bank's.'

He glanced across at the photos and visibly winced. Maybe not that delicate, then.

'Yes,' he managed, swallowing. 'Partly, at least. He was my guest, but he was also the guest of the players, in acknowledgment of his efforts in keeping them funded over the years. Not so much patron as patron saint.'

'So they're a professional company?'

He looked at her for a moment as though she had asked him the question in a foreign language, or that he was baffled as to the relevance. She recognised the condition: he was baffled as to the relevance of *anything*, given the way his world had just been turned inside out. She was about to reiterate when he seemed to gather himself and managed to answer.

'Ehm, no,' he began distractedly, like he couldn't believe he was talking about it, couldn't believe he was talking about anything. Then he began to expand, as though finding unexpected solace in doing so. After that kind of shock Catherine had often seen people put themselves together

182

again only very slowly, and sometimes it appeared as though they were surprised to discover each function that still worked. 'More accomplished than your average amateur-dramatics society— mostly down to Eric and Veejay, I think—but not professionals.'

'But presumably you pay them for their performances here?'

Again that look: 'what the hell does this have to do with anything?'; and again as he answered he found something in the distraction.

'I do, yes. Eight hundred pounds per show this year. That's a lot more than when it all started, but given what it brings in I don't quibble.'

'Yes, I heard you charge five hundred pounds a head. Thirty-six seats minus you and your guest. That's what, seventeen grand? Must help pay the bills.'

He nodded blankly, thoughts somewhere else again.

'Cragruthes has been in my family for close to four hundred years,' he said, his voice so quiet it seemed to be coming from far inside him. 'Posterity carries with it a burden of duty. A place like this can't be preserved in aspic, but preserved it must be, so it has to pay for itself, which is not always easy. I inherited when I was just twenty-three, when my father died.'

He glanced at the black-and-whites with an apologetic sadness.

'Managing an estate was a far cry from what I imagined myself doing, but when it comes to duty I appreciate I got off lighter than most. There have been a few ill-starred attempts to bring in revenue over the years, but you've got to try new things

183

because you just never know what's going to work. Or rather, *I* never know what's going to work.'

He managed a self-deprecatory smile, but it only lasted a moment before being enveloped in sadness again.

Catherine looked away, giving him respite from her gaze, taking another scan of her surroundings. Up close everything looked a little tatty, care-worn and frayed at the edges. As he shifted in the armchair she caught another waft of fustiness and deduced that his jacket was the source of the smell. It probably cost a fortune twenty years ago, and may not have been dry-cleaned since. Surely he had others, though. Perhaps it was his favourite, a garment he wore for physical reassurance. He certainly looked in need of comfort.

'They approached me with the idea for the moonlit plays back in 2003. Did you meet Veejay Khan and Eric Watt?'

Catherine had seen the still-shaken troupe of performers sitting together in one of the public rooms but hadn't spoken to any of them individually or caught any names. There was an Indian-looking woman among them, but Catherine had thought Veejay was a male name.

'Not yet, but I will. We'll be speaking to everyone in time. Are they in charge of the company?'

'In so far as anyone is in charge. They're not terribly official about anything; that's theatre for you. Eric cooks the books but Veejay is the one who whips the cast into shape. They came to me about ten years ago with the notion of staging *A Midsummer Night's Dream* in the grounds. They knew I was an enthusiast as I had come along to a few of their plays at the Ardnabruich village hall,

184

and I'd often caught further performances of the same pieces up in Fort William.

'Of course, I thought it was a lovely idea. Initially they put on just the three shows for local audiences, plus a coachload one night from Fort William. But then towards the end of the same week, I had a corporate booking for what was supposed to be a seminar followed by dinner. I thought to myself, why don't we have dinner and a play?'

He glanced towards the shots of him with the players, then closed his eyes and shook his head. Catherine could see what was going through his mind. He had loved the plays, and not just for the money, but evidently what he was contemplating was that had it never been set in motion, then what happened last night would never have come to pass. Or maybe he was wondering if he'd ever see such performances again.

Either way, it seemed an appropriate juncture to steer the conversation around to the subject of who was really to blame.

'Sir Angus, as you may be aware, we have told the media that we have not ruled out the possibility that this was an accident.'

He straightened a little in his chair, something resembling optimism suddenly legible in his features.

'Yes, so I gather. Have you found any . . .'

'The truth is, we have no grounds at this stage to rule it in either. So unless and until I receive very strong evidence to the contrary, I am going to proceed upon the assumption that this was murder. I realise this is difficult, but can you think of anyone with a motive, anyone who might have had reason to wish—'

185

'No,' he interrupted, insistent, appalled. It wasn't just an answer, it was a denial of the reality of what she was suggesting. It was a final futile attempt to shore up the internal defences that had been all but demolished the night before.

'Why would anyone?' he asked in disbelief. 'How *could* anyone? Do you know who this man was? Have you any idea of his contribution to the arts world and beyond? The projects he's made possible, how many people he's helped?'

'Nonetheless, he moved in a world where there can be a lot of jealousy, a lot of resentment.'

'It must have come with his job, that he's had to say no to a few people who didn't want to hear it, but . . .' He sighed. 'No. Just no.'

Catherine wasn't expecting to hear much of a response to that one. She was really just forcing him to confront the ugly idea by way of preparation before she sprung something worse.

'Sir Angus, I realise this is very disturbing to consider, but what happened last night involved a shot from distance in the dark. If you are so certain that nobody could have had a motivation for harming your guest, I therefore have to ask whether it's possible the gunman could actually have been aiming at you?'

Burned

Jasmine had plenty to mull over on the drive back up through Ayrshire, her thoughts on the journey down having been dominated by the single question of whether she'd get there before Sanquhar left, occasionally interspersed with a moment's anxiety about whether her urgency was making a lasting impression on the average-speed cameras. She turned off the stereo so that she'd have peace to think, then turned it on again a couple of miles later because the clunking noise was back, and whenever she could hear it she couldn't think about anything else.

Her reflections were also derailed by the sight of a silver Passat in her rear-view mirror, spotted slotting into a gap three cars behind as it exited the fast lane. There were too many vehicles between it and the Civic for Jasmine to get a good look, but she had no doubts over the make and model. She thought about pulling out into the fast lane to see whether it followed, but between the yellow vultures monitoring her speed and the clunking sound beneath the bonnet she decided it wasn't a viable option.

Jasmine was approaching the big roundabout where the roads to Ayr, Prestwick and Kilmarnock converged, so she decided it would be wisest to defer any manoeuvres until she was sure the Passat was taking the same route. She was held at the lights on the roundabout and the curve of the approaching traffic allowed her to confirm that the Volkswagen was in the same lane, still three cars back.

Flooring it was even less of an option now. The first few miles of the Kilmarnock road were restricted to fifty miles an hour, still enforced by the average-speed cameras. People didn't take chances with those things, not even the boy racers in their souped-up ned-mobiles. So if no one was going to speed up, her only option was to slow down.

She dropped to forty, then let the needle creep further anti-clockwise until it was approaching thirty-five. Nobody was going to tolerate that pace driving anything other than a tractor, or maybe a Micra. The Passat was going to have to pass or make its intentions obvious and either way she was going to get a look at the driver, as overtaking was a slow process when you were limited to fifty miles an hour.

She glanced back and saw the Saab immediately behind her begin to indicate, waiting for an opportunity to pull out. When a space appeared, it swung right, followed by as many preceding cars as could fit themselves in before an approaching lorry closed the gap.

Jasmine held her pace steady and kept her eyes front, flitting between the road and the mirror. In her peripheral vision she was aware of a few turned heads in the passing vehicles, as their drivers sought a look at what idiot had been pootling along so unnecessarily slowly. She hoped she lived up to all their prejudices. Then, finally, the Passat was pulling alongside.

Jasmine stepped a little harder on the accelerator, upping the speed to prolong the time spent side by side, and this time it was the slower driver who turned her head to get a look at the passing motorist.

She saw a blonde-haired woman, mid-thirties, eyes on the road, head swaying and mouth wide as she sang a song, presumably for the benefit of the two toddlers perched in child seats in the back. The blonde woman was the only driver in the overtaking convoy who didn't turn and look at her like she was an idiot, something Jasmine considered profoundly ironic.

At least this particular panic had been precipitated by a Passat, rather than merely a silver car. That was progress but she needed to let it go, and not react until there was something to react to.

In the days since she was followed the truth was that she hadn't spotted anything further to be genuinely suspicious of. She'd seen a hundred silver vehicles and been wary of all of them, but that wasn't vigilance, that was paranoia, and it was potentially counterproductive. With her so hung up on this silver Passat, if the guy knew what he was doing he could have been invisibly following her for days via the simple expedient of driving any other vehicle.

The thought of it made her shudder. Why would anybody be tailing her? Her principal suspicion was Hamish Queen, or rather someone working on his behalf. He had lied, he had made the assumption that Tessa Garrion was missing and he had the wherewithal to make things happen quickly. However, according to Sanquhar, Queen had called all of the surviving Glass Shoe players as soon as he'd finished talking to Jasmine. If one of them had something to hide it could have been any of them who had organised a tail, or even followed her themselves. It wasn't as though she'd have been hard to track down: Sharp Investigations was in the Yellow Pages, as well as linked on a thousand websites following last summer's press.

From what Sanquhar had said, it sounded like they all might have something to hide, as well as reputations well worth protecting. He had hinted at repercussions, or at least how she wouldn't be popular for excavating this period of their collective pasts. Finlay Weir was a teacher, Sanquhar had suggested maybe even the head of a school, and in this day and age even trace elements of scandal could be toxic. You could get fired for pretty much anything except being a rubbish teacher.

Murray Maxwell had become a Scottish household name back in the eighties by appearing in Scotia Television's long-running soap, *Darroch Glen*, then established his acting credentials more seriously during the nineties as Inspector Kelvin in the same channel's Glasgow-set police drama *Raintown Blue*. It was still going, fifteen years after Maxwell left it, but his character's name remained the one everybody referenced whenever the show was mentioned. He had moved to the other side of the camera after that, producing new programmes for Scotia and eventually becoming its head of drama. It was said he was in the running for the vacant top job as the channel's chief executive, his chances of which would not be augmented by revelations of venal excess, even if it had been three decades ago.

Russell Darius, as a horror-film director, was arguably the one who had least to lose from stories of sex, drugs or even Satanism, but he was also known to be fiercely protective of his privacy.

When she was reading the coverage of the spat over ACS's funding rejection, Jasmine, who had barely heard of Darius before, was surprised by his list of credits. It turned out that she knew many of his films by reputation, though she hadn't seen them, and certainly couldn't have said who directed them prior to clicking the article's link to the IMDb. According to one sidebar, despite being regarded as something of an auteur, Darius's

190

reluctance to sell *himself* had contributed to his dwindling commercial success during an era when the cult of personality reigned and selling your films purely on their own merits seemed quaint to the point of naive. He had given precious few interviews in recent years and made even fewer films. It seemed he had gained great notoriety back in the early eighties, when his work fell foul of the tabloids' 'video nasty' hysteria, and this had made him very shy of the British press ever since.

Contemplating this line-up, Jasmine almost laughed out loud at just how staggeringly bare-faced Hamish Queen's lie had been. The only two names he could be forgiven were Finlay Weir and, ironically, Tessa Garrion. She'd give Hamish this much though: it certainly bore out Dot Prowis's testament to his talent-spotting ability. Of this small company, all but two of them had gone on to very big things: a West End producer; a film director; two television stalwarts, one of them now a major player at a regional ITV franchise; and the ex-head of Arts Council Scotland, waiting in the wings for a place on the BBC Trust.

However, just as striking was the fact that nobody seemed aware of their common connection. Jasmine hadn't seen it mentioned anywhere; the link between Darius and Sanquhar was a particularly glaring omission in light of the funding controversy. How many awkward questions would that have posed had it come out at the time, especially for Sanquhar? Was it personal? Was there a long-standing grudge? If so, Darius had been very magnanimous by not revealing a fact that would have mired Sanquhar neck-deep in the brown stuff, restricting himself to a dig about

191

his elitism.

All these famous names had once worked together in the same fledgling theatre company. It should have been a well-known item of trivia, like how everyone knew Billy Connolly had once been in a band with Gerry Rafferty, or that Francis Ford Coppola, Martin Scorsese and James Cameron had all worked for Roger Corman. That nobody knew the original Glass Shoe Company included Hamish Queen, Julian Sanquhar, Russell Darius, Murray Maxwell and the late Adam Nolan indicated that none of them had ever mentioned it, because it would only have taken one to do so, especially in the Wikipedia age, for it to go viral.

There had to have been a conscious decision never to invoke this connection: either a collective vow or, perhaps more disturbingly, they had each independently reasoned that they had too much to lose. Either way, each must have known his counterparts' silence was guaranteed by the prospect of mutually assured destruction.

Why?

What had been so awful that Sanquhar still seemed spooked by it thirty years later? As he said himself, he wasn't some nutter. He was a hugely respected, intimidatingly intelligent and thoroughly sober individual, yet there he was, talking about something that responds to human darkness, something that feeds off the worst in men, and he wasn't being entirely allegorical.

* * *

Jasmine took a detour to East Kilbride and stopped off at Galt Linklater's premises to fill in some

192

paperwork concerning the job in Perth earlier that day. It was twenty past six by the time she got there, but there was usually somebody around in the evenings, sometimes all night if work required it. She had to buzz to be let in, but she could see lights on inside. When she walked through reception and into the offices there was a small cheer and some applause. She saw Rab Forrest, Andy Smith and Johnny Gibson gathered around one desk, grinning at her. Andy was miming his hands on a steering wheel, then a sudden shudder. Clearly they had heard about this morning's events. Even Grumpy Gibby looked tickled.

They were eager to hear her version of it and she obliged, not least because she wasn't going to get peace to file her paperwork until she'd done so. Their attention felt slightly patronising, as the story was clearly all the more amusing to them for it being 'the wee lassie' who had pulled this stunt, but nevertheless, the unequivocal sentiment coming from all of them was that the wee lassie had done well.

'They've already started referring to you as "Crash",' Rab informed her.

She rolled her eyes, as if to say 'what are they like?' and to acknowledge that this die was now cast, but she did so to conceal a degree of relief at having acquired this new nickname. As she became a more familiar face and the barriers of formality started to break down, some of them had occasionally referred to her as Jazz, which had uncomfortable associations, so she was really hoping it wouldn't stick.

Her paperwork filed, she set off for Arden and the office. It was after seven and she was getting hungry. She'd leave the transcription to the morning, but she wanted the recording of her conversation with Sanquhar copied and backed up. 'Your day's work's never over until you've secured the evidence,' Jim had once said, and she abided by this no matter how tired or hungry she was.

As she drove past a supermarket on her way through Clarkston, she thought about stopping briefly to pick up a take-away salad or a sandwich, but forced herself to keep driving. She knew that if she did that, she'd end up eating it in the office—transcribing the Sanquhar interview. She could already hear her internal logic: might as well while I'm here. Not as though I've anything else to do with my evening.

She really would need to get herself a life, and she fully intended to, but chances were she'd probably get herself that new office furniture first.

I *will* do *something* with my evening, she vowed as she slowed to a stop behind the office, a sentiment made all the more compelling by having every space in the car park to choose from. A quick bite and a trip to the cinema. Even if the only thing she'd be showing up in time for was some no-brain blockbuster, she'd force herself to go. This was important.

She switched off the engine and reached down into the passenger-side footwell for her bag. As she gripped it and sat up straight again she felt uneasy, as though she'd done it too fast and made herself light-headed. It was far more than that, though. The hairs on her arms were pricking up, a nauseating sense of unease coursing through her. She felt claustrophobic all of a sudden and reached for the door by reflex rather than intention. It was what

Fallan had described as 'a sudden, unarticulated sense that something about your immediate environment is disturbingly wrong'. Something told her to run. Not drive, run. It was fear, and Fallan said to listen when it speaks.

As she climbed out of the Civic she saw a man running towards her, his head covered by a hood, all but his eyes obscured by a black scarf. Something twinkled and shimmered in his right hand, a flickering pale blue light.

Jasmine ran for the building. She had enough of a start to know she'd get there first, but her keys were in a pouch in her bag and there were two locks to the main door. She tripped on the topmost of the front steps as she tried to delve and run at the same time, her eyes on the bag instead of on her footing. She stumbled for a pace and, unable to brake or recover her balance, slammed into a full-length double-glazed panel next to the door, throwing her arms up to cushion the impact. Her bag fell to the ground, scattering some of its contents on the flagstones, but the office keys remained pinched between her thumb and fingers on her right hand. She steadied herself and stabbed the cylinder key into the lower of the locks. As she did so, she saw a flash of colour, a reflection in the glass of something arcing and spinning through the air. She heard a shuddering crash but kept her eyes on the locks and the keys, concentrating solely on getting that door open. She turned the second key, squeezed herself inside through the minimum width of an opening, then turned around and slammed the door shut again, the mortise lock clicking home to secure her inside.

Through the glass she saw that the small blue

twinkling light had been transformed into a big, orange dancing glow.

The man hadn't pursued her. He was standing a few yards behind her car, glass fragments sparkling on the concrete from where the driver's side window had been shattered. He was unmoving, but from that distance, with his eyes beneath the hood, Jasmine couldn't tell whether he was staring at her or at the Civic.

Inside the Honda the orange glow continued to dance, then there was a jolt, a pulse of greater ferocity, and she saw flames begin to lick around the interior. The hooded man took this as his cue to depart. He began to run, charging flat out towards the street, ducking to the right at the junction and disappearing out of Jasmine's sight. Then, a few moments later, she heard an engine gun and a vehicle sped past the car park entrance, headed for the main road.

It was a silver Volkswagen Passat.

Jasmine watched as the blaze inside the Civic intensified. She heard the side windows shatter and saw the smoke begin to vent from the openings, the flames burning all the fiercer for the sudden inrush of fresh oxygen.

She was losing another small piece of her mum. It wasn't just a car, it was a little time capsule, a place where she could still smell her, still feel her. All those memories, the places they'd gone together, the journeys they'd shared, the conversations they'd had.

Other people went to gravesides to think about their lost loved ones. Not Jasmine. She'd only been back once since the funeral because there was nothing about that place that connected her with her living mother, only with the empty numbness and the hollow ache of a horrible morning in the drizzle. The headstone was meaningless. Her mum had many memorials that meant far more to Jasmine. The Civic had been the most immediate of them, the most direct, something that transcended life with her and life without her.

Now it was burning before Jasmine's eyes.

She slumped down at the foot of the stairs and cried.

*   *   *

Jasmine wasn't sure at which point she realised DI Gormley was insinuating that she may have torched her own car as an insurance fraud, but she was acutely aware of the precise moment when she understood that the situation was irretrievable.

It was nothing explicit, more a series of questions that seemed irritatingly tangential until she worked out what they were driving at.

It was rather an old model, was it not? Was it a second-hand purchase? Third-hand? A dealership or a private sale? How did it run? Did you have a lot of trouble with it lately?

She deduced that these were questions intended to knock you off your guard if you were pulling an insurance job, by subtly conveying that the polis knew you were at it. She didn't know how an innocent party was supposed to react according to the police's playbook for these situations; whether they asked these questions every time or only when they had their suspicions.

She mentioned her connections with Galt Linklater and dropped a few names, hoping at least

197

to put herself in a context other than fraudulent chancer or attention-seeking hysteric, and at most for that brightening of the features that came with the recognition of a common acquaintance.

'I know who you are, Miss Sharp,' Gormley said darkly.

That was the moment.

When a young uniformed PC first arrived on the scene he had begun taking details, then got a call on his radio and was evidently told to hang fire. He informed her that there was someone more senior on their way, someone who had heard about it over the radio and wanted to handle it personally. Jasmine had been pleased, thinking maybe this meant there was a connection to something they were already working on.

There was a connection all right, but not to anything new. Jasmine didn't know what version he'd heard, or whether Gormley was one of those cops who would simply have preferred if she'd just let it lie. She hadn't been an agent of mischief over the Ramsay case, really just the bearer of bad news, but he looked like he would have no problem shooting the messenger.

DI Gormley's face was, Jasmine reflected, a development opportunity. He looked like he'd spent much of his life in a bad mood, the lines on his visage indicating a near-permanently sour expression.

Once he said he knew who she was, she grasped that there was no point in trying to convince him of the truth of her case, because whether he believed her or not was immaterial. He wasn't going to help her.

'This silver Passat, did you get a registration?'

'No.'

'So you couldn't be sure if it was the same car as you think has been following you?'

'No.'

'And the man had his face covered, that's right?'

'Yes.'

He said they'd look into it, in a way that suggested it would be placed on the task list right behind investigating alien abductions and the hunt for Sawney Beane.

Then as a parting shot, almost as an afterthought, he asked:

'Can you think of anybody you might have upset, Miss Sharp? Anyone who might wish you harm?'

It was part going through the procedural motions and part a reminder that though she might know a few ex-cops, she hadn't made many friends on the force.

She imagined herself answering.

'It could be Hamish Queen, the multi-millionaire West End producer; Murray Maxwell, the big TV star; Russell Darius, the horror-movie director; or maybe Julian Sanquhar, the former head of Arts Council Scotland.' Why not chuck in Alex Salmond, Mark Zuckerberg and Bill Gates and slap on a tin-foil headscarf for good measure. Gormley would lap it up.

'No,' she said, trying to hold back a new onset of tears as she watched him leave.

She felt all of a sudden very vulnerable and very much alone. Her car—her mum's car—was gone, and the police weren't going to do anything about it. She had nobody on her side. It put it into perspective that she was merely one girl confronting some powerful and, it would appear, dangerous people. As she said to Sanquhar, she was just asking some questions: that was all she had in her armoury. If they were responding with intimidation and violence, then what option did she have to return fire?

Stings and Barbs

As Jasmine placed the handset back on its cradle she reflected on the unlikelihood of video-call technology ever becoming standard, rather than a novelty allowing people who actually liked each other to gawk into webcams. The inability to see each other's faces was not something that the humble telephone was missing: it was in fact one of its greatest strengths.

It seemed to be the morning for awkward calls. So far she'd been involved in three, and it wasn't yet eleven.

First Jasmine called Polly Seaton at Centre One, chasing up her request that Polly delve into the PAYE archives and dig out information on who else the Glass Shoe Company had paid a wage during its mayfly lifespan. Polly confirmed that Murray Maxwell, Russell Darius, Adam Nolan and Finlay Weir had been alongside Tessa Garrion on the payroll. Even more helpfully, she was also able to inform Jasmine that Finlay Weir was these days earning a salary from the Logie-Almond Academy Charitable Trust, thus saving her the bother of finding out where he taught. Logie-Almond Academy was a private school in rural Perthshire, and a quick browse of their website revealed that

Finlay Weir was its headmaster.

The awkward part had come when Jasmine's memory and conscience finally combined at the right time to prompt her to suggest she and Polly go out for a drink some time. There was a pause that endured just a little too long to represent Polly carrying out a quick check of her mental diary, followed by a response of '. . . eh, yeah, I suppose. Why not?'

Even before her unmistakably equivocal words, in those milliseconds of silence Jasmine realised first how stupid she'd been, then how pitiful she must look. Her unease at taking a loan of Polly, of cashing in on her goodwill despite their never being big pals, combined with her reluctance to socialise with the girl had made Jasmine blind to the possibility that Polly might not much fancy socialising with her either. It was a gut-deadening moment as she suddenly realised how unconsciously arrogant she'd been in thinking she'd be doing Polly some kind of favour, but that particular discomfort was soon dispersed as she grasped that Polly's more likely interpretation was that Jasmine was a sad act with no friends. It was no great consolation that it wasn't entirely true. Jasmine did have friends, but where she and Polly undeniably differed was that when she clocked off Polly had a life.

Once more, with feeling: Jasmine screws up.

There was no way of getting this toothpaste back into the tube, so she had to endure several knuckle-biting minutes of arranging a time and venue for a date that neither of them particularly wanted to keep.

Jasmine had just about finished beating herself

201

up about it when she got a call from Charlotte, who had recently returned from France and had just heard from her dad how his meeting with Jasmine went. It was safe to say she wasn't best pleased. At a later date, once Charlotte had calmed down, Jasmine might be allowed to explain that she wasn't working for Hamish Queen's third (imminently ex) wife, and might even be able to outline how she hadn't asked her father anything deceitful, sleazy or impertinent. But even if she managed both, she reckoned it was safe to assume that Fire Curtain wouldn't be offering her a part any time between now and the heat-death of the universe.

Jasmine's awkward call to Polly had at least yielded comparatively direct contact details for Finlay Weir, for what that was worth: a number she could call, ask to speak to the man and have some hope of being put through, however briefly.

She had left a message for Murray Maxwell at Scotia TV's studios at Pacific Quay on the south bank of the Clyde, but she had no guarantees that the receptionist had forwarded it to the right department, far less that it would ever land on Murray Maxwell's desk. And as for Russell Darius, that was only a couple of stages superior to a message in a bottle. So far the only route open to her was via his representation at Agents United, where they probably had a special hopper for binning the thousands of inquiries they got, asking for messages to be passed on to their talent roster.

The content of her requests had been quite explicit: she identified herself as a private investigator wishing to ask questions about an actress by the name of Tessa Garrion who had worked with Mr Maxwell/Mr Darius/Mr Weir under the auspices of the short-lived Glass Shoe Company. She reasoned that, given Hamish Queen's ring-around, there was no point in being coy or attempting to mislead them. If she was overt about what she was investigating and about what she already knew, it would be unambiguously overt on their part if they refused to speak to her. It was as much pressure as she could bring to bear for now. She'd keep the requests coming and, if she got nowhere, her next gambit would be to subtly imply that their refusal to respond wouldn't look good when she went public. She didn't actually have anything much to go public with at this stage, but they might not know that, and besides, it was early days.

When she called Logie-Almond Academy she was surprised to be told by the receptionist that she was being 'put through to the headmaster's office', but that turned out not to mean the headmaster himself. Instead she spoke to 'Mr Weir's secretary', to whom Jasmine dictated her carefully worded but explicit request. Her heart sank a little. She had been half hoping for a direct line, or at least to be told when Weir would be available to take a future call. Instead she had encountered another protective layer of bureaucracy for another subject to hide under, meaning there was no chance of her dialling the number one time and getting lucky with him simply picking it up.

She imagined him reading the message, like she had imagined Maxwell and Darius, if they ever got theirs: the stern expression and maybe even a little lurch somewhere in the stomach as Hamish Queen's warning was confirmed to be valid. What then, for each of them? A quiet resolution to thwart all approaches. A vague and undramatic little lie to a secretary or PA to paint Jasmine as an undesirable. A block on calls, an instruction not to pass on any further messages. And perhaps for one of them something more: a sudden hollow fear that a dark secret wasn't buried quite so deeply as he'd believed.

Or they could just phone her back within the hour, as Finlay Weir did.

*   *   *

Jasmine travelled up to Perthshire in Jim's old surveillance van, a clunky ancient diesel that still smelled of cigarettes and fish suppers nine months after Jim last drove it. It was Jim's recommended practice only to drive a surveillance vehicle when you were actually on surveillance, as opposed to merely getting from A to B, in order to minimise the number of times you were seen getting in or out of it. Plus, if you drove it to meet somebody, you were pre-burned with regard to following them in future.

Jasmine didn't have much of a choice at that moment, as her insurance company had reneged on their promise of a hire car, saying they were suspending this service in her case until they had 'further investigated the validity of the claim'. This meant that that miserable dick DI Gormley had been on to them. He wouldn't have said outright that the police believed she had torched her own car, as that might lay him open to repercussions. More likely a mixture of vagueness and innuendo, nod-and-a-wink stuff. Or Plod-is-a-wank stuff, as far as Jasmine was concerned.

The state of the van made her feel all the more self-conscious as she drove slowly down the broad tree-lined avenue that wound through the school grounds to the auspicious main building. She passed immaculately maintained playing fields, manicured verges, woodland pathways, outlying sandstone terraces with distinctive house badges identifying them as individual boarding houses, and a more modern sports hall the size of her old primary school. If she had sold her Honda Civic before it got petrol bombed she would have been doing well to raise enough to pay a week's fees for this place, but nonetheless, she always felt quite robustly herself when she climbed out of that vehicle. Showing up in a purposely nondescript van made her look—and feel—like the hired help.

She reported to the school's reception and was greeted by a formidably stern secretary who looked dubiously at her, as though readying herself to escort Jasmine from the premises, until she stated that her business was with Finlay Weir and she was expected. The secretary's manner softened a little as she instructed Jasmine to take a seat while Mr Weir was informed of her arrival, but from her overall demeanour Jasmine could vividly imagine that she'd have preferred the escorting from the premises resolution. The headmaster's stock had probably taken a hit too, if he was entertaining the likes of Jasmine.

She sat on a wooden bench and glanced at the framed photographs on the wood-panelled walls: strapping girls and ebullient boys, thrusting, healthy and oh-so-confident as they wielded lacrosse sticks, grappled for a rugby ball, sang in the choir, played in the orchestra.

A girl walked past in a grey uniform with purple trim. Despite being garbed in pleated skirt, buttoned-up blazer and school tie, she still looked older than Jasmine. It was something in the way she carried herself; something in the way they all carried themselves.

Growing up in Edinburgh, Jasmine had known no shortage of private-school kids, but this place was something else entirely. According to the website, they did have day pupils but, being out here in the wilds of Perthshire, it was principally a boarding school: the kind of place only a certain class of family sent their offspring. The kind of place Hamish Queen and Julian Sanquhar had first met.

Finlay Weir ambled into the reception area with the unassuming grace of a man who already knows he's going to be treated as the most important person in the room and thus doesn't need to sell it.

'You must be Jasmine Sharp,' he said, a subtle gesture dismissing the secretary's intention to stand up and mediate introductions.

Weir was tall and slim; not skinny, just thinner than Jasmine had expected, albeit those expectations had been coloured by the proliferation of photographs of rugby players on the walls. He had a full head of grey-flecked brown hair, which he appeared to have made no effort to dye, and was dressed in a dark brown suit, not altogether businesslike but not ageing-geography-teacher-with-PVC-elbow-patches either. Jasmine's eye for detail spotted a tiny hole in his left earlobe where a stud must once have sat, but there were more explicit reminders of his more bohemian previous career at his wrists, where he wore cufflinks in the shapes of tragedy and comedy masks. She had

206

found out that Queen and Sanquhar were both roughly one year his senior, but he looked a few years younger than them; could maybe even pass for late forties. He was attractive in a distinguished way; not trying to maintain a look whose time had passed, but chiselled enough to suggest he must have been very handsome once upon a time.

'Would you like a cup of tea or coffee? A cold drink?' he asked, gesturing towards a corridor.

'No thank you. But I wouldn't mind some fresh air. I've been cooped up driving for a while. Could we stretch our legs a wee bit?'

'Certainly. I'll give you the tour.'

Jasmine could have murdered a cuppa right then, but it was a greater priority to keep him out of his office. There were times when it was expedient to make the subject feel relaxed and comfortable, and times when you didn't want them enjoying the reassurance of home advantage. This was definitely the latter. If she wanted Weir to open up, she had to take him away from the trappings that reminded him he was at the centre of this little world, not least because at a moment's notice he could summon the scary secretary and grant her transparent wish of huckling Jasmine right out the front door.

In keeping with his stated intention, he gave her the tour, walking first all the way around the main building and then out towards the playing fields. He talked about the history of the school, famous alumni, the construction dates of various buildings, and informed her that he had boarded here himself in his schooldays. He had an easy manner but it felt professionally courteous rather than genuinely warm. Jasmine detected a certain intensity about

207

him, a steel behind the smile, and decided she wouldn't want to get sent to this headmaster's office if she was in trouble.

Not that she imagined discipline was a big problem at Logie-Almond. It was hard to imagine some of the scenes she'd witnessed at Canonmills High being replicated here.

As if to emphasise the point, they had to give way at one point to a man with two rifles slung over each shoulder, accompanying a troupe of a dozen boys in cadet greens.

Jasmine's face must have shown surprise, and quite possibly alarm.

'They're off for some shooting practice,' Weir explained. 'We have a rifle range, on the fringes of the woods.'

'With live ammunition?' she asked, trying not to sound horrified.

'Oh no,' Weir said. 'Those were only third years.'

What he left unsaid negated any reassurance his actual words might have offered.

It really was another world.

'I believe you'd like to ask me some questions about the rather ill-starred Glass Shoe Company,' Weir said as they resumed their walk along a neatly defined gravel path.

'Yes,' Jasmine answered, relieved that the foreplay was over. 'Though I was given the strong impression you might be disinclined to answer them.'

'Oh yes? By whom?'

'Julian Sanquhar, for one. And Hamish Queen, though less explicitly. I broached the subject with Hamish first, and by the time I spoke to Julian he informed me that Hamish had been phoning

208

everyone involved with Glass Shoe to warn them that I was sniffing around. Julian seemed certain that nobody would be in a hurry to revisit that part of their past. Thus I confess I was surprised when you called back.'

'It seems I didn't get the memo,' he stated, a wryness to his tone that was born more of bitterness than humour. 'I shouldn't be surprised. I don't know if Hamish Queen would even remember my name.'

'He claimed he couldn't,' Jasmine told him, watching for a response. His eyebrows rose sardonically before she added: 'He in fact claimed he couldn't remember the names of anybody in the original Glass Shoe Company except Tessa Garrion, whom I had just asked about, and Adam Nolan, of whom I could ask nothing. Among those whose names he had apparently forgotten were Julian Sanquhar, Murray Maxwell, Russell Darius and yourself.'

Weir gave a small sigh and glanced away towards the woods, Jasmine detecting a slight shake of the head. Regret and something else that lingered just as long.

'In my case it might be true; or at least halfway plausible. He certainly worked very hard on forgetting me after the company broke up.'

'Hamish suggested that the cast shied away from each other because of a kind of shared professional embarrassment. People not wanting to be reminded of their failure while it was still raw, that sort of thing.'

'Hmmm,' Weir replied, but Jasmine couldn't tell whether it was in agreement or dispute. She suspected there was a bit of both, but she knew this much: he wasn't going to leave it hanging. Weir wasn't reluctant to revisit this part of his past, he was champing at the bit.

'I think it suited Hamish to forget certain things,' he added, unprompted. 'I was with Dundee Rep for a year, which was where Hamish saw me. I was Christian in *Cyrano de Bergerac*. It got me a lot of very good notices and some very tempting offers, including a place in the Lyceum Company in Edinburgh. I turned them down because Hamish sold me on his idea for Glass Shoe. I was rather torn—who wouldn't want a job at the Lyceum?—but Hamish pushed all the right buttons, including a clever mixture of flattery and guilt.'

'He told you his planned project just wouldn't work without you?' Jasmine guessed.

'Bang on the money. So I signed up, walked out on Dundee Rep, said a very polite thanks but no thanks to the Lyceum and headed for the Highlands.'

'Oh dear,' said Jasmine, letting him know he could skip this part. For now.

'By the time the dust had settled over the rubble of Glass Shoe, everyone was already cast and rehearsing for their autumn seasons and I had missed the boat. I was out of work for a long time, just the odd bit part here and there. Meanwhile Hamish got busy with a new venture and a little way down the line he's got a musical in the West End. I was getting desperate and I reckoned he owed me, so I approached him for a part. Nothing big: a place in the chorus, anything, just something to deal me back into the game.'

He gave a rueful smile, devoid of humour.

'No can do. I *just wasn't right for it*.'

Weir stopped for a moment where two paths met, briefly undecided which route to continue their walk. He opted for the right, taking them around the playing fields.

'I hasten to add that I'm not bitter. Hamish set me on the road to here, put me out of my misery. If he hadn't, maybe I wouldn't have this.'

He gestured expansively at the school and its impressive grounds, the sprawling domain of which he was ruler.

But he sounded bitter, and saying he wasn't just drew attention to the fact. Jasmine knew what it was to be working towards a future in the theatre then to have to rebuild your life around a different career altogether. Yes, Weir had done well for himself, and yes she might do well with Sharp Investigations; she was already earning more than she would had her more modest dreams come true and she'd landed a part with a rep. But even those modest dreams would always seem more desirable than compromised reality, and Weir had enjoyed a true taste of living his dreams before they were taken away.

He might even believe himself that he wasn't bitter. He probably wouldn't rant about it after a few too many, probably didn't get maudlin and bore the missus with his 'coulda been a contender' speech. Nor would he ever have gone to the press with anything compromising towards Hamish Queen or the others, as that simply wouldn't be becoming for a man in his profession, nor conducive to career preferment. But in Jasmine, finally he had a chance to discreetly share some information that could make life just a little less comfortable for Hamish Queen. That was why he'd phoned back, and so soon. He had been bottling this up for years and she was the first person to come along offering a corkscrew.

'Still, at the time it must have stung,' she suggested, giving the handle a twist.

Weir shrugged, not denying it, but saying: what can you do?

'That's Hamish. I've heard the same story over and over from other people. Once you cease to be useful to him he discards you.'

'I think it runs in the family,' Jasmine replied, thinking of Charlotte and deciding to tempt Weir with an intimacy.

'What do you mean?'

'I know his daughter. She's got her own company now.'

'Fire Curtain,' said Weir, showing he still kept an interest in Scottish theatre.

'Yes. It's been said Charlotte has a discerning eye for recognising talents but only in so far as envisioning how they would augment her own.'

'How do you know her?'

'We were at the SATD together.'

'You trained as an actress?'

'For a while. I had to drop out because my mum died. She was an actress too. Theatre runs in my family.'

Jasmine knew there was no need to share this, but she couldn't stop herself. It was his age and his theatre background. She'd be embarrassed to admit it, but she had said it on the off chance that Weir had known her mum, just throwing out a line and hoping to get something back. Ever since Dot Prowis said she'd seen her perform it had opened up a whole unexplored area of her mum's life. Her

212

heart had soared to hear Mum described, and she wanted to feel that way again, to unearth those hidden archives. Mum had friends who worked in theatre, but Jasmine had often heard as much as they were prepared to say. Plenty of others must have worked with her though, or at least seen her act, so surely it wasn't folly to hope that one day she'd mention the name to somebody and it would bear fruit. Any memory would be cherished, a photograph would be like the Holy Grail.

The name evidently meant nothing to Weir, but then he was already out of theatre and into teaching by the time her mum was on stage.

'I'm convinced it was more than professional embarrassment that led to Hamish and the other members of Glass Shoe shunning each other,' Jasmine said. They were skirting the playing fields, passing the all-weather surface with its high fence and approaching the rugby pitch. 'What happened up there at Kildrachan House that would have him lying to me about forgetting people's names, then phoning those same people to warn them I was asking questions? Julian Sanquhar all but suggested I'd be putting myself in harm's way by digging this stuff up. He made it sound like you'd all been raising hell, and I don't mean that purely as a figure of speech.'

Weir let out a laugh, and for the first time she saw genuine amusement in his face.

'God love Julian. For a man who prefers working behind the scenes he's always been the biggest drama queen of the lot. Give him his due, he's the most gentle-natured fellow, but with it the most sensitive and therefore the most inclined to take everything too seriously. But yes, you're right: it

213

was a little more than professional embarrassment, especially between Hamish and me.'

'You had a falling out?'

'Oh, everybody had a falling out. We were a theatre company on the road! Well, not on the road yet, but certainly at close quarters. Rehearsals were often a battleground. Hamish and Julian hired us and promptly forgot that we might have minds of our own. Being a fledgling company, and everybody having comparable levels of experience, we all felt we had our own ideas to contribute, but in truth the last thing we needed was a democracy. We needed a dictator, and that should have been Hamish. He wasn't strong enough though: neither in himself nor in his conviction. He could have said, quite literally, "my house, my rules", but I don't think he was comfortable with that. Hamish liked to be liked. He needed a bad cop, and that certainly wasn't Julian.'

There was a strong breeze picking up now that they were well away from the shelter of the trees: not exactly an icy wind, but cool enough to remind Jasmine that June in Perthshire didn't always mean shorts and T-shirts.

'Looking back,' Weir went on, 'it's easier to see how Hamish was torn between his natural instincts and some high-minded ideals that he thought he ought to be observing. Inside, at gut level, I think Hamish always wanted to put on glossy spectaculars, but at that time he still thought there was something vulgar about it, almost something too easy. He maybe hadn't learned by then that what comes easiest often does so because it's what you're best at.'

'Were there aides de camp in this conflict? I mean, was Julian the advocate for the more elitist aesthetic?'

'I strongly suspect so, but not in any confrontational way. He would have been influencing Hamish subtly, privately, *behind the scenes*, where Julian was most comfortable. The stand-up rammies and blazing arguments were all between Hamish and Darius. He was the production designer. I mean, he had parts too—we all did, even Julian—but he designed the set, the costumes and the props.'

Jasmine wondered a little at Weir's reference to Russell Darius by surname. It had been Hamish this, Julian that, then Darius. There was something of the public school about it, but he sounded less like a headmaster and more like a pupil referring to his peer. Was there something in that? Did it suggest camaraderie or distance?

She noticed the word 'rammies' get special emphasis too. Weir spoke in an almost neutral accent, identifiably Scottish but shorn of regionally specific pronunciations. He had chosen the word and spoken it with remembered relish as though it required something more colloquially Glaswegian to convey the ferocity of the arguments.

'Darius would remind us all that Shakespeare was competing for audiences with public executions, so you could say that he was the one trying to appeal to Hamish's instinct for spectacle. I remember he devised these fantastic spring-loaded arrows that fitted into a tunic. The archer would twang a bow and the actor in the costume pushed a button to suddenly pop these things up. It looked for all the world like you'd really been shot. One day Hamish decided that such visual effects were a sideshow detracting from the text and off we went, fifteen rounds.'

Weir smiled again at the memory, though she could tell that it was only the distance of time that made it amusing.

'Lilliput and Blefuscu,' she suggested.

Weir nodded.

'Arguing over which end to slice an egg, quite. But it seemed so terribly important at the time. God, we argued over everything. Fortunately, outside of rehearsals, the social side of it was going well. Too well, some would say.'

'Julian Sanquhar certainly intimated as much. He wouldn't elaborate, but he made it sound like the last days of Sodom and Gomorrah.'

Weir rolled his eyes.

'Julian, bless him, has a brain the size of Perthshire and a heart to match, but he was never the most worldly. He was twenty-five and a strange mixture of prudish old fuddy-duddy and immature adolescent. I suspect he shed the latter part eventually and more fully grew into the former. At the time it wouldn't have surprised me if he was still a virgin. That was one thing that didn't run in his family, right enough.'

'I don't think virginity runs beyond one generation in any family.'

Weir gave a dry laugh and continued.

'I meant the opposite. His father was quite the swordsman, reputedly. In fact, I think it was around about that time that Julian's parents got divorced. It upset him a great deal. He was very close to his mother but he thought the world of his father. A painful business for anyone, but as I said, Julian was more sensitive than most. I think starting out on this theatre venture was a response to that,

216

taking himself away to the Highlands and building something new.'

They had reached the end of the last pitch. Weir gestured to his left with a querying look, checking Jasmine was happy to leave the path and continue along the grass at the touchline. She acquiesced, grateful for the recent dry spell and the resultant absence of mud. As they turned she saw a group of girls trot down from the school building in hockey gear, one struggling with her arms full of white protective pads.

'So you and Hamish,' she said. 'What did you fall out about?'

'Tessa Garrion,' he replied, fixing Jasmine with a neutral but intense stare, as though warning her they were on sensitive ground.

'I was captivated by her. Let me be clear: I don't mean she was some cute young thing I developed a crush on. She was wonderful to work with, by far the best thing about those rehearsals. I admired her professionalism as well as her natural talent, and she was great company. She lit up the room, brought the best out in me too, I felt. We got on so well, and I hoped it would turn into something more, but it became clear she wasn't interested in me that way.

'I was all right with it. I could take being "put in the friend zone", as they say these days, because she was the kind of woman—the kind of person—I was thrilled to have as a friend. But then, a couple of weeks into rehearsals, she was sleeping with Hamish and I wasn't best pleased.'

'You couldn't stand back and wish the other guy good luck?' Jasmine said drily.

'The other guy was married.'

217

'Ah.'

'It's been another recurring theme with Hamish: he can't keep his hands off the cast. That's why he's on to his third divorce.'

'They do say he has an eye for talent.'

'I cared about Tessa. She knew he was married, she wasn't misled, but I couldn't help thinking she didn't really know what she was getting into either. It must have dawned on her soon enough. We were all in the same house so we could hear the arguments.

'She broke down in tears a couple of times during rehearsals. She became rather short-tempered too: less tolerant of all the aggro and of the lack of professionalism being exhibited in certain quarters.'

Weir stopped and looked across the pitches, over the heads of the girls now practising passing and dribbling.

'Tessa and Hamish had a blazing row on the night she left. There were a lot of things coming to a head around then, not just between the two of them.'

He took a breath and sighed through his nostrils, biting his lower lip.

'You ever been in a situation where, deep down, you all know something's over but it takes somebody to point it out or something to happen to make you all see it? For us, that was it: Tessa leaving. I think we all recognised it when it came; we just didn't realise it was going to be so messy.'

'Messy how?'

'I remember I got up quite late. The house was strangely quiet, a real morning-after feel to the place. None of us was ever up with the lark, but someone normally went around the rooms waking people, getting everyone roused so that we could

218

commence rehearsing. It was usually Hamish, Julian or Tessa: the first two because they were paying the wages and Tessa because she simply lived to work.

'I wasn't the first awake: I found Hamish in the kitchen, looking very overwrought. He told me Tessa was gone. They'd had a big argument, as we knew, and she had walked out. I asked where she had gone and he told me she didn't say: just packed her things and left. The last bus passed through Balnavon just after eleven, and he reckoned she must have taken it. It went to Inverness, where you could get the midnight sleeper train south, all the way to London.'

'Where she'd been planning to go all along,' Jasmine stated.

'How do you know that?'

'Hamish said she'd gone down for some auditions and then come back north to consider her options. He likened it to a gifted footballer playing out the season with Elgin City when there were offers from Man United and Barcelona waiting for his signature.'

'Well, in this case, Elgin City were buggered without their star player and we all knew it. We had a crisis meeting, where it was suggested that we could ask Saffron to take over.'

'Saffron? Who's that?'

'She was this Kiwi hippy chick who kind of fell in with the company. She worked in the bar at the Balnavon Hotel. We rehearsed at the church hall across the road from the hotel; well, strictly speaking it was the community centre, but it was next door to the church and everybody called it the church hall. The local minister certainly

219

liked to play on the ambiguity. He was a joyless, shrivelled little Wee Free, and was vociferous in his disapproval of our whole undertaking. The fact we were doing, you know, *that* play seemed to exercise him all the more. *Witchcraft and blasphemy*,' Weir mimicked, wagging an angry finger and screwing up his face into a pinched expression.

'I think the fact that it was for pleasure and entertainment was his principal objection. Hamish's father had funded the construction of the community centre, so the minister couldn't stop us: he just had to protest from the sidelines. Anyway, Saffron came to watch us work and just gradually insinuated herself into the group. She was a few years older than us, maybe in her mid-thirties, and a bit of a drifter. She'd lived all over the world, left New Zealand years back. God knows how she ended up in Balnavon. She was a passable actress, though. We gave her Lady MacDuff.'

'So she became part of the company?'

'Not officially. She got some cash-in-hand payments, probably not Equity rates. She was "in", though. She'd have dropped the bar job to come on tour if it had got that far, and she hung around with us at the house when she wasn't working.'

'But her name would never have appeared on any paperwork,' Jasmine stated, thinking of Julian Sanquhar's reluctance to name names. He hadn't mentioned her, only the people he knew would have been listed on the payroll.

'No. I couldn't tell you her name, in fact. Her surname, I mean. I don't think I ever heard her referred to as anything other than Saffron, and I wouldn't be surprised if that wasn't her given name either. She was rather New Age. Very liberal-minded, easy to imagine dancing naked at Woodstock with flowers in her hair.'

Weir smiled quite warmly at this memory, like a break in the clouds.

'I volunteered to ask her. I think I was the most desperate to keep things going, as I would be out of a job if the tour didn't happen. I went to the little house she rented, a one-storey terraced place on the main road out of the village, but no dice.'

'She said no?'

'No, she didn't say anything. I saw her through the window, but she refused to come to the door. She told me to go away. She sounded upset and rather apprehensive. When I went back and reported the situation, Darius came over a little sheepish and confessed that things had perhaps gone a bit too far the night before.'

'What things?'

'He didn't say and frankly I didn't want to know, but the whole time at Kildrachan, Darius was on this Aleister Crowley trip. He always had an interest in the occult, so living in some big spooky mansion in the Highlands—not to mention consuming a great volume of various proscribed substances—he was dabbling in all kinds of bizarre stuff. It didn't bother me either way: he could sacrifice goats in the living room as far as I was concerned, if it kept him and his drugs out of my way. It was a lot of arrant nonsense, though the mere discussion of it was usually enough to disturb Julian. Saffron shared Darius's appetites, both for drugs and for ritualism. I don't know what they got up to that evening, but clearly it had been a step too far for her.'

They had circumnavigated the playing fields and

rejoined the system of gravel pathways. Jasmine was concerned that Weir was about to guide her back to the main building and draw their discussion to a close. Instead, he led her in the opposite direction, towards the dormitories. He wasn't done.

'Drugs and occult rituals? Is that what Hamish Queen was hoping to prevent me from finding out about?'

'No,' he replied. '*This* is what Hamish doesn't want anyone finding out about: the next day, the police turned up at the house. They took him in for questioning and he was there for the best part of two days.'

'Questioning over what?'

'Tessa Garrion's disappearance, though we didn't know that at the time. She'd only just left and nobody had reported her missing. All of a sudden the cops were hunting all over the house. It was very weird. They didn't turn up asking if Tessa was there, they just took Hamish away and began rooting around the place. They wouldn't tell anyone anything, but that's the police for you. You never know what information they have or what their agenda is. They found bloodstains in the front hall and in one of the big drawing rooms, and they began questioning everybody about what they'd seen and heard.'

'But for the police to have taken action, and so soon, they must have had reason to suspect something had happened.'

'No doubt, but as I said, they weren't telling us what they knew. Until they questioned us we didn't even know it was Tessa they were concerned with. They questioned us separately, so it was only when we spoke to each other afterwards that we discovered nobody had actually seen Tessa leave. We only had Hamish's account of her departure.

'All of a sudden those arguments we overheard took on a darker hue and it threw a different light on Saffron shutting herself away. Nobody actually put it into words, but we were all wondering the same thing: was it purely in reaction to what she and Darius had been involved with, or had it been something else? It was a horrible time. Horrible. And of course there was no means of getting in touch with Tessa to see if she was all right.'

Jasmine could see an echo of the company's shared angst on Weir's face as he remembered the helplessness of not knowing.

'No instant messaging or mobile phones in those days,' she said, though she couldn't help but think of how little difference modern technology had made during her fruitless attempts to contact Jim.

'No,' Weir said. 'But then, just as suddenly, the police dropped the whole thing. Just like that: nothing to see here, just go about your business, citizens.'

'Why?'

'I spoke later to the younger of the two police officers, who seemed very bemused by the whole thing. He said his boss got a phone call, went out for a few hours, and when he came back Hamish walked. He wouldn't tell him anything about it, just said the inquiry was over.'

Weir picked up a stray stone from the grass and tossed it back among the gravel.

'It was all over for us too. When Hamish got back nobody even suggested carrying on. We couldn't get out of there fast enough. We all knew what one another had been thinking. The atmosphere was toxic. We went our separate ways and largely endeavoured to keep them separate. That's why it was a measure of my desperation that I should ever get in touch with Hamish and go pleading for a part. Probably why he found it easy to decide he didn't owe me anything, too.'

Weir sounded like he was being philosophical about it, but Jasmine knew he wouldn't be so bitter if he really believed Hamish was justified in blanking him. Something rankled still: deep and raw.

'In my inquiries, I've sourced a number of Tessa Garrion's official records,' Jasmine told him. 'She hasn't paid tax, claimed benefit, phoned an ambulance or shown up on any kind of database after summer 1981.'

Weir stopped where he stood and a shudder passed through him. He turned to look at her, glowering, almost accusatory. A palpable energy emanated from him, making him seem bigger for a moment.

'You seem more angry than surprised,' she observed.

It took him a moment to find his voice, as though he had to restrain several less temperate representatives of his thoughts before nominating a spokesman.

'The police dropped the whole thing, so one just assumes there was nothing to it, but I never saw Tessa again, never even heard her name spoken until you called. Her name should have been up in lights, known across the land. I always had a lingering suspicion something about it was rotten. One phone call and the son of the local laird walks free. See, that's the thing with people like Hamish:

they have the connections and the resources so that the normal rules don't apply. And when they do get into trouble, there's always somebody who comes along and makes their problems go away.'

Mystery Guest

Catherine was glad to get outside into the heat and light, away from the claustrophobia of the laird's sad little chamber. It was like being stuck inside the man's head, surrounded by his memories and regrets. Stepping out into the open air again, she felt as though she was breathing out for the first time since entering the cold and fusty study.

As she strode through the grounds, her taxpayer horror fantasy of the investigation resembling some massive police jolly was grossly exacerbated by the sight of every cop not actively engaged in a specific purpose wandering around carrying paper plates bounteously laden with canapés.

She found Beano and Zoe over by a decorative fountain, the former balancing a quite inappropriately immodest selection on his plate in a pyramid formation. It was further testament to the quality of the fare that the latter had been tempted into having a nibble too, as the depressingly athletic Zoe seemed to live almost entirely on fruit and raw vegetables; albeit enough fruit and raw vegetables to feed a football team.

'You managing a wee bite there, son?' Catherine asked, feigning the tones of a concerned mother worried about her child's faltering appetite.

'Best crime-scene catering we've ever had,' Beano replied, proffering the plate towards her. 'They're

225

giving it away at the kitchen's back door. Obviously tonight's corporate gig is off and the chef didn't want this stuff to go to waste. Beats the usual greasy burger from some dodgy van.'

Catherine helped herself to a vol-au-vent, and had to concur.

Beano went back to his conversation with Zoe, comparing notes on how they had spent their last days off and apparently trying to outdo each other in terms of confessing to having no life. Zoe at least had some kind of purpose going on, training for a forthcoming marathon, but she bemoaned how this was the ideal hobby when you had no mates, or at least no mates whose schedules overlapped with your own.

Beano probably edged it, admitting to having spent an unhealthy number of hours playing video games with his flatmate.

'What makes it worse is that it was the new *Mortal Kombat*. I think it has worrying implications for my personal growth that I'm still playing essentially the same games as when I was about ten. Graphics are a bit better these days, but nothing else has changed, which is kind of embarrassing. When I was first playing it on my Super Nintendo I thought that by this point in my adult life I'd actually be living *Mortal Kombat*, some kind of action hero, but naw: there I am, all growed up, a polis on his day off still sitting on the couch mashing buttons.'

It was an unwelcome reminder of last night's conversation with Drew, about which she was feeling a little guilty today, not to mention embarrassed. It was that final remark, comparing the game Duncan wanted to the situation she'd been called to deal with: pompous and over-

226

dramatic, essentially 'my job is so important and I'm the only one who understands what's real'. Precisely the kind of shit she hadn't ever wanted to hear coming out of her mouth, the cards she had never wanted to play in her marriage.

She was worried, though. Something about this bothered her, prodded at her deepest maternal instincts. It wasn't always about protecting your kids from danger, but about protecting them from the worst that could happen, and that didn't necessarily mean something happening to them.

Maybe it was disproportionate, maybe it was irrational, but the fear that filled her mind whenever she thought of her boys playing violent games—even kidding on they were soldiers with their toy guns—was that this would foreshadow a future reality. She was horrified by the prospect of one of them one day hurting somebody. As their mother, there would be the responsibility of knowing she could have stopped whatever had got into their heads. And as their mother, she bore a fear of what it suggested was already inside them as her sons.

But perhaps worst of all was her knowledge of what they'd be carrying forever once they had done something irreversible.

'Did you say you played violent computer games when you were *ten*?' she asked Beano to confirm.

'Yeah. Like I said, graphics weren't up to much in those days, but according to the press a wee red blob representing blood was going to warp my fragile young mind. Turns out they were right.'

'How?' Catherine inquired.

'I joined the polis, didn't I? Must have been mental.'

227

Catherine remembered why she seldom sought out Beano for serious insight into anything, and wondered what it ought to be telling her that she had done so today.

'How'd it go with the laird?' asked Zoe.

'Worse than useless. He's in bits. Huddled in his wee study, surrounded by his creature comforts.'

She thought back to her final question, one that he gave the very strong impression he had never considered. What colour there remained had drained from his face and Catherine feared for a moment that he was going to be sick. He was a picture of shock, and not a little fear.

'That said, it being good practice to disclose all my observations, I should mention that his creature comforts seem to revolve around the theatre, and that there's photos of him creeping the boards as a student.'

'Meaning what?' Zoe asked.

'Probably nothing, but there's a couple of things I'm reluctant to overlook. One is that Sir Angus is no stranger to stagecraft. He had to give up his dreams a long time ago, but maybe still has the gift for a performance.'

'And what's the other?'

'That if you wanted somebody killed, the best alibi in the world would be standing right next to the victim when he gets shot.'

'Anyone ever tell you you're a very cynical person, boss?' Beano asked.

'Aye. Mother Teresa, when I lifted her for soliciting.'

He let out a dirty laugh then resumed tucking into his pile of canapés with unseemly alacrity.

'Christ, don't let DI Geddes see you guzzling like

that,' Zoe told him. 'It'll give her another possibility to ask if *that's* that why we call you Beano.'

Catherine smiled. Poor Laura, she had never worked it out and, this being the Glesca Polis, nobody was ever going to tell her.

Despite a reputation for being outspoken to the point of abrasive, Laura had been surprisingly withdrawn when she first arrived from Edinburgh, but had gradually emerged from her shell over the year or so since. Catherine had initially thought it was to do with getting used to being on a new force in a new city, but gradually deduced it was more to do with what Laura had left behind, and she didn't mean the job.

Laura didn't talk about it explicitly, but there were allusions that Catherine couldn't fail to pick up on. Suffice to say, Catherine would have given a great deal for half an hour in a locked interview room with Laura's ex, whoever the bastard was.

'Speak of the devil,' Beano said through a mouthful of choux pastry.

Catherine watched Laura march towards them, having emerged from one of the tradesmen's entrances at the side of the building. She looked both flustered and perturbed, a sight all the more discomfiting for its rarity.

'Something vexes thee?' Catherine asked, the lighter tone an attempt to offset the fact that Laura looked in genuine fear of a bawling out.

'The numbers don't add up,' Laura said.

'What numbers?'

'The RSB junket. We got everybody's details, didn't let anyone leave until we had verified ID, addresses, all contact details. We did it exactly as you ordered.'

'But?'

'When I checked the list, there are only thirty-three names on it.'

'How many should there be?'

'There's thirty-six seats on that mobile gantry, and when I asked the chef he said it was thirty-six covers for dinner.'

'Is there a means of verifying whether thirty-six people actually showed up for dinner, and whether all the seats on the gantry were occupied?'

'That's what's "vexing" me, boss,' Laura said, dropping her voice a little, as though afraid of being overheard. 'The maître d' says he had a list of place settings to show everybody where they were sitting. There was one pinned up on display for the guests, but his staff had a copy too, for laying the tables. Not only could he find neither of them, but when he went to print me a fresh copy the file had been deleted from the computer. So, as it turns out, had the finalised list of guests the bank emailed to the castle. Bottom line is, there was a person here last night that somebody on the inside doesn't want us to know about.'

Catherine turned to Beano.

'Cynical, you say?'

Convergence

Jasmine met Polly for their mutually reluctant drink in a basement bar on Bath Street called Kave. The place was Polly's suggestion, a regular haunt of hers. It was large and spacious, booths lining the outer walls, sofas tucked into cosy corners, benches

230

and long tables for bigger groups either side of the oval-shaped bar in the centre. The music wasn't too loud, which would make conversation easier, though that might not turn out to be a blessing as the evening wore on.

She found Polly at one of the booths, waving to her from the back of the leather-upholstered horseshoe. Polly needed to gesticulate because Jasmine hadn't spotted her on the first pass. This was partly because she hadn't physically seen her in four years and partly because she'd been looking for someone sitting alone. There was another girl sitting at the booth with Polly, her face just as familiar now that Jasmine saw it close up.

'You remember Carol?' Polly said. 'Another Canonmills High refugee here in the west.'

Jasmine placed her now; she had been in her class for French in third year. She gave her a smile and offered to buy them both a drink while she was on her feet. Inside, she was fuming slightly. Polly had called in back-up. What was doubly annoying was that Jasmine had thought about doing the same. She had considered phoning her schoolfriend Megan, who was now a junior doctor at Glasgow Royal Infirmary, but then decided it was a bit off to spring a surprise, not least because Polly hadn't known Megan very well. Jasmine hadn't had much to do with Carol at school, but Polly had decided to bring her along, presumably in case she and Jasmine couldn't find anything much to talk about. In that case, maybe Jasmine should be grateful.

She told herself to get a grip as she placed her order at the bar. It was a few drinks and a blether, not a peace summit.

A couple of rounds in, her trepidation was just a

slightly awkward memory. She had thought about staying on the mineral water, especially given it was a school night, but as she didn't have a car to drive anyway she decided she might as well make use of the disinhibiting properties of a few scoops. Whether or not it was the alcohol, Polly and Carol turned out to be easy company.

Jasmine found herself doing most of the talking early on, as Carol launched into a bit of grilling on the subject of her 'interesting' job. They were questions Jasmine was becoming familiar with, and thus more experienced at answering, so she was able to keep it general and, more importantly, keep it light. Everyone became more relaxed and comfortable once they moved on to the common ground of their school years, a subject that proved largely inexhaustible for the remainder of the evening. Jasmine found it pleasant to be able to reminisce about what now seemed simpler, easier days, though at the time they felt anything but. She enjoyed hearing different perspectives upon the same incidents and the same people, sufficient to make Jasmine wonder whether she'd been going around with blinkers and ear-muffs for five years, as so much seemed to have been going on beyond her notice.

It was interesting to learn a little about what had happened to some of the characters she remembered, but it only served to emphasise the separation she felt from those times and those people. They had once loomed so large in her world; now they were merely names and stories, drifting away on the tide of life and getting smaller as the distance grew. It made her grateful to have cultivated this contact with Polly, grateful too to

Polly for bringing Carol, as Jasmine often felt she'd been left a little isolated by the events of recent years. She had a compelling urge to ensure they got together and did this again soon, an impulse not entirely down to the vodka.

The music had become louder as the evening wore on and the place grew busier. They ended up talking at the tops of their voices to be heard, huddled all the closer in their booth, increasingly oblivious of their surroundings except when going to the bar or the toilets.

A girl rather purposefully approached their table and for a moment Jasmine thought she might be handing out fliers for a club, but when she got Polly's attention, she stood up and welcomed her with a hug. The girl slid into the booth next to Polly as she sat down again, perching on the outside edge to indicate she wasn't joining them for long.

Polly introduced her as Katrina, her former flatmate. They ran into each other in Kave fairly frequently, so there wasn't a great deal of catching up. Katrina was just saying hello, as well as informing Polly with an impish grin that there was 'a guy pure checking you out'.

'Where?' Polly asked, interested and wary at the same time. There was mischief here, as there always was around this subject, but she couldn't quite read it.

'We're over in the alcove,' Katrina said, gesturing towards a darkened niche at one end of the room where purple drapes and velveteen pouffes were arranged in a way intended to suggest ancient Araby, but conveying more camp than Bedouin. 'I could see him watching you. Couldnae take his eyes aff, in fact.'

233

'Where's he sitting?' Polly asked.

'At a booth over there,' she indicated, gesturing with a nod to a spot over her shoulder. 'Don't look,' she added.

Polly was leaning around anyway, desperate to see.

'What's he like?'

'Seemed quite mature,' Katrina replied, smirking.

Polly craned her neck and finally worked out who Katrina meant.

'Ya bitch, he's pure ancient,' she said, and they both burst out laughing. 'Must be in his bloody fifties. Oh, shite, he's getting up.'

It was Jasmine's turn to crane her neck, while Polly and Katrina returned their attention to the table lest they make eye contact. She was too late: she only saw a figure disappear around the curve of the bar, catching a glimpse of the back of a grey-haired head and a long dark coat.

Jasmine looked to the table where the man had left a half-finished drink.

'Nursing that same pint the whole time as well,' said Katrina. 'Stingy bastard.'

Jasmine faked a laugh, concealing the complete change in her mood. She had quickly triangulated the sight-lines and concluded that the unfinished pint was on precisely the table she'd have chosen if she was surreptitiously surveilling the occupants of this booth.

He'd been nursing the same drink for a long time, staying in position, not returning to the bar, not going to the toilet and not consuming much alcohol. He had got up and left as soon as he realised he'd been noticed, moving swiftly out of sight, quite possibly leaving the premises, and doing so via the door on the blind side of the bar, from Jasmine's point of view.

Pure ancient. In his fifties.

Suddenly Jasmine wasn't having fun any more. A big part of her wanted to leave, but she didn't want to take off at short notice, not when everything had been going so well. Nor did she want to admit defeat and have her evening ruined by this. It was, after all, still possible that the guy had been just some bloke whose date didn't show, or even some old lech perving on the sight of some young women who were oblivious of his rapt attention. In either instance he might well have bailed in embarrassment when he got caught looking. However, Jasmine's instincts insisted otherwise.

She switched to mineral water as a precaution, though she had sobered up very fast anyway. The conversation kept flowing but she felt disconnected from it now, faking responses to conceal that she could only think about the man who might be following her.

Polly asked if she was getting tired, observing that she hadn't said much for a while, and she seized the opportunity to make her excuses, citing a long run of early starts.

Promises and phone numbers were exchanged on the pavement at the top of Kave's stairs, the trio's parting proving an extremely protracted affair. Carol seized Jasmine's mobile at one point, expressing incredulity that she wasn't using certain social networking utilities, and drunkenly demonstrated how to set up accounts on her phone. She launched several applications that Jasmine didn't even know the device had, and which she had no intention of launching again once Carol handed it back.

A black cab was passing with its yellow light on as Polly and Carol began meandering towards Hope Street, trying too hard to look sober as only tipsy people ever do. Jasmine was about to hail it when Polly announced that they were headed to Central Station and asked if she was going that way too.

Her more cautious instinct told her to grab the wee black bus and get herself delivered to her front door, but the memory of her initial flight from the silver Passat still itched. She was on to this guy tonight. In all probability he would have given it up when he was noticed in the bar, but if not, there was a chance she could burn this bastard. She wanted a face.

Hope Street was very quiet at that time of night, making it impossible for anyone to conduct a foot-follow without being seen. She stole a few backwards glances as they progressed, but the only people visible further back were two older women dressed for a night out. There were other options, however. A group of three girls, moving as slowly as they were, would be easy enough to track from a parallel street. He could skip a block east to Renfield Street and keep pace, stopping at each junction to watch them cross as they made their progress down the hill. Besides, if he had any brains, he'd have worked out where they were heading and would be waiting at Gordon Street to acquire them there, or maybe inside the station itself.

Polly and Carol said some more goodbyes, then they finally parted company with Jasmine, heading off to the low-level trains that would take them to Uddingston and Hamilton respectively.

Standing on the concourse all alone, drunks meandering past like malevolent bumblebees, all of a sudden Jasmine didn't feel so bold about noting anybody's face. She glanced at the station clock on the departure board: she hadn't realised it was quite so late. The last trains were leaving, a time of the evening when it was sensible to avoid all eye contact, so scanning strangers to see if they might be the man from the bar was quite definitely contra-indicated.

She just wanted to get home now, and to make sure she wasn't followed as she went.

She got on to the rearmost carriage of the Cathcart Circle train and remained standing by the door, though there were plenty of seats. She didn't see anybody in her carriage who looked a candidate for the man who'd bailed out of Kave, and she kept her eye on the platform, watching who else was getting on further forward. The carriage got busier in the last couple of minutes before departure, and her view further down the platform was obscured as an arriving train disgorged a surprising number of passengers presumably heading for the clubs or for nightshifts.

She got off at the first station, dawdling on the platform, then skipped back on again just before the doors closed. The train pulled away and she caught the eye of a middle-aged man in a long coat, staring at her through the windows as the train pulled away. Could have been him, she supposed, or it could simply have been someone having a closer look at the daft lassie who couldn't seem to make up her mind where she was getting off.

Her station came up next. This time she waited on board as the rest of the passengers disembarked, then hopped off when the urgent bleeps warned that the doors were about to close. The train pulled away, leaving Jasmine the furthest person back on the platform, from where she could see the last of the passengers making their way to the top of the stairs up ahead. Ordinarily, she felt vulnerable when she found herself walking through the station alone when it was late and dark, but tonight she only felt relief at the isolation, that finally she could be sure there was nobody following her.

Jasmine reached the top of the stairs and turned right on to the narrow passageway that spanned the tracks. As she did, she saw that the tree-lined lane leading to the station entrance on the main road was cut off by the figure of a grey-headed, heavy-set man in a long, black raincoat. Pure ancient. In his fifties.

He moved surprisingly fast but it was largely immaterial. Jasmine had nowhere to run but back down the stairs to the platform, and she had just got off the last train of the night. In any case, the paralysis of fear stifled the urge towards flight. She froze against the wall, cornering herself, her legs threatening to buckle.

Never mind run, she was doing well to remain standing.

'Jasmine Sharp,' he said. 'Ever get that feeling when you realise you're out of your depth to a quite catastrophic extent?'

His accent said London. Not pearly-king cockney; somewhat less of the lower orders than that, but definitely the capital. Quietly authoritative, a voice used to being listened to.

'Four words. Glass Shoe: leave it. Understand?'

He thrust his face close to Jasmine's and stared

into her eyes. He had a big thick neck and a head so solid-looking she imagined you could hit it with an iron bar and the bar would bend.

She said nothing, her voice too dry to speak.

'I've got four words too,' said a second voice somewhere behind him. 'Can I help you?'

This time the accent was local, the voice quiet, a polite inquiry.

Thick-neck didn't turn around, barely took his eyes off of Jasmine. He glanced to the side only briefly, checking the position of the third party rather than giving him a full up-and-down.

'This doesn't concern you, mate. It isn't what you think. The lady and I are just talking, and I don't appreciate interruptions, so I strongly suggest you fuck off before you get hurt.'

'And there was me about to say the exact same thing. What were the odds? You and I are on a wavelength, I can tell.'

Jasmine recognised more than just the accent this time. She couldn't see past her tormentor but she knew who was standing behind him. Hope and release flooded through her and she issued an involuntary blubbing sound, part nervous giggle, part tears.

Her sense of relief was instantly truncated as thick-neck took a step back and his right hand slipped inside his coat. It emerged again in one swift, unbroken motion to extend in a straight line from his shoulder to the muzzle of a pistol.

Jasmine could see past him now. He was pointing the gun straight at Glen Fallan.

This was *strongly* contra-indicated.

Fallan looked thinner than she remembered, but perhaps this was because the man in front of

239

him was squat. Fallan was built like a sprinter, the Londoner like a shot-putter. It was speed versus solidity, but it didn't matter while thick-neck was holding a gun.

Fallan understood this, but seemed unnervingly relaxed. He explained why.

'You're not going to shoot me. I know that for two reasons. The first is that you reek of cop. I'm figuring ex, as you're no spring chicken, and going by that accent you're a long way off your old manor, so you do not want to end up explaining this to the Glesca polis.'

'And what's the second reason?' thick-neck asked testily.

'That you're standing there listening to me talk.'

This was when Fallan demonstrated vividly that unless you're going to use it, a gun is just something extra to carry. With his arm extended and an unnecessary weight at the end of it, thick-neck was off-balance and encumbered as Fallan made his lightning move. He seemed to hit his opponent in four or five different places in blindingly rapid succession, so quick that he didn't even have time to reel from one blow before he was sustaining the next.

Fallan pinned him to the concrete face down, a foot on the small of his back, his arm stretched out behind him, locked straight in a strained and twisted-looking hold. The man's face was pale and dazed, his breathing one elongated, broken gasp. Pain hadn't fully registered yet: this was still the shock of impact.

The gun lay a few feet away, but Fallan didn't seem interested in it right now.

'I'll give you this much,' Fallan told him, his voice

240

calm and quiet, 'you chose your spot and your time really well. Late night, quiet and isolated. Statistically very unlucky you got interrupted. And statistically very unlikely I will either.'

Fallan gave the slightest tweak on the man's fingers, eliciting a strangulated groan.

'There are two hundred and six bones in the human body Do you know which one is the most painful to break?'

Jasmine saw the strain on his face as he summoned up a response.

'Why don't you tell me?' he spluttered. It was intended to sound defiant, but his voice was too strained to suggest he had much in reserve by way of stoicism or nihilistic rage.

'Sure,' Fallan replied. 'The answer is none, if you're the one doing the breaking. As for which one is the most painful to *have* broken, well, that's something we're going to find out together over the next wee while unless you explain in detail who you are and what you want with my acquaintance Miss Sharp.'

'It's not me,' he said immediately. 'I'm just doing a job. And I wasn't gonna lay a finger on her, I swear.'

'Your name,' Fallan prompted.

'Rees. Darren Rees.'

'Who are you working for?' Jasmine asked.

'Hardwicke Chambers. It's a law firm.'

'You don't look like a silk to me. Jasmine, fire up your phone and look up that name.'

'I'm not bleeding lying. It's a law firm. I'm ex-Met. I do jobs for them, but I'm not going to hospital for them.'

Fallan gave Rees's fingers another slight twist,

causing his spine to arch and his head to rise in pained response.

'You may have taken that out of your own hands when you started threatening young women in railway stations.'

'I wasn't gonna lay a finger on her, on my mother's life. I don't do anything illegal. Close to the line sometimes, but I stay inside of it. It's a law firm, for Christ's sake. Sometimes I find out information for them, sometimes I find people. Somebody's making a nuisance of themselves, I let them know it's in their best interests to back off. Make them think it's more trouble than it's worth. I'm not allowed to do anything that's against the law. Course, the subjects don't know that, but that's how it works.'

Jasmine had found Hardwicke Chambers on her phone. They were a major legal outfit based in Holborn. Their official website wasn't giving much away, but further down the screen she could see search results referring to libel cases and super-injunctions.

'Nothing illegal?' she asked. 'I realise Scots law is different, but I'm pretty sure petrol-bombing cars is against the law in London too.'

A note of confusion found its way on to Rees's face amid the sweat, strain and ruddy-cheeked agony.

'I don't know anything about that. I seriously don't. I got sent here today with the instructions to find Jasmine Sharp, give her that message and let her know I meant business.'

'Who are you working for?' she demanded.

'I told you: Hardwicke Chambers.'

'I mean who are they representing: who is the

242

client?'

'I don't know. I don't even know what the message refers to. That's how it works.'

'Two hundred and six bones,' Fallan reminded him, digging a heel into his spine.

'They never tell me,' he spluttered desperately. 'I don't get told the client's names. It protects them, it protects me.'

'Not tonight it doesn't,' Fallan growled.

'He's telling the truth,' Jasmine said, to which Fallan responded by relaxing his grip a little. 'You can let him go. I think I know who the client is.'

'Who?'

A person who had the connections and the resources so that the normal rules didn't apply. And when he did get into trouble, there was always somebody who came along and made his problems go away.

Except this time.

*　　　*　　　*

'You fair chose your moment,' Jasmine told him.

Fallan was sitting at the square pine table in her little kitchen, a stillness about him that was far from reassuring. It was like the surface of the deepest river, concealing a dozen deadly undertows. Once you had slipped beneath its waters there would be no trace of you ever found again.

He was seated precisely where he had sat almost a year ago, back when she had wondered at the mirror-world she found herself in, in which she was dodging the police and inviting a confessed murderer into her home. This time it was worse than that: he wasn't just a confessed murderer,

243

he was the man who had confessed specifically to murdering her father. It was bloody *Star Wars* in reverse. She had come to believe that Fallan actually was her father, only to be shattered by the revelation that he was the man who had killed him.

He had denied her the chance to know her father, to ever meet him; and even if he was so bad, the chance to change him.

Fallan had taken from her something irreplaceable, committed something unforgiveable. This latter was immaterial as he had not sought forgiveness for this deed, nor shown any remorse. And yet he was the man she had turned to in her time of need.

That had been the third awkward phone call of a few mornings ago: a phone call she'd sworn she'd never make, back outside the refuge when he told her it was all she had to do if she was ever in trouble.

'Fuck you,' she'd told him. 'When I leave here, you'll never hear from me again.'

But even in her tears and anger, even as she cursed him to his face and made her vow, she'd kept the number.

As she'd watched the flames consume the inside of her beloved Honda, her mum's beloved Honda, she had asked herself: if they were responding with intimidation and violence, then what option did she have to return fire?

Only one.

'I got here earlier,' he replied. 'I wanted to get the lie of the land, and it's easier to watch for who's watching someone else if you observe from a wider perimeter. I clocked the guy well before he started following you. He was parked along the street from here, chose a spot with good sightlines to your front close. People on surveillance take great care to make sure they're not seen by their subject, but they can sometimes forget about everybody else.'

'Were you in the bar tonight?' Jasmine asked, wondering how she could have failed to recognise him.

'No. But I knew he was. I'm as patient as I am practised at stalking my prey from a distance. So, you want to tell me who you've been upsetting this time?'

Jasmine began to recount the events that had transpired since the morning Mrs Petrie walked through her office door. As she did so, she was surprised and a little dismayed to discover just how much at ease she felt in Fallan's company, and how quickly so. Despite how she urged herself to detest him, how she tried to think of what he'd taken from her, she felt strangely comforted by his presence. Truth was, he had taken away a man she'd never met, so there was no face, no memory to fuel outrage or bitterness. But most of all, the reason she found herself relaxed enough to open up and confide in this man was that, sitting close to him, she felt safe. Despite all she knew him capable of, and very possibly because of it, she felt more secure than she had since, well, since the last time he'd sat in this kitchen.

She had to admit that at some fundamental, instinctive level she trusted him; her instinct vindicated by the hard evidence of experience. In fact, appalling as it was to consider, given what she and Fallan had been through, she couldn't name anybody else alive whom she trusted more.

Thus it was only in talking to him that she felt

able to bring forth something that had been lurking in her mind for days, growing all the larger the longer she tried to pretend it wasn't there.

'She's dead, isn't she?' she said. 'Hamish Queen killed her back in 1981, but he was to the manor born and it got covered up. Now I've threatened to unearth the story all these years later and he's released the hounds. First somebody starts following me, then they petrol-bomb my car, and now I've got some ex-cop working for a major law firm being sent to put the frighteners on me.'

'Who is this Hardwicke Chambers mob, then?' Fallan asked.

Jasmine spun her laptop around on the table so that the screen was facing him.

'They appear to be a firm that specialises in making rich people's problems disappear. Libel cases, Mary Bell orders, privacy injunctions, anonymity super-injunctions . . .'

'And we can assume that's only for the cases that get as far as legal recourse,' Fallan said. 'I wonder how many problems are quietly resolved as a result of warnings from the likes of Mr Rees. Is there a list of their clients anywhere?'

'Not that I've found,' Jasmine replied. 'And I can't imagine there would be, as that would somewhat defeat the purpose of a super-injunction.'

'True enough,' Fallan conceded. 'Which Premier League footballer has been caught shagging the nanny: the press can't tell you because of a super-injunction issued by Hardwicke Chambers, whose clients include . . .'

'The information will be out there, though,' Jasmine insisted. 'Google Hamish Queen's divorces and throw in Hardwicke Chambers as a cross-

246

reference.'

Jasmine watched the reflected glow of the screen play across Fallan's face, his eyes narrowed in concentration as his fingers tapped the keyboard.

'It would be nice to have confirmation,' she said, 'but even without it, I'm one hundred per cent certain he's their client.'

Fallan's fingers stopped tapping and his head moved backwards just a centimetre.

'Not any more,' he said, turning the laptop around so that Jasmine could see the screen.

It was showing the BBC website. The story was linked from the top search result, less than thirty minutes old.

Hamish Queen was dead.

PART II

PART II

Prelude to a Kill

Tessa was somewhere else, in a place outside her physical form, a spectator upon what was happening to her. So often she'd heard the term 'out-of-body experience' and thought it so much mumbo-jumbo. She knew what it meant now: a defence mechanism, detaching you from your present circumstances because you couldn't bear the view from within.

She had been drugged, she was sure. Something in her tea, most likely. Everything was slightly out of focus, but this effect wasn't merely chemical.

She wasn't seeing herself, not her face, but she could see a woman there and she knew the woman was her. She could see what was being done to the woman. She knew the woman's name was Tessa Garrion, but something inside wouldn't let her connect Tessa Garrion to herself. It wasn't happening to someone else, it was happening to someone she once was, and someone she would have to be again, but not someone she was right now.

She had been so many women. Lysistrata, Katherina, Miranda, Clytemnestra. She knew how to step in and out of all of them. Now she had stepped out of Tessa, because it was the only place to go to.

It wasn't safe here, outside herself. It wasn't comfortable. There was not sanctuary and there was not reassurance. There was only nothingness, but this state of oblivion was a temptation. It called to her, offered to soothe, to take away the pain.

Perhaps absenting herself was a form of resistance. It would be her body, but it would be a mere vessel, devoid of what made her Tessa, like she could void it of what made it all the characters she played. It would not be her. She would not be here.

She felt anger at herself for being so foolish as to have trusted him.

She had been seduced. What he was doing to her body was rape, but her trust had been seduced, and she'd been an easy mark. He had manipulated her, manoeuvring her to exactly where he needed her in order that he could do this. There had been others involved too; were they complicit or oblivious, willingly playing their parts or used and manipulated like she had been?

He had talked about his art, talked about his vision and the place he saw for her in it. It made her feel so foolish when she found out what he really saw in her, and that it was all he really saw.

He had been stronger than her; quicker too. She knew further resistance would only bring further violence, and that terrified her, as she had never experienced violence quite like the brutality with which he had subjugated her.

He was inside her already: there was no preventing that now, no undoing it. Why do anything that might prolong the act? She could float further and further away, deeper into this inviting state of delirium, hide there until this was over. Hide this whole event away inside her mind forever.

Except she knew she couldn't do that. She'd always know where it was kept. She'd always know this happened, always know she had been beaten into submission and treated as meat. She'd always know how the worst of men saw her, and she'd love every man a little less because of it.

She had to act, and to act she had to become herself again: had to admit what was happening.

She let it pour in, felt it flood her soul: the fear, the horror; the rage.

It proved futile, though. She was too well restrained.

She had become herself, she had acted and she had failed. Worse, he had seen the fight in her eyes.

He relished it.

He savoured it like nectar.

And that was when she felt his knife.

Enemies

It was the lead item on the news the next morning, but the story was still sketchy and contained little more detail than the earliest reports Jasmine had read on the web. Hamish Queen had been shot yesterday evening in the grounds of Cragruthes Castle in Argyll, where he was attending an outdoor performance of *A Midsummer Night's Dream* as the guest of the castle's owner, Sir Angus McCready.

At this stage, according to a statement, the police were 'not ruling anything out and not ruling anything in'. Among the theories currently enduring this indeterminate status was the possibility that Queen's death had been an accident. The Cragruthes estate was apparently renowned for its hunting, with corporate clients paying exorbitant prices for exclusive access, but with such prized game to be had, the lands were also known to attract poachers. It had therefore been suggested that Queen may have been hit by a stray shot from someone trying to bag a deer under cover of darkness.

At the less innocent end of the scale, the BBC reporter mentioned that the majority of the audience at this moonlit spectacle had been top-level business executives, there on a corporate-hospitality junket as guests of their bank. It was hinted that the bullet may have been intended for one of them, or perhaps more likely their hosts, given that not everybody shared the banking sector's belief that the time for contrition was over.

All of these possibilities appeared to be given credence because the more obvious framing of events—that somebody had wanted Hamish Queen dead—was seemingly unthinkable.

'A popular and flamboyant figure,' the reporter described him, 'much-loved in the world of show business and greatly admired beyond it for his charity work, Hamish Queen was not a man known to have enemies.'

'He wasn't known to have been questioned over the disappearance of a young woman either,' Jasmine said to Fallan. 'And as for enemies, Finlay Weir didn't look too chuffed when I told him that there was no evidence of Tessa Garrion living happily ever after. They've a shooting range at that school. He mentioned the older kids get to use live ammunition.'

She recalled the image of the man carrying rifles, then the presence of Hamish Queen sitting opposite her in the bar upstairs at the Edinburgh Playhouse. She couldn't only see him, she could

254

remember his smell, his sing-song accent, the almost crackling sense of self-assurance and dynamism that had emanated from him.

Suddenly she thought of Charlotte. Poor Charlotte. She was about to be inundated by the ocean of hurt that Jasmine had spent a long and desolate time adrift upon. Then it hit her that she may have played a part in precipitating this. Yes, it could have been an accident and it could have been a bullet meant for someone else, but what if the shot had been fired by Finlay Weir to exact some belated justice for Hamish getting away with murder? What, indeed, if Hamish hadn't killed Tessa Garrion, but rather knew too much about who did? Either way, his death lay at the end of a chain of events that Jasmine had set in motion.

She thought of Julian Sanquhar, how scared he'd been, how he had tried to warn her that her actions might have dire consequences.

You will only succeed in disturbing a great deal of long-buried hurt and shame, but what worries me is that you might awaken something worse.

If she had heeded those words, then Hamish Queen might still be alive. Charlotte might still have her father.

Jasmine screws up didn't quite cover it this time.

'I have to go to the police,' she said.

She looked to Fallan for a response. He just stared back, saying nothing, but there was a hint of dubiety in his otherwise stony expression.

'What?' she asked. 'You think I shouldn't? I know how you feel about them, but this just got way out of my depth. I need to tell them what I know.'

'You don't need to tell them anything,' he finally replied. 'And if you do, you'll be dealing yourself out. Your own investigation will be over. You won't get to find any answers for Mrs Petrie and I won't get to have a quiet word with the guy who torched your car.'

'But in all likelihood this is going to turn into a murder investigation and I've got information they won't be aware of. I've even got a suspect.'

'Which is all the more reason to tread carefully and quietly, and find out as much as you can on your own. If you go to the cops now, if they think what you've got is relevant you'll be used and discarded. And if they think what you've got is mince, they'll take action to neutralise you in case you scare off the big game. Either way, you won't be permitted to pursue your own agenda any more.'

'Somebody may have just died because of my agenda. Julian Sanquhar was scared, really scared. I've got people following me, not just that ex-cop Rees. No disrespect, Glen, I don't underestimate your capacity for beating people up and I'm grateful for you coming to my aid, but I'd sooner it was someone else's problem. This game is becoming too rich for my blood, so dealing myself out seems the safest option.'

'Not as safe as you think. Sure, this shooting might not be about what happened up in Balnavon in 1981. But if it is, given that you've reason to believe there was high-level complicity in covering up Tessa Garrion's disappearance, maybe the police are the last people you want to be telling how much you already know.'

In the Blood

Jasmine had considered Fallan's advice and ultimately decided that it would be in her best interests if she did speak to the police regarding the Hamish Queen investigation—just not the *current* Hamish Queen investigation, and not current police either.

It had taken a couple of days, but Harry Deacon had drawn upon his contacts on the force and succeeded in finding out which officers had been at Balnavon nick in the summer of 1981. Finlay Weir had told her how a younger cop had been displeased by the impression of higher-level influence facilitating Hamish Queen's release, so she was hoping to get a first-hand account of the investigation from someone not bound by covert loyalties. Harry was able to furnish her with contact details for a retired officer by the name of Callum Ross, who now ran the outdoor sports facilities at the Culfieth Hydro hotel down in Wigtonshire.

'Did he do his thirty?' Fallan asked, driving them south through Ayrshire in his bashed and bullet-blasted Land Rover. The last time she'd accepted a lift in it things hadn't gone very smoothly, so she was surprised to feel so comfortable back behind its dashboard, its same scents filling her nostrils and piquing her memory. It smelt of diesel and chopped vegetation, like the inside of an old shed, smells she was surprised to find both pleasant and comforting.

'Must have. Harry said he retired from the force in 2007.'

'And he was in one tiny Highland cop shop the

257

whole time? How come he ended up down here at the other end of the country?'

'No. Perhaps significantly, Harry said he transferred out of Balnavon in October 1981, only a few months after Tessa Garrion's disappearance.'

'And where did his transfer take him?'

'That's rather interesting too. He became a police marksman.'

Harry had smoothed the way for Jasmine by getting in touch with Ross first and telling him he would be helping out his fellow former officers if he could spare some time to speak to 'one of Galt Linklater's associates'. Ross had thus needed little persuasion, and Jasmine had been given the all-clear to come south and visit the Hydro's outdoors centre.

She had enjoyed no such luck in pursuing the remaining two listed members of the Glass Shoe Company. The closest she had got to Russell Darius had been a brief chat with his agent, Wallace Charlton, when her third phone call to Agents United was (perhaps mistakenly) transferred directly to him instead of his assistant. Charlton had been both polite and understanding, and Jasmine believed him when he assured her that he had passed on both of her previous messages to his client. Unfortunately she also believed him when he said, with some weariness, that even as his agent he often found it difficult wringing a response out of Russell Darius, so she shouldn't hold her breath.

Murray Maxwell was offering neither politeness nor understanding. A little digging had at least got her a direct number for his office, rather than having to take her chances with the lucky-dip that was the Scotia Television switchboard, but on each occasion Jasmine had called, the phone had been answered by Maxwell's PA. The first time, she had been given a breezy but neutral 'yes, I'll pass that on'. The second time she could tell words had been exchanged. There was an unmistakable hardening to the assistant's tone as she said 'oh, yes,' in response to Jasmine identifying herself, followed by: 'I did pass on your previous message, but Mr Maxwell has been extremely busy of late.'

Third time was most certainly not the charm. Jasmine was told in icy tones that 'if Mr Maxwell was interested in speaking to you, he would have responded in person. I must warn you that if you persist in making these calls, we will consider it harassment, in which case we are prepared to take vigorous legal recourse.'

'To be fair,' Fallan had stated, 'it's probably not the best time to be asking him if he wouldn't mind discussing his hitherto secret past links to the recently murdered Hamish Queen.'

'But couldn't I use that?' Jasmine suggested. 'You know: talk to me about this or I talk to the press about Glass Shoe.'

'I wouldn't play that card quite yet: you don't know enough. He could call your bluff. And if you did broadcast his connection to Queen, the polis would be all over it.'

The sun was shining on the Culfieth Hydro as Fallan's Land Rover drove past it, making for the outdoors centre which was situated a mile up the hill. The granite sparkled in the sun, giving the grand Victorian building something of a fairy-tale look, but Jasmine could imagine it would look far more forbidding in clouds and rain. It was all turrets and balustrades, austere and imposing, like an insane asylum in some Gothic psychodrama. It had been an asylum of sorts once upon a time, a place where the Victorian infirm were sent for the fresh air and to take the waters, and later where the Edwardian dipsomanic were sent for fresh air and to take *only* the waters. As a legacy of those days, the hotel had remained unlicensed until the nineties, but in recent times it had reinvented itself as an all-year, all-weather leisure resort, with the outdoor sports HQ located adjacent to the first tee of the hotel's nine-hole golf course.

Jasmine didn't need to ask for Callum Ross or have him pointed out. She was getting good at recognising ex-cops when she saw them, though in his case it probably helped that he was holding a gun. Rather disturbingly, he appeared to be pointing it at a child of around ten. As she drew closer, Jasmine could see that the gun was in fact some kind of laser-tag weapon, the use of which Ross was merely demonstrating. His instruction complete, the child gleefully took hold of his ray gun and went charging off to catch up with a group of children and adults in camouflage overalls, all headed for an area of woodland.

Ross seemed equally adept at recognising his visitors without introduction. She guessed this may have been assisted by their being the only people in the vicinity not dressed in some kind of sports or pseudo-military attire, or it could have been that Harry had provided a few details regarding his young 'associate'.

'You must be Jasmine Sharp,' he greeted her. 'And this is?'

'Glen Fallan,' she said.

'Are you with Galt Linklater too?'

260

'I'm with Sharp Investigations,' Fallan answered, and Jasmine had to suppress a smile at the conviction with which he uttered it.

'You look kind of familiar,' Ross said. 'I worked with Harry Deacon a couple of times back in my Strathclyde days. I was just wondering if I knew you from the job as well.'

'It's possible,' Fallan deadpanned.

'What were you? Drugs? Murder?'

'Bit of both. Glad to be out of it now.'

Ross nodded sagely. He looked like he'd be in agreement. He was dressed in a blue polo shirt bearing the hotel's logo, the material stretched across a muscular frame, his skin tanned and healthy, his features bright and alert. He didn't seem like a man who was missing his old job, and God knows Jasmine had seen a few of those, though some of them were probably just as miserable then too.

'So, I gather there's something I might be able to help you with?' Ross asked. 'Harry didn't give me any clues, so I must confess I'm quite intrigued. Always a pleasure to take a trip down felony lane, as long as it's not concerning any incidents in which police shots were fired. I can't disclose anything about those, you understand.'

'No,' said Jasmine. 'It's going back a bit further than that. It's concerning your time in Balnavon, and the recently departed Mr Hamish Queen.'

The easygoing jollity fell from his face.

'Let's go somewhere a bit more private,' Ross said.

Somewhere more private turned out to be the hotel's shooting range, situated in a disused quarry a quarter of a mile down a dirt track from the outdoors centre. Ross announced that he had been heading there next anyway, as he had work to do in preparation for guest sessions later that day.

He took them there in a Land Rover almost identical to Fallan's, and it struck Jasmine as remarkable how two such similar vehicles could make her feel so different. The Hydro-liveried four-by-four felt colder, less cosy, more bumpy, and the smell of diesel was cut with that of wet clothes and musty fruit. She wanted out of it as soon as possible, the short trek down to the quarry seeming to take ages. Maybe it wasn't the vehicle so much as the uncomfortable memory of her last trip down into an old quarry with Fallan beside her and an old polisman at the wheel.

This time, at least, the guns were only air rifles. There were eight of them lined up on a rack inside one of two wooden enclosures at the near end of the quarry, various targets and pellet-catchers dotted about the ground at different ranges. Ross took one of the rifles and began stripping it down, preparing to oil and clean the weapon along with its seven sisters on the rack.

'I grew up in Glen Kerse,' he said, slipping a cleaning rod into the barrel. 'Six miles outside Balnavon. I knew, or rather I was aware of Hamish Queen since I was about four or five. I say aware because he was the laird's son, and though we were roughly the same age and lived close by we were never going to be round each other's houses to play, you know?'

'I can imagine,' Jasmine replied.

'It's weird. Rural life, village life back then— you hear folk talk about how everybody was quite close and knew each other's business, but not while the class partitions stood so firm. I mean, nothing against the guy, but that's the point: nothing for him either. I didn't know him. Like everybody, I knew who he was and who his father was, but I don't think either of them could have picked me out in a photograph, even when I was one of the local polis.'

'And what about your boss?' Jasmine asked. 'Could they have picked him out?'

'Dougal Strang? Oh aye. Fergus McQueen always enjoyed good relations with the sergeant, but as long as he was on first-name terms with the organ-grinder, he didn't need to pay close attention to the monkeys.'

'Fergus *Mc*Queen?' Jasmine queried.

'Aye. That was the laird's family name. Hamish changed his when he became an actor. He was Hamish McQueen right up until his early twenties.'

'How many monkeys were there?' asked Fallan, prompting an askew look from Ross as he glanced up from where he was bent over a gun.

'Just the one, at any given time. It was a real shoestring operation. The geographical area we covered was so big it was ridiculous, but it wasn't like we were dealing in gang wars and riot control.'

'Do you want a hand there?' Fallan asked, nodding towards the other guns that were awaiting attention.

'Would you know what you were doing?'

Fallan nodded and lifted one of the rifles, breaking it with barely a flick of the wrist.

'Cheers,' Ross said, ripping a rag in two and offering him one half. 'I'm still trying to place you. Did you do firearms training on the force?'

'No. It was more of a recreational thing.'

'Just target shooting, or game too?'

'I always liked to hunt,' Fallan replied.

'Aye. Once it's in the blood, it's with you forever.'

Fallan said nothing to this, and Jasmine could only guess at his thoughts. He was trying to put Ross at ease though, so for that much she was grateful.

'In July 1981,' she said, 'Hamish Queen was held for questioning over the disappearance of a woman by the name of Tessa Garrion. What can you tell us about that?'

Ross nodded to himself, as though in confirmation that he had always known this was where the inquiry was headed.

'Plenty,' he replied. 'And very little. That whole business played a big part in my deciding it was time to spread my wings and move on. Something else about village life: different rules for different people, and not just the McQueens. It was young Tormod who kicked it all off. He came in and said he wanted to speak to Sergeant Strang. He wouldn't talk to anyone else. So Dougal took him into his office and they spoke, but he wasn't entirely forthcoming with the details of what was said.'

'Who was this Tormod person?' Jasmine asked.

'Sorry. Tormod McDonald. He was always known as young Tormod because his father was Tormod too. His father was the minister.'

'The Wee Free?' Jasmine asked, recalling Finlay Weir's unflattering impersonation of him.

'Actually, he wasn't, but it's a common enough misperception of anybody who only had cursory dealings with him. He was a poisonous and curmudgeonly wee bigot who disapproved of just about everything, so I can understand where the confusion arose. He could actually have outdone the Wee Frees in the fire-and-brimstone stakes as well. He's long dead; and if there is a heaven he'll be outside the gates protesting. He always took a dim view of joy, you see.'

'And what about his son?'

'Oh, you can read his dim views on joy in the paper these days. He followed his father into the ministry, but he writes a column for the Scottish edition of the *Daily Mail*. I've only seen it the odd time, but it's clear the apple didn't fall far. Of course, you can't get away with ranting about Catholics these days, so homosexuality and secularism appear to be proving able surrogates.'

'Sounds like a *Mail* columnist right enough,' Jasmine agreed.

'The big difference is, the others write about asylum seekers as if they were Satan. He writes about Satan as if he was an asylum seeker: a nefarious incomer who threatens our way of life, but I mean like a real person, not some woolly concept. Between that and the Young Earth Creationism, I think there's enough for him to be sectioned, but then I always thought he was a weirdo.'

'So what did he have to do with Hamish Queen being brought in for questioning?'

'He told Dougal he thought there had been a murder up at Kildrachan House the previous night.'

'And how would he know this?'

'Well, this is why he would only talk to Sergeant Strang, and why Dougal was cagey about the details of what he was told. Young Tormod knew he could rely on the sergeant's discretion. Dougal was as easygoing as he was experienced, and he knew that in a place like Balnavon, such discretion could save everyone a lot of bother.'

Ross snapped the rifle back together and replaced it on the rack, taking another to begin work on.

'From what I can gather, Tormod had been up at the house not just the night before, but several nights: him and his younger sister, Mhairi. Old Tormod had been kicking up a stink about Hamish and his troupe using the church hall; he was just shouting at the rain, to be honest, an angry wee dog barking to look aggressive but succeeding only in reminding everybody how powerless he was. And what he also succeeded in was cultivating his children's fascination with this forbidden fruit. Tormod and Mhairi were all over those rehearsals like a rash. Tormod would have been eighteen, Mhairi sixteen, maybe seventeen, so they were at an age when their father could neither rule them nor keep track of them.'

'So everybody in the village was aware of what was going on at the church hall and Kildrachan House?' Jasmine asked.

'Aware? Most of us had already bought tickets. Not a lot of nightlife options around there, especially in those days, and we were aware that Hamish, for all he was the spoiled laddie, had gone off and become a proper actor, and had brought other proper actors to put on this play. There was a barmaid from the Balnavon Hotel who latched on to them.'

'Saffron.'

'Aye, that was her name. She'd only been in town a couple of months so nobody really knew her, apart from Charlie Aitken at the hotel. Flower-power type, as far as I gather. I didn't know her myself: I drank in the Stag. I heard she was quite arty, so it was unsurprising she got herself involved with the actors, but the minister's two were in there all the time as well. I think they started off just hanging about and watching, but as time went on they got more and more involved. Mhairi was handy with a sewing machine so I think she was appointed their unofficial wardrobe mistress, and I heard Tormod started off helping with set painting but ended up getting a non-speaking part: Banquo's son.'

'Fleance,' said Jasmine. 'So he was a little more flamboyant in his youth.'

'Aye. Always a little strange, but who wouldn't be, growing up with that oddity for a father.'

Without discussing it, Ross and Fallan had developed a little production line, Ross rodding and cleaning the guns before passing them to Fallan for oiling.

'He certainly didn't want his father knowing that he wasn't merely hanging around rehearsals: him and Mhairi were going up to Kildrachan of an evening, and I don't think everybody was just sitting around reading stanzas and sonnets to each other.'

'No, I was given a rather different impression by other witnesses.'

'That was why young Tormod would only speak to Dougal. He had been up there late on that night and seen something, but there was drink involved, and possibly more. The epitome of unreliable testimony, I'd have said, but he was very scared; scared enough for Dougal to look into it.'

'But look into what?'

'He thought he'd seen a woman being stabbed, then someone dragging her body through the woods. And if that sounds vague, then welcome to my world circa 1981. I'm sure Tormod told Dougal more than that, but Tormod was the minister's son and so was extended special privileges of discretion not entirely consistent with standard police practice.

'We went up to Kildrachan to investigate. Tormod had given Dougal a list of everyone who had been there the previous night. From that, the only person who couldn't be accounted for was Tessa Garrion, whom we subsequently learned had been in a sexual relationship with Hamish Queen, one that had ended acrimoniously that very night.'

'And is it true you found traces of blood?'

'No,' Ross replied. 'We found what could have been bloodstains, but they were never properly analysed.'

'Why not?'

'Because it wasn't a murder inquiry. We were just following up a vague and possibly hysterical report from one witness. Believe me, it would have taken more than we had before Dougal ordered any course of action that involved digging chunks out of Fergus McQueen's walls and floorboards.'

'But he was okay with arresting Fergus McQueen's son?'

'Hamish wasn't under arrest, though he knew he wasn't going anywhere either. Not until Dougal got to the bottom of whatever had happened.'

'Were you aware that Hamish Queen was married at that time?'

'Yes. To the daughter of some duke or life peer or whatever from Englandshire. Which was another reason Dougal was keeping a tight cordon around his inquiries. Scandal meant headaches and messy

268

complications.'

Jasmine waited until Ross glanced up from his work and looked him in the eye.

'Are you saying Sergeant Strang would have preferred if the whole thing just went away?'

'Undoubtedly,' he replied. 'But not in the way you're implying. I had my reservations about how Dougal ran his show, but I never worried about his integrity. In fact, he could have released Hamish sooner than he did. Tormod came in again and tried to recant his testimony, such as it was, admitting his imagination might have got the better of him. And the barmaid, Saffron, I went to question her and she told me she saw Tessa Garrion getting on the last bus to Inverness at ten past eleven. That didn't satisfy Dougal, though. He thought she was a bit flaky.'

'So why did Hamish finally walk?'

Ross ceased rodding the barrel of the gun he was holding and let the weapon rest in his lap.

'To this day I don't know. Dougal got a phone call. He picked it up in the main body of the kirk and then transferred it to his office, where he took it with the door closed. Shortly after that he went out. He was gone for a few hours, and when he came back he said Hamish could go. He wouldn't say where he'd been. He said the whole issue was closed and hadn't to be brought up again.'

'Just like that?'

'Like it never happened. Dougal made it clear he didn't want anybody even talking about what may or may not have been going on at Kildrachan. We weren't to tell anyone that Tormod and Mhairi had been up there, far less that Tormod had sparked this investigation.'

'And what about Tormod himself? What was his take on this?'

'As I said, he recanted his testimony, except there was no official testimony, just a private conversation he'd had with Dougal.'

Ross resumed rodding the barrel and sighed.

'Aye, the vicissitudes of life at Balnavon nick. I had been thinking about a change for a while, but that whole business was what lit a fire under me. The spoiled son of the laird and the weirdo son of the minister: special rules for special people. Dougal's policies of judicious discretion. He took the secret of that phone call to his grave, and I'm nearly as bad. In thirty years, you're the first people I've told about it.'

'You mean since Finlay Weir.'

Ross gave her a confused look.

'I told nobody.'

'Then how does he know about it?'

Ross was halfway into a 'search me' shrug when he realised he knew the answer.

'It was a very small station. He must have overheard.'

'Why, what was he doing there?'

'We were questioning him too. The way we heard it, Garrion had snubbed this other guy's advances in favour of Hamish.'

'Funny he didn't mention this. He didn't mention Tormod and Mhairi becoming involved in the production either. Why is everybody I talk to about this so reluctant to name all the people involved?'

'Well,' said Fallan, 'considering the first guy you asked about it just got shot in the head, I don't imagine anyone is about to start getting more garrulous on the subject.'

270

Jasmine frowned.

'Do you know where I would find Tormod McDonald?' she asked Ross.

'Depends. If you're lucky, at Balnavon Parish Church, carrying on his late father's fine work.'

'And if I'm unlucky?'

Ross winced.

'Iraq. I heard he serves some of the time as a chaplain in the armed forces.'

Ross handed the last gun to Fallan for oiling, then lifted one of the cleaned rifles from the rack. He broke it, placed a pellet in the breach, primed the spring and snapped the barrel home again. Then he turned to Jasmine.

'So, seeing as you're here, do you fancy a wee go?'

'I've never done this before. I'm not sure I—'

'Just give it a whirl.'

Jasmine accepted the weapon principally out of politeness, though she would have felt less awkward and reluctant had he been handing her a large salmon.

'Don't be scared,' he told her. 'This thing wouldn't stop anything bigger than a rabbit. I'll just set you up a target.'

As soon as Ross exited the enclosure Fallan stepped in behind her, gently supporting her arms and guiding her into a stance. His hands were on her arms, her shoulders, her back. The hands that killed her dad. She didn't recoil, didn't flinch. Something inside her regretted this: wished she could feel instinctive revulsion at his touch because to feel hate, she'd know what it was to feel *something* for her father.

His hands were gentle, a stillness flowing from him into her like a current.

271

Ross approached a metal frame about ten yards away, removing a shot-peppered paper target from a pellet-catcher and replacing it with a new one.

Jasmine put her eye to the scope, seeing only a green blur. Fallan's hand touched her cheek.

'Keep your head back from the scope. It'll kick when you fire.'

He nudged the stock up a little in her left hand and suddenly the target appeared, crosshairs bobbing and swaying around the red and blue concentric circles. The view through the scope showed how every little movement at her end would be magnified at the point of impact. She had thought she was standing fairly still, but she might as well have been on a boat.

'Breathe slow and steady,' Fallan said, his voice itself a soft breath. 'Watch the crosshairs rise and fall. Don't try and freeze, don't hold your breath, just get used to the rhythm.'

She felt the outside world melt away, only the crosshairs and the circles in her view, only the sound of her own breathing in her head.

'Fire on the outward breath, but don't *pull* the trigger: squeeze it, smooth and fluid.'

She watched the hairs bob a couple more times, the amplitude of their movement always reducing, then squeezed firmly and steadily against the trigger's resistance. She felt a sudden kick against her shoulder and heard the plink of the pellet hitting the back of the catcher. There was a small hole about a centimetre above the red circle at the centre of the target.

Fallan showed her how to break the gun and ready another pellet.

'A little too high,' she said. 'I'll aim lower next

272

time.'

'No,' said Ross. 'Don't compensate. Keep aiming for the centre. The important thing first time is to get a good grouping.'

She fired four more shots, all of them about a centimetre high of the bullseye. They were all roughly in the same place, at least.

Ross returned to the frame and replaced the target, examining the used one as he walked clear.

'Aye, very good,' he said rather drily. 'Never done it before, my arse.'

'I haven't,' she insisted. 'I missed every time.'

'Look at that grouping,' Ross indicated to Fallan, pro to pro, like she wasn't there.

Fallan took the paper card and examined it. Something bright crept into his expression, but whatever it was, he promptly hid it again.

'Tight,' Fallan observed. 'Scope's zeroed for a longer distance.'

'That's right,' Ross said. 'Last shooter must have been set up for the far targets, back of the range. I generally don't re-zero these because you never know what level the next guest is going to be.'

'And what does any of this mean in English?' Jasmine asked.

'That you're a natural, hen,' Ross replied.

He made an adjustment to the scope and handed Jasmine the rifle again.

'Try now.'

She began another grouping, still aiming dead centre. This time the pellets found their mark.

It was strangely calming. She could lose herself in the view through the scope, putting everything else from her head.

She had no idea how long she'd been there, but

she was snapped back to the here and now when Ross mentioned the death of Hamish Queen. Suddenly the view through a rifle scope meant something else entirely.

'Heard some scuttlebutt from a shooter I know who's still on the job. They haven't found the slug yet, but from the damage it did they reckon Hamish was killed by a very high-powered rifle, something with serious distance capability.'

'So it could have been a hunting accident after all?' Jasmine wondered.

'I sincerely doubt it. The theory that the bullet might have been aimed at one of the bankers is bollocks as well. A long-range shot, cover of darkness: this was someone who knew what they were doing.'

She caught just a hint of professional admiration in Ross's tone, like he knew it was inappropriate but he couldn't help but give the shooter his due. And with that, she realised what that brief flash of brightness on Fallan's face had been.

It was pride.

Version History

Catherine hated these mobile incident rooms. They made her feel like she was about to give blood in some supermarket car park. Truth was, she was merely going to sweat it. They also reminded her uncomfortably of temporary toilets, like you'd find at fairgrounds and festivals. The one time she and Drew had gone to T in the Park, back before Duncan came along, she had decided just to hold it

274

in rather than bare her nethers to the abominations of the cubicle she'd found herself in. They were only there for the day and her bladder was already well trained by the job. She had thought she could hang on until she got home, but didn't make it past the first motorway services area on the M8. The relief bordered on a euphoria that eclipsed everything she'd felt all day, except perhaps when she heard Steven Lindsay play 'Swimmer' live for the first time since her teens.

Given the manpower she'd been allowed to commandeer, it was a squeeze fitting so many detectives into the cramped and flimsy little space, and she was glad to be doing it early in the day, given the paucity of the ventilation. Right then, shampoo, deo and body spray were still winning. Nonetheless, cramped, crowded or sweaty, she knew this part was the cornerstone upon which any investigation was built. Sometimes it was repetitive to the point of seeming redundant, but it was an indispensable practice, the importance of which had been instilled in her by her old mentor, the redoubtable Moira Clark: 'Make sure everybody else knows what everybody else knows.'

She checked her watch. It was just coming up for ten. She'd give it a minute, then clear her throat and bring the room to order.

The drive had taken more than two hours. The first time she'd come up, with Zoe at the wheel, she had thought it quite a picturesque trip, a nice change from motorway tailbacks and grey housing schemes, but she could see it getting old fast if she had to keep coming here. The road was rapidly becoming over-familiar, and she was already fed up with blue-lighting it to get past caravans.

She wouldn't be seeing a lot of Drew and the boys this week either. She had crossed paths briefly with Duncan this morning, as he was an early riser, but all she'd managed with Fraser was a groggy kiss, waking him up for school as she was heading out the door.

Duncan didn't ask about *Trail of the Sniper*, which meant Drew must have had a word. He had, however, been staring at an advert for it in a magazine when she walked into the kitchen, his expression baleful despite it being the day before school broke up for the holidays. She deduced that he'd assembled the pose for her benefit; it was no coincidence she just happened to walk into the room and find him there with that page open. Dad had said no; was he trying to melt Mummy's heart, thinking she might be good cop on this occasion? Or had he read something in Drew's explanation that pointed the finger back at her? Maybe it was a consolation to be out of it. By the end of the week he'd have moved on to obsessing about something else anyway.

What was all the more galling about coming up to Alnabruich was that her role here was nothing she couldn't do over the phone from Glasgow. This was political: this was about the TV and press cameras shooting her outside Cragruthes Castle instead of outside Govan police station when she made a statement later today. That said, she'd feel a lot more justified in whining about it if she could argue that the travelling was getting in the way of all her rapid progress.

Ten years ago, this would have been considered early days. Now she was serving under the tyranny of ever-accelerating news cycles, of people hitting

276

refresh on a browser and expecting the story to change from minute to minute. When it didn't, it wouldn't be long before the politicos began asking whether the investigation had stalled. Progress wasn't measured in days any more, but in hours. That was why even she was conscious of having seen the same footage over and over again: cops in hi-viz vests combing the grounds and the woods beyond; the same statements from her and from a spokesman for the Cragruthes estate.

The bank had put forward nobody, wanting their part in it to be quietly buried. Given the recent revelations about former Royal Bank of Scotland boss Fred Goodwin taking out a super-injunction to conceal what he was getting up to when he wasn't flushing billions down the toilet, it was no surprise that his counterparts at the RSB weren't firing salutes over Hamish Queen's body.

The interviews with the bank's delegates and guests were ongoing, but they were all telling the same story. There were no accounts of anybody acting suspiciously or sneaking away during the show. Drink was flowing, and that meant urine would have been too, but there had been toilet breaks between acts. When there are only three rows, and not a lot of leg room, it's hard for anybody to take their leave without being noticed. And yet there were only thirty-five guests accounted for, including the host and the late Mr Queen, and someone had taken pains to erase the paperwork.

She had gone back and pressed Sir Angus on this. He said he had been sure they were full, though he added that in the past the bank and other clients had booked the full complement of places while keeping one or two free in case they had to add someone at short notice. Plausible enough, but it didn't explain why somebody had deleted the lists from the Cragruthes computer.

A copy of the final booking emailed to the castle had been requested from the RSB, as the original outgoing version would still be on their system. When it arrived, Catherine suspected it might pose some awkward questions for somebody, and she was going to enjoy asking them.

One of the local officers spoke first, a sandy-haired outdoorsy type she could easily have made a fool of herself over once upon a time.

'DC Brian Frazer, ma'am,' he identified himself. 'We've been bracing folk known to be fond of a wee moonlight trek with a gun on them purely for defending themselves from animals. Alibis all round, which is to be expected, because it's standard practice that you always have somebody to vouch that you were in the pub while you're out bagging an unauthorised bit of game. Further to that, the consensus is that nobody goes shooting during the fortnight that these plays are on, because there's just too much activity.'

'I hope I'm hearing a "but" here,' Catherine observed by way of urging him to get to it. You didn't pipe up first just to tell everybody you had nothing.

'Indeed. I spoke to a younger guy called Andy Philips. He's seventeen. It was his dad I was there to talk to, Donny, but it turned out his boy had been out doing a bit of late-night fishing. It's not just the woods that are well stocked on the Cragruthes estate, you see. He was on his way out here along the Oban road when he saw somebody getting

278

into a black Range Rover some time after ten. He didn't take note of the time; he was just estimating according to when he left the house and how long it normally took him to get there.'

'Please tell me he got a plate.'

'Sorry. The boy wasn't wanting to be seen, so he was more concerned with staying out of sight at that point. But the driver emerged from the woods on the side of the road nearer the castle.'

'Did he get any kind of look at him?'

'Not much. Says he was dressed in dark-coloured camo with a hat pulled down ever his eyes. Weird thing is, he said he didn't see a rifle. The bloke was running, though. Got into the Range Rover and took off in a hurry. Andy ditched his tackle at that point and was thinking of turning back because he thought the bloke might be running from gamekeepers. He'd heard a shot a wee while before; he thought maybe fifteen minutes but, as I said, he didn't check his watch. He lay low for a while and when no keepers appeared he proceeded as planned. He didn't know about what happened until I showed up, as he was fishing half the night and then sleeping.'

'So do you know where the vehicle was parked?'

'Aye. I drove Andy up to show me. It's estate land on either side of the road at that point. The Range Rover was parked in a layby, about a kilometre from the castle as the crow flies, maybe a kilometre and a half on foot.'

'Are you familiar with the territory?'

DC Frazer gave a coy smile.

'I may have strayed on to it when I was Andy's age, with a fishing rod purely for protection from the salmon.'

'Perfect. I want you to take charge of a second ground search. Start from where the Range Rover was parked and work back towards the locus along the probable routes.'

'Yes ma'am.'

It was a positive start, and just as well, because Catherine suspected the next part would be less dynamic.

'Have we got anything new on the victim?' she asked, for which, read 'motive'.

All eyes fell on DI Malcolm Gillan, who did very well not to wince at being put on the spot. Nonetheless, his body language was clearly apologetic for what was about to follow. On a major investigation such as this, there was always going to be at least one job that would turn out to be like nailing jelly to a wall, and he had been assigned it. There was no way of knowing that in advance, so she hoped he understood amid his frustrations that giving him this beat was an endorsement, not a booby prize. She knew it was going to be crucial, so she needed someone who could get the job done.

'A whole load of bugger-all at the moment,' he admitted. 'No business deals gone sour, no drug habit connecting him to the wrong people, no debts, obviously, and no Jekyll-and-Hyde public face versus business face stuff. So far I'm getting the impression Barney the Dinosaur had more enemies.'

'*I'd* shoot Barney the Dinosaur,' Catherine said, partly to offer Malcolm a boost and partly in bitter memory of the cloying dreck she'd had to sit through when the boys were very small.

'Detectives have spoken to the family,' Malcolm went on, 'and we're also using their information to spread our inquiries to close friends and to his professional associates. Nobody's jumping up to point any fingers, so no obvious candidate has leapt to anyone's mind. The one thing that sticks out so far is that Queen was in the middle of his third divorce. It's possible his latest flame had a rival suitor—or even a husband—who was the jealous type, but at this stage we don't know if there even *was* a latest flame.

'Three wives and counting also implies that he was given to flinging it about; certainly if there's a vice to be looked into, it would appear to be women. However, the main thing is we're aware that the dirt and the grudges don't start coming out until the eulogies are all finished, so we might have to be patient.'

'It's early days,' Catherine agreed, trying to sound supportive, but everybody knew this was bad news. It was early days, but in another sense it was already very late. They were way past the twenty-four-hour mark and moving into the exponential stage, whereby the longer it took, the longer it was going to take.

Nobody was pointing fingers, no names were leaping to anyone's mind. Nobody had a motive. Nobody had a clue.

'What about our secondary angle?' she asked the room. 'The possibility that the shot was wide and Sir Angus McCready was the target?'

It was Laura's turn to look apologetic.

'Nothing coming in to support that so far, boss. A dispute with a property developer where he'd agreed to sell off some land then changed his mind, that's the only controversy in his recent past, and it wasn't that recent: 2006. A lot of lawyer sabre-rattling on either side, then it died away. He's mouthed off about the animal rights lobby a few times in the local papers, so that might be worth pursuing, but he's not exactly Huntingdon Life Sciences. He seems popular enough with the punters around here, mostly getting "decent cove" and "harmless old duffer" type reviews. We're digging into his private life as discreetly as we can manage.'

'Keep it that way,' Catherine said. 'We don't want the political fall-out from our aristocratic innocent bystander discovering he's being investigated. And in the event that he *was* the intended target, then nor do we want the shooter to know we're on to that possibility.'

'Yes boss.'

'Now, anything else we need to share?'

Catherine scanned the faces around the rapidly heating room and noticed that one of them wasn't giving her his undivided attention, being instead bathed in the glow of an open laptop.

'Beano, I've told you before: you can bring in games on the last day of term, but no earlier.'

'I'm sorry boss,' he responded. He raised his head dutifully, but his attention was still partly on his screen. 'It's the RBS guest list. It just pinged into the inbox the second you called us to order, and I wanted to bring us up to speed if there was anything we should know.'

'And is there?'

'Yes. The bad news for us is that I've double-checked my count and it currently shows thirty-three names.'

'Shit,' said Catherine, then she picked up on Beano's key word. 'Hang on, what do you mean "currently"?'

This prompted a grin from the Detective Constable.

'Because the bad news for the guy who sent it is that, working for the RSB, I'm guessing they teach you a lot more about using Excel and PowerPoint than about using Word. This document was edited about two minutes before it was sent.'

'That's as may be,' Catherine countered, 'but if he just opened it to check it was the right file, it would say it was last edited at that point, wouldn't it?'

'Only if changes were made. I'm guessing he's never clicked on the Review tab, or he'd know that the Track Changes option had been enabled.'

'And does that show that something's been deleted?'

'Better than that. Not only can I tell you for sure that there was a thirty-fourth person on that list, I can tell you his name and, just as importantly, who deleted it.'

Rite of Passage

The village of Balnavon was clouded in a light and misty drizzle as Fallan drove Jasmine through it in his Land Rover. The dreich weather was having the opposite effect of the sunshine upon Culfieth Hydro, rendering what ought to have appeared a couthy and charming little rural settlement gloomy and oppressive. Tearooms and tourist shops that might otherwise have appeared cosy and colourful looked washed-out and claustrophobic, venues for interminably miserable afternoons on ill-judged day trips.

She could understand why Callum Ross got out; the only question was how he'd stuck it here so long. The surrounding countryside was no doubt spectacular, when you could see it through the clouds of rain and clouds of midges but, having grown up in the comforting anonymity of cities, Jasmine couldn't imagine walking down the same wee streets every day, seeing the same faces, knowing every one of them and every one of them knowing your business.

They had passed the Kildrachan estate on the way into town, its broad entrance sweeping away from the road between two redoubtable stone gateposts. There was no visible sign of the house itself, the track quickly vanishing into dense and mature woodland. Jasmine couldn't stop herself wondering whether Tessa Garrion's remains lay somewhere behind those gates and beneath the dark of those trees, waiting for discovery and the justice it might bring. Little that she had uncovered about this case had given her reason to believe Tessa had survived the summer of 1981; and only the flaky testimony of a hippy-chick barmaid suggested she had ever made it out of Balnavon. Whether she had got on that bus or not, what was indisputable was that she'd never been seen again.

Jasmine knew from a conversation with Charlotte that Hamish's elderly parents still lived at Kildrachan with a small housekeeping staff. She felt dreadful for them. She didn't imagine losing a child was any easier when he was fifty-five than if he was a tenth of that and, coming towards the last years of your own life, surely you'd want the comfort of knowing that those you had brought into the world were going to keep thriving.

The thought of Charlotte had given her more pause. Charlotte had grown up at Hamish's own handsome Highland pile, about thirty miles away in Ardcruich. She was most likely with her mother down south, but Jasmine couldn't help but worry in case she was visiting her grandparents for mutual comfort and support.

Their last words had been in anger, mainly Charlotte's. It had been ten minutes of stream-of-consciousness invective, circular and repetitive, fired by that unique indignation felt by the over-privileged on the rare occasions when the world didn't bow to their expectations.

'I can't believe it,' she kept saying. There wasn't any particular detail she was incredulous of, so much as the revelation that a nobody such as Jasmine could do anything other than kiss her Pilates-sculpted arse. Gotta watch this breed, Charlotte, they'll turn on ya.

'I can't believe you would betray me like this,' was her opening salvo. As in, before even identifying herself to the person who had answered the phone. 'You're working for that bitch, aren't you? I put myself out for you and you're just a muck-raker, sifting through the dirt for that gold-digger. I can't believe it. I thought you were a friend. I thought you were somebody I could trust. You made your job sound all clever and exciting but it's just sleaze and innuendo. I can't believe it.'

It didn't sound like Hamish had told Charlotte much, or indeed anything, about what they had actually discussed. As far as Jasmine knew, he may not have lied outright to his daughter either: it seemed to be Charlotte who was drawing her own

285

conclusions, revealing a few of the chinks in her armour as a result. Hamish Queen was divorced from Charlotte's mother, who had been his second wife, and it turned out he had been in the throes of divorce number three. Charlotte, needless to say, wasn't galpals with her mother's successor, and was clearly still bearing a lot of scars from the break-up.

If Jasmine ran into her up here, it wouldn't so much be awkward as utterly sordid.

Jasmine had placed a call to Mrs Petrie to give her an update. It was just a means of checking in and making sure she was still content for Jasmine to pursue her inquiries; she had no intention of telling her what those inquiries were unavoidably pointing to.

She didn't get to speak to her. Mrs Petrie's daughter answered the call and informed her that her mother was in hospital 'again'. Alison, as she gave her name, had come down to Cornwall to help out.

'She has peaks and troughs,' Alison said. 'We're hoping she'll be back on her feet in a few days, but you always worry how much each bad spell is going to take out of her.'

'I understand,' Jasmine had told her.

She gave Alison a vague and neutral message to pass on regarding her progress. Making inquiries, developing a picture of Tessa's life as an actress, following up solid leads. She worded it carefully: 'solid' rather than 'good'. Solid made it sound like reliable information; good made it sound like it would lead to a positive resolution.

On one level it was a relief not to talk to Mrs Petrie direct, not to have to hear the guarded hope in her voice as she asked questions, and not to feel

286

like a sleaze for stringing her along and keeping back the truth. On another level, her call to Alison brought home how painful this was all ultimately going to be, when she would have to tell Alice, like all those other clients before her, that she had acted too late in trying to find her sister. Thirty years too late, in fact.

She recalled her mum's deterioration, the way she'd look like she was slipping into the final throes, but somehow kept finding it in herself to rally. What would it do to Mrs Petrie when the one thing she had pinned her hopes upon was taken away?

The church hall, or rather the 'community centre' was right on the main drag, the church itself set back from the road up a short but steep banking. Even allowing for the greyness of the day it was the epitome of nondescript: Calvinist austerity extending even to the architecture. If buildings could have emotions, this one looked like it was in the huff, tucked away from the passing traffic and sulkily determined not to catch anyone's eye.

Across the street and just a few yards further north was the Balnavon Hotel, a more welcoming sight partly due to its brighter aesthetics, but as much down to the chalkwritten promise of a pub lunch after the best part of three hours on the road.

Fallan went up to the bar to order while Jasmine sat at a wooden table and took in the surroundings. The walls were bare stone, hand-hewn rocks rather than kiln-fired brick, the floor a matt sheen of dark grey slate. It might have seemed a little cold but for the fire in the grate, which instead added to an atmosphere that was both warm and somehow timeless. It was easy to imagine the place having changed little in maybe a hundred years.

She would have been completely wrong, though. Framed photographs betrayed how the interior had looked not so long ago: plaster and paint on the walls, swirly carpets on the floor, beaten-copper tabletops and garish tartan upholstery. She saw images of smiling groups posing for the camera to record big nights: grinning, tipsy men holding up a huge fish; a man with a golf ball in one hand and in the other a cardboard number one with a hole through it; footballers displaying signed jerseys or just posing with the regulars.

Fallan returned with the drinks and some encouraging information.

'Checked the licensee certificate on the wall,' he told her. 'It says Mr M. Aitken.'

Callum Ross had told them that back in 1981 the hotel was run by a Charlie Aitken. With any luck, like the establishment across the road, they had kept it in the family.

A waitress brought their food; she was a young girl in her late teens or early twenties. She spoke with a soft and lilting Highland accent, warning them to watch their plates as they were very hot.

Jasmine asked if the owner was in, and if so could she speak to him.

The girl said she'd just go and get him, but didn't leave without first making sure they had all the condiments and drinks they needed.

Jasmine watched her withdraw into the corridor leading to reception, and heard her call out as she walked.

'Dad, you busy?'

A brawny and bearded man emerged into the bar a few minutes later, approaching their table with a helpful smile. He looked late forties or early fifties, and Jasmine immediately pictured him halfway up a mountain when he wasn't behind his bar or his reception desk.

'I'm Murdo Aitken,' he introduced himself. 'Is everything all right with your meal?'

'It's fantastic,' Jasmine replied truthfully of a very welcome plate of beer-battered haddock and chips. 'The decor is lovely too. Did you renovate it recently? It's very striking. A real improvement.'

'You look a bit young to remember it before, but thank you.'

'I saw the photos,' she said.

'Aye, right enough. No, it was done about, God, is it really ten years? Aye, ten years ago now. I took over from my old man in ninety-six, and I meant to change it sooner, but you know how it is.'

Jasmine agreed, thinking of that office furniture she was going to buy before she retired.

'We kept the photos, wee bit of continuity, keep the old spirit of the place. Was there something I can help you with?'

'Perhaps. Did you work here a long time before you took over?'

'All my days. Started off washing dishes and I was behind the bar as soon as I was legal. Why?'

'We're trying to find out a bit about a woman who worked here in 1981. She was from New Zealand, went by the name Saffron.'

Aitken screwed up his face in thought for only the briefest moment. His eyes lit up in recognition before an equally swift change in his expression brought on a hint of rather furtive concern.

'Aye, I remember Saffron all right. She wasn't here long, just a couple of months. Looked like she'd just come in from Woodstock, or maybe *Lord of the Rings*. Seemed very exotic to me, though I was about eighteen and never been further than Perth.'

'You don't happen to remember her surname, by any chance?' Jasmine asked, her tone almost apologising in anticipation of being rebuffed. It was, after all, a long shot at thirty years.

'Simpson,' he replied almost instantly, a little smile creeping across his face. 'And her real name was Veronica.'

'That's some memory,' Fallan observed. 'Can you rhyme off everybody who worked here?'

'No,' Aitken replied, looking a little coy. 'But her name was easy to remember, because she told me some people used to call her Roni.'

Jasmine's blank expression must have begged an explanation.

'Ronnie Simpson,' Fallan offered. 'Celtic goalkeeper. One of the Lisbon Lions.'

'That's right,' Aitken confirmed, a little bashfully.

'Do you remember when she left and where she went?'

'I remember she left pretty suddenly. She didn't turn up for work, just phoned to say she was packing it in and moving on. Gave absolutely no notice. Her landlord said much the same thing: she called him and told him she was shipping out. Lived in one of the wee places just along the street, on the road north. We wondered if she'd got bad news or something. We were all pretty disappointed. She had the sort of personality that lit a place up, really outgoing, priceless in a pub.'

Aitken had that furtive look again, like he'd given something away. Fallan read it better than Jasmine.

'I'm guessing it wasn't just her name that made

her easy to remember,' he said, once Aitken had retreated back to Reception.

'What do you mean?'

'I mean he was eighteen and she was a woman of the world. I'm guessing he was just a boy when Saffron started working here, but a man shortly after.'

The Deceiver

They located the Reverend Tormod McDonald a little while later, via Fallan's suggested strategy of wandering across the road to his churchyard and making themselves sufficiently conspicuous that someone would inevitably come out and inquire as to what they were doing there. Discreet inquiries had suggested they were more likely to find him in Balnavon than Baghdad, but Jasmine was surprised that it was the man himself who appeared in the grounds and very politely asked them if he could be of any help. After recent weeks, it was quite a relief to encounter a veteran of the Glass Shoe debacle who wasn't protected by the human firewall of a PA or secretary; and nor was he likely to have been on Hamish's round-robin advance warning list.

He was thin and angular, a gawkiness about his posture like a small man trapped in too tall a body, or as though he had never quite outgrown the physical awkwardness of his teenage years. The effect seemed all the more pronounced alongside Fallan, who carried his stature so effortlessly that it was easy to forget just how big he was. Jasmine was reminded of Aunt Spiker in *James and the Giant*

Peach, though Tormod lacked the harshness in his face that she had always imagined on Roald Dahl's monstrous creation. Nor did his features suggest the pinched and curmudgeonly figure Callum Ross had described as having sired him.

Jasmine had done some reading ahead of her trip, acquainting herself with 'young' Tormod's works and world view. He had proven a predictable hit with a constituency that was reassured to find a churchman under seventy who didn't have any truck with all the wishy-washy liberal views increasingly espoused by his peers in the Church of Scotland and its southern counterparts. However, she had discovered that he was also an occasional theatre critic, both as a regional stringer for the *Mail* and in a blog, and in these writings the picture became far less black and white. Jasmine perceived a serious disconnect between the more compassionate and insightful perspective underpinning his appreciation of drama and the priggish curtain-twitcher ranting about 'feral youth' and 'sexual incontinence' in his columns.

Would the real Tormod McDonald please stand up.

'Are you looking for a grave?' he asked, which Jasmine considered might seem a very threatening opening gambit from anyone not dressed in a dog collar. Her expression must have said as much.

'People are sometimes looking for a particular headstone: an ancestral figure. Have you come far?'

'Glasgow.'

'We've had visitors from all over, who had their roots in Balnavon. So what brings you here?'

Jasmine composed a look of the utmost innocence and sincerity.

'We were wondering whether there's going to be any kind of service. You know, for Hamish Queen. I was at drama school with his daughter Charlotte,' she added, for further benign context.

'I see,' he replied. 'Dreadful, dreadful business. Unspeakably tragic, and unimaginable for the family. But no, there will be no service. We'll pray, for sure, and there are those of us in the village who would like there to be a service, but the family are not religious. It's a pity, for they'll have no comfort now.'

A pity, yeah, thought Jasmine. Because back when Mum died, having some guy in a dress mumble glib platitudes about a non-existent super-being would have made all the difference. However, Tormod's tone wasn't glib, and nor could his sentiment be described as a platitude. In fact, there was a certainty about it that was disarming. He truly believed there was comfort to be had from his God, his faith, and he sounded regretful that Hamish's family were denying it to themselves.

'I saw him only recently,' Jasmine said. 'I spoke to him in Edinburgh, when he was at the Playhouse ahead of his *Grange Hill* musical going on tour. Were you familiar with his work?'

'I must confess I've never seen one of his productions. I've very seldom been to London, so opportunities have been scarce.'

He sounded apologetic though not regretful, as though he had been remiss in his duties by not catching one of Hamish's shows, but that they wouldn't have been his natural choice.

'My time is mostly spent around here. I've been overseas a bit in recent years, but never anywhere you're likely to see a big musical. One of my duties is as an army chaplain at the base over in Glen Fynart. The regiment have been heavily involved in Iraq, so they've flown me over there a few times. It's a humbling and disturbing experience.'

'But you are a fan of the theatre generally, aren't you,' Jasmine stated. 'I've read your reviews.'

'Oh, you have?' he said, his face brightening. He seemed very pleased but stopped himself from breaking into a smile, self-conscious about skipping onto the subject of himself so directly from where they'd been only a moment before.

'Yes. You're very passionate about it. Some critics write like they hate the theatre and resent having to sit through the plays. You always seem to find something positive to say.'

'I can't help myself. I'd sooner sit through a bad play in a theatre than a good film in a multiplex. Are you involved in theatre yourself? You said you trained with Charlotte Queen. I've seen a few of her Fire Curtain productions on tour at Eden Court.'

'No, I had to drop out. It runs in the family though: my mother was an actress, back in Glasgow in the late eighties. Had to give it up when I came along. Yvonne Sharp was her name.'

There she was again, throwing out her line. She felt doubly self-conscious doing it in front of Fallan, but she could not help herself.

She didn't catch anything, however. Tormod did seem to search his memory for a moment, then gave her an apologetic wince.

'I would have just missed her. I was at Glasgow University eighty-one to eighty-five. I went to see quite a few plays back then. I was studying theatre as well as theology.'

'A curious combo,' Jasmine observed.

'Well, yes. I applied and was accepted for theology and philosophy, but when I got there, I found you had to choose a third ordinary subject for first year. There were places in theatre studies, so I chose that and got the bug. Ended up dropping philosophy and did my honours in the other two.'

He allowed himself a smile now, relaxing into reminiscence.

'And have you ever crept the boards yourself?' Jasmine asked.

'Oh, goodness no,' he answered, issuing a little chuckle at the absurdity of the suggestion. 'The pulpit is as much of a stage as I'm cut out to inhabit.'

'What about when you were younger? Like maybe summer 1981?'

The smile vanished, a guarded expression coming down to replace it like the curtain dropping over a set.

'Who are you?' he demanded.

Jasmine handed him a card while Fallan stiffened, folding his arms to reinforce that the pleasantries were over and now they meant business.

'My name is Jasmine Sharp, Sharp Investigations. I'm looking for a woman called Tessa Garrion. She was last seen in summer 1981, here in Balnavon, where she was working with Hamish Queen's Glass Shoe Company, rehearsing for a tour of *Macbeth*. You and your sister were also involved in the production. Your sister was helping with costume and you even had a non-speaking role. That was until it all fell apart one night, when Tessa Garrion disappeared. Hamish Queen said she walked out after an argument, but the next day you told the police you had seen a woman stabbed at Kildrachan House and someone dragging a body.'

'I have things to be getting on with,' he said, turning away. 'I am not prepared to discuss this.'

As he turned, he found Fallan blocking his path.

'What did you see, Reverend?' Fallan asked. 'You can tell us. You don't have to worry about Dougal Strang any more.'

'Please step aside, or I shall be forced to call the police. I haven't spoken about these matters in thirty years and I'm not about to start now, not to two strangers, with Hamish Queen dead and not yet buried.'

Fallan didn't step aside, but nor did he move to block Tormod when he opted to walk around him on to the grass.

'Have you considered the possibility that his death and what you saw that night might just be related?' Jasmine asked.

This stopped him in his retreat towards the church.

'How could they be, after all this time?' he asked.

He wasn't saying this to dismiss the idea. There was palpable anxiety in his voice.

'I don't know. That's why I'm trying to find out what I can about what happened here, but nobody wants to talk to me. When I met Hamish Queen in Edinburgh it was to ask him about Tessa Garrion. He told me lies and then he phoned the surviving members of the Glass Shoe Company in an attempt to stop them speaking to me. Julian Sanquhar did agree to talk, but only so that he could urge me against pursuing my inquiries. He warned me it would have the direst consequences, and with Hamish Queen now dead it looks like he was right.'

296

Nothing she said appeared to be giving him any solace. He looked increasingly concerned, and increasingly trying to conceal it.

'You met with Julian Sanquhar? Who else have you spoken to?'

'I'll answer your questions when you start answering mine. What I will say is that Sanquhar was genuinely afraid, like by probing into this I was likely to raise the devil himself.'

Jasmine had chosen her words carefully and they had their impact. She saw him flinch: nothing pronounced, but there was a noticeable flash of alarm about his eyes.

'We don't mention such things lightly, Miss Sharp,' he replied, his voice dropping as though afraid of who might overhear. 'And certainly not on sacred ground.'

'I'm sorry. No offence intended: it was a figure of speech. I'm just curious as to why nobody wants to talk about what happened here, and why Julian Sanquhar seemed so concerned.'

'It sounds to me like you should have heeded his advice. I'm heartened that nobody wants to talk to you about this. It proves they feel shame. Remorse. There was something wanton and corrupt in those people, and they sought to corrupt us too. We were innocents. My sister was just a girl, yet she was taken advantage of in the most squalid and disgraceful way.'

'What happened to her?'

He shook his head gravely. Jasmine couldn't tell whether it was in refusal to answer or in bitter remembrance.

'There was evil abroad in that place. They both summoned it and were consumed by it, willingly so. People talk about being seduced, about giving in to the darkest desires they wouldn't admit to even harbouring. I can forgive that: it is human weakness. But when those desires are not their own, when they are driven by something that did not come from within and they become something other than themselves . . .'

He glanced away to the west, towards the ancient woods that bordered the Kildrachan estate, his face grey with loathing and anxiety.

'Miss Sharp, people like you don't fear Satan because you think science and psychology have explained him away. In truth, you're falling for his disguise. I did too. Satan walked among us at Kildrachan as surely as you have walked through this churchyard. We didn't recognise him until it was too late, but then, that's how he works. He is the Deceiver.'

*　　　*　　　*

'I think we should take a detour via Logie-Almond,' Jasmine said as they hit the road back south. 'I'm guessing there was quite a bit Finlay Weir neglected to tell me.'

'Aye. Almost as much as Creeping Jesus back there.'

'True, but he wasn't going to give us anything else, whereas we can put the screws on Weir because I'd wager much of what he didn't tell me concerns Creeping Jesus, or more accurately his kid sister. He gave us Saffron, probably because he reckoned she would be untraceable, but made no mention of those two.'

Jasmine had suggested to Tormod that they ought

298

to go and talk to his sister instead, hoping to elicit some angry and hence unguarded disclosure, but he had snorted dismissively.

'Good luck with that,' he replied. 'She lives in Sydney, has done for twenty years. She works in television, making costumes.'

So not *that* traumatised by her brush with the decadent thesps, Jasmine thought. She'd got away from here, though, *tout de suite*: glimpsed another life when the circus passed through town and decided she was having it. Tormod had glimpsed something that scared him, and ultimately retreated. He had been drawn to the Glass Shoe people by the irresistible allure conveyed by his father's disapproval, but ended up filling his robes.

The retreat hadn't been total, however. He started at Glasgow Uni in 1981, which would have been the September after whatever had happened at Kildrachan. Despite that, when he had to find a third subject he still chose theatre, and took an interest to this day. Perhaps it had shown him a side of himself he didn't want to admit to, but nor could he entirely free himself of it.

'You know,' said Fallan, 'this shit used to be a lot easier back in the day. You would just tie somebody to a chair, show them a selection of power tools and a site transformer, and all of a sudden they'd get this cathartic urge to tell you everything you wanted to know.'

Jasmine said nothing.

'That was a joke, by the way,' he clarified.

'Yeah, you'll probably find that kind of humour works best on people whose relatives you didn't murder.'

It was Fallan's turn to respond with silence.

299

She felt bad for saying what she had and was about to apologise, then saw the situation for what it was and asked herself what the hell *she* was feeling bad for. She couldn't help it, though. She did feel bad.

'I'm grateful to you for sticking around,' she told him, her voice threatening to catch in her throat. 'You don't owe me anything. Well, you do, but I'm not holding you to any obligations. I won't pretend I don't need your help right now, though.'

'Needs must when the devil drives,' he said, and she saw a little glint of humour in his smile, amused by their mutual awareness of who was at the wheel.

It made her think of the Reverend Tormod McDonald again, and of Julian Sanquhar. Both men were disturbed by the belief that Satan was more than just a name we gave to the worst in ourselves.

'Sanquhar gave this interview to the *Sunday Times* a few years back,' she told Fallan. 'He said: "You go and ask the soldiers who were in Bosnia, in Kosovo, in Rwanda. They'll tell you there are evils in this world greater than man." I'm guessing you've seen some very bad things in your time, and done some truly dark deeds. Do you believe there's something outside of man that can make him worse than he would otherwise be?'

'Yes,' Fallan replied. 'Drink.'

'I'm being serious here.'

'So am I. Entirely. But if you want to know about Satan, let me tell you a wee story. Guy I knew, back in very bad times, name of Malky. Bad, bad bastard. A brutal reputation even among men for whom violence was a way of life. He'd been in the game a long time before I met him, by which point he'd become a born-again Christian. It was an AA thing: he'd been on the programme and he was very committed to everything he did. Never did anything by half, so if he was going on the wagon he was riding it all the way. Anyway, the twelve steps were kind of a gateway drug to Christianity, and he took that very seriously too. Everything stopped for church.'

Fallan dropped a gear and accelerated. He was taking advantage of a break in the oncoming traffic to overtake a tractor, but it turned left into a field as he did so, through a gap in the hedge that had been invisible upon their approach.

'Malky worked for Tony McGill, remember him?'

'The self-styled old-school gangster?'

'That's the one. Some chancer had ripped Tony off on a deal, something to do with smuggled cigarettes. The guy was seriously taking the piss and wasn't listening to reason, shall we say. Malky had been Tony's man on the deal, so I remember Tony asking Malky what he was going to do about it. Malky's response was these exact words:

'"Tomorrow's Sunday, so I'm going to church to pray to the Lord that He'll make this guy see the error of his ways and do what's right. Then, if that doesn't work, first thing Monday morning it's balaclavas and a van."'

Jasmine covered her mouth, though she wasn't sure whether she was trying more to stifle her shock or her laughter. From Fallan's expression, she could tell the story had ultimately ended with plan B.

'The point is, religion doesn't change what's inside. People just use it to make sense of what's already there. I think Tormod is scared—scared now as he was scared then—and this is how he

301

convinces himself that it's all right to be afraid, because he was dealing with something that was too big for him to fight.'

Instruments of Darkness

Tormod had never known such torment.

He had known pain. He had known shame. He had known guilt, anguish and fear. He had no inkling they could all assail him at once, each one multiplied to the power of the last until he was tossed in the tempest of his own silent screams.

Never in his life had he more sincerely wished he could turn back the hands of time. Never had its flow seemed so irreversible, events marking him with a stain that could not be cleansed. Never had he felt so wretched, so condemned. This was something far worse than fear, because fear was a mere part of it. This was true horror, that only a damned few would ever know.

There were beliefs he had been brought up with from infancy, cautionary teachings handed down by his father that he had dutifully acknowledged, but only tonight did he realise that, until now, he had never really had faith in them. He had merely professed to believe in them, as was expected of him as a good son. Like the stories of the Old Testament and even some of the New, these stories of ancient evil, of demons, of Satan, were remote and fantastical, unrelated to the world he had grown up to understand.

He didn't truly believe in them because he didn't think he was expected to truly believe in them. He didn't even think his father truly believed in them. They were statements to be affirmed as a matter of identity; myths to be considered on a metaphorical level. They were not something you ever expected to encounter. Not something you ever expected to feel.

But now he had truly felt, and now he truly believed.

He had suffered possession, and now that it was over he understood that the possession itself was not the worst of it: merely the beginning.

What had passed before had been mere madness. He had endured the helplessness of watching in a state of delirium, confusion and fear as something else made a vessel of his body and he became a mere passenger.

He had felt desires that were not his. He had watched himself carry out deeds that were not the will of his own mind.

Then the devil's true cruelty was revealed as it passed from him once more.

It had left him, but when the scales fell he saw that the world was forever altered, and he was doomed to live in it.

The house felt different. He wandered through its corridors like a wraith, seeing agonised faces wherever he looked: every painting on the walls was staring at him in condemnation, every potted plant morphed into a chimera. He saw this place for what it was, and understood that the evil that had taken him was still here. He could feel it all around: it had passed from him but it had not departed and, worst of all, he knew it would seek out others.

Too late he ran to find Mhairi: sweet, innocent Mhairi.

He discovered her naked in the arms of a man. She was already in its grip, no longer herself. She was scornful of his words: wanton, cruel, flaunting not just her body but her lust.

His failure was complete, his anguish absolute. He didn't think anything could bring him lower. Then he heard chanting, and saw the flicker of candlelight spilling from an open door.

That was when he learned that it had not been he who summoned this evil; learned that he simply couldn't have. It took more than mere thoughts, mere will. It took what he saw beyond that door.

The ritual. The altar. The knife.

The sacrifice.

Saturnalia

They made it to Logie-Almond Academy a little before six o'clock. As Fallan drove slowly through the grounds they passed groups of pupils in their uniforms making their way from their dormitories along the paths and pavements towards the indoor sports hall.

'Will he still be around?' Fallan asked.

'Their term runs a week later than the local prole schools, and as it's a boarding school, the show isn't over when the bell rings at four.'

The last time she was here, Jasmine had spotted a notice in the reception area advertising office opening times of nine until six, as well as a phone number for out-of-hours inquiries. As it looked like there was something going on this evening, she was confident Weir would still be present.

304

Unfortunately, so was his secretary. New visitors are seldom a welcome sight when they show up five minutes before you're planning to close for the day, so it was with considerable relish that this torn-faced woman came off the phone to her boss and informed Jasmine that 'Mr Weir isn't available to speak to you.'

'We'll wait,' she said.

'No, you don't understand. Mr Weir has instructed me to inform you that he has extended his cooperation already on this matter and now wishes to be left in peace. We are about to close the office for the day, so I must ask you to leave the premises, and I am obliged to inform you that you are not at liberty to return. This is not only private property, but it is a school, and we have obligations to our pupils and their parents that . . .'

She wittered on for another few seconds, trotting out more official policy and milking the moment. Jasmine had stopped listening back at 'Mr Weir has instructed me'. She waited patiently for the woman to finish.

'That's fine,' she said, offering a breezily polite smile, no hard feelings. 'I understand. I do have a very important message for Mr Weir, but I'm happy for you to pass it on as long as you do so right now. Then we're out of here, okey-doke?'

Jasmine scribbled the words and numbers down on a piece of paper. The secretary put it to one side, then picked it up again when Jasmine made it clear she wasn't leaving until it had been relayed to its intended recipient.

The secretary picked up the phone and pushed a button.

'Yes, I'm sorry to disturb you again, Mr Weir. I've

305

been asked to pass on the following message. It looks like some sort of code, but I'm assured you'll understand what it means. It says simply: "Mhairi McDonald, Balnavon, five, eleven, sixty-six. Eighty-one minus sixty-six equals fifteen."'

It was not so much a code as a password, and it gained them full access about ten seconds later.

'You don't know Mhairi McDonald's date of birth,' Fallan said under his breath as they were escorted to the headmaster's office.

'Neither does Weir.'

Weir's office was bigger than Jasmine's whole flat, and its furniture was probably worth more. Leather-bound volumes lined the shelves of towering bookcases either side of a fireplace she could have driven her old Civic through. It certainly vindicated her previous strategy of speaking to him away from his power centre. Under most circumstances, this kind of environment would have provided a quite formidable home advantage to the host, but it wasn't going to do him much good today. When you're a boarding-school headmaster staring down the barrel of an underage sex accusation, you can't really get much further on to the back foot. Furthermore, home advantage or power centre, nobody could be said to be in their comfort zone when Glen Fallan was sitting opposite.

'None of it was what you think,' Weir said, having waited until he was sure his secretary was well back down the corridor before opening his mouth.

'Well, people do rush to fill in the blanks when you withhold information,' Jasmine replied, outlining her agenda. 'Nature abhors a vacuum.'

'She told me she was eighteen.'

'But you didn't believe her, did you?'

306

Weir sighed, glancing around as though there might be a secret exit he could slip through. Ordinarily, sitting at that great antique desk he'd be in his element, but right then he just looked trapped behind an immovable obstacle.

'You're right. I didn't believe her. I thought she was lying about her age because of the drink. I knew she was trying to act more grown-up than she really was, but I'd never have believed she was under sixteen.'

'Yes you would. Otherwise why would you leave her and her brother out of the story?'

'Because I'm a headmaster here in this place, and any kind of moral question mark, however tenuous, can be toxic. But I would never have allowed myself to get involved with her if I'd thought she was underage.'

'Tormod McDonald said she was taken advantage of. Was Mhairi an easy score after you struck out with Tessa?'

'Tormod knows nothing. She wasn't taken advantage of; far from it. I could see what she was; I could see what they both were: small-town kids who were thrilled to be getting to play at being grown-ups. We didn't patronise them and we didn't lead them anywhere they didn't want to go.'

'And where did Mhairi want to go?' Jasmine asked.

'Further than I was prepared to take her,' Weir replied sternly. 'When I realised Tessa was only interested in Hamish I was a little wounded. The last thing I was looking for was to get involved with somebody else. I was quite withdrawn, in fact, but Mhairi kind of snuck in under the radar because she wasn't someone with whom I thought anything

307

would happen. Then all of a sudden it did.'

A hint of a sad smile played across his face.

'She was a sweet girl. More mature than Tormod credited anyway, and with her eyes set on the big wide world. But I could see she was trying a little too hard to be something she was not; or at least something she was not yet. She was a virgin. And she stayed a virgin, though she wanted it to be otherwise.'

'So you did have your concerns that she was underage?'

'I really didn't. I just felt that it wasn't my place. It would have spoiled what we had together, because although she said she wanted to, I knew she only thought she wanted to.'

'Why did Tormod think something more had happened?'

'Tormod knew Mhairi and I were an item, shall we say, for a few days, and had no problem with it. But on the same night that Tessa disappeared, he freaked out. He burst into my room and found us in bed together. I thought he was drunk, but I suspect he was on more than just booze. He seemed physically erratic and emotionally strung out. He tried to drag Mhairi from the room, even though she was naked. I restrained him and he started ranting and raving at me, accusing me of corrupting his sister. She told him to fuck off. I don't just mean that as a figure of speech: Tormod clearly had an issue with "cursing", as he called it, so she was choosing her words to drive the point home.'

'And did he, as requested, fuck off?' Fallan asked.

'Yes. He seemed all the more distraught that his sister had rebuffed his rescue attempt and preferred to stay in the clutches of evil and depravity. He went wandering off like a wraith and Mhairi slammed the door behind him.'

'Did the police ask you about this?' Jasmine asked. 'You know, when you were being held for questioning, as you neglected to mention the last time we spoke.'

Weir sighed with exasperation.

'They questioned everybody,' he said.

'Not at the station.'

'They took me in because someone must have told them about me and Tessa. They were struggling, and it was about the only narrative they could work with: the jealous suitor angle. It was nonsense and they knew it. They didn't ask me about Mhairi, though.'

'Strange,' Jasmine said.

'Strange how?'

'It was Tormod who sparked the police inquiry. He told the sergeant, confidentially, that he'd seen a woman being stabbed and then somebody dragging a body in the grounds. But despite his overwrought condition, and how angry he must have been, he can't have told them about you and Mhairi.'

'No. He must have been protecting her, afraid for her reputation or concerned she'd get into trouble. He was very fond of Mhairi: sibling allies against the rule of their father. But you say he told the police he saw someone stabbed? This is the first I've ever heard about it.'

'The sergeant kept a very tight lid on who knew what. He was keen to avoid a scandal, and he had his doubts over the reliability of Tormod's account for the same reasons you just described: he was distraught and possibly intoxicated.'

309

'He was pretty out of it,' Weir agreed. 'We all were, but neither drugs nor alcohol were the most potent part of the cocktail. We were intoxicated more by feelings of abandon and saturnalia because we knew it was all coming to an end. Even before Tessa left we knew it was falling apart. It's where the word decadence comes from: to fall away. I think people pushed things further that night because they sensed it was over.'

'Where were the drugs coming from?' asked Fallan.

Weir swallowed, looking like a kid who doesn't want to grass on his mates.

'Darius,' he eventually replied. 'He had all sorts of stuff.'

'You guys were up there the best part of a month. That would have to be some size of stash. Well-hidden too, if the police didn't find anything.'

'I suppose. It wasn't really my thing. And I'm not just saying that because I have to distance myself from drugs. They've never interested me.'

Fallan nodded understandingly. Jasmine wondered why he'd asked; professional curiosity perhaps. Then he spoke again.

'Mr Weir, we both appreciate the importance of your reputation and we're grateful for you taking the time to speak to us. I think it's only fair to inform you that Miss Sharp here just made up a date of birth for Mhairi McDonald, whom we believe to have been at least sixteen and possibly seventeen in the summer of 1981. You don't have anything to worry about with regard to that story going public.'

Weir's eyes flashed with a combination of relief and anger at this revelation, but his outrage at her

310

deceit—not to mention Jasmine's own dismay at Fallan giving up this leverage—was stemmed by the sense that there was a qualification still to come.

'However,' he resumed, 'if in our subsequent inquiries we find out that you have been withholding further information from us, then we will be making the press aware of your connection to Hamish Queen, the various motives you might have for wishing him harm and the fact that you have ready access to rifles and live ammunition.'

Fallan said nothing for a few moments, letting the silence grow, watching carefully to see what was in Weir's eyes.

'If you've told us everything, then we really have nothing to fear from each other.'

An expression of resignation fell upon Weir's face.

'I haven't done anything wrong, and I haven't hurt anybody,' he said. 'I want to know what happened to Tessa, same as you, but I don't want to be collateral damage on your quest. There are two things I can't afford to be tainted by: sexual impropriety and drugs. There was no impropriety about what happened between Mhairi and I, but rumours and innuendo can be enough. As for drugs, same goes. There's no statute of limitations when it comes to boards of governors.'

'Surely they wouldn't fire you over a few tokes when you were in your twenties, even if you did inhale?' Jasmine suggested.

'Have you seen the fees for this place? Do you think parents are going to spend that kind of money sending their children to a boarding school where there's that kind of question mark over the headmaster?'

311

'How big a question mark are we talking? More than just a few tokes?'

'Not so much the volume as the supply. As your colleague here seemed to divine, Russell Darius wasn't the source. I'm going to tell you who was, but on the understanding that my name is kept out of this. Being revealed to have a connection to this man, however tenuous, could be disastrous for me.'

'We're not here to blackmail you, Mr Weir,' Jasmine assured him. 'We're just trying to get to the truth. Who was the dealer?'

Weir swallowed.

'Sammy Finnegan.'

The name didn't mean anything to Jasmine, but Fallan let out a wry chuckle that suggested he understood why this was a flag Weir wasn't happy to wave.

'He was the final member of the team at Kildrachan. He was a joiner, to trade, and Darius brought him along as set-builder on a cash-in-hand basis. Sammy was a very cash-in-hand kind of guy. He wasn't a bad chippy, but that wasn't why he was hired. He was Darius's dealer and principal drug buddy. He had connections in Glasgow and drove down to score new stuff when he needed it.'

'You knew him?' she asked Fallan.

'Showbiz Sam,' he replied. 'Cultivated a niche market that was about quality over quantity, and I mean the quality of the customer and therefore what he could charge them because he guaranteed discretion and reliability. He sold to people who couldn't afford to be caught scoring off some wee ned in a nightclub.'

'Sells,' corrected Weir. 'Present tense. Which is why it wouldn't help me to point out that my

312

involvement with him was thirty years ago. He supplies drugs at the high end of the market. Discretion assured, yes, but if people find out I've a connection to a guy like that, then innuendo would take care of the rest. As far as anyone knows, he could have been quietly supplying me for decades.'

'He was also known as Snobby Sam,' Fallan added. 'He was effete and pretentious, which in that game you can't get away with unless you're also hard as nails and have a couple of guys on your payroll who are also hard as nails. He'd a genuine taste for culture, though. Other folk couldn't muscle in on his market because they couldn't move in the same circles, didn't know how to speak the language.'

'He learned that at Kildrachan,' Weir said. 'When he first showed up he'd have thought Chekhov was just a bloke in *Star Trek*. Now I gather he's quite a fixture on the scene: all the opening nights, all the gallery exhibitions, a reputable patron of the arts, a respectable family man who's on first-name terms with all the movers and shakers.'

'Movers and shakers such as Murray Maxwell, perhaps?' Jasmine suggested.

'I didn't say that. Murray certainly partook back then, but we all did. A few spliffs to wind down with, a bit of speed if we were wanting to work on something through the night. Darius was into his trips, though: always interested in altered states. He was fascinated by what transforms consciousness, what makes you who you are, whether if you alter the mind you alter the person so that it's someone else inside the same body: the same themes he explored in his movies.'

'And how did Hamish feel about all this going on

in his house?' Jasmine asked.

'All right at first. He didn't mind a bit of blow, and I think he'd have been okay as long as he knew his family were out of the country, but it was Tessa who really objected. It was getting in the way of the work, and if she wasn't happy, Hamish wasn't happy. She and Sammy ended up having a stand-up argument in which there was only ever going to be one winner. Hamish fired him, part of a doomed last-ditch attempt to hold everything together and get the rehearsals back on track. That's why the police never found any drugs: Sammy was gone, which was another reason everybody went for it that night. We were blowing what was left because we knew the party was over.'

The Fugitive

Catherine's hackles were well-risen by the time she had made it from the front entrance of the Royal Scottish Bank's ostentatiously plush Edinburgh headquarters to the reception desk on the far side of the lobby, across an expanse of marble floor larger than her garden. Clearly not everybody was quite so struck by the building's interior splendour as management would like, as there was scaffolding up on two sides as part of a controversial multi-million-pound refit. Having been bailed out by the taxpayer to the tune of eleven figures, in their chastened state it was heartening to see the banks embracing a new era of corporate austerity. We were, let's not forget, all in this together.

Looking at the opulence of her surroundings, she

couldn't help but think of the condition of most police stations she'd been in recently, and more to the point the state of Duncan and Fraser's school. It was a flimsy eighties-built one-storey structure that looked like a temporary building-site headquarters, an effect enhanced recently by a proliferation of men in hard hats who had concluded that the place was literally falling apart.

Mustn't go down that road, though, she thought. That's the 'politics of envy'. If anybody in this country ever deserved a slap in the dish with a dead salmon, it was whichever smug and spoiled little prick came up with that one. Execs were trousering bonuses of several million pounds, even for the years in which their companies had recorded a huge loss, while freezing wages down the line where they weren't simply laying people off. But if you pointed out the inequity of this, that phrase was their catch-all comeback.

She thought of the joke Drew had told her the night before, when she informed him of the next morning's first port of call.

A banker, an asylum seeker and a *Daily Mail* reader get shipwrecked and end up floating on a raft with nothing but a ten-pack of Mars bars to sustain them. The banker announces that he is an expert in resource management and so for everyone's good he should take charge of the food. He proceeds to open the pack and stuffs nine of them into his mouth. Once he's swallowed the last he gives the remaining bar to the *Daily Mail* reader, saying: 'I'd keep my eye on that asylum seeker, if I were you. He'll be after your chocolate.'

'My name is Catherine McLeod,' she said. 'I'm here to see Gavin Shields, your head of marketing.'

The receptionist glanced at her computer screen, scrolling with her mouse, then fixed Catherine with a polite but steely stare.

'I can't see any appointment listed for today. Are you sure he's expecting you?'

'I'm pretty sure he's not,' Catherine replied, producing her warrant card. 'But why don't you phone upstairs and see if he can squeeze me in.'

* * *

Gavin Shields' office looked north, with a view of the castle to the left and Princes Street Gardens spread out beneath at the foot of the Mound. Catherine guessed that you could see across to Fife on a clear day.

He had escorted her inside without delay, and had his secretary offer her freshly brewed tea or coffee. She wasn't thirsty, but accepted, wanting to give the impression this was little more than a polite visit. When you say no to the drinks, they know they're in trouble.

Shields was putting on a false face too, but in his inexperience he'd chosen the wrong one. He was being friendly and cooperative, polite to the point of solicitous. From the moment he'd come down to the lobby—in person—he'd been acting like her visit was no imposition, or if it was, that he entirely understood the importance of it and was extending his assistance accordingly.

A busy man who had done nothing wrong would have every right to seem just a little miffed at having the police show up unannounced and insinuate themselves into his working day. A man with nothing to hide, and who had already given

316

the police a statement, might betray a hint of resentment that they were back for more on his time, as opposed to theirs.

Of course, it was always possible she was misreading this, due to having failed to factor in bank executives' natural humility.

'Did you know Hamish Queen?' she asked him.

'No, not personally. I'd only ever met him once before the other night.'

'And when was that?'

'Same place, same circumstances. A previous trip to Cragruthes for the moonlight Shakespeare thing. It was, let me think, 2007.'

'Did he have a connection with the bank? Was there a reason he was there on the same night as your corporate booking?'

'No connection that I'm aware of. Just coincidence. I'm told he came to one performance of the moonlit play each summer. Chances were we'd cross paths, as we've had at least one trip every year since it started.'

'*At least* one?'

'Yes. It's a very popular event. There have been years when we've had multiple outings. We've cut it back to one since the, er, late unpleasantness.'

'We've all had to tighten our belts,' Catherine said, trying to keep the pH of her voice not too far below seven.

If Shields picked up on the dig he wasn't going to show it. He was too intent on being the cooperative witness.

'I'm guessing that made the places all the more coveted,' she suggested. 'A Wonka's golden ticket.'

'Absolutely,' agreed Shields. 'I realise some people would make a fuss about us spending five hundred pounds a head on a hospitality junket, but that's what Oscar Wilde was talking about when he said people knew the price of everything and the value of nothing. You've no idea how valuable a trip such as this one is in terms of keeping business flowing.'

'So who decides who's all coming?'

Shields gave a good-natured sigh; or at least his best impression of a good-natured sigh.

'That's a more complex and delicate political process than Middle East peace negotiations, believe me.'

'Perhaps you could talk me through it, give me some examples. Can you get this year's list up on your computer?'

'Sure,' he said.

Catherine stepped around the back of his desk and stood alongside him as he opened the document.

'What kind of notice do people have?' she asked. 'I mean, would they know they were coming a month back? Longer?'

'We try to invite people six weeks in advance, which allows us to re-allocate places if anybody can't make it.'

'Yes. Sir Angus told us you sometimes keep places empty right up until the last minute. Is that in case you have a blue-chip VIP show up at short notice?'

'It has been. Or as likely somebody we need to compensate for a screw-up,' he suggested, laughing. 'It's just a question of leaving a little slack in the system. Sometimes it goes empty, as this year. You can often fill it at literally the last minute—tell somebody that if they can pack a bag and be there on time, the place is theirs—but sometimes it's just not practical.'

'I see. I was just curious because of *this*. Do you mind?' she asked, taking the mouse from him.

'No, go ahead,' Shields replied, sounding a little unsure.

Catherine did as Beano had shown her, clicking on the Review tab at the head of the document, which changed the array of icons laid out across the top of the page. She then pulled down the Show Markup sub-menu and placed a tick against the Insertions and Deletions option.

The previously neat document was suddenly a mess of coloured fonts, shaded underlays and outlined bubbles.

'Wee trick I learned. It shows all the revisions that have gone on. I guessed it would tell quite a tale in terms of who was added and subtracted at various stages.'

'Yes,' Shields said, giggling, trying to sound in amused agreement rather than nervous. He still thought he might be getting away with it, though. 'It would be serious blackmail material round here if it showed who took certain names out.'

'Ah, but it does show that. See? There's even a different colour for each user who's edited the document. And the reason I'm showing it to you is that before sending us the copy we requested, user GShields—that's you, I take it—removed the name John Smith. Can you see it there? See the scoring-out marks to indicate it was a deletion?'

She turned her head to clock his response. He looked like she could have been showing him Goatse.

'Both printed copies of the seating plan for your corporate dinner were removed from the

319

Cragruthes dining room and the document deleted from the castle computer, as was the earlier version of this list sent to finalise the booking. Right now I could do you for concealing evidence from a murder investigation, and I reckon I could easily bump that up to conspiracy to pervert the course of justice, because I'm sure you're not the only person who's lying about this. So I'm only going to ask you once: who is John Smith?'

Shields seemed to deflate, his head slumping to his elbows on the desk, his face disappearing into his interlocked fingers. He took a couple of breaths, then straightened himself in his chair.

'This is not what you think,' he said, his voice barely above an apologetic rasping whisper.

'That's not what I asked you. And if the next two words you issue are not—'

'Francis Wyngarde. Our mystery guest was Francis Wyngarde. Do you get it now?'

Francis Wyngarde. The man who had presided over the Royal Scottish Bank's tailspin into crushing debt, all the while still lining his pockets in a manner that would have shamed most third-world dictators. He was the poster-child for the credit crunch and, in Catherine's opinion, along with Fred Goodwin something of an Aunt Sally whom the financial sector were content to abandon to public flogging because hatred of individuals lessened the impetus to attack the system itself.

Several years on, Wyngarde was still fiercely reviled by the public, but apparently retained certain connections in high places. The bank evidently knew it was way too early to begin any attempt at rehabilitating his reputation, but they were dipping their toe in gentle waters at

Cragruthes, where he would be in the company of RSB executives and certain highly favoured business people whose discretion could presumably be relied upon. Perhaps sounding out the latter group's response had in fact been the purpose of the exercise, knowing that if they disapproved they would do so quietly. And perhaps they just wanted him to know he still had friends.

'We kept his name secret because all sorts of people see this list,' Shields explained. 'This was not a public event. It's not like we had him in our sponsors' box at the Scottish Cup Final.'

'I understand the distinction,' Catherine said, disguising her growing anger.

'When Hamish Queen was shot we knew we had to get Francis out of the picture. He was gone before the ambulance or the police even arrived. We had a driver and a limo up there; we always do, in case somebody suddenly has to be somewhere fast. It was already going to be toxic from a PR point of view, but if the media got wind that Francis Wyngarde had been our guest, that night of all nights . . .'

'Quite. I can certainly see why that would be your number one priority, with a guy lying dead on the grass near by.'

'With respect, there was nothing we could do about that.'

Catherine took a moment, making sure she didn't respond in anger. She forced herself to smile, an invaluable exercise in screwing the nut that Moira had taught her. Not only did it help stem the flow of emotion and allow her to compose herself, but she lost nothing in terms of conveying her dismay. Shields found it all the more disturbing than if she

321

was blazing in rage.

'You don't see it at all, do you?' she said. 'The arrogance. It's quite breathtaking. Thinking your business is so important that it doesn't need to pay its respects to a dead man, and prizing its reputation above the needs of our investigation into that man's murder. That's why I could think of no more fitting redress than to make sure this appears on every front page tomorrow; every news bulletin.'

She took in the horror in Shields' face for a few moments, letting him truly contemplate what that was going to feel like.

'But I won't.'

He stared at her, his expression confused and apprehensive, as though afraid to believe this was for real. Eventually he found his voice.

'Detective Superintendent, I don't think I need to say how much I appreciate—'

'Save it,' she interrupted. 'But understand this. One day, Mr Shields, I am going to come to the RSB in my professional capacity to ask for a favour; most likely a very, very big favour. And when I do, you are going to be the bank that likes to say "yes".'

* * *

Catherine was still fizzing with rage as she made her way back across the marble tundra towards the exit. She was so furious she had half a mind to go back on her word and tell the media anyway. Fortunately, professional caution intervened. She knew she didn't want *that* media nightmare all over what was already a high-profile investigation. Besides, she knew that her real anger was down to the fact that the missing name had turned out to be nothing. They'd all wasted their time over a red herring and up at Cragruthes they were literally scrabbling in the dirt looking for a clue.

Her phone rang as she emerged on to the street, a light drizzle blowing towards her from the east. The display read DI Geddes.

'This better be good news, Laura, because I just hit a brick wall here.'

'Then allow me to shunt you back on to the track. We've found the shooter.'

Drug Culture

Jasmine was waiting in the circle bar of the Theatre Royal, watching Sammy Finnegan and his wife enter for their pre-ordered interval drinks. He'd have been difficult to pick out if she hadn't seen some recent photographs, as nothing about the man's appearance said 'drug dealer'. Indeed, it said it all that the pics were from the society pages of a glossy called *Caledonia Life*, captioned pap-snaps of the great and the good at a black-tie charity fundraiser held inside Kelvingrove Museum and Art Gallery. Not for him the ned-with-cash vulgarity, sun-lounger orange complexion and threads at least a decade too young for him.

In the course of her work Jasmine had seen a few of Glasgow's bad boys made good, and those who had cultivated an air of respectability tended to look like retired boxers or football players: smartly dressed, nothing to prove to anybody any more but still carrying themselves with a certain bristling edge. Finnegan was known to be able to look after himself, but there were no exterior indicators. He looked like this was where he belonged. His wife did too. She was older than him, dressing elegantly for her age, no evidence of Botox or lip-filler. She looked very much at home, unselfconscious, double-kissing friends as Finnegan headed to the bar.

They were here for an RSC touring production of *Othello*. Jasmine had called her friend Michelle and got her to browse the Theatre Royal's box-office database, hoping to get an address for Finnegan. Michelle was able to do better than that, informing her that he had bought two tickets for the touring show the following night. In the meantime Jasmine had put in a couple of shifts for Galt Linklater, some very boring bread-and-butter surveillance stuff. She'd spent the best part of two days sitting in a van watching a house, from which the subject never emerged. It could happen like that sometimes. On one level it was easy money, but she felt the boredom all the more pronounced as it was like being in limbo, suspended in nothingness while she waited to resume her investigation into what had happened at Kildrachan House.

She knew that if Mrs Petrie suddenly phoned up to call it off she'd keep going anyway. She had a need for answers now, rendered all the more pronounced by having so many people evade, stall and outright lie to her. She wanted to know who had torched her car, or perhaps who had ordered it to happen, and not least because she wanted to be able to ram the facts of it down that arsehole polisman's throat.

The fruitless surveillance had at least given her the time to make some calls to the UK Border

324

Agency. She didn't have an 'in' there, so she was wading through treacle in terms of negotiating the bureaucracy, but she had eventually spoken to someone who had agreed to delve into the archives on her behalf. Roni Simpson, aka Saffron, was a New Zealander, so there had to be record of her entering the UK. Given her well-travelled and rootless lifestyle, Jasmine was conscious she may well have left it again following her midnight flit from Balnavon, and she wanted that confirmed before she started looking in a haystack for a needle that had bailed thirty years ago. The bloke at the Border Agency said he'd see what he could do, but she wasn't holding her breath.

She sidled up to her mark as he reached the bar, her mobile phone in hand.

'Mr Finnegan?' she asked brightly.

He turned, giving her a practised greeting smile, but she could see the flicker of uncertainty in his face provoked by his failing to recognise her. His eyes flitted to one side, perhaps checking for somebody. Fallan had said he would have back-up in the vicinity; nobody conspicuous, nor evidently in Finnegan's company, but they would be watching. They'd be young, fit, game and probably tooled. She wondered what they made of having to sit through Shakespeare of an evening, but then their job wasn't to watch the stage.

'Yes?' he replied, calm and curious, unthreatened by what he found before him. But that was why she was the ninja.

'I think you should have a look at this email,' she said, passing her phone to him.

It was addressed to Detective Superintendent Catherine McLeod, and CCed to several

325

journalists, the subject header stating: 'Society drug-dealer's secret link to Hamish Queen'.

The body copy was prefaced by a list of bullet points summing up Finnegan's involvement in the Glass Shoe Company, his clash with Tessa Garrion, his subsequent firing by Hamish Queen and the troubling fact that Tessa disappeared two days later and had never been seen since.

She could tell Finnegan was a past master at putting a calm face on things, a man who knew that giving way to his base emotions was an unaffordable indulgence, but he still looked rattled.

'Who are you?'

She passed him a card with a name and address scribbled on the back.

'My associate and I would like a wee chat after the show. We'll be at this café-bar on Hope Street. And just so that you're not tempted to do anything rash, that email is in an outbox scheduled to refresh in a few hours. We can't stop it from sending if anything happens to us.'

He regained his composure, visibly relieved to learn that these things didn't have to go public and the price was just some information.

'A wee chat about what?' he asked calmly, managing a cold smile.

'Kildrachan. Summer of eighty-one. People don't want to talk about this for some reason.'

'Maybe it's because it was the Scottish play,' he replied sardonically.

'Well, apologies for the ambush tactics, but I'm sick of being stonewalled. Enjoy the rest of the show.'

'Could have been worse,' he deadpanned. 'You could have threatened to tell me the ending.'

326

Finnegan turned up at the basement café-bar less than ten minutes after final curtain, no longer accompanied by his wife. He appeared to be unaccompanied by any wingmen either, but a smartly dressed man in his thirties had cased the place a minute or so before, John the Baptist to his Jesus Christ. Finnegan went to the counter, ordering a double espresso and a repeat of whatever the place's only other two customers were drinking, then made his way across to their booth.

'How was that ending?' Jasmine asked as he sat down.

'"Oh bloody period",' he quoted. She waited for a quip in keeping with the line's capacity for juvenile amusement, but he didn't seem in the mood for levity. Even if they hadn't been shaking him down for information the man had, after all, just sat through *Othello*.

'There's part of me kind of wishes he'd never written it,' Finnegan said. 'I mean, there's tragedy and then there's *that*. One poisonous individual bringing out the worst in good people, spreading so much unnecessary suffering. I'll always go, but I never look forward to it.'

Finnegan was definitely not what she was expecting. He wasn't some player who had learned to talk the talk merely in order to blend in with his rarefied customer base. He lived this stuff. However, Glen had warned her that it would be catastrophic to mistake a degree of artistic sensitivity for weakness. Plenty were bound to have done before, and he wouldn't be where he was if he hadn't put them straight.

With that in mind she thought she'd best remind him that she had her own recourse should things turn less cordial.

'This is my associate, Glen Fallan.'

Finnegan began instinctively extending a hand and then hesitated as the words hit home. The pause only lasted a fraction of a second, but they were all aware of it.

'We never had the pleasure,' Finnegan said, recovering to meet Fallan's grip across the table. 'But your reputation precedes you. And, rather confusingly, part of that reputation concerns you being dead for about twenty years.'

'I got better.'

One of the bar staff brought their drinks. Finnegan took a sip of espresso and sat up straight.

'So,' he said, 'what can I do for you?'

'Tell us about Kildrachan,' Jasmine replied.

'Why don't you tell me what you already know so that I don't waste any time. I don't want you being late back to wherever that email is waiting for a cancel command.'

'We know you were there, ostensibly as Russell Darius's construction carpenter, but mainly as his drug supplier.'

'I would dispute the balance of that,' he said, taking another sip of espresso. As far as she could tell, he wasn't being facetious, and despite his awareness that he was on a clock, this was clearly a distinction he felt it important to make. 'I spent a lot more time building sets than scoring dope.'

'Nonetheless, I'm led to believe Tessa Garrion thought that the latter activity was impacting disproportionately on the entire production. You

328

had what has been described as a stand-up row with her, after which Hamish Queen fired you. Two days after that, Tessa was gone and the police were investigating reports of someone dragging a body through the grounds of the house. Then, thirty years later, I start digging around these incidents and suddenly Hamish Queen is dead.'

'I think even the Glasgow polis would consider that thin.'

'So thin you came running here to prevent us sending that email.'

'It wasn't the polis I was worried about, and I'm sure you know that. My business relies upon discretion.'

'You're not denying what happened, though.'

'Why would I? It's true. Tessa and I did have our arguments, more than one. What's thin is to imagine I'd be creeping about two days later, killing her in revenge for being given my cards. And as for what happened to poor Hamish, this is the first time I've heard it suggested the two things might be related. I've never killed anybody, Miss Sharp. Had to do a few things I'm not proud of to protect my interests, but never that. Not everybody at this table can say the same.'

He eyed Fallan warily as he took another sip of coffee, as though concerned he might have spoken out of turn. Jasmine noted that for all his measured composure and control, he was very defensive about his own sense of integrity. A man caught between worlds, able to move in the higher one but largely because of what he could bring from the realm beneath.

'Tessa didn't need Hamish to fight her battles,' he said, almost in a hurry to put some distance

329

on his last remark. 'She was tougher than she looked, very driven. I didn't like being painted as the bad guy, though. I was a convenient scapegoat for everybody's excesses, and some were more excessive than others. She found it easier to blame me than to confront Darius. I called her bluff, though. She threatened to phone the police about the drugs and I said go ahead.'

'Ballsy call,' said Fallan. 'Especially when the Highland plods would have found it very easy to railroad a wee Glesca keelie out of town rather than upset the laird's son and his Oxbridge chums.'

'A calculated risk,' Finnegan replied. 'I got the impression she was more concerned about the law than I was. One of her frequent complaints about the drugs was that they were going to bring the cops down on us all. I called it right: she backed down.'

'And so she got Hamish to fire you instead,' said Jasmine, watching carefully for what emotions his recollection might betray.

'I didn't bear Tessa a grudge. For one thing, I knew Hamish didn't fire me because of her: he fired me to try to undermine Darius. They were always at loggerheads, and I reckon in his desperation Hamish convinced himself Darius could be reined in if he got rid of his drug-pushing blue-collar bad influence. It wasn't me who was the problem, though. I wasn't *pushing* drugs; that wasn't why I went in the first place and it wasn't why I stayed. I was happy enough to be involved with what was going on; I'd never been part of anything like it.'

He stared into his little white cup, a pleasant recollection turning sour like the last gritty dregs at the bottom.

'When I was fired I wasn't sad to get out of there.

330

I'd had a good time, but we were well past the point where it stopped being fun. It was all coming to an end, anyone could see that, and it was a relief not to be witnessing the final throes, let me assure you. Darius was starting to scare the shit out of me.'

There it was again: the man with a redundant first name.

'I notice you refer to him as Darius,' Jasmine observed, 'but you called Hamish and Tessa by their first names. Why is that?'

'I called him Russell when I first knew him. Early days at Kildrachan, I was still calling him Russell. But I was calling him Darius by the end, like everybody else. To his face, at least. Behind his back they started calling him Dangerous.'

'Was there a kind of Smeagol/Gollum thing going on with him?' Jasmine asked.

'You could say that. Not a split personality, but there were definitely two sides he could choose to show you. Russell was the softer side, the name his mother called him, the name Tessa called him when she was trying to appeal to his better nature. Darius was what he got called at school and I think he embraced it as the name of his more public self. A face he could show to the world, a mask he could wear, and you can misbehave if you're wearing a mask.'

'Are we talking about drugs here, or something more?'

'Let's just say that Darius is the reason I don't deal in hallucinogens, but it wasn't the drugs per se, more what was driving his use of them. He was looking for something within, wondering what might be already hidden inside or what he might will into himself. He was obsessed with the idea of transformation, of different selves that could inhabit the same mind. Drugs were part of that, but not the whole. It was not so much what he was doing as the fact that it evidently wasn't enough, so what was disturbing me was the worry of what he might do next.'

'Was his behaviour increasingly erratic?' Jasmine asked. 'Volatile?'

'Did he have a temper?' queried Fallan.

'Oh, he had a temper all right, as anyone who witnessed his battles with Hamish would attest, but no, he wasn't erratic or volatile. He was driven, and that was worse, as far as I was concerned. I have to admit, this is more about me than about him. I liked being part of things at Kildrachan, but the place itself could creep me out sometimes. It was my childhood vision of a haunted house. Add to that the fact that we were spending all our days working on *that* play and the atmosphere could become infused. I'm not a superstitious person, but you spend all day thinking about "reeking wounds, horrible imaginings" and being "from the crown to the toe top-full of direst cruelty" then you don't necessarily want to be spending your dark evenings with Darius.'

He stared at his cup again.

'Do you want a refill?' Jasmine asked.

'No, I think I could use something stronger.'

He summoned the barman and ordered a large malt.

'So who did want to spend their dark evenings with Darius?' Fallan asked. 'People don't like to trip alone.'

'Murray wasn't averse to a bit of experimentation. Used to make me laugh whenever I saw him play

332

that straight-edge Eliot Ness cipher on TV.'

'Do you supply Murray Maxwell still?' asked Fallan.

'I won't answer that question.'

'That's a yes.'

'No, it's an "I won't answer that question". You could ask me if I supply Alex Salmond and I'd give you the same response. If I answer it for one person, even in the negative, it compromises me for precisely the reason you've illustrated.'

'"Reputation is an idle and most false imposition,"' Jasmine quoted. '"Oft got without merit and lost without deserving."'

Finnegan eyed her with a strange mixture of suspicion and admiration.

'Iago,' he identified. 'But then, you were an actress, weren't you. I Googled you. It came up in the Ramsay reports.'

'I trained, didn't finish. I was raised on Shakespeare, though. My late mother was an actress. She had a quote for every occasion.'

'"Good name in man and woman, dear my lord, is the immediate jewel of their souls." So if you're looking for leverage to get Murray to talk, then my name plus Kildrachan should be enough. Especially for a man with designs on the top job at Scotia. He'll cooperate to keep this quiet. It was thirty years ago, but it was acid. That never plays well.'

'Anyone else?'

'Yes, Saffron. She was up for anything. That said, she'd done a lot of drugs in her time so she had kind of seen the show before. She was as much attracted to the other stuff Darius was experimenting with: the rituals.'

Jasmine sat forward involuntarily, primed by her

frustration at what Julian Sanquhar and Tormod McDonald had only alluded to.

'It started off as a laugh—a makeshift Ouija board, chants and candles—but Darius kept taking it further. He was videotaping it all too. He was interested in the theatre of the ritual: of how ritual itself was empowering. He wanted to know what it could unlock within yourself to play certain things out. He was staging these affairs with as much care and planning as putting on a play; arguably more, given that Hamish kept ditching his more *Grand Guignol* stage effects from the production.'

Finnegan took a large mouthful of whisky, about half the glass, letting it play on his palate for a moment, seeming to savour the burn, like the pain of it might be medicinal. He winced a little as he swallowed.

'I found it distasteful. I didn't believe the mumbo-jumbo was going to summon anything, but what bothered me was this fascination with evil, with blood, with death. I'm with Mr Sanquhar on this. I don't like horror movies and I'm instinctively suspicious of people who do.'

'It's not every day you encounter a squeamish drug dealer,' said Fallan. 'And a prudish one's rarer still.'

Finnegan allowed himself a small smile, like he was taking Fallan's remarks as a compliment.

'I know all too well what people are capable of, and I know what *I'm* capable of. I'm not in denial or retreat from the darker aspects of human nature. But nor do I necessarily want to be reminded of them on a night out. I prefer work that allows me to contemplate how much more we can become, what we can aspire towards.

'Darius was another little rich kid, same as Hamish and Julian, though not so old money. He never had a grounding in the everyday horrors you and I did, Mr Fallan, of growing up in places where violence can become almost banal. Darius can put an arterial spurt of blood on the screen because to him it's just an image. He'd never been there to actually smell the stuff when somebody got glassed. It's easier to fascinate upon it when it's at a remove. Horror is an escapism for him, just as beauty became an escapism for me.'

'Would you say he was seduced by the idea of evil?' Jasmine asked, thinking of the escalating process Sanquhar had described.

When there is a wanton will in man to seek the darkness, then there is something out there that listens, and it whispers back.

'The idea, yes: inasmuch as it was a nebulous concept he was too naive to understand. He was seduced by the idea of notoriety too, another little-rich-kid misbegotten aspiration, something he thought he wanted right up until the point when he got it. Notoriety is not such a desirable thing to actually *have*, as myself and Mr Fallan here could attest. Darius learned about that the hard way.'

'How?'

Finnegan shifted a little in his chair, stealing a glance at his watch, his thoughts still partly on that outbox.

'It was early in his movie-making career,' he said, 'maybe around the time of his second picture coming out. He was living in London in those days, trying to make a name for himself, get noticed. He gave an interview to some foreign underground horror cinema magazine—German, maybe, or

335

Italian—in which he said he was in possession of a snuff movie. The journalist might even have claimed to have seen it, I can't remember. It gave him a certain cachet anyway, among film-makers and audiences alike. The more you're in touch with the darkness, the more scary a person you're perceived to be, then the scarier your movies are going to seem. That was the logic, and it worked for him for a while, but there was a sting in the tail, in the shape of the video-nasties hysteria. You're too young to remember this, but it had the British tabloids in their element.'

'I remember it,' said Fallan with a curious smile. 'Served me well, in fact. A friend and I had a pirate-video rental racket going on, a dial-a-film deal: used to drive them around to folk's houses in this dilapidated van. The tabloids were in a state of high dudgeon and suddenly all these cheesy old horror movies nobody previously wanted to rent were like gold dust because the press were demanding they be banned.'

'It was a convenient distraction for the Thatcher government too,' Finnegan added. 'Nothing like a moral panic to take people's minds off mass unemployment and riots on the streets. I'll admit I have my own reservations about these films, but I also know what it is to have the authorities decide what you're selling for other people's private recreation is a gross threat to the moral order.'

This was met with a wry smile from Fallan, something Finnegan acknowledged by briefly tipping his glass to him before taking another sip.

'There was a witch-hunt, and inevitably in the midst of it some hack stumbled upon this foreign article about Darius. The Department of Public

336

Prosecutions had already got involved in the fiasco, so suddenly he had Scotland Yard kicking his door in, searching for this snuff movie.'

'Did they find anything?' asked Jasmine.

'Of course not,' Finnegan scorned. 'These days you can find executions and beheadings and all manner of real death with a few clicks of a mouse. Back then, though, the myth of the snuff movie was one of the things that helped drive the hysteria: people are being killed for entertainment! But for all the raids and confiscations, funnily enough, nobody ever produced one in court.

'That didn't bother the tabloids, of course. Darius ended up their poster-boy for everything that was evil and depraved about the video nasties. That's why he doesn't give interviews and won't be returning your calls. He got the notoriety he had wished for and found he couldn't live with it. He went off to make movies in America after that.'

'Does he still live there?' Jasmine asked, aware that this would take him out of the equation for recent events.

'No, he lives down in the Lake District, I believe, out in the wilds.'

'For the privacy,' Jasmine suggested.

'Yes. That and the fur and feathers. I gather his time in the States made him very adept at the hunting and shooting.'

Hardware

The weapon sat isolated on a sterile worksurface in the forensics lab, like the table was a display plinth for the world's ugliest cultural artefact. It was a sculpture in black metal, a little over a metre long, resting on bipod legs and a spike at the rear, a study in lethality from its butt to its muzzle. It even looked dangerous to brush against, the serrations of the picatinny and forend rails above and below the barrel looking like razor wire.

'We found it in the river,' Laura had explained. 'About a quarter of a mile from the layby where Andy Philips saw the Range Rover.'

'Someone was sharp-eyed,' Catherine replied.

'Jammy too. The hydroelectric power station a few miles upstream was undergoing a maintenance procedure and they dammed off the water. The river level dropped two or three feet as a result; less churned up as well, so the riverbed was visible. You'd normally see nothing.'

Finally they had caught a break. Now she was going to find out whether it could tell them anything and, given how this case had panned out so far, she wasn't taking that for granted.

At her request she had been met at the lab by Sergeant Mark Brooks, who had instructed her when she did her firearms training. As well as a police marksman and instructor, he was also the resident weapons anorak, all of which added to the incongruity of Catherine's previous contact with him outside the job. His two daughters, Amy and Rosie, had gone to the same nursery as Duncan and

Fraser. It was going back a few years now, though it felt like a heartbeat. She hadn't seen Amy and Rosie since Fraser started primary school, but the sight of Mark in civvies, these two delicate little princesses clambering all over him in their lilac-print dresses, was about as far removed as she could imagine from the world of the device that sat before them right now.

He was carrying a long black tube, which she assumed to be some kind of gun-tech equipment that he would be geekily excited to demonstrate to her later.

Boys. She bet he'd let his kids play *Trail of the Sniper* if they'd been sons not daughters. Probably caught himself wishing his kids were the opposite gender as often as she did. Maybe they could organise a trade.

'It's an AX338,' Mark said. 'British-made. Rifle of choice for the army sniper programme these days. It's made by a firm called Accuracy International, and they're not kidding. It's tested to be first-shot accurate at six hundred metres, and useful for harassing fire at ranges well above a thousand.'

'At the risk of asking a daft question, is this definitely our murder weapon?'

'It's a fair one to ask, given that you don't have the slug yet.'

'No. It passed right through the victim's head and we don't yet know where it ended up.'

'Still some distance away, probably, given this thing's stopping power. It fires a .338 Lapua round, with a muzzle velocity of more than three thousand feet per second. This rifle only entered production in 2010, though, so it's not like some hunter accidentally dropped it in the water several years

339

ago and it's lain undisturbed ever since. This is your gun, no question.'

'So what can it tell us?'

'For starters, that your killer is a pro. This scope is zeroed for nine hundred metres. The guy is taking a night shot at almost a full click, using a Zeiss optic lens: no black-light infrared imaging. So that means you can rule out the possibility that Sir Angus McCready was the intended target.'

'Why?'

'Because a sniper capable of shooting someone from close to a kilometre doesn't miss and hit the guy standing three feet away. Given the range, the conditions and the hardware, you're looking at a highly skilled operative.'

'A professional assassin?'

'Possibly. Unless you come up with a plausible motive connecting Queen to someone with sniper training and access to this standard of firearm, then it could well be a contract hit.'

'Shit.'

This was a worst-case scenario in development. A hired third party put them at one more remove from the truth, because any evidence they found pertaining to the shooter was unlikely to tell them much about who hired him.

'So why did he drop the weapon in the drink?' Catherine asked. 'I mean, even allowing for our stroke of luck in the water level dropping enough for us to spot it, why chuck it in the river less than a mile from the murder scene? Why not a river a hundred miles from here? Why chuck it at all?'

'If you're getting paid enough it's no great loss to discard the weapon rather than risk getting caught with it later. From that we can also assume it won't have been used in any previous hits. If a guy was to use the same rifle on multiple jobs, then we could match the shell cases to the weapon and put a signature to his work. Whereas if you ditch the weapon each time, as long as you haven't left any prints you're preventing the murder weapon ever being connected to you.'

'As opposed to it being found in your house—or in your black Range Rover.'

'You've got it.'

'Christ. Have you any good news for me?'

'Yeah. You don't need to worry so much about finding the shell casing because you already know which gun fired the shot.'

'Would it just make you laugh out loud if I said: "Yes, but there might be a print on it"?'

'I would exercise discretion,' Mark replied, meaning yes. 'But I can help you find it anyway. We know the range, so we can work out where he took the shot from. I'll take a drive up there later, but I've had a look on an OS map and I already think I can narrow it down.'

With this, he popped the cap off of the long black tube and revealed it not to contain anything gadget-tastic after all. The geeky excitement part she called dead on, however. He unrolled the aforementioned Ordnance Survey map of the Alnabruich and Cragruthes area and weighted its corners down with reference texts on a nearby worksurface.

'At a distance of nine hundred metres you're never getting an unbroken line of sight through all those trees,' he said, pointing to the woodland bordering the castle gardens where the play had ended. Then he indicated an area to the north-west, not far from the layby.

341

'Up the slope here the gradient is steep enough that you would have a clear view over the trees. There are a few rocky outcrops that would be ideal for cover too. If I was taking this shot, that's where I would set up.'

Yellow and Blue

'Slasher movies are synonymous with innocence to me,' said Fallan.

Had it been anyone else, it might have seemed a bizarre thing to say. Coming from Fallan it seemed to make its own kind of paradoxical sense even before he explained himself.

He had driven home to Northumberland and returned with several Russell Darius DVDs from his apparently extensive horror movie collection, and they had been watching them together so that Jasmine could at least acquaint herself with Darius's work while the man himself remained out of reach.

'They remind me of innocent times, back in my teens.'

'Before the killing became real?' Jasmine asked, trying to sound merely curious but not quite succeeding in keeping the accusatory acid from her tone.

'A lot of bad things were already real. I preferred to spend as much time as I could out of the house. My pal Flea's family had a Betamax video recorder, first VCR I'd ever seen. Flea's mum worked nights a lot and so did his dad, in a manner of speaking.'

'What do you mean?'

'He was a burglar. Hence the VCR.'

'Ah.'

'When we had the telly to ourselves we used to hire pirate tapes off the ice-cream van, always a horror if you could get them, because these were films you wouldn't be allowed in to see at the pictures. We'd watch them over and over again, rewinding the gory bits—and the dirty bits,' he added with a sheepish expression so unfamiliar it was like seeing a different person, or at least a different aspect of this person for the first time.

'You could tell there was a good bit coming up, blood or nudity, because the tape went all fuzzy from folk doing the same thing, winding it back and re-playing over and over. People talked about them being corrupting, like you couldn't tell the difference between the films and what was real. Mary Whitehouse should have come round my house of an evening. I knew all too well what was real.'

He spoke quietly, trying to sound merely reflective, but he couldn't hide the bitterness and a fragility she had only glimpsed in him a precious few times.

'The slasher movie was the sub-genre in vogue, so that's what we saw most of, and that's what I associate with escapism, with simpler times, with innocence.'

'And what about now? Do you have all these movies because they remind you of those times?'

'Partly, yes, but partly because they're still escapism to me. I'm not like Sammy Finnegan. I got what he was saying but I like them because they're a million miles away from the things he mentioned, from puddles of blood on the pavement and stabbings in your home-town streets. The killing is theatrical, ritualised, stagey, *spectacular*: all the things that killing isn't in real life. But it's the motives that make it truly innocent for me. The motives aren't real either. They're abstract, Gothic, just a cheesy back-story to explain a maniac with a knife deciding to go on a rampage: bereaved mother killing summer-camp attendants as surrogates for the ones who were negligent when her son drowned. Vengeance played out to absurdly extrapolated degrees. Not someone getting their face opened and bleeding to death on a pub floor because they did the same thing to the assailant's mate two weeks ago.'

The motives in Darius's movies were as unconvincing as Fallan described, to the point where they struck Jasmine as being perfunctory. As a film-maker he seemed less interested in what drove a person to kill than what made them capable of doing so. From the movies she had seen, and the synopses of others that she'd read, he kept coming back to the questions of whether you had to become something else in order to kill, or whether killing itself transformed you; whether to kill you had to tap into a source inside yourself, or whether what was inside you was forever destroyed by the act of killing.

She felt like a student again, sitting there in a T-shirt and jogging bottoms, watching DVDs for hours on end. She wondered guiltily whether it was billable: technically, it was research, and she had her laptop open on the couch, scouring websites for what she could learn about Darius. It was this exercise that made her appreciate what the over-used terms 'cult movie' and 'cult director' truly

344

meant. There were dozens of websites and fan forums either dedicated specifically to Darius's movies or at least paying their dues to his place within the genre. The content ranged from the excitable spoutings of fan-boys and gore-hounds, to serious and even academic appraisals of his work.

There was also some eye-opening material on one site regarding the video-nasty hysteria of the early eighties, leading to the infamous Director of Public Prosecutions list and ultimately the Video Recordings Act of 1984. In among the web pages covering this, she found a video clip more jaw-dropping than anything that had played on her TV screen that day. It showed the then MP Graham Bright, who was campaigning for stricter censorship, confidently telling a television news reporter: 'I believe that research is taking place, and it *will* show that these films not only affect young people, but I believe they affect dogs as well.'

Jasmine had to play it again to make sure that he really had said that, all the while trying to decide whether anyone who said in advance what research '*will* show' was shamelessly dishonest or just plain stupid. She was coming down on the side of 'both' when she suddenly spied a link at the side of the page that stopped her breath.

The link read: 'The infamous snuff interview: *Giallo* magazine, September 1983.'

She called Fallan over and together they read the piece, the English translation side by side with scans of the appropriately yellowing pages from the original magazine. Finnegan's memory hadn't failed him regarding the nationality of the interviewer. The journalist was German, by the name of Jan Neumann, but the magazine itself was

Italian. Giallo was the native term for a particular class of lurid and exploitative movie, in reference to the distinctive yellow covers sported by the films' pulp-fiction predecessors.

The tone of the piece was giddily enthusiastic, more towards the fan-boy than the academic end of the critical spectrum. It recounted conversations from a day spent with Darius in London, starting off with a trip to Smithfield market to watch butchers at work, followed by a pub crawl around significant locations from his then two movies to date, *The Ritual* and *The Birth*. This led on to a coyly non-specific account of drug-taking back at Darius's place in Fulham, and ultimately to the moment when, in his inebriated and unguarded state, Darius showed a video tape to his equally intoxicated interviewer.

Neumann described a grand, high-ceilinged room: dimly lit, close-curtained. There were many paintings on the wall but the ones the camera lingered on were all themed around hunting or conflict: an eagle taking a fish from the waters, a shooting party on the moor, two stags locking antlers. Then the camera lit upon two figures in hooded robes, their faces never seen, standing before a table, or perhaps an altar, upon which a naked woman was restrained. There were sheets on the floor, crudely daubed with occult symbols, the outside edges dotted with burning candles.

Neumann then described watching in revulsion, disbelief and not a little awe as one of the robed figures murdered the woman, stabbing her several times with an elaborately designed sacrificial dagger.

These were images Jasmine had seen already

346

that day, aspects and details of them revisited several times in the Russell Darius movies she had watched.

Neumann claimed that Darius had then precipitately become altogether less hospitable, switching off the VCR and insisting that the journalist had to leave. 'He was like a girl who has realised she's let you go too far when she hears her father's key in the lock,' Neumann put it. 'She can't get rid of you fast enough. Or perhaps I was the girl who had gone too far, as I later felt a little squalid and ashamed.'

At the end of the translation a further link took Jasmine to a 2003 retrospective piece by Neumann twenty years on. From the perspective of distance and maturity he questioned what he had really seen. He had been drunk and high, and wondered whether the whole day hadn't been set up by Darius to put him in the position of maximum susceptibility. The man was, after all, an expert at creating convincingly gory visual effects. The format may have played a part too: the immediacy of video gave an authenticity, a live-ness to it, a sense of true events being captured, whereas graded film tended to put a polish on what it depicted and thus render it more obviously a fiction.

He had been rebuffed by Darius in all attempts to secure a new interview, but was confident in concluding that the whole thing had been an elaborate publicity stunt, albeit one that had ultimately backfired upon its perpetrator.

Neither Jasmine nor Fallan were quite so sure.

There was little doubt Darius wanted the notoriety, but he may have believed it would come at no cost. He didn't need to tell Neumann how the video had come into his possession, and nor was there any danger the German could identify the location or the girl. They needed to talk to someone who could tell them what went on that last night at Kildrachan.

It was time for a phone call Jasmine had been very much looking forward to making.

'Hello, this is Jasmine Sharp of Sharp Investigations.'

'Miss Sharp, as I've warned you before, I've been instructed to consider—'

'Yeah, I heard,' she interrupted. 'I'll be brief. Tell Murray Maxwell I want to talk to somebody about Sammy Finnegan, Hamish Queen, Kildrachan House and a shitload of LSD. My first choice is your boss, but I'd settle for a journalist.'

*   *   *

'*Murray wasn't averse to a bit of experimentation. Used to make me laugh whenever I saw him play that straight-edge Eliot Ness cipher on TV.*'

Jasmine clicked her mouse and stopped the playback, glancing across at her guest. Murray Maxwell was sitting in the cramped confines of Sharp Investigations, looking precisely as comfortable as Jasmine wanted him to be. He was a man who looked like he was used to spacious, uncluttered office suites, broad windows, a view of the Clyde, conversation-piece lobby furniture and fresh-brewed coffee on tap. The absence of all those things was the least of what was making him uncomfortable, however.

He wasn't like she had pictured him. Now in his mid-fifties, she was expecting someone who

348

looked like that most familiar of sights to Jasmine: a retired cop. He was businesslike in his attire, but most certainly did not look like a businessman. There were subtle hints of flamboyance about his appearance, the cut of his suit, the shade and style of his shirt. A man who knew what looked good on him and what didn't. There was no danger of anybody thinking he was an executive in an accountancy firm, for instance.

He was undoubtedly good-looking, a handsome figure still. You could see the younger man who had been Inspector Kelvin, but there was no suggestion of faded grandeur about him, of his best days being at his back. Jasmine imagined that ordinarily he would exude an easy confidence stemming from being the most important or even just the best-looking man in any given place.

She'd bet he was an accomplished networker, the hand everybody wanted to shake, an expert at working the room.

He wasn't going to do so well working this one.

He had tried to turn on the charm, complimenting her on the Ramsay case and asking her about her own acting experience. He had done his research, even knew her mum had been an actress. This had threatened to do a job on Jasmine, tempting her off track, until she remembered that one of the broadsheets had included an almost intrusively in-depth background piece on her and it was presumably still available online.

She stared at him, not challenging him for a response to the recording, just curious to see how he'd react.

'At least I know you must grasp why I haven't been very keen to talk to you,' he said. 'I apologise for that, but you have to understand what's at stake right now. I have put so much, so much of my life into my work in television. This kind of opportunity doesn't come around often, and it's so delicately in the balance. Any hint of scandal and it's gone. You know what the papers are like.'

He spoke the truth. She had read up on him and been intrigued by his unorthodox but ultimately astute career path. He had given an interview in which he explained his move into production as being born of an awareness that he had a limited shelf life as an actor, especially when he was so strongly associated with one particular role. 'I thought being on the production side would allow me to create drama that might offer new roles for me, but I got so engulfed by the process, just too busy. Plus I realised it would just seem so obvious that I'd parachuted myself in.'

Prior to that, he explained, he had feared he'd struggle to get work elsewhere, and anyway didn't want to uproot himself and his family from the west of Scotland. That said, he cited a downside to life in his home town that was also a factor in moving behind the cameras.

'Once you're a fixture in a programme like *Raintown Blue*, an almost iconically Glaswegian show, you're no longer an actor: you're part of the landscape, part of the furniture. It's the friendliest city I've ever been in, but people can act like they own you. That's why I decided I'd rather find something else to do than end up with an annual pay packet from panto just because I used to be Inspector Kelvin.'

For someone who had otherwise proven himself a politically smart operator, this had turned out to be a particularly ill-chosen remark, the tabloids seizing upon it and spinning it to sound like he was slagging off all of Glasgow's esteemed pantorati. It had taken a lot of finessing to put out this particular fire, so Jasmine appreciated why allegations of drug-taking and a long-concealed link to the victim of the most high-profile murder of the year were not complications he wanted to be dealing with at the moment.

'I had no idea Tessa was still missing until you told me just now,' he stated. 'I remember the police coming to the house and Hamish being taken in for questioning. I think Finlay was taken in too at one stage. But then it blew over just as suddenly as it had begun and I just assumed everything had been sorted.

'After that, we all went our very separate ways. Not much chance of a cast reunion: it was something we all wanted to put behind us and forget about. And by that I don't just mean the police or the arguments or the drugs, but the all-encompassing sense of professional failure. I really had barely thought about it again until you got in touch, and then of course that was massively compounded by what happened to Hamish.'

'You never worried over someone blabbing about the drugs?' asked Fallan.

'It was a very distant, vague fear, a niggling thought in the middle of the night from time to time, but only once the storylines in *Raintown Blue* became more drug-oriented and Kelvin became what Sam Finnegan so flatteringly described as "an Eliot Ness cipher". It would be far more damaging now. Actors are allowed a bit of hedonistic indulgence; it's almost expected of you. But once

351

you go corporate, it's different rules.'

'Did you have any contact with Russell Darius after Kildrachan?' Jasmine inquired.

'No. We were working on different things and then he went off to America. I didn't know he was even living in the UK until that spat over funding.'

'Back in the early eighties, were you aware of the rumours that he was in possession of a snuff movie?'

'Vaguely, inasmuch as it was a story I only paid even cursory attention to because it was about Darius. I thought it was bollocks. Snuff movies were an urban myth, but I do remember thinking that if anybody ever actually had one in their possession it would be him.'

'Do you know what this movie was alleged to show?'

'No. The news stories I read were big on outrage and short on detail. Where are you going with this?'

From the increasing guardedness in his tone, Jasmine could tell that he thought he already knew.

'According to the German journalist to whom Darius screened the video, the snuff clip shows a woman being stabbed to death by one of two figures in hooded robes, in a big grand room. The reason the police came to question everybody at Kildrachan was that Tormod McDonald told Sergeant Strang he had seen a woman being stabbed and someone dragging a body through the grounds of the house.

'The next day, Saffron refused to answer her door and told Finlay Weir to go away. When asked why she might be behaving this way Darius suggested that what they had done the night before may have gone too far. Saffron's next move was to tell

352

the police that she had seen Tessa get on the last bus out of town. She was the only witness to this, and therefore the last person to claim to have seen Tessa alive. She then quit her job, vacated her rented house and left town for good.'

'You're saying you think this snuff movie is *real*, that it shows Darius and Saffron killing Tessa? That's ridiculous. How would you know it was even shot at Kildrachan? It could have been made anywhere, two years later or five years before.'

He was saying this but the shock on his face said he feared it was true and he was looking for something to cling on to as the deluge threatened to swamp him.

'There were paintings on the walls. An eagle taking a fish from the river, a hunting party, and—'

'Rutting stags,' Maxwell interrupted, his face suddenly pale and drawn.

Jasmine gave him a moment, but just a moment. His thoughts were far away, in place and most definitely in time. She had to press him while he was reeling.

'We need to know what you remember about that night. Finnegan said you did drugs with Darius and Saffron, and took part in these rituals.'

'I did,' he admitted. 'But not that night. I was with Julian, in the kitchen mostly, other end of the house. Darius was getting increasingly strange and so around Julian was always the safest place to be. A few single malts was as hardcore as it got. I was hiding, really. I'd had enough.'

'Of the drugs, or of the rituals?'

'Both.'

'Were they getting out of hand? Escalating?'

'In a way, but I wasn't freaked out or anything,

353

I just thought it was all a bit silly. Candles and pentagrams, all that Aleister Crowley crap. It was funny at first, even quite excitingly spooky, but all that black-magic stuff very quickly becomes self-evidently daft. Sitting around, burning incense and chanting meaningless incantations: might as well be in church. That's why Saffron was the perfect foil for Darius. Any new-age nonsense, or even dark-age nonsense, and she was in there.'

'You're saying you were at the other end of the house, and so saw nothing, heard nothing,' recapped Fallan. 'Convenient.'

'I didn't see or hear nothing: just nothing pertaining to Darius, as was my firm intention. I saw and heard Tormod: that's the person you should be pressing on this. He's the one who was behaving erratically that night, bouncing off the walls and acting like a man possessed. Or perhaps like a man who has just been released from possession and is distraught at discovering what has happened while his conscience wasn't minding the store.'

'What are you saying?'

'Well, it's clear you know Tessa was with Hamish, Finlay was with Mhairi, Saffron was with Darius and now I'm telling you I was with Julian. Aren't you forgetting somebody?'

'Adam Nolan,' Jasmine replied.

'Adam Nolan. He was the only veteran of the Glass Shoe debacle that I had any real later contact with. We remained friends, and even worked together when I was in a couple of episodes of *First Do No Harm*. He was tickled when I told him I'd learned young Tormod had become a man of the cloth, and a fire-and-brimstone, morally censorious one at that. As Adam so memorably put it, "For a Presbyterian, he could suck cock like a Catholic altar boy."

'He was always hanging around Adam, in the thrall of a fascination he either didn't fully understand or more likely didn't want to give its true name. Adam didn't do anything about it. He was experienced and wary enough to know it might come to nothing, with dangerous consequences. The age of consent was still twenty-one in those days. But that night, amid the widespread awareness that everything was falling apart, a sense of abandon was abroad. Tormod finally took a taste of what he wanted, and then, like many males in the possession of lust and ardour, as soon as he came the spell was badly broken.'

'Hence then charging into Finlay's room,' Jasmine suggested. 'Accusing him of corrupting his sister. Major transference.'

'Self-disgust is a hell of a comedown. But it would be wrong to say he sobered up instantly. He'd had a lot to drink, as well as some speed and some poppers too. His head was all over the place. He was wailing like a banshee, pinballing in and out of rooms, totally out of control. He might not have been in a condition to make a reliable witness, but if anybody saw anything that night it would have been him.'

He wasn't very forthcoming when we asked him about this stuff before.'

'Oh, I think he might be a little more open once he realises you're aware that the Reverend McDonald of Balnavon, one of Fleet Street's professional homophobes, secretly loves the boabby.'

355

'What a helpful man,' Jasmine said as soon as Maxwell had departed. 'Do you think he was lying to us?'

'Yes, but helpfully,' Fallan replied. 'I don't know quite what, but there was something very specific he was lying to us about.'

'He was way too reasonable all of a sudden, for a guy who had been so evasive—and even too keen to explain *why* he'd been evasive.'

'He was very quick to give up somebody else too: threw us Tormod—something he's kept his silence on for decades—just like that, which means he wanted the heat diverted away from wherever it was headed.'

She thought back to what they'd been talking about, searching for what it might have been that had precipitated his emergency manoeuvres. Rather than replay the discussion in her head she remembered she could replay it on the covert recording she'd made. That was when she realised her tactical mistake. And just when she thought she was being clever too.

Jasmine screws up.

'Shit.'

'What?'

'I shouldn't have played him Finnegan's recording. It just reminded him that Finnegan wasn't there that night. That meant Maxwell could say he was at the other end of the house with Julian and therefore had nothing to do with whatever happened. He knows Darius isn't going to talk to us and that we've no idea how to get in touch with

356

Saffron. So he chooses Julian as a plausible alibi, knowing we're very unlikely to get a second pass at him either.'

'Still,' Fallan said, 'he's tossed us a hell of a chip.'

'Quite,' she agreed. 'We can finally find out exactly what Tormod told the police. And maybe what he didn't.'

The Gift of Motive

Catherine didn't spare the horsepower as she drove back from Cragruthes one more time, determined to make it home before the boys were in their beds, but a series of tailbacks had her revising her hopes downwards in twenty-minute increments. When she drove out of Alnabruich she had estimated that with just an acceptable degree of naughtiness concerning the speed limit she could be home in time to sit and watch them both play in the garden for a while; maybe let Fraser stay up a bit later than usual if it stayed dry. Duncan generally got to stay up longer than his younger brother, but had been made to understand that it wasn't a hard and fast rule.

Sitting stationary for ten minutes a time at a contraflow, her aspirations had become more and more modest: be back in time to give Fraser his bath; back in time to tuck him in and read a story; back in time for Duncan's bath; for Duncan's lights-out time.

With Glasgow finally rising in the middle distance she told herself she'd settle for finding Duncan hadn't yet nodded off, so that she could get a kiss and a cuddle.

She needed the reassurance of her children's touch, her family's presence, being one of the things she could rely upon to make sense and keep everything else in perspective. It was, she well understood, an indication that she knew this investigation was gradually slipping away. Another Moira-ism: 'When the job's doing your box in, remind yourself what really matters.'

And it surely was doing her box in.

It was no longer, by any definition, 'early days', and they were still chasing shadows, searching for anything that might resemble a plausible motive for killing Hamish Queen. They were still waiting to hear somebody say a bad word about him, with even his ex-wives blaming his workaholism rather than any more venal reasons for their marriages breaking up.

'We were all just mistresses,' one of them had put it, in an appropriately luvvie way. 'Hamish was married to the theatre.'

And in that relationship, it seemed, he had been slavishly faithful. It was his first and only true love, one to which he was devoted above anything else. He made millions but lived to work. One ex claimed their four-night honeymoon had been the only holiday he accompanied her on throughout their eight-year marriage.

The sharpest tones had come from his second wife, Julia, the mother of his daughter Charlotte. She had bemoaned the fact that Hamish had so seldom been around for their little girl; her anger compounded by the fact that Charlotte, perhaps inevitably, grew up to worship him.

There was some anger. There was some

bitterness. There was no hate. There was nobody who *hated* Hamish Queen. There was nobody who wanted him dead.

They had discovered the gun, but that turned out to be something of a mirage. The bullet had been found, embedded in stone at the foot of the castle walls, the hole covered over by ivy. It was a .338, as Mark Brooks had predicted, and ballistics matched it to the rifle from the river, so they had the murder weapon but, crucially, not the means of death. If the killing was the work of a hired professional, then the AX rifle was not the murderer's instrument. The *assassin* was, and the trail of this sniper was very cold.

Catherine knew nobody was blaming her, but that didn't feel like any kind of consolation. In fact, she'd had a call from Graeme Sunderland while she sat in that interminable tailback, the content of which would have been less disturbing had it constituted a demand for progress and an old-fashioned chewing out.

He was being unreasonably reasonable, which had set her on edge, because she could tell he was uneasy. And yet he claimed he wasn't getting leaned on. The political pressure had eased, and that in itself, he said, was indicative of how nobody had a clue what was going on here.

'Sometimes the pressure's useful because you can trace where it's coming from,' he admitted, 'follow the ripples back to the source of the disturbance. It can point you in interesting directions: suspicions people have, worries, grudges, even plain paranoia. But over this? Nothing.'

'Surely you're not talking about them backing off, trusting our judgment and letting us get on with doing our jobs?'

'I'm more inclined to fear it's the calm before the storm.'

'I don't follow.'

'Are you in the car alone?' he asked.

'Yes. Why?'

'Because this is a conversation we're not having, about a possibility we didn't discuss. Understood?'

'Understood. So what are we not talking about?'

'The nightmare scenario.'

Sunderland didn't have to spell it out. It had been on the edge of her consciousness in recent days, the thought she wouldn't entertain. It was one of those fears you didn't admit to yourself that you'd had until someone else came out and named it.

The nightmare scenario: the random sniper; the apparently motiveless killer, striking from distance, in darkness, like some god of chaos. Nobody knowing why the target had been chosen, and nobody knowing who might be next.

As Catherine well understood, delivering a motive was one of the most crucial ways in which the police served the public. Whenever people heard about something dreadful, something horrific, they needed the reassurance of being able to tell themselves there was a reason why it didn't happen to them; why it wouldn't happen to them. It was drug-related. It was gang-related. The victim and the accused had been on a three-day drinking binge. The stabbing was in retaliation for a previous incident. And, of course, everybody's favourite comfort blanket: the victim was a prostitute.

Most of the time, motive adhered to the tenets of Moira's Law.

This is Glesca. We don't do subtle, we don't do

360

nuanced, we don't do conspiracy. We do tit-for-tat, score-settling, feuds, jealousy, petty revenge. We do straightforward. We do obvious.

Catherine thought of the two cases she had submitted to the Procurator Fiscal just days before the Hamish Queen shooting. They were both horrific crimes, but rendered all the less scary for the public at large once a motive gave them a framework to make their own kind of albeit twisted sense.

A twenty-nine-year-old woman, Emma McTaggart, was found stabbed and her body partially burned in woods near Bishopbriggs, murdered making her way home from a party. Initially a seemingly random killing, until the investigation uncovered the break-up with her serially abusive boyfriend a few days previously.

A forty-one-year-old divorcee, Maureen O'Connel, was discovered dead in her home, strangled and naked in the bedroom of her flat in Mount Vernon. Initially it looked like the worst fear of every woman who lived alone: a random assailant who struck in the night once the lights were out and the doors locked. However, there was no evidence of a break-in, and neighbours said they had heard drunken voices in the close, a couple in high spirits.

Laura Geddes secured the confession of a forty-eight-year-old accountant named Colin Anderson. They had gone out on a date, their second, and in their mutually drunken state, he had been invited back to Maureen's flat for sex. When they got down to it Anderson was unable to maintain an erection, a recurring problem exacerbated by the alcohol, the consumption of which he found necessary to

361

overcome nervousness precipitated by fear of this chronic affliction. As the porter had it, 'much drink may be said to be an equivocator with lechery: it makes him, and it mars him'.

The drink marred Maureen too. She laughed at him, unknowingly making herself the vent for years of pent-up rage at a series of sexual humiliations.

It was brutal, it was squalid and it was unforgivable, but it made its own kind of sense, and it absolved those single-dwelling women of their fear. *They'd* never take a comparative stranger home for sex, and if they would, *they* wouldn't laugh at him if he couldn't perform. *They'd* handle it better. *They'd* do it differently. *They* wouldn't get murdered.

'Is this a conversation you've "not had" with other people?' she asked Sunderland.

'No comment.'

For which, read 'yes'.

'It's a bit early to worry about something as out-there as that,' she said, trying to make it sound like the thought hadn't even occurred to her.

'I'm not worrying about it until I have to worry about it; I'm just worried that I might have to worry about it. The longer we go on without any sniff of a motive, the more people start to think the unthinkable. Add to that the fact that it's now known in certain circles that this shooting involved serious hardware, military training . . . Nobody's actually used the words "Washington sniper" yet, but you can tell they're thinking it. The idea of someone who could strike at any time, just as we hit the height of summer, is a recipe for hysteria. Factor in the profile of the target and the idea of a nameless shooter picking off the great and the good is starting to trouble certain people's thoughts.'

Catherine understood what Sunderland meant regarding being 'worried that I might have to worry', but despite his admission she was going to persist with banishing this idea from her thoughts until such time as there was a second victim. Meanwhile she was determined to get a grip on the case once more. It wasn't like they didn't have any evidence; just that all the evidence they did have wasn't pointing them anywhere in particular.

Unlike some laboured investigations, it didn't feel as though there was something crucial that they hadn't yet found; more that there was something they simply weren't seeing. She couldn't help but suspect it was like some three-dimensional visual puzzle: look at it from just the right angle and it would suddenly resolve itself into a picture that made sense. This concept seemed all the more tantalising given that this was the first murder case she'd ever worked in which she was in possession of multiple photographs of the victim taken a fraction of a second before the bullet struck.

With that thought, the puzzle twisted just a little in her hands. The picture did not come into focus, but there was one thing she could be sure it wouldn't show.

This was not a random killing. Whether he or she had done it personally or paid a hitman, whoever wanted Hamish Queen dead had to know what was going to happen at the end of the performance. The clue was the photograph itself.

First-hand or from information given to assist the hit, the shooter had to know the target would come down from the audience and pose with the cast, like he'd done in all those previous photographs hung in

Sir Angus McCready's private study. If he hadn't, surely the assassin would have set up somewhere else, with a black-light scope, and taken his shot while Hamish sat in the audience watching the play. It would be a tricky shot: dozens of people huddled close together in the dark, making the target hard to distinguish among the other infrared blobs. Instead, the killer had known that his mark would stand perfectly still under the spotlights at the end.

Everybody say cheese.

Altered States

This time, Tormod McDonald was not to be found at the Balnavon parish church or its community centre, nor the manse, which they had tried first. Their visit to the last had given Jasmine pause, the possibility of meeting Tormod's wife forcing her to contemplate the uncomfortable ramifications of ever actually using their leverage. The woman had done nothing to deserve all that this would precipitate, and Jasmine didn't think it was her place to rain it down on Tormod either. She would be bluffing here and she knew it. That said, she was still entirely confident that her bluff would not be called.

Venturing inside the church building, having been drawn by a familiar sound, she was confronted by the incongruous image of a cleaning lady vigorously vacuuming between the pews with a Dyson upright. Jasmine had always found it a spell-breaking juxtaposition to see someone hoovering away inside a theatre auditorium, even more so than to see what lay behind the flats backstage, so there was a particularly disarming bathos about the supposed house of God getting its carpets spruced.

'Are you looking for the minister?' the cleaner had asked.

'Yes. Is the Reverend McDonald around?'

'No, sure he's away to the barracks, but he has a service at six so he should be back in a couple of hours.'

Fallan walked outside into the churchyard, staring fixedly across the street to where the Balnavon Hotel stood diagonally opposite. He then proceeded forward between two rows of headstones and leaned over the black metal railings atop the grass banking leading down to street level, his head turned to look west. Jasmine joined him to see what he was looking at, seeing only the main road, which bent out of sight as it led back out of town.

'What are you seeing?' she asked.

Fallan turned around and gazed back beyond the church building towards the meadowland bordering it at the rear, to the north.

'That's still the Kildrachan estate there, isn't it?' he asked.

'I think so. The grounds go on for a couple of miles all around, far as I know. Why?'

Fallan gave a noncommittal grunt by way of reply and wandered off towards the far end of the churchyard, in the opposite direction to where he'd been facing. He came to a short stone wall, about chest height on him, and clambered up to look either way along it.

He dropped back down with the softest thud, the lightness of his impact at odds with the weight of his frame. She really would not want Fallan

365

sneaking up on her. His size didn't appear to be any impediment to his stealth nor his agility.

He led her back out of the churchyard, left along the main street and into the narrow lane he must have been looking along.

'I remembered seeing this wee pathway when we came out the hotel the other day, leading up the side of the graveyard. I want to know if it goes where I think it might.'

She followed him down the lane, moss-covered crumbling concrete giving way to gravel and then hard-packed earth strewn haphazardly with patches of grass and weeds. About a hundred and fifty yards from the main road, past the walls hemming in the churchyard, they came to a stile, flanked by fencing on either side. The fencing was of simple construction, three lengths of steel wire running between regularly spaced upright wooden spars, its purpose really just to denote the borders of the estate than keep in livestock or keep out trespassers. Beyond the stile, the path continued, snaking along the side of a dry-stone dike until it disappeared under cover of trees.

'Shortcut,' he said.

'Bound to be more than one route in and out of a place like that,' Jasmine mused, but Fallan seemed more intrigued by it than she could quite appreciate.

She was concerned for a moment that he was about to lead her forward on to the Kildrachan property, as specifically forbidden by a small weatherbeaten plastic sign next to the stile. It wasn't the trespassing aspect that worried her so much as the possibility of running into Charlotte while trespassing on her family's land.

366

Fortunately, Fallan proceeded no further, but as he turned around to retrace his steps she saw a familiar sudden alertness about his face that had her fearing she was about to be thrown to the ground amid a hail of gunfire. There were no evasive manoeuvres, however. He simply stood still, his gaze fixed on the path ahead, or something he had seen at the end of it.

'What's wrong?' she asked anxiously, still not confident the getting-thrown-to-the-ground part could be entirely ruled out.

'Saw somebody.'

'Where?'

'He's gone now. Gone fast. He didn't want to be caught looking.'

'Have you seen him before?'

'No, but once was enough to recognise what I was looking at. A pro.'

'Another investigator? Like Rees?'

'No. A different kind of pro.'

'And what kind would that be?'

'The ex-military kind. The kind who's not going to get caught looking twice, so we probably won't see him again. That won't necessarily mean he's gone, though, which troubles me.'

'Why?'

'Because he's also the kind who would "really know what he was doing" with a high-powered rifle.'

Fallan led her back to the main road, Jasmine as reluctant to catch up to this mystery stalker as she was curious to see whether there was a silver Passat parked somewhere near by. She wondered whether they might pop into the hotel again and wait for Tormod there, but Fallan turned right and strode on purposefully past the church.

He continued all the way along the narrow main street, beyond the last of the tourist shops, until they reached the point where the road broadened to accommodate a layby and an adjacent Perspex shelter denoted the bus stop.

There was an old punter standing there, plastic bag of library books in one hand and in the other a lead tethering a hairy white Westie.

'Has this always been the bus stop?' Fallan asked, indicating the modern transparent and graffiti-proof shelter. 'For Inverness, I mean.'

'Naw,' he replied. 'This is the new one. Used to leave from outside the chemist's, but they changed it to here.'

'When?'

'Ach, not long. Would be about seventy-four maybe?'

'Cheers,' Fallan replied, flashing Jasmine a grin in acknowledgment of the fact that 1974 constituted 'recent' in the old man's perception of Balnavon's history.

Fallan looked south, towards where the main entrance to the Kildrachan estate was tucked away out of sight of the road.

'That hotelier,' he said, 'Murdo Aitken, told us Saffron lived in one of the wee houses past his premises at the other end of the village, didn't he?'

'Yes,' Jasmine agreed. 'I think it must have been that wee terrace just before the pavement runs out on the road north. What are you getting at?'

'The quickest route home from Kildrachan House to where Saffron lived would be the back way, down that path by the meadow and along the lane at the church.'

368

Jasmine got it now, and asked the question for him.

'So how could she have seen Tessa Garrion getting on that bus?'

*   *   *

They intercepted Tormod McDonald as he made his way from the manse around to the church. He checked his stride, halted for just a moment by the sight of them before proceeding unabated, and conspicuously trying to *look* unabated. He had an expression of mild irritation, as if he had nothing to fear from them and it was their own time they were wasting.

'I have to prepare for a service,' he said as he reached them, intending to brush past. 'I told you as much as I'm prepared to.'

'Adam Nolan's family were a little more cooperative,' Jasmine lied.

That stopped him like a Taser.

'They even let us look through his private diaries.'

'That would prove nothing,' Tormod ventured, a little hastily.

'True. But it does beg the question, why would he make it up? Nowadays, different story: you've a public profile and a reputation to uphold, but back then you were nobody, and apart from anything else, you were underage.'

'Private diaries can be private fantasies,' Tormod argued.

'Obviously they're just his word against yours. But we've got more than his word.'

'Hell of a story,' added Fallan. 'Adam Nolan, the admired and lamented RSC actor turned TV star,

369

practically a gay icon, and Tormod McDonald, the man of the cloth and moralising newspaper columnist. Can't think of an editor in the country who wouldn't want this as an exclusive. Apart from yours, obviously.'

Tormod's expression withered, his lower lip trembling like he was just a wee boy getting a row from his mum. Jasmine felt sorry for him, but it was pity she couldn't afford.

'What do you want?' he asked, his voice wavering.

'You know what we want,' she said. 'Tell us what you saw that night.'

'You can take the earlier part of the evening as read,' Fallan added, drawing a glare. 'It's what happened after that that we're interested in. Like when you barged into Finlay Weir's bedroom and your sister told you to fuck off. The way he told it, it didn't sound like she was being taken advantage of, as you put it.'

'My sister *was* taken advantage of. We both were. We were young and impressionable. We were in thrall to those people.'

'I'll give you that,' Fallan replied. 'They must have seemed very impressive, very sophisticated. They encouraged your curiosities, you and your sister. They let you join in: let you drink, try some drugs, but their company itself must have been intoxicating. Altogether a disinhibiting environment. Maybe brought out desires you never knew were in you.'

'Yes,' Tormod agreed, looking less adversarial towards Fallan. 'A lot of that is true. But there was more than intoxication involved. Those were not my desires, don't you see? They came from somewhere else, somewhere outside. Possession.

Through those other indulgences my wantonness cried out and announced my vulnerability to something that is ever-listening. I was weak, and in my weakness I let it in.'

Jasmine and Fallan shared a look, mutually understanding that they should say nothing, let him speak. Clearly he needed to believe this, or the rest of his world would fall in on itself.

'It truly felt like possession,' Tormod went on. 'Something else in control, something that would not be denied. Then suddenly it was gone, and like Adam and Eve I was aware of my own nakedness, of my sin.'

He looked down at the ground, not wishing to meet anyone's eyes for a moment.

'I went to Finlay Weir's room, it's true. I wanted to intervene before it was too late, to save Mhairi from the moment of awakening I had just suffered. I failed. I was distraught and, I will admit, still very drunk. More than drunk. I was uncontainable. Adam tried to calm me, I think, but I didn't want him near me. I went staggering through the house in a daze.

'Eventually I stumbled into the doorway of one of the grand rooms downstairs. The door was open, a strange light coming from within. The doorway was as far as I got, though. What I saw caused me to turn and flee. I saw figures in robes. I think there were two of them, but my attention was drawn almost entirely to the one who was holding a knife, a sacrificial dagger. I saw him stab a woman who was strapped to an altar. She was naked apart from the bindings. There were candles everywhere, symbols painted on sheets. I only glimpsed those for a moment, but I can still see them now, imprinted. And I can see the blood. It gushed like a burst pipe, dark red. The woman strained against her bonds but she didn't scream. It was as though she was in a trance, or sedated.'

'Did they see you?' Jasmine asked.

'No, I don't think so. Perhaps. They could have, but I don't remember them reacting. It felt as though it was happening somewhere else and I was only having a vision, like I could have walked over but not been able to touch them. I fled, though. I ran in panic, thinking I was lost in my own nightmare. Then I realised I was going to be sick, so I found a toilet. I vomited, and then after that I must have fallen asleep on the bathroom floor. I woke up maybe an hour later, an hour and a half perhaps. It was about quarter to eleven.'

'So the festivities had started quite early that night?'

'Earlier than usual, yes. Rehearsals just kind of broke down at about four o'clock and things deteriorated from there. I was very woozy, probably still drunk, but much calmer. Everything was calmer. There was music playing somewhere, but the house seemed still. I started to remember what had happened before I passed out, but the problem was, I couldn't decipher whether I was remembering elements of a drunken dream or actual events.

'With some trepidation I went back to that room, where I had seen the stabbing. There was no sign of what had been there: just an ordinary, or rather very expensive and possibly antique oak table with carved legs and a candelabra in the centre. The curtains were drawn, there were a few empty wine bottles around the mantelpiece and a smell of

372

snuffed candles.'

'No sheets? No bloodstains?'

'No. I began to think I must have imagined it. I went outside. Part of me wanted to go home but another part felt I couldn't leave the place. Mhairi might still be in there, as far as I knew. Plus there were things I wanted to understand. I didn't want to see Adam right then, but I felt like it would be worse to just disappear, like he might be laughing about me or, worse, telling somebody. I ended up wandering in the grounds not knowing where to put myself. That was when I saw somebody dragging a body; dragging it by the legs.'

'Did you recognise them?'

'It was dark. I just saw shapes.'

'How close were you?' Fallan asked.

'Twenty or thirty yards.'

'Where? Were they on open ground? Gravel? Grass?'

'The woods. They were among the trees.'

'They? More than one person?'

'No, I mean whoever it was and the body. But I had seen more than one figure in robes back in the room, which is why I ran when I heard someone else coming. I heard the door to the house close and footsteps on the stone stairs. I ran as quickly and as quietly as I could, all the way home.'

'Which way?' Fallan asked.

'What do you mean?'

'The main road or the back way?'

'The back way. It was the shortest route home to the manse.'

Tormod glanced towards the path at the side of the churchyard, remembering his flight.

'I spent a tortured and largely sleepless night,

373

perhaps the worst of my life. I didn't trust my own memory or my own senses. I didn't know what was real and what was down to intoxication, and I wondered whether what I had seen was a manifestation of my guilt. If I had allowed something to possess me, then what might the residual effects be? But my conscience wasn't to be denied. I had to tell the police in case what I had seen was real.

'I spoke privately to Sergeant Strang, because I didn't want anything down in black and white. I didn't tell him about the drugs because I feared there would be hell to pay if the police went up to Kildrachan and seized stuff. I think he read between the lines, but I knew I could trust him.'

'So why did you try to recant your testimony?' Jasmine asked. 'Callum Ross told us you came back and claimed you'd been imagining things. Why would you do that when you could trust Sergeant Strang's discretion and when he already knew your account was potentially unreliable?'

'Someone leaned on you, didn't they?' said Fallan. 'Somebody told you to change your story or they'd broadcast your wee secret.'

Tormod swallowed, decades of doubt and regret etched upon his face. He nodded.

'Who?'

He looked away, past the back of the churchyard, past the stone walls and the meadow, towards the woods, beyond which lay Kildrachan House. Then he answered: a single, simple word.

'Darius.'

First Person Shooter

Duncan was in bed by the time Catherine made it home, but fortunately not yet asleep, so she went in for a few soft words and a cuddle. Six months ago she'd have been at risk of waking Fraser by allowing herself this wee indulgence, but the boys each had their own rooms now. What used to be the playroom had long been earmarked as Fraser's future bedroom, but he was not enamoured of the idea of finding himself alone after lights out and clung to the comforts of sharing with his big brother way past his big brother's tolerance for such a cohabitation.

She asked him what he'd done with his day. He and Fraser had been at a summer club, as although Drew wasn't in the office this week he really needed some peace to make headway on his current project. Duncan told her at length about playing rounders, and how much more he enjoyed being on the fielding side because they'd been using proper baseball mitts. She suggested he might want to use some of his report-card money to buy a catcher's glove of his own for playing in the garden, then made the mistake of asking, 'Or have you already thought of something else you'd like to buy?'

He went quiet for a moment. She thought she wasn't going to get an answer, and when he spoke again she assumed he had moved on to another subject, as was typical of his capricious thought process.

'Greg Paterson was at summer club today,' he began.

'Oh yes?'

'Well, you know you said he was a nice boy?'

'I did. He is.'

'Well, *he's* got *Trail of the Sniper* for his Xbox and it's not made him, you know, disturbed or anything.'

Oh God. It wasn't over.

'I know Dad said it wasn't suitable for my age, in case it puts horrible thoughts in my head, but Greg's had it for like a month and he's still normal. In fact, he's about the only boy who doesn't go in a rage when he gets caught out at rounders.'

Catherine had to suppress a smile at the logic and the way he put it, but she was also suppressing her annoyance, and not at Duncan for his refusal to let it lie.

Drew had had words, as promised, but Duncan had read equivocation between the lines. Normally he understood that Mum and Dad were two heads on the same hydra. The boys grasped that there was little point in trying to play one off against the other when they were resolutely in agreement. Unfortunately, both Duncan and Fraser were adept at detecting the fault-lines. Drew had said his piece and handed down his ruling, but Duncan had detected his lack of conviction, same as Catherine had the night she picked a fight over it.

As she softly closed Duncan's bedroom door she was already saddling her high horse in preparation for sallying downstairs into battle. The smell of what he was cooking wafted up to meet her, and the thought of turning dinner into another argument was enough to give her pause. Drew had done as he said he would; she couldn't take him to task for being insufficiently convincing. That would be ridiculous.

376

Get a grip.

She thought of Duncan's words, hoped she could quote them to Drew for the humour without him thinking it was an overture to digging him up.

'Greg's had it for like a month and he's still normal.'

There was her fear in a nutshell, and it looked pretty silly all of a sudden.

She had argued with Drew about this, she had even been desperate enough to probe Beano about his experiences, yet she hadn't sought the opinion of the mother and time-served police officer whose judgment she respected implicitly. Deep down she understood that this was because she already knew what Moira would say.

'Are you daft, hen?'

Placenta-brain never wears off: you can't think straight when it comes to your own kids. Nothing stays in proportion. Catherine had spent a life garnering first-hand knowledge of what drove people to kill, and of what it took to execute such acts. There were a lot of things in this life that could damage children, that could take away their empathy and their innocence, and ultimately render them capable of brutal deeds in later life. Software was going to be well down that list.

She saved Duncan's remark until they'd finished dinner, and as predicted, Drew's laughter was tempered by a look of trepidation that he was about to be taken to task once more.

'I did tell him that *we* had decided,' he insisted. 'I didn't say "your mammy won't let you".'

'I know, but I've been thinking about what you said that night, about people who disapproved of violent games never having played them. I realised

377

it was more than just a polite way of saying I didn't know what I was talking about. I thought just seeing them over somebody's shoulder was enough, but the truth is I *have* never actually played one. I've never been interested; I'm not particularly interested. But I should examine the evidence.'

Drew grinned.

A few minutes later she was sitting in front of one of Drew's computers, her husband leaning over her shoulder, launching the game for her.

'Is this something comparable to *Trail of the Sniper*?' she asked.

'God, no. I'm not letting you near anything like that until you've grasped a few principles and immersed yourself properly in some gameplay. Otherwise all you'll see is the blood and gore.'

'So what is this?' she asked, before the word *Doom* appeared on the screen, answering her question.

'Is this the one that had you shouting at the *Today* programme, when John Humphrys was going on about killing people with chainsaws?'

'No, that was *Doom 3*. This is seriously old-school.'

Drew showed her how to control the cursor and movement with her right hand on the mouse and her left on the keyboard, and she haltingly began manoeuvring around the virtual environment, assailed every so often by a blob of coloured pixels in a vaguely humanoid shape.

'The graphics are like something you'd play on your phone,' she observed.

'I do play it on my phone,' Drew replied. 'But these graphics were supposedly so disturbing that the game was given an eighteen certificate at the time.'

He was serious about immersing her in the gameplay. He made her work her way through several levels, saying she wouldn't be allowed to move on to anything else—or indeed stop—until she could make it through a map without getting killed.

'Objective achieved, sir,' she reported once she had lain waste to another onslaught of less-than-disturbing pixel-rendered hell-spawn.

'Let's move you forward a few years,' said Drew. 'With a wee bit of *Serious Sam 2*.'

This was one of the games he let the boys play, though in the interests of not prejudicing the experiment he didn't spare her the blood and gore. It was a riot of colour, a romp across a cartoonish landscape through the eyes of a knowingly cheesy macho protagonist. She fired grenades, rockets, laser beams and cannonballs, all a simple matter of pointing and clicking.

'When do I get to see the under-the-counter hardcore stuff?' she asked.

'Keep playing. I chose this because there's a sniper rifle later in the game.'

'Where?'

Drew brought down a command console and keyed in some code. A rifle suddenly appeared on the ground in front of her. She moved over it to pick it up, then switched to using it.

Catherine felt a moment's unease as the wide perspective changed to the bobbing, narrow view through the simulated scope. She thought of Hamish Queen's head, framed between similar crosshairs, but it was difficult to maintain the image when she was looking at some kind of mutant space

379

zombie. She clicked the mouse and the zombie's head exploded. It was hardly tasteful, but she had to concede it was unlikely to inure her to the psychological trauma of taking another human life.

She zoomed out, found another target and repeated the drill.

'How you getting on?' Drew asked.

It was only when she noticed him place down a refilled wine glass for her that she realised he had left the room and come back. She'd become engrossed, and she had to admit she was enjoying herself.

'It's laughably facile,' she said, administering another long-distance headshot with her sniper rifle. 'No matter the range, you just zoom in with the scroll-wheel and click. Dead-shot every time without having to bother about zeroing the . . .'

Christ.

And there it was: the tiny adjustment in perspective that caused the picture puzzle to look completely different.

'What?' Drew asked, as she hadn't spoken, moved or even blinked for several seconds.

'Nothing,' she said, getting up from the PC. 'I just need to make a quick call, then I'll be right back.'

'You just worked out Serious Sam is the man who can help you crack the case?'

'Something like that.'

Moonlight Theatre

There was a clanking noise coming from somewhere as Fallan's Land Rover made its way along the A66 into the Lake District national park. It piqued a moment's sadness in Jasmine, as she found herself bizarrely nostalgic for the unsolved rattling sound that used to disturb her at the wheel of her lost and lamented Civic.

It was weird to think about how much the noise had worried her, what its consequences might be, what it might ultimately cost her. Every time she turned up the stereo she knew she was procrastinating, running away from a problem that would eventually have to be solved, but she had been wrong. Now the issue was completely moot, and she'd never find out what it was.

She hadn't found out who the bastard in the silver Passat was either, but she'd stopped worrying about him too, for now at least. Maybe that was another question Russell Darius could answer.

Fallan pulled over into a layby and climbed out of the vehicle.

'Where you going?' she asked.

'I keep hearing a noise, something rattling against the chassis. I'm going to take a look underneath, make sure my wee emergency kit isn't about to come loose.'

'Your emergency kit?' she asked, then realised what he meant. 'Oh. You mean you still keep a gun stashed under there,' Jasmine said, trowelling on the disapproval in her tone.

Fallan eyed her sternly.

'How did you say you got this guy's address?' he asked.

'Police contact, via someone at Galt Linklater. I figured Darius would have rifle permits, so his details would be on file.'

'And did you figure he would also have rifles?'

She had to concede it was a fair point.

When they were investigating the Ramsay case Jasmine recalled telling Fallan that she didn't want him carrying guns around her. She also recalled subsequently telling him, once they'd been shot at a few times, to ignore her if she said anything so daft in future.

They were on their way to challenge the man who had killed Tessa Garrion, and most likely Hamish Queen too. It was unlikely that the mere revelation of their knowledge would cause him to cower in shame and surrender. A gun would probably help.

Jasmine had reckoned she would be a very long time waiting for a reply from Darius, far less an invitation to pop round for a chat, and had decided just to brazen it out and confront him. In terms of the investigation, there was really nothing else left that she could do.

She *had* found a possible lead buried amid what little information the police had revealed about Hamish Queen's murder, but it was tentative, not a matter she was in a position to move on until she had received confirmation of something from an official source. If there was one thing she had learned on this investigation, it was that people wouldn't talk until you had something on them. Thus she knew she wouldn't get anywhere by door-stepping someone with a theatre connection simply because her name was Veronica, especially when

382

Jasmine's next question was regarding her part in a drug-fuelled satanic ritual that ended in murder.

'Oh no, I think you must have me confused with somebody else, dear.'

Fallan popped back up from under the vehicle, his inspection complete.

'It's the exhaust,' he announced with a frown. 'It's ready to fall off.'

Fallan turned the Land Rover around and drove back ten or twelve miles to a town where he'd noticed a Kwik-Fit garage as they passed through. He left the vehicle with the mechanics and suggested they grab a bite to eat while they waited for the exhaust to be replaced.

About a quarter of a mile from the garage they found a pub that looked like a Constable painting with a beer garden. They ordered food at the bar and it was brought to them outside, where they sat at a trestle table, Fallan facing the street, Jasmine with a view of what the menu informed her was an eighteenth-century coaching inn.

They sat and ate, easy in each other's company. They could have been two more tourists, enjoying dinner outside on a warm summer's evening as the sun began to dip. She wondered what they looked like to the people at the other tables. Good friends, perhaps? Lovers? God, no. Please don't anyone be thinking that.

Father and daughter?

Jasmine was finishing off the last of her lemonade when Fallan's face did that thing, a sudden alertness to his features, like a dog that's just smelled trouble long before the humans will see or hear anything. However, he didn't throw her to the floor or initiate any other dramatic action. Instead, he bowed his head just a little lower over his plate and took a mouthful of food, as though nothing had happened.

'Look at me and keep looking at me,' he instructed.

'What is it?'

'The bloke I saw in Balnavon. I just spotted him on the other side of the street.'

'He's been following us?'

'Yeah, but I don't know how. I've been keeping an eye out for a tail, and we doubled back to get here.'

'He's good, then.'

'Maybe not that good. I just made him for the second time.'

Fallan waited a few moments and then got up, handing her some cash.

'Wait five, get the bill and I'll meet you back at the garage,' he said, his voice dark with intent.

'Hang on, this isn't going to be one of those situations where you come back with blood on your hands and give me a one-liner, is it?'

'I just want to find out what he's driving, maybe get a plate.'

'Oh.'

*   *   *

Jasmine sat in the reception area of the garage and waited, trying not to keep checking the clock, trying not to admit she was worried. Ten minutes passed. Fifteen. Twenty. The guy behind the desk was starting to look antsy, the Land Rover all fixed up in the forecourt and the clock edging nearer and nearer eight o'clock and closing time.

Her mobile rang and she almost leapt in her seat, fishing it hurriedly out of her pocket. She felt a little sick when she saw the caller wasn't Fallan.

Her phone didn't recognise the number.

'Jasmine?' asked a male voice. 'It's Callum Ross, from Culfieth Hydro. We spoke a few days ago about Tessa Garrion. Listen, I've got some new information, if you're still interested.'

'Very. Fire away.'

'Actually, its old information, but it's new to me and that's kind of the point. Your visit fair got the old cogs turning. Us retired polis hate it when we remember unanswered questions, especially from the cases when you were told to stop asking them. I made a few calls, looking to dig up what was on file regarding Tessa Garrion.'

Jasmine was doubly curious now, as there had been nothing on STORM, but she had been warned it only went back twenty years.

'You mentioned she'd gone to London for a while, so I got an old mate of mine in the Met to do a search. She was on their files. They wanted to speak to her as part of a murder investigation, summer of 1981.'

'She was a suspect?'

'No. They thought she might be a witness. If she'd been a suspect we may have got a bulletin about it, though communications between different forces was haphazard in those days. It was still the age of steam. These days, if another force was seeking her as a witness it would have been flagged up the second we put her name into a computer, but back then not a lot trickled down to a backwater like Balnavon.'

'What was the case?'

'Reginald Sutton, a film producer. Low-budget crap: soft-core *terribly British* sex comedies and cheesy horror films. Found dead in his office, stabbed through the neck with a letter-opener. They arrested his missus for it. Forensics found . . . I hope you don't mind me being graphic here.'

'No, go on.'

'Forensics found traces of vaginal fluid on his genitals. He was known for playing away, making use of the old casting couch and all that that entails. The Met cops reckoned the wife had walked in on him shagging some budding young actress and just lost the plot.'

'So did they do her for it?'

'No. She had a solid alibi, plus everyone the police spoke to said she was long past being bothered by the fact that her husband was a philanderer. They reckoned it more likely to have been a hit. Turned out Reggie had a lot of dodgy gangland connections. There was bent money pumped into all his films, partly laundering, partly so the villains could go to a few parties and premieres. He owed money to some dangerous people.'

So that explained why Tessa had apparently changed her mind and taken up Hamish's offer to join his fledgling touring company. She wasn't the future star sought by Man United, playing out the end of the season at Elgin City to get his head straight. She was sought by the police—and, more worryingly, quite probably the mob—because she had seen something that held the key to a murder.

That was why Finnegan had been able to call her bluff. She wasn't going to phone the police about his drugs because she didn't want them hearing her name, didn't want them learning where she was. Tessa didn't know that her name actually meant nothing to the cops in Balnavon, or at least she wasn't taking any risks. If she came forward as a witness in a gangland murder investigation, then she knew she'd be a target; and if she had actually seen this bloody slaying first-hand, then she would have a gruesomely vivid picture of what might happen should the perpetrators ever catch up with her.

*   *   *

Finally, Jasmine saw Fallan come around the corner and into the forecourt. There was blood on his hands. And his nose. And his mouth.

She hurried outside to meet him.

'What happened to you?'

'He made me. Must have got too close. He doubled back without me seeing. I came around a corner and bang, there he was waiting for me. Put me down. Fair to say I didn't get the plate.'

'Are you all right?'

'I can take a beating,' Fallan replied sourly. 'It's one thing I can thank my late father for teaching me.'

The sky was turning to dusk as they reached Blackwater Cottage, the location Jasmine had been given as Darius's address. It was signposted from the main road, but as the main road was barely worthy of its 'B' status, she was glad of the sat-nav to have got even this far.

Inside, she was cursing the Land Rover, as she would very much have preferred to be making this approach two or three hours ago, with the sun still bright in the sky.

Despite the modest-sounding classification of its name, the cottage looked a fairly sizeable property,

387

sheltered in the cleft of a steep and narrow valley. They could see it nestled below them, once they had turned, past the Private signs, on to a tight single-track road that wound down the incline in switchbacks. Fallan guided the Land Rover cautiously on its descent, aware that the hedges and trees flanking both sides might make it hard to see if something happened to be approaching around the next corner.

In the event, something was, and when it did they could hardly miss it; in fact, missing it was going to be the main problem. They heard the sudden gunning of an engine and the crunch of tyres on a loose surface, and turned the final bend in time to see a black BMW coming head-on at speed.

'He's not going to stop,' Jasmine realised in alarm.

'Get the plate,' said Fallan, braking and turning the wheel.

'What?'

'Get the plate!' he repeated, slewing the Land Rover as far into the side as he could manage, making room for the BMW to pass, which it only managed at the cost of a wing mirror to each vehicle.

The dazzle of headlights prevented Jasmine getting a bead on the plate before the car crunched along their flank, but she managed a good look from the rear, repeating the registration to herself until she could get out her phone and key it into a note.

'I hope that wasn't Darius,' Jasmine said.

'I doubt it. Didn't you see that guy?'

'No, I was looking for the plate, remember? What about him?'

'Ski mask. I suspect naughtiness.'

Jasmine phoned Rab Forrest at Galt Linklater with the plate and requested he get her a PNC check post-haste.

Fallan drove the Land Rover slowly and softly as he covered the rest of the distance to the cottage. The four-by-four rolled over the final few yards at walking pace, the engine already off.

'Get out quietly,' he said in a near whisper. 'Don't close the door.'

Jasmine climbed delicately from the vehicle, watching where she put her feet, holding the door carefully so that it didn't fall shut. As she looked towards the cottage she heard a creak and saw the front door swing inwards, then froze to the spot as a figure emerged on rapid but unsteady feet, holding a shotgun. He was male, short, slight of frame, bearded, wild-eyed, jumpy and bleeding.

Russell Darius.

Jasmine turned to look across the Land Rover and saw that Fallan wasn't there any more. He had disappeared from view as surely as if he had just teleported out of there.

It took Darius a second to see her, as though in his frantic and enraged daze he had been so intent upon the person he expected to find that he needed a moment to register the one who was actually there. Once he'd clocked her, though, he had eyes for nothing else. He levelled the shotgun in his hands, his eyes glaring down the barrels.

'Who the blazes are you?' he demanded. 'What do you want?'

Jasmine couldn't speak, couldn't move, other than to raise her hands in surrender.

Blood was trickling from his hairline. It ran into

his left eye and he raised a hand to wipe it, cradling the shotgun in the crook of his right arm. The barrels dipped a little, then jerked upwards sharply as the gun was wrested from his grasp and a pistol placed at the back of his head.

Fallan.

'We're private investigators,' he said, sliding the shotgun away across the earth with his foot and beckoning Jasmine forward to take it.

She found the catch and broke the gun, pulling out both rounds. Fallan moved away from Darius, stepping around to face him but keeping the pistol trained, thumb on the safety. Darius looked threatened but less manic, as though it was easier being the one under the gun than waving it.

'We're looking for an actress named Tessa Garrion,' Jasmine said, finding her voice. 'She disappeared thirty years ago from Kildrachan House near Balnavon, where she was part of the Glass Shoe Company.'

Darius looked quizzically from her to Fallan.

'You came to talk about Shakespeare but you brought a nine-mil?' he asked, his well-travelled accent betraying just the subtlest remnant of Geordie. 'They take theatre seriously where you come from.'

'Glasgow audiences are pretty merciless,' Fallan replied. 'Bear that in mind when the lady starts asking you questions.'

'Can't we discuss this civilly, inside?' he pleaded. 'I've just had somebody break into my house and I've taken a very nasty bang on the head. I'd like to clean up the wound, maybe have a seat, make sure my brains aren't falling out.'

'No,' ruled Fallan. 'Let's stay as we are. I'd say a

bit of moonlight theatre would be appropriate.'

Darius put a hand to his bleeding scalp.

'And I'd say that was in rather poor taste.'

'You would know,' said Jasmine.

'Not a big horror fan, then?' Darius replied sardonically.

'Horror, I don't mind. Snuff movies, not so much.'

Darius seemed guardedly contemplative in response. He had lost the look of wild-eyed fear, but he was still on edge, and this remark had clearly got a lot of wheels moving behind the scenery.

'Assuming you're not from a new paramilitary wing of *Mediawatch*,' he said wearily, 'can I ask what you think snuff movies might possibly have to do with me?'

'You know fine,' Jasmine fired back. 'You made one, at Kildrachan House, summer of 1981. You and a woman named Veronica Simpson, a drifter from New Zealand who called herself Saffron. You killed Tessa Garrion. You drugged her, stripped her naked, stabbed her to death and filmed the whole thing. Then when Tessa couldn't be found, Saffron lied to the police about seeing her get the bus out of town, while you blackmailed Tormod McDonald to change his story about what he saw. It's over, Mr Darius.'

He looked to Fallan, then back at Jasmine, fixing her with a particularly penetrating gaze. If it was possible to be *be*mused and *a*mused at the same time, then Darius was pulling it off.

'And if I admit to this, do you feel my confession would have greater or lesser veracity through having been obtained at gunpoint?'

Fallan took a step further back and lowered the pistol.

'You came at us first,' he said. 'With a shotgun.'

'I had just discovered an intruder in my home, for God's sake. I don't habitually go around waving guns at people.'

'Did he attack you?'

'No. Yes. Sort of. I disturbed him. I came home and saw this car outside. I wasn't expecting visitors. I saw that there was nobody in the car and nobody waiting for me in the garden. I noticed that there was a light on inside, so I was a bit concerned.'

'So you went for your guns?'

'No. Not at first. I opened the front door pretty carefully, I'll say that. Then I called out, asked if anyone was there, precisely because I didn't want to startle him if there *was* an intruder.'

'Especially if he'd got to your guns first,' said Jasmine.

'No. I keep them in a secure room with a six-digit PIN on the lock, so I wasn't worried about that. I heard no response, so I began to suspect I'd left the light on myself, but then the door to my viewing room opened and suddenly I'm staring at this six-foot guy in a ski mask.'

'Your viewing room's soundproofed, yeah?' suggested Fallan.

'Indeed. That's why he didn't hear me. I don't think he was here to attack me, he was looking for something. But suddenly I'm between him and the exit, and he just barrelled into me.'

Darius rolled his eyes a little in self-recrimination.

'Looking back, I may actually have got in his way by trying to dive out of it. We grappled in the hall and he threw me off. I rattled my head pretty hard against the edge of a radiator.'

He gave his head another delicate pat, blood

sticky on his fingers. Fallan's eyes remained vigilantly monitoring his movements.

'I lay there in a daze for a little while. At first I was relieved, but then I felt this combination of fear and boiling rage, so I went for my shotgun. If he'd still been there I wouldn't have fired, though. I just wanted the bugger on his knees, with his bloody mask off, telling me who he was and what he wanted.'

'What do you think he wanted?' Jasmine asked.

'He was rooting through my library.'

'He was after a book?'

'Films. DVDs and videotapes. I don't know why. I have a few rarities but nothing you're going to be able to put under the hammer at Sotheby's. Look, sincerely, can we go inside? I need some painkillers.'

'Maybe he was looking for a snuff movie,' Jasmine stated.

Just then, her phone chimed, alerting her that she'd received a text. A glance at the screen showed it was from Rab, and Jasmine's eyes widened involuntarily as she read the succinct datum it conveyed.

'What?' asked Fallan.

'It's the BMW. It's registered to Murray Maxwell.'

Darius's head lifted sharply in response, his eyes briefly narrowed in thought before his look of concentration was replaced with one of grim satisfaction at whatever he'd concluded.

'You've been talking to Murray about my snuff movie, haven't you?'

'Yes,' Jasmine confirmed. 'He dismissed it as an urban myth until we told him a little more. He became considerably less sanguine when we shared

393

some of the details from Jan Neumann's account.'

'I'll bet he did,' Darius said with bitter amusement. 'Sufficiently that he came charging down here looking for it. He didn't find it, though. So why don't you both come inside and I'll *show* you my snuff movie.'

Horror Show

Darius led them through his house to the viewing room towards the rear of the property, past testament to his various enthusiasms. Serious outdoorwear hung on hooks above walking boots and waders; fishing tackle lay on the wooden floor between bookshelves heaving with philosophy volumes and collected works of film criticism. Upon the walls there were framed posters of his movies, many with the translated titles of foreign-market releases, interspersed with photographs of his son and daughter, from infanthood through to wedding shots. Some even showed his ex-wife Margaret King, a one-time 'scream queen' who was these days a regular on an American detective series. Jasmine had read that they were still on fairly amicable terms, and that Darius had directed a few episodes of the show.

Fallan stayed with him as he helped himself to painkillers and fashioned an ice pack for his head, while Jasmine took a seat in the viewing room. Three of the walls were lined with literally thousands of videotapes and DVDs, the fourth accommodating a huge plasma TV and a pull-down screen for cine-projection. There were dozens of cassettes and empty cases scattered about the floor, evidence of Maxwell's apparently fruitless search.

'He'd have been here a while,' Darius said, taking an elephant stool from the corner and climbing to reach one of the topmost shelves. 'But happily I know precisely where the needle he was looking for sits in this haystack.'

He picked a single black DVD case from the shelf and placed the disc into a player underneath the plasma screen.

'He was looking for a tape. The original is on Betamax. Far superior quality to VHS, better enduring too. The tape itself was in perfect condition, but with the player becoming obsolete I transferred all my cassettes to DVD because I knew that once my machine packed in I wouldn't be able to replace it. All the originals are in a box in the attic.'

Jasmine watched as a screenful of static suddenly resolved itself into a crystal-clear picture, showing the grand room at Kildrachan as described by Neumann.

It was so unnervingly sharp that it looked like it could have been taken yesterday. She saw the paintings, the furniture, the wood-panelled walls, curtains so long and so plush they probably weighed more than she did. The camera then picked out two figures in robes, one a good six inches taller than the other, and finally the woman.

It focused first upon her face, partially obscured by long hair that was thrown about by her writhing movement, then moved down her body, lingering voyeuristically on her naked breasts and tarrying again when it reached her pubic mound. It panned out to show her bound to a makeshift altar, though her spastic motion indicated delirium rather than struggle. Jasmine looked for tell-tale lines on her naked flesh: borders where latex overlapped skin that should have been easier to see on this huge, blown-up image and with such crisp picture quality. She saw none.

The shorter of the robed figures produced the dagger, its oversized handle intricately ornate, its blade long and grey. Jasmine felt a shudder as he brought it down, physical revulsion coursing through her as blood first sprayed and then pumped in rhythmic cardiac spurts from the wound.

'Jesus,' she said, and glared across at Darius.

He stared back with an expressionless, penetrating gaze, one that looked right inside her; the most uncomfortable aspect of which was wondering what he saw.

The blade struck again, with similar results, and as it did Jasmine forced herself not only to keep watching, but to look for the previous wound. She saw it: a raw slit, red-rimmed, blood smeared all around it.

The woman strained against the bonds each time the knife went in, then seemed to slip under, her strength failing, until she was still, her head rolling around to face away from the camera.

The figure bearing the knife stood with his head bowed, his hands raised and spread, a gruesome parody of a priest at his altar. He chanted some kind of incantation over the motionless corpse, then walked slowly away off screen, the body remaining in the centre of the shot.

Jasmine stared in disbelief and disgust for a few seconds. She wanted to look at Darius, to read his expression, but she had learned that the abyss gazes also into you.

Then there came another sound from the speakers, a voice on the tape.

'You all right, dear?' it said.

The woman turned her head.

'I think my foot's gone to sleep,' she replied in a Kiwi accent.

The two robed figures approached the table once more and undid her bonds. As soon as they were loose she righted herself and hopped off the table, but she made no move to get dressed. Instead she began a conspicuously drunken attempt at dancing seductively in front of the taller figure, before pulling him into a kiss.

She turned and did the same to the shorter one, tugging back his cowl. It was Darius: younger, clean-shaven but unmistakably the same man who was sitting across the screening room.

The second figure pulled back his cowl also, revealing himself to be Murray Maxwell.

'It's a fake,' Jasmine said with some relief. 'How did you manage it? It was a single shot.'

'That's theatre for you,' Darius explained. 'You don't get second takes or multiple angles on stage, so it's all in the equipment and a bit of misdirection. The initial shot showed Saffron's skin so that you didn't see any latex, but it got slapped on there by Murray each time the camera was dwelling on that lingering upstroke of the blade. The knife itself was the real star, though. The blade retracts, and there was a pump system feeding trick blood into it through a tube in the sleeve of my robe.'

'Did you tell them you were planning to pass this off as real?'

'No. I was in an embarrassingly indulgent

397

experimental phase back then. I had a credulous interest in ritual and the occult at the time, and I was doing way, way too many drugs. I wanted to act out the ritual and have an artefact of it that would look real. It was only later I had the idea of generating a bit of mystique. Worst idea I ever had.'

He shook his head, years of weary regret on his face.

'This is first-generation,' he added. 'A digital copy of the original tape. Not what I showed to Neumann. I had to dirty it up a bit, make it look like it had been passed around and copied from a copy from a copy in forbidden circles.'

'But if he knew it was a fake, why would Murray Maxwell be desperate to get his hands on it?'

'Keep watching.'

Jasmine turned back to the screen, where she could now see the woman Darius identified as Saffron drop to her knees and begin unzipping Maxwell's fly.

Darius hit Stop, for which Jasmine was most grateful.

'It gets a bit graphic from here on in. We were all pretty out of it and we got a bit carried away. Very carried away, in fact. So I didn't make a snuff movie, but I did somewhat inadvertently make a porno. Murray and I both had sex with Saffron, and it's all on this tape.'

'So why did you lean on Tormod McLeod to recant his story? Why didn't you just tell him what he'd seen was staged?'

'I tried telling him it was fake, but there was no convincing him once he'd decided what he'd seen with his own eyes was true, especially someone raised on tales of satanic evil. I strong-armed him

398

as a last resort.'

'Couldn't you have just shown him the tape?'

'No, because I'd already told Murray I'd destroyed it. The day after, we were all aware things had gone too far. I think Finlay Weir went to talk to Saffron at one point and she was so embarrassed she wouldn't even leave her house. I lied and told Murray the tape was erased. So a few years later, when the snuff story broke, all he would have known about it was what was in the tabloids. He'd no idea the infamous snuff movie was actually the tape we made until you told him about it. Now he's worried the existence of a skin flick with him in it could torpedo his career.'

Like it had just torpedoed Jasmine's investigation. The ramifications hit her hard: what Darius had shown her meant her quest may well have met its final end down a narrow, winding lane in the Lake District. Not only was her snuff-movie theory dead in the water, her one other possible lead had also been wiped out by what she'd just seen.

The police reports had said Hamish Queen was watching an outdoor play when he was killed. It had taken Jasmine moments online to deduce that the performers must have been the Loch Shiel Players as, according to their website, the amateur company had been putting on 'Moonlight Shakespeare' at Cragruthes Castle for almost a decade. One of their leading performers was named Veronica, but even allowing for ageing and theatrical make-up there was no way the woman Jasmine had seen in the website photos was the same person who appeared in Darius's video.

'Shit,' she said, which barely began to cover it.

'Bollocksed your little theory, have I?' asked

Darius, less than sympathetically.

'Little bit.'

He looked puzzled for a moment, as something occurred to him.

'You thought I *killed* Tessa Garrion at Kildrachan. Are you saying she never appeared again? Because I always assumed she must have pitched up somewhere safe and sound, given that the police just dropped the whole thing.'

'Saffron told the police she saw Tessa getting on a bus that night, but we're pretty sure she was lying. We just don't know why any more. Saffron blew town herself shortly afterwards, but none of it adds up now.'

'For what it's worth I can show you some footage of Tessa, if you like.'

He sounded apologetic, aware it was barely above worthless.

'Yeah, that would be great,' Jasmine replied, trying to sound more grateful than she felt. It was a sad little consolation prize: all this way down the line and the most she'd recover from Darius's house was a digitally transferred replica of a memory.

He climbed back up to the same shelf and produced another disc, popping it into the machine and carefully replacing its potentially explosive predecessor inside its plastic case.

'This was shot during rehearsals,' he said as the plasma screen was once again filled with light.

Jasmine saw the interior of the church hall. She could see the graveyard outside through the windows, recognised the view of the street beyond. Balnavon didn't look like it had changed much in thirty years, but the same could not be said of the cast.

The actors were preparing to rehearse, milling around, waiting to be called to order by their director. Jasmine saw all of the people she'd spoken to recently, pictured clearly and in close-up: Finlay Weir, a little more gawky and less handsome than she had assumed; a surprisingly androgynous Tormod McDonald standing next to his very pretty sister (whom Jasmine was relieved to observe looked less likely to get carded on a night out than she did); Hamish Queen, glancing with mild annoyance at the intrusion of the camera; and Julian Sanquhar, a slight and apologetic figure whom she'd never have taken for a future political heavyweight.

Then, finally, the camera found the woman Jasmine had been looking for: Tessa Garrion.

She looked mature for her years: confident about her posture, comfortable in her own skin, unselfconscious; yet she was also clearly young, still girlish, the adolescent within her not buried so deep in her past. She was standing next to Saffron, both of them in medieval dresses. They were of similar height and build, but Saffron was easily picked out with her flowing blonde locks, Tessa's chestnut hair in a then-trendy crop Jasmine's mum used to refer to as a Purdey.

Saffron said something about the first time she saw 'the Scottish play' performed in Dunedin, and in response Tessa produced a blonde wig and turned to the camera to repeat what Saffron had said, mimicking her accent. Mimicking more than her accent; she got the intonation, timbre, pace, emphases, the lot, as well as mirroring her body language perfectly too, the way Saffron held herself

401

physically as she spoke.

She was a prodigious mimic. She would impersonate the voices she heard on the radio.

She was a suspect?

No. They thought she might be a witness.

Tessa was incomparably adept at playing women older than herself.

She was tougher than she looked. I got the impression she was more concerned about the law than I was.

When the revelation struck her, Jasmine could barely breathe as the truth of it flooded in and threatened to drown her where she sat. In that moment everything altered. Everything looked completely different.

'"I have deceived even your very eyes",' Jasmine said, her voice collapsing into a whisper. '"What your wisdoms could not discover, these shallow fools have brought to light".'

She had come here to confront Russell Darius as Tessa Garrion's murderer, but now she understood: she didn't merely have the wrong killer. She had the wrong victim.

Point of Impact

Mark Brooks was waiting for Catherine outside the training range. It was a dry, bright afternoon, the kind of day it felt good to be outdoors, almost like she wasn't working. The sense of bunking off was enhanced by them having the place to themselves. The school holidays being underway, Drew had taken the boys swimming, but if they had any idea where their mum was headed, then they'd have far rather been with her.

No pointing and clicking. Real rifles, real scopes, real bullets.

'Where's the gun?'

'Inside the range,' Mark answered, opening the gates for her. 'All set up.'

'Lay on,' she said, stepping inside and inviting him to take the lead.

'I've got some news for you,' he told her. '*Big* news. I've been trying to find out where this rifle could have been sourced. State-of-the-art weapons like this, there's usually a traceable route from the legal into the grey market, before it goes black.'

Mark handed her a pair of ear protectors as they marched towards where the AX338 was set up on a dusty and largely denuded patch of turf at the near end of the enclosed field.

'I put out feelers among my fellow gun geeks, went through some delicate back channels, let people know sources would be protected. I was hoping for a lead: know a guy who knows a guy kind of thing.'

'Mark, get to the money shot.'

He grinned.

'Okay. Guy emailed me last night with his number. David Armstrong, as in the owner of Armstrong Fabrics and Textiles. Family business goes back to the days of dark satanic mills, and he owns about half the Borders. He's got a vast private estate and he's into his hunting, into his guns. He reckons the AX338 is his. Stolen.'

'Did he voice any suspicions regarding who took it?'

'No. He only noticed it missing three days ago,

403

but the last time he used it was a week before that, so he doesn't know when it was taken. Thing is, he didn't report the theft because he couldn't admit to owning the weapon in the first place. It's illegal.'

'Calibre too high?'

'You can own a rifle up to any calibre if it's single-shot, but semi-automatics are only permitted up to .22 rim-fire, which is a lower-velocity round. The AX338 is a semi-auto shooting .338 Lapua centre-fire high-velocity rounds.'

'What was he doing with it?'

Mark gave a slight shrug, like it was a daft question.

'He likes to shoot. He's got a lot of land. Wanted to try his aim at longer distances.'

'Longer distances like nine hundred metres?'

'Not *like* nine hundred metres. Precisely nine hundred metres, when he last used it. Target practice.'

Catherine nodded with open satisfaction. This latest development didn't just back up her hypothesis, it might even bear her a suspect list. How many people would know there were weapons to be had chez Armstrong?

'So, you want to tell me what we're doing here on this fine day?' her companion asked.

'Proving that, for once, you were wide of the mark, Sergeant Crackshot.'

'With what?'

'Your expert assassin theory.'

He looked amused and intrigued, his expression saying bring it on.

'Okay. Let's say you're the shooter, and you're not some military-trained pro, but you know where you can get hold of a rifle and some ammo. You take the gun from the home of David Armstrong and you set yourself up for your shot in the grounds of Cragruthes Castle during the moonlight play. If you're not an expert, you're not going to try your hand from almost a kilometre away. You're going to position yourself much closer. Still under cover, obviously, but as near as you can get: maybe just inside the tree line. That's a hundred and eighty, maybe two hundred metres tops.'

She knelt down next to the AX338.

'You've used a rifle before, under careful supervision, probably on a range like this one. It was all set up for you, the instructor talking you through it at first, but you grasped the basics and maybe even surprised yourself how accurate you were. So you know what you're doing as you lie down in the woods, lining up your victim in the crosshairs of this phenomenally powerful, precisely accurate long-range weapon.'

'Through a scope that's zeroed for nine hundred metres,' said Mark, letting out a wry and slightly embarrassed chuckle as he got it. 'Face-palm.'

'The shooter thinks where you're looking is where you're shooting. We're about two hundred metres from the targets there, right?'

'About two-twenty. You know, I could have just worked it out using the tables if you'd said.'

'Never mind the ballistics,' Catherine replied. 'I don't want theoretical. I want to know for sure, using the same rifle as the shooter.'

Mark got himself prostrate on the ground and took hold of the weapon.

'You're going to want to put those muffs on,' he warned, lining up a shot at a concentric-circle target roughly two hundred metres away.

'Aim for the bullseye,' she said.

Mark flipped off the safety, took a moment and fired. He shot five rounds to get a consistent grouping.

'You couldn't hit a coo's arse with a banjo,' she told him.

All of the shots were high, embedding in a tight pattern at twelve o'clock in one of the outer rings.

'I'd put that at forty-five to fifty centimetres,' Mark estimated. 'Begging the question why the bullet hit Hamish Queen instead of comfortably clearing his head and cracking into the castle wall.'

Catherine produced her phone and loaded up the clearest image she had of the fateful group photo, handing it to him.

'It's because Hamish Queen wasn't the target. When the killer pulled the trigger, his crosshairs were on Veejay Khan.'

The Fate of that Dark Hour

Fallan drove in though the south entrance to the multi-storey at the Buchanan Galleries, parking on the fourth floor before he and Jasmine made their way swiftly downstairs to the second, where the hire car he had parked there first thing that morning was waiting. Roughly four minutes after entering at Bath Street in a green Land Rover, they left again via the Killermont Street exit driving a blue Mondeo, making for the M8 and heading north.

The subterfuge was necessary to ditch their stalker, the ex-military-looking creep who had decked Fallan down in the Lake District.

'I'm sick of this guy showing up wherever we go and yet we never see him on our tail,' he had said. 'It's like we've emailed him our itinerary for the day so he knows where to be before we even get there.'

Today's itinerary would take them all the way to the Ardnamurchan peninsula and finally, Jasmine was sure, to the answers she was looking for.

They made it there by early afternoon, not long after two. The journey took a little less than three hours, the last twenty minutes of which was down a single-track road with passing places, which were largely redundant as the only things they had passed in ten miles were on four legs. The sat-nav on Jasmine's mobile showed a monotonous solitary line surrounded by nothing, like an asystolic reading on an ECG.

They'd had to use her phone for navigation as the Mondeo's cigarette lighter didn't match the plug on Fallan's device, and he didn't have an adapter. She had pre-cached all the maps before they made it out of Glasgow, and her contingency was vindicated by the falteringly weak signal out here; though by the time the signal was flickering between one bar and nothing they were already on this final road with no navigating left to do. It was something she did out of habit, mindful of the possibility that the phone signal might be lost at the same time as she was. The GPS would have tracked them regardless of the mobile reception, but without pre-caching the maps it would have been tracking them across a blank screen. Ironically, even with the maps loaded that wasn't far from the truth.

The house came into view as they crested the hill they'd been climbing for the past two miles, the loch shimmering in the middle distance behind it. It was about half a mile from the water, on a plateau that was like a natural half landing midway up the mountainside. The road descended a steep diagonal, skirting a tree line that also snaked part of the way down the slope then stopped abruptly, giving way to scrub, boulders and scree.

'Jeez,' said Jasmine, 'and I thought Darius lived in the middle of nowhere.'

'Bugger being *her* postman,' Fallan agreed.

It was a handsome, mostly wooden building, a Scandinavian-style structure on two storeys, flanked by timber balconies and walkways. The road passed what Jasmine deduced was actually the rear of the property, as it had been built facing the loch. As they approached, Jasmine was assured to spot a four-by-four parked at the near side of the house, meaning someone was home. Then as the Mondeo rose over another undulation in the track, Jasmine saw her, pruning a bush where the edge of her property met the road.

The woman glanced up at the sound of the vehicle's approach, turning to face it once it became apparent that it was coming to a halt rather than passing through. Jasmine found it amazing that there could be anywhere beyond here that they might be on their way towards. In her case, it was definitely the end of the line.

Fallan parked the Mondeo in the passing place adjacent to the rear of the house, next to a large cylindrical oil tank, another indicator of their remoteness. No gas mains way out here. The back garden was very expansive and there was plenty of room behind the four-by-four, but the long driveway was only one car's width, so Jasmine guessed Fallan didn't want to make the woman edgy by boxing in her vehicle.

She walked slowly towards them as they got out of the car, almost as though she was heading them off before they reached her property. The shears in her hands looked pretty threatening to Jasmine's eyes, but only because she had watched *The Burning* a few nights ago, Fallan having mistakenly picked it up along with his Russell Darius collection.

'Can I help you?' they were asked. The tones were firm and polite, Jasmine detecting disguised apprehension. This house was probably Hamish Queen's first phone call after Jasmine's meeting with him at the Playhouse. That was why she hadn't rung ahead.

'We're looking for Veronica Simpson.'

The woman narrowed her features in concentration, as though Jasmine had asked for someone who might live at the next house, another five miles into the beyond.

'That's you, isn't it?' Jasmine added, making it sound like she might have some doubts. She didn't, but she was playing nice. To begin with.

The woman shook her head, but it wasn't a denial.

'Yeah, sorry,' she said, like she was coming out of a daze. 'It's just nobody's called me that for a very long time.'

Jasmine noted the accent: soft hints of New Zealand, diluted in a region-neutral Scots.

'We're actually interested in what you called yourself before that.'

She gave Jasmine a puzzled, almost amused look.

'You mean Saffron?'

Jasmine glanced past her for a moment, to where the loch was shimmering at the foot of the gentle

409

slope beyond the house.

'No,' Jasmine said. 'I mean Tessa.'

*   *   *

Fallan proved the keenness of his reflexes, responding in a twinkling to cover the ground between them as Tessa Garrion collapsed. It was not some theatrical swoon; more like a sudden draining that began in her head and worked downwards. First her mouth made this wavering, stroke-like expression, which was perhaps Fallan's cue to move, a fraction of a second before her legs went.

Jasmine had planned to pre-empt any denials by taking out her phone and displaying a screen-cap from Darius's rehearsal video: a shot of Tessa and Saffron side by side. It proved everything: who she really was and who she really wasn't.

Tessa's reaction indicated it wouldn't be necessary.

Fallan set her down in a faint-recovery position, resting her head gently on the grass and beckoning Jasmine to elevate her feet. After a few minutes they let her climb slowly upright and made sure she was steady to walk.

'You'd better come inside,' she said.

They helped her through the hall and down a broad pine staircase into a split-level open-plan room with vast double-glazed panes affording a stunning view down to the loch. There were toys lying scattered around the floor, evidence of a recent family visit. Jasmine logged the photos on their way through the house and around the big public room: shots of the same person as a

410

schoolboy, as a rangy teen, in graduation gown, wedding portraits, as well as several collages of what she took to be the grandchildren.

Tessa rested herself delicately upon a sofa, putting her feet up as Fallan directed, then he went off to fetch her a glass of water.

She took a sip like it was whisky, cradling the glass in her hands in a way that further suggested she was nursing a spirit. The colour was starting to return to her face, but her hands were still trembling just a little.

'You want to know what happened to Saffron,' she said, as though steeling herself for this task. Her voice retained its Kiwi traces despite her admission: thirty years of pretending must have hardwired it.

'Ultimately, yes,' Jasmine replied. 'But first we want to know what happened to Reginald Sutton.'

She saw Tessa flinch. It was a mere glimpse in her eyes, like a subliminal message appearing on the screen for a solitary frame, but if you were looking for it, it was unmissable. Then she nodded to herself, resignation mixed with bitterness, a draught she had no choice but to swallow.

She lifted her head and sat up straight, like a proud matriarch about to direct two generations about their business. When she spoke, Jasmine understood that she was drawing on her pride to get through her humiliation.

'Reginald Sutton raped me,' she stated, her voice strong and unfaltering, a theatrical proclamation from which she was not shrinking. 'In his grubby little office in a mews in Ladbroke Grove, he raped me. I thought it was a call-back. I had auditioned for him a few days before, for a thriller he was producing, some *Straw Dogs* rip-off. The call came

411

from his secretary, so I thought it was above board. She said Reggie and the director would both be there, but when I turned up there was no secretary, no director, just him.'

She tutted, as though reproaching herself for her naivety over some trivial matter.

'He started off all nicey nicey, or at least his idea of what passed for charm, but he was phoning it in. I wasn't the first. I doubt I was even just the tenth. He'd been at this for years, and looking back it was almost like he couldn't be bothered lingering over the formalities. He made his overtures, told me what I had to do to "nail the part". He was very practised at what he was about, though. He had already cut off my exit so that I couldn't "make my excuses and leave", as they used to say.

'I said I wasn't interested in working for anyone who wasn't hiring me for my acting abilities. He laughed, told me not to give myself airs. He said that, in many languages, the word for actress and the word for whore are one and the same. He told me better actresses than me had been on his couch at one time or other, and I should start to understand the game if I wanted to get ahead in it. He also said he'd make sure I had no future at all if I walked out without giving him what he wanted.'

Jasmine could see her shudder in anger, tears appearing at the corners of her eyes.

'I told him he was kidding himself if he thought anyone in the British film industry was going to blackball somebody on the word of a sleazy little nobody like him. That was when he hit me, harder than I'd ever been hit before. He wasn't even angry, though: that was the thing. I'd just given him his cue. He'd done this so many times before. He told

412

me it would be worse if I struggled, reminded me that nobody knew I was there. He said he'd told his secretary the appointment was cancelled and got her to erase it from the books.'

She wiped away a tear, but her voice stayed strong, drawing on an actor's skill to deliver the lines despite how they were making her feel inside.

'I did struggle, but he was strong, and he was brutal. When you encounter that kind of brutality you feel helpless and so scared. Part of me threatened to withdraw into myself, pretend it was happening to someone else and crawl out again when it was over, but as he lay on top of me, something desperate took over, some kind of instinct that knew I had to get him out from inside me.

'The couch was close to his desk. My hand was scrabbling about and it found something metal. I grabbed it and struck out at him, trying to hit him in the side of the head. I remembered somebody telling me the way to knock someone unconscious was to hit them in the temple. I didn't hit his temple, though.'

'You hit his neck,' Jasmine said.

Tessa nodded.

'I just wanted him to stop. It went right through, so easily. I thought I'd missed him, or caught him a glancing blow and lost my grip. He fell off the couch on to the floor, and it was only when I got to my feet I saw what I'd done. Even then I told myself it must have looked worse than it was. But it was on the news that night that he was dead.

'I was so scared. I was twenty-three years old and I was facing life in prison if I got caught. I didn't believe my plea of self-defence would win me much

413

mitigation, not in those days. This was a year before a judge fined a rapist two thousand pounds because of his victim's "contributory negligence" in hitch-hiking wearing a short skirt.'

'So you decided to lay low at the other end of the country,' Jasmine said, filling her in some more on what they knew, 'and belatedly took up Hamish Queen's offer to join the Glass Shoe Company.'

'I thought I'd be safe, be hidden, among friends.'

'More than friends, in Hamish's case.'

Tessa bowed her head a little, shielding her pain from view.

'Yes,' she said, swallowing.

'Were you lovers before that?'

'No. We were friends, and there was a spark for sure, but he was married and I respected that. When I first got to Kildrachan I spent more time with Finlay.'

'He told us you were close, but it didn't come to anything.'

'Finlay was a dear friend and a decent, decent chap. It helped to have the companionship of such a good man after what happened, but it also helped that it was a chaste companionship. There was no physical chemistry there; perhaps that's why I initially sought him out. But in time I needed tenderness, to be reminded of a lover's touch so that it might help erase . . . Well, no, you simply can't erase that, but it's like when you hurt yourself and you rub the sore spot. It works by inundating the nerve with sensory information, so it carries fewer pain signals to the brain. I needed to overwhelm the nerves that carried those signals and I was selfish in my need so, despite his wife back down the road, Hamish and I became lovers.'

414

'Fighters too, we heard.'

She gave a sad smile, knowing but not regretful.

'It was very overwrought, what went on between us. We'd never have worked out together, even in better circumstances. Both too passionate about everything: about our work, about ourselves, just turned up to eleven all the time. We argued over trivia and we argued over the biggest things too.

'I confessed to Hamish what had happened in London. I only told him by way of letting him know I was going to have to leave, to go abroad. He wasn't having it; thought it could all be sorted. His father knew great lawyers, contacts in the police, et cetera et cetera. Hamish was used to everything being fixable. He wasn't the one looking at a murder charge, though. I just felt I had to run, and run a lot further than Balnavon. Hamish begged me to stay, made me all kinds of promises and assurances, which was when I played the trump card of reminding him he was married.'

She took a long look into the distance, towards the loch. Jasmine could seldom remember ever being anywhere quite so still. She heard the call of a bird that could have been just outside or quarter of a mile away.

'I said no goodbyes, except to Hamish. No farewells meant no need for explanations to anyone. We all knew the production was falling apart, so my leaving wouldn't be a total bolt from the blue. I planned just to slip away while everybody was . . . otherwise engaged, and catch the last bus to Inverness. I think I told Hamish I was taking the sleeper south overnight, but that was so that he'd think I was gone by the morning. I intended to get a bed for the night and catch a flight to Heathrow the next day from Inverness airport, then take the first stand-by I could get to the continent.'

'So Saffron *did* see you getting on that bus?' Jasmine asked, puzzled by the timeline.

'No.'

Tessa sat very still for a few moments, and Jasmine thought she detected a couple of false starts before she finally brought herself to speak once more.

'I slipped away as quietly as I could, as I didn't want to bump into anybody. But as I made my way through the grounds, I heard someone moving among the trees. I don't know if you've been to Kildrachan—'

'Not inside the estate, no.'

'Well, the road winds through some dense woods, very mature, much older than the house. I could hear somebody breathing heavily, from effort. I came off the track and approached very cautiously. As I said, I didn't want to bump into anybody and I certainly didn't want to bump into a stranger in the woods at night, but I wanted to see who was there. With the straining and heavy breathing, I was concerned someone might be trapped, or having a heart attack or God knows.'

She took a sip of water, swirling the glass and gazing down into the clear liquid.

'I saw Saffron. She was only a few yards away, lying on the ground. I thought she saw me, because she seemed to be staring right back, but she wasn't. Her eyes were wide open, but she was dead. There was someone standing close by, wearing a hooded robe. He didn't see me and I never saw his face. He had his back to me, bent over, like he was getting his breath back. He was like that for a few seconds, during which I was just frozen; frozen in fear and almost frozen in time. Then he took hold of Saffron by the feet and began—or I should say resumed—dragging her body.

'I stayed where I was, perfectly still, barely breathing, and I watched him take her away, slow and laborious, every yard an effort. Saffron always seemed to me like she would weigh nothing: she was so effervescent, so light on her feet. But this wasn't Saffron any more, just a dead weight, a broken vessel. I knew where he was going, too. There was a well in the grounds, an ancient thing. It was all roped off because part of the upper wall had collapsed and they were afraid someone might fall down it. Hamish had shown it to us so we would know to avoid it, and said his family were planning to have it filled in once they returned from their travels. I knew that was where he was taking her, and I knew she'd never be found.'

'Unless you told someone,' said Jasmine.

Tessa nodded numbly.

'I thought I was undone. I would have to come forward with what I'd seen, and by doing so I would deliver my own fate into the hands of the police. And that's when I realised I had a choice.'

Tessa's eyes were glazing, staring without focus. She wasn't looking at anything in the room or through the window. She was looking at a dead body in a moonlit wood thirty years ago.

'I took her life,' she said. 'I cannot deny it, never have done, at least not to myself . . . I took her life. I saw an opportunity before me, a chance to escape. I became her. I knew I still had to run, but I could run as someone else.'

'So the next day, when Finlay came to Saffron's

417

house and she wouldn't answer the door, that was you?'

'Yes. I went straight to her place and let myself in. I'd been there before and I knew she didn't lock the back door. Nobody locked anything much around there. I was able to sneak into the church hall and take a wig. I put on her clothes, looked out her passport and all the documentation I could find. She had been travelling for years so she had all sorts of official stuff she might need for visas and the like. Even a copy of her birth certificate.'

'Identity theft for the analogue age,' said Fallan.

'Finlay came around the next day, to say Tessa had left and to ask Saffron if she'd take over her part. I can't remember what I said, but I told him to go away, said I needed some time alone. I faked Saffron's accent, speaking to him through the door. I had intended to pack up and leave right away, but having spoken to Finlay, albeit briefly, I realised that it would cover my tracks better if more people encountered who they thought was Saffron, to give the impression she was still here for at least a couple of days after Tessa was gone.

'I phoned up the hotel and quit, said I couldn't do that day's shift. I think I said it was a family emergency or something. I found her rent book and called her landlord too, though I waited and did it the following morning, so that was one more witness, on still another day, that Saffron was still alive. I was planning to leave later that day. I had a taxi booked, partly so that it was another witness, but mainly so that I wasn't out there standing at the bus stop when someone I knew walked past.'

'The bus stop being close to the main gates of the Kildrachan estate,' said Jasmine.

418

'Exactly. So when the doorbell rang I thought it was the taxi driver come early, but when I opened it, it was a policeman, a young guy. I thought I was ruined, so it was the performance of my life to conceal how scared I was just for those first few seconds until it became apparent that he assumed I was Saffron. He was there to ask about Tessa's disappearance, as he'd been told Saffron was involved with the theatre troupe.'

'And that's when you, as Saffron, told Callum Ross that you saw Tessa get on the last bus to Inverness.'

'Yes, but that wasn't the end of it. Obviously I was rather disturbed to learn that my own leaving was being investigated as suspicious, so I asked him why all the fuss. I learned two things. The good news was that the name Tessa Garrion meant nothing to the local cops beyond this current inquiry, but the bad was that they had reason to suspect something bad had happened and they were holding Hamish for it.

'I took the taxi, as planned, and spent the night in Inverness. I was too late for the last shuttle. I think there were only two a day back then. I got booked on to the later of the next day's flights; the earlier one was full. I was concerned about Hamish though, as he was obviously keeping quiet to protect me, and if there was suspicion surrounding my disappearance, then it was only a matter of time before police beyond Balnavon started looking for Tessa Garrion. So the morning of my flight, I phoned the police station in Balnavon and spoke to the officer in charge.'

'Sergeant Dougal Strang,' said Jasmine.

'That was him, yes. I told him I knew where he

419

could find Tessa Garrion, but that I would only tell him in person, alone, and that I needed absolute, guaranteed confidentiality. He drove straight to Inverness to meet me. We spoke at the hotel. I ditched the wig and showed him my own passport to prove I was Tessa Garrion, safe and sound, and I told him I was pregnant by Hamish.'

'You were pregnant? How could you know so soon?'

'I wasn't pregnant. I told Sergeant Strang I was so that he'd agree not to tell anybody he'd seen me. I said Hamish didn't know about the baby. I wanted to go it alone, and if Hamish found out he'd try to do the right thing by me, and I didn't want him suffering all the shame and scandal that would come with it.

'The sergeant was as good as his word. As far as the police were aware, both Tessa Garrion and Saffron Simpson were alive and well. I flew to London that day, then on to Brussels.'

'Why Brussels?'

'It was the first flight with stand-by seats available when I reached Heathrow. I flew out on my own passport as I looked nothing like the photo in Saffron's, but after I got there I became Veronica Jane Simpson for keeps.'

'Until you became Veejay Khan,' Jasmine said.

'That was my husband's name for me. I met him in Brussels a few months after I arrived. I got an office job. I spoke French and had decent secretarial skills from part-time work in my drama-student days. Jaffir was a lawyer. He was from Edinburgh originally, though his family hailed from Sri Lanka. He was based in Brussels but he worked for a British firm. We got married in 1982.'

420

'Making you officially V. J. Khan, and a British citizen. Where is your husband now? Are you still married?'

Tessa nodded.

'He's in Amsterdam. Phoned me about half an hour before you arrived. It's the first time he's been away overnight since what happened to Hamish, so he was checking I was holding up all right.'

'How did you end up here?'

'We lived in Brussels until 2000, when our son, Michael, went off to university. He did law, like his father, and he chose Glasgow. We'd talked about coming back to Scotland and decided it was the right time to do it. Jaffir travelled a lot on his job and could increasingly do the rest of it from home, so we relocated. We had actually rented this place for a holiday a few years before, and it came on the market at just the right time.'

'When did you get back in touch with Hamish?'

'I ran into him in Brussels, in about 1995, at the theatre, unsurprisingly. I was there to see a production of *Woe From Wit* and he was there to check out the venue itself ahead of exporting one of his musicals. He was already doing very well and I was pleased for him. Not so well on the marriage front, but that was always Hamish's problem. I told him my married name and how I'd already ceased being Tessa Garrion as part of my disappearing act. We kept in touch.'

'Did you act again?' Jasmine asked.

'Not until I got involved with the Loch Shiel Players. There were possibilities in Brussels, but . . . I saw it as kind of a penance for what I'd done. Then once I had become a mother, it all got too complicated, and you'd be amazed how fast the years passed after that. I missed it terribly, but I knew it was a small price to pay for the life I had, compared to the one I'd have ended up with. I had Jaffir and I had Michael, and I had my freedom.

'But when we moved here I saw this amateur dramatics group performing down in Fort William and I decided to dip my toe again. Or more like the recovering alcoholic's first sip: he can't have just one sip, and I couldn't just dip my toe. I got very heavily involved, and then when funding became really tight I asked Hamish to sponsor us, which he kindly and generously did. He was the most loyal of friends, in every way.'

A tear ran down her face as she stared into the distance again, this wound still very raw. Jasmine felt Tessa's pain all the more keenly due to her growing awareness that it was her investigation that had set the dominoes falling.

'Did Hamish call you recently?' Jasmine asked. She had to lay her cards on the table here.

'Yes,' Tessa replied, her tone indicating that she was only now reminded of this. 'He called to warn me that a private investigator had been asking about Tessa Garrion. It was only a few days before he was killed.'

'We don't believe these two events were coincidental. Hamish didn't just call you, he phoned everybody who was in the Glass Shoe Company to warn them about me.'

'He didn't want them to talk. He was still trying to protect me.'

'They all had their own reasons not to talk. One more than the rest. Whoever killed Saffron knew you were still alive, knew that you had taken her identity, but also knew you'd never say anything

422

because you would incriminate yourself. But when I started digging into what happened at Kildrachan the stakes changed.'

'But how would the killer know I'd taken Saffron's identity? Are you saying it was someone from the company? I had always thought it was some local weirdo. Who else would be going around in a robe like that in the dark?'

Jasmine told her all that they'd learned about that night, the sum of all her recent efforts still lacking its final answer.

'Jesus,' Tessa reeled. 'Talk about sex, lies and videotape.'

'So despite the snuff movie being fake,' Jasmine said, 'Darius or Murray could still have been the killer. Maybe something happened as one of them walked her back to her house.'

'Murray told us he was with Julian in the kitchen, drinking whisky,' Fallan said. 'We now know for sure that part was a lie. So maybe there's another reason why he drove down to the Lake District in a desperate attempt to destroy the tape.'

Tessa shook her head.

'It couldn't have been Murray. The person I saw wasn't tall enough. Murray could probably have carried Saffron over his shoulder. He wouldn't have needed to drag her along the ground.'

'Then it had to have been Darius after all.'

'Not necessarily,' Tessa argued.

'But there's no one else it could have been,' Jasmine replied, exasperated. 'I've seen the tape myself, and it was Murray and Darius in those robes.'

'On the tape, yes,' agreed Tessa. 'But who was holding the camera?'

Stars, Hide Your Fires

He had hidden himself away behind the camera, cowering in the sanctuary of that invisible fourth wall, too scared to step beyond it and into the frame. He was supposed to be part of the ritual, he and Murray flanking Darius, an unholy trinity in the robes that had been intended for the weird sisters of act one, scene one.

He'd only have to stand there, Darius explained, for visual symmetry. No speaking part, no action. Easy enough, he'd thought; easier still after a few drams. But the second she took her clothes off and stood there naked before them, he felt this near-paralysing sense of intimidation and selfconsciousness.

He couldn't be up close. He couldn't do this.

'It's okay,' Darius had assured him, trying to stem his apologies. 'You can get us some hand-held shots, add to the impression of "found footage".'

So he had stood and watched, only stood and watched.

The violence barely registered; it meant no more to him than any other stage trick. When you were party to the technicalities, that was all you saw: equipment doing its job. You sometimes had to blind yourself to the spectacle, because your attention was already supposed to be on your next task: your blocking, your dialogue, a scenery change.

Her nakedness ceased to register too, her body becoming just another part of the performance, nudity itself a costume.

424

But then, when it was over, she began to dance. She was no longer the character of the sacrificial victim, no longer an element of Darius's tableau. She was Saffron again, but Saffron to the power of ten. Shameless, wanton, venal, lustful. Dancing naked, flaunting her nudity, pulling them into kisses, pulling both of them into a writhing embrace.

He hated her.

He wanted her.

He hated her because he wanted her, and he wanted her because he hated her.

He hated how she carried herself, draped over the men with easy familiarity. He hated how she went barefoot, bare-legged, in loose skirts that always seemed to be riding up, flashing her underwear. He hated how she seldom wore a bra, breasts always partly visible in those strappy sundresses that she favoured.

She was a disgrace. She was just like the tauntresses who had led his father to stray, preying on a good man's weakness, their shameless sins also a merciless predation upon his innocent mother.

Women like her had ruined his parents' marriage. Women of low morals, without respect for themselves, without respect for the codes, the decency of those around them. They resented those codes, that decency, resented the better lives those people were trying to live. Their conduct was an iconoclasm.

And now this, this was everything he suspected about her, writ larger than he could have imagined. Yet he could not walk away, could not look away, could not stop filming as she writhed and cavorted.

Darius and Murray became as faceless as if they

had kept up their hoods: he only saw her.

Every so often she would look towards the camera, look towards him. She was humiliating him in his exclusion, taunting him by not inviting him to join too, yet taunting him also because she knew he was too afraid to come forward should he be beckoned.

The more he watched, the more he wanted her. The more he wanted her, the more he hated her. The more he hated her, the more he wanted to watch her degrade herself in animalistic frenzy.

*   *   *

He strode out into the night, just a minute or two behind her. Murray and Darius had gone off to the kitchen in search of whisky and some food. He moved at a brisk jog; it would be unseemly, even alarming, should she turn and see him sprint.

He knew the route she'd take, and caught up quickly. She was still pretty drunk, walking in no great hurry.

'Hey, what's up?' she asked, turning to take in his approach.

'Let me walk you home. It's late and dark.'

He just wanted to walk her home. Be solicitous. See what happened. 'You're a dear, Julian, but I'm all right. Just need my bed.'

He wanted her. She'd want him too. She couldn't get enough. He just had to show willing, show he wasn't scared.

'*I'll* put you to bed,' he said, and leaned in to kiss her.

She turned her head and stepped to the side. She had this look of both amusement and distaste.

426

'God, no, Jules. I've had quite enough of that for one evening.'

Amusement and distaste. It was so unthinkable to her as to be ridiculous. She was laughing at him. Taunting him. Tempting him, flaunting herself in the most obscene ways possible, then spurning him when he rose to the bait.

Hate. Want. Hate. Want.

Something took possession of him there among the ancient trees, a demon of the woods. Something that had lurked there for aeons, older than humans: something that feeds off the worst in men and further emboldens them. When there is a wanton will in man to seek the darkness, then there is something out there that listens, and it whispers back. The ritual had summoned it forth. There was no need for the sacrifice to be real: the wickedness at its heart was real enough. It called out to evil and invited it inside.

He was no longer himself.

Hate. Want.

He wrestled her to the floor. She went down so easily, resistance and coordination dulled by drink and drugs. There was something almost compliant about it, accepting, resigned. It was proof of what she was: she didn't even have the dignity to struggle.

But as he pulled her legs apart, her face inches from his, she spoke.

'Enjoy it, you prick. This is the only way you'll ever get a woman.'

Hate. Hate. Hate.

He grabbed her head and banged it against the ground; banged it again and again and again. The hood slipped further forward in his throes of rage, rendering him faceless. He was not himself. He was the instrument of the demon, the demon of the woods.

Then in its final, calculated malice, it suddenly departed. He was himself once more, but a self changed utterly, cast into hell.

*   *   *

God forgives. If there was a single most vital underpinning to all faith, all hope, it was this: God forgives. Julian did not merely believe this, though: he knew it, because God had made His forgiveness known in the shape of a gift.

The next day, as he sat there, wretched in his numb horror, hoping his crime was not readable upon his very countenance, there came a miraculous revelation. Hamish informed them all that Tessa had walked out, abandoning the production, and as they attempted to solve the crisis it was suggested Saffron might be a suitable replacement. Finlay had gone to Saffron's house, and the discovery of her absence should have been the beginning of the end. Instead Finlay reported that he'd spoken to her. He'd found her home, but she would not come out. Darius confessed that things had gone a little too far the night before, he and Murray assuming Saffron was ashamed to face them after what they had all engaged in together.

How could he have spoken to Saffron? How could she be alive? He had killed her, dragged her body to the old well and dropped it down where he hoped it might never be discovered.

That was when he realised he'd been seen. Hamish said Tessa had left to catch the last bus to

Inverness. She would have been walking towards the main gate as he laboured to transport Saffron's body to its final resting place. She had seen and yet she had stayed silent; furthermore, she had gone to Saffron's house and imitated her voice when Finlay came to call. She had walked out on the company and on Hamish. The production was falling apart, nobody would deny it, but why would she leave without notice, under cover of night?

She was running from something, he did not know what, but she had found a perfect place to hide. She would not come forward, because to do so would be to instigate mutually assured destruction.

He was reprieved. A gift from God.

God forgives.

But a sin this black still called for great penitence, and he would pay it willingly. He would dedicate his life to others. He would lead a life of humility, of endeavour, of sacrifice. He would seek no glory, but be the conduit, the facilitator by which others may succeed. He would never forget his crime, and never cease paying his debt.

The Tyrant's Power Afoot

'The cameraman had to be Julian Sanquhar,' Jasmine said. 'Murray lied to us about being with him in the kitchen. He was with him all right, but he was a safe alibi to give because he knew Julian would never admit to us what they were both really doing. And he said Tormod came charging in at one point because he knew Tormod had been in such a state of hysteria that he wouldn't remember either way.'

'So why didn't Darius mention to us that Sanquhar was involved?' asked Fallan.

'He was protecting Julian's reputation,' said Tessa. 'Darius learned first-hand what it's like to be monstered by the press, and he knew it would ruin Julian if it could be spun that he'd once been involved in making horror and porn.'

'Would he do that?' Fallan asked. 'Spare him, I mean. He didn't owe him anything.'

'It's consistent,' Jasmine said. 'Darius could have had him on toast back when there was that Screen Scotland controversy.'

'Darius was a bit wild and arrogant in his day,' said Tessa, 'but he was never spiteful. I recall during that funding row he said in his statement he didn't believe Julian had ever actually seen a horror movie. I can see now that that was him letting Julian know he could have thrown him to the lions.'

'But maybe there's a reason Darius didn't want that can of worms re-opened either,' Fallan suggested. 'We know Darius can shoot. Can Sanquhar use a rifle?'

'He was in Afghanistan,' Tessa replied. 'He made two radio series over there, *Voices of Camp Bastion* and the follow-up, *Voices Beyond Camp Bastion*. It's possible somebody gave him some training. But why would he shoot Hamish? Nobody but me knew Saffron was dead.'

'Maybe he missed,' said Fallan darkly.

'What do you . . .' Tessa began. Then she understood.

'Oh God. He was standing right behind me. The cast were in a kind of tableau, and I was crouched on one knee.'

430

'You were the target all along,' said Fallan. 'Once Jasmine started asking questions about Tessa Garrion, the killer knew he had to eliminate the one person who knew the truth.'

Tessa looked sick again, the memory of Hamish Queen's murder presumably now taking on an even more disturbing aspect for her.

'Darius and Julian are about the same build,' Jasmine said, weighing up what they might now deduce. 'So it could have—'

'It was Julian,' said Tessa with grave certainty. 'He knew where to find me. He knew about the Moonlight Shakespeare performances: he'd been to one, a few years back. I never saw him, but I heard somebody say he was in the audience that night. You know: "Ooh, the head of Arts Council Scotland. Maybe we'll get a grant." I was terrified he'd recognise me. Only Hamish knew who I was. I thought I'd be all right in make-up, but we always mingled after the show. Fortunately, I heard he left before the end.'

'Because he was as scared as you of meeting face to face,' Jasmine said. 'He had worked out what you'd done, but he couldn't be sure how much you had seen. But if he left before the end, how could he know there would be a photo call? You were in the spotlight half the night, but he took his shot after the final act.'

'There's often a photo call at the end of an amateur show, and Sir Angus has lots of previous ones hanging up in his study. It's possible he saw those and knew it was coming. But if you ask me, that wasn't it. Knowing Julian, he probably thought it impolite to kill me before the play was finished.'

'The show must go on,' said Fallan.

431

Jasmine got to her feet. She'd heard enough.

'I think it's time to call Catherine McLeod. Tell her to cross-reference whatever they have on the Queen murder against Julian Sanquhar.'

She looked to Fallan to see if he felt otherwise.

'Call her right now,' he said. 'If he's come at Tessa once, he'll come at her again.'

Tessa clutched her hands to herself in response, looking anxiously towards Jasmine.

Jasmine glanced at the screen on her mobile. There was a little 'x' where the signal indicator usually sat.

'Do you mind if I use your landline?' she asked.

'No, by all means.'

Jasmine picked up the handset and pressed the green dialling button. There was no tone.

'It's dead,' she reported.

'It was working fine earlier. Jaffir called me from Amsterdam about half an hour before you arrived. Did you press the—'

'Green button, yes. There's nothing.'

'They must be working on the line. It'll come back on in a wee while, or you can usually get a signal if you drive up to the brow of the hill.'

'I'll do that,' she said, making for the stairs.

Fallan got up and blocked her path.

'Do *not* go out that door,' he said in a tone that was not to be argued with. 'And I'd tell you to stay away from the windows, except this place is nothing *but* windows.'

'What's wrong?' Jasmine asked.

'Jolly bad luck there's a fault on the line just when we've tracked down the one person who could tell us what happened at Kildrachan House.'

Multiplying Villainies

He had been paying this debt for thirty years before he was confronted with what the true price might be.

He felt a chill to the heart when he got the phone call from Hamish, but he knew not to panic. There had been small scares before, glimpses of a possible confluence of events that might conspire to precipitate discovery, not least sitting in an audience one evening and realising Tessa Garrion was among those performing before him.

It was when he met the girl, Jasmine, that he knew the situation was dire. He agreed to speak to her in order to find out what she already knew, and more importantly find out whether she was capable of getting to the truth. On that score, he saw very quickly that he could have no doubt.

He recalled those headlines after the Ramsay story broke last year. For the first time, he was forced to contemplate how much worse it would be now, than had his crime been discovered back in 1981. He had so much more to lose.

He had a father's responsibility to his children, a husband's duty to his wife, to protect them, to provide for them and ensure their futures. He could not allow this fate to fall upon them. He had no choice but to act, to eliminate the one element that held the key to everything else.

He knew her name. Knew where she lived. He had been invited to watch an outdoor Shakespeare performance at Cragruthes Castle and had sat there in the audience in cold horror when he recognised not only her face but her voice, her stage presence and her talent. He had slipped away before the final act so as not to have to be introduced to her during the informal gathering that was scheduled to follow.

He knew where he could get a rifle. He had been shown how to use one, and proven a good shot too. He couldn't target her at home, though. If he did that, the police would pull apart her life in every detail as they tried to find a motive. That was when he realised the moonlit play would present the perfect time and place. A death under such circumstances would cloud his purpose in confusion, calling doubt upon whether the victim was a specific target, collateral damage or merely a random victim.

Collateral damage. Friendly fire.

He killed Hamish. He didn't understand how. The rifle had not slipped in his hand, his aim had been steady and true. Yet Hamish lay dead, not Veejay Khan. Not Tessa Garrion.

He had scrambled away in panic and fear, tossing the rifle into the dark depths of the river for fear it should be discovered on him, or that he had left some invisible trace of himself despite the gloves and all the other precautions he'd taken.

He had been rash and impulsive, and in doing so he had made everything so much worse. He had killed a man who had once been his closest friend, a man he still respected and admired though their lives had taken different paths. The only consolation was that he had further disguised his intentions. Everyone assumed Hamish was the target, and nobody understood what really lay behind the shooting. That would change, however, if the girl found what she didn't yet know she was looking for.

It was all an even bigger mess. One that would require a professional to clean up.

He had been assigned a personal escort in Afghanistan when he made *Voices Beyond Camp Bastion*. In recording its predecessor he had barely had cause—or leave—to travel out of the military compound and, satisfied as he was with the programme, he knew a companion series was required to tell the stories of the people on the other side of the fence. The British Army offered their own personnel as escorts, but he knew that people would not speak to him honestly—or indeed at all—if he appeared to be under their authority. He needed to travel with some autonomy, and to that end (abetted by a stack of awards for the first series) convinced the money men to finance a private security contractor.

His bodyguard was a former army captain from Bristol named Len Holt, a career soldier who had 'served his country and thus earned the right to serve himself'.

They spent a lot of time together over the course of a month, two men from different worlds who grew to share a mutual respect. From the off, Holt was impressed and surprised that it was just Julian and an interpreter. No entourage, no kit, no crew. He only needed his digital recorder and a microphone. Holt, for his part, impressed and surprised Julian with the depth of philosophy with which he approached the complexities of morality as they were presented by his job. He appreciated the fact that Julian wasn't judgmental, that he understood that there were those who had to undertake brutal deeds so that the rest could remain secure in the impression that they lived in a civilised society.

Towards the end of their time working together, late one night over a few drams, Holt passed him a business card. It was an odd gesture as Julian already had all his contact details, but he inferred that there was something symbolic in it, particularly as Holt was keeping one finger on the card, where he'd slid it closer to Julian on the tabletop.

'I kill people for money,' he said. 'That is the inescapable truth of my business. Sometimes certain people have to die so that the world is better for those who are left.

'They say history is written by the victors. I'd go further and add that, half the time, morality is the sheen the victors polish on the surface of a world shaped by conflict. And the other half, morality is just the self-righteousness of people who have never had to take a hard decision. Sometimes it is simply a matter of being the man with a gun, as opposed to the man without. A matter of how much further than the other guy you are willing to go in order to survive. About what you are prepared to do, what you are prepared to *pay*, in order to make the world the way you want it.'

With that, he lifted his finger from the card, inviting Julian to pick it up.

Given the rather shocking confidence that was implied in Holt's words, in truth he was rather scared not to.

'Thank you,' Julian said. 'I'll hold on to this, though I couldn't imagine ever needing it.'

'Well, that's just the point,' Holt replied. 'I hope you don't. But if you do, it'll be because you have needs you couldn't imagine.'

*   *   *

Julian was chastened by the disastrous consequences of his previous panicked response, and ensured Holt understood that his role was merely a watching brief until such time as hard decisions might be required. He told Holt only what he needed to know, the bottom line of which was that he could not afford the girl making contact with the woman who these days went by the name Veejay Khan. If that contact never took place, then further action might be counterproductive. It was possible, for all her passion, that the girl would fail. But if she reached her goal, it must prove a final one.

He got the call he was dreading at around two o'clock in the afternoon.

'Subject is en route to the primary address. No question that's the destination. ETA approximately twenty minutes. I need a decision. Do you wish me to proceed?'

There was no other choice. It wasn't about him, but about his family. About his life's work. His legacy.

He profoundly regretted that it had to be like this, but she was the one who had ignored his warnings, stirring that long-buried evil, summoning forth once more the demon of the woods. Didn't Hamish Queen's death prove to her that these matters should not have been disturbed?

'They mustn't be found together. Afterwards, I mean.'

'They won't be found,' Holt replied. 'Not ever.'

437

Dread Exploits

'Do you have a telescope?' Fallan asked Tessa. 'Or a pair of binoculars?'

'Yes,' she said, getting up and hurrying to a pine chest sitting in the corner, like a fort besieged by toys. She slid back the lid and rummaged for a moment, tossing out some waterproofs and then producing an expensive-looking pair of field glasses.

'I think these are fairly new. They're Jaffir's. He likes watching the wildlife.'

Fallan took them from her and popped off the lens caps.

'Don't suppose he likes shooting it too?' he asked.

'Oh, I see. No. There's an air rifle that belongs to my son, just for target shooting.'

'That may have to do.'

'Don't you have, you know, your wee emergency kit?' asked Jasmine.

'It's in the car.'

'So?'

'So that's why I need the binoculars.'

Fallan got Tessa to show them to one of the upper rooms, where he crouched at the side of the window, looking through the binoculars from the bottom-right corner of the pane.

Jasmine waited in the doorway while Tessa went off to retrieve her son's air rifle from his bedroom along the hall. She could see the mountainside rising beyond the rear of the house, the tree line climbing away to the left. What was he looking for?

Then, suddenly, she was sure she saw something

438

flare, which caused her to start and stumble against the doorframe.

'What?' asked Fallan.

'I saw a flash. Sorry, I was spooked and thought it might be a gunshot. It was actually more like something sparkling in the sunlight.'

'Where?' Fallan asked impatiently, beckoning her down close to the window.

She pointed.

'To the left. Just at the edge of the trees.'

Fallan scanned carefully with the binoculars, which moved in his hands across the most minute and steady of axes, like his wrists were precision-motorised. Then they stopped.

'Shit,' he said.

'What is it?'

'It's that prick who's been following us. I have no earthly idea how, given we were the only vehicle on about ten miles of single-track road, but somehow he's found us again. Tessa said Sanquhar was in Afghanistan, right? I'm guessing he met some private contractors, made some very useful connections. Some of these guys are psychopaths. Glorified hitmen. This one not so glorified.'

'So why can't we get in the car and make a run for it?' Jasmine asked, knowing she wasn't going to like the answer.

'Because he's dug in up there with a rifle trained on the back door. Probably been there a while already, but he'll be patient. I figure he's waiting for us to leave, and his plan is that when we do, he'll put the first round in my head as we walk to the car. You won't know why I've just fallen down, so you'll stand nice and still on the spot in confusion for a moment while he drops you too. After that, maybe

439

Tessa comes out to see what's going on. Maybe she runs for her car, and maybe he just saunters down the hill in his own time and takes her out up close, quick and clean. Then he washes away the bloodstains, slings the bodies in the back of his ride and buries us in the hills.'

'Jesus, Fallan, don't sugar-coat it. Is there a good news bit?'

'Not really. We got lucky as it is. The flash you saw was the reflection of a scope as he moved the weapon. Ideally he would have the sun behind him, but the angle of the hillside meant it was a choice between that and having the cover of the trees. He's playing the percentages. Lens flash is really only an issue if you're worried another sniper might shoot back.'

'How do you know this stuff? Don't answer that. What are we going to do?'

Tessa returned with the air rifle, which she was in the process of removing from a canvas carrying bag. It looked just like the one Callum Ross had taught Jasmine to shoot at Culfieth Hydro: single-shot, spring primed by breaking the barrel. That weapon had felt heavy and powerful in her hands, but she remembered him saying it 'wouldn't stop anything bigger than a rabbit'.

She looked at the puny little tin of pellets Tessa was holding, and thought of this man, whoever he was, who had been big enough to floor Fallan. She hadn't seen him, but he had to be just a bit larger than the average bunny.

Fallan took the gun, broke it and loaded a pellet.

'What are you hoping to do with that?' Jasmine asked.

'Only thing I can do: what every good mother

440

warns you about when you're playing with these things.'

Jasmine didn't follow, but Tessa was just such a good mother.

'Take his eye out,' she guessed. 'You'd have to get very close.'

'If I can flank him, I can get close enough. Maybe even close enough to rush him while his focus is on what he's looking at through his scope.'

'Fallan, this is the guy you took a beating from yesterday, when he *didn't* have a gun.'

'He got the drop on me. Saw me coming. This time it'll be the other way round. I need to get a handle on the terrain around here, though. Mrs Khan, do you have any maps?'

'I don't think so, but I can look.'

'The maps on my phone any good?' Jasmine asked.

'Better than nothing.'

She handed him her mobile and he began working the screen with his finger.

'"You have activated Friend Flag",' he read. "This service notifies—"'

'Yeah, it says that every time,' she told him. 'I don't know how to deactivate it, so just click to acknowledge.'

'No,' Fallan said. 'This is how the bastard always knows where we are. Your phone is effectively functioning as a GPS homing beacon.'

Fallan picked up the binoculars and looked again at their stalker.

'Guy's got his mobile right beside his rifle. He's using it as a range-finder. Your phone is telling him exactly how many metres away you are, so he can accurately zero his scope for the shot.'

441

Jasmine remembered Polly's friend Carol fiddling with her phone as they left Kave, wittering about all these social networking apps that she had but wasn't using.

'I'm sorry. I'd no idea.'

'No, this is good,' Fallan said. 'This is very good.' He turned to Tessa.

'You've got grandkids, right? I saw toys.'

'Three of them. They were just here at the weekend. God, what if this guy had come then?'

'Don't think about it,' he ordered her. 'Do you have any remote-controlled vehicles?'

'Yes. Connor's got this thing that bounces off the walls like it's got a mind of its own. What do you want it for?'

* * *

It was Jasmine's job to watch from the window, crouched with the binoculars close to the bottom of the frame, her focus fixed on the man in the camo gear who was making his way down the hill. He was going for it, aware his prey was on the move, possibly worried that there might be boats out of sight, the edge of the water not visible due to bushes, trees and the undulations of the land.

Fallan had taped her phone to this remote-controlled 'tumble-twister' car, then taken it outside to the front of the house and left Tessa to guide it. Upon his instructions, she kept it at walking speed, monitoring its progress from the upper tier of the split-level front room, from where she could see it make its way down the dusty pathway that led towards the loch. The toy vehicle had dual-axial motion systems, allowing it to navigate its way

442

over or around just about any obstacle, so it didn't get stuck in any potholes, ruts or even the cattle-grid she had expressed concerns about. There was going to come a point when she couldn't see it any more, upon which Fallan had advised her to simply keep the joystick pointed forward. Past a certain distance, as long as it was still moving, that was the main thing.

Fallan stood at the back door, awaiting Jasmine's cue. She watched the gunman continue his descent, alarmed by the pace of his progress, because the faster he moved, the smaller was Fallan's window. The gunman proceeded briskly but carefully, his torso maintaining the same level despite the rugged terrain. His legs were functioning as a suspension system, keeping the rifle in his hands rigidly horizontal at all times, like it was fixed to a steadicam rig.

He made a sharp diversion, avoiding a ditch or a stream, and for a moment she feared he was going to alter the vector of his approach so much that he'd miss the blind spot. Fortunately, once past the obstacle, he corrected again and resumed his previous trajectory.

He hit the mark Fallan had pointed out, and Jasmine gave him his call.

'Go, go, go.'

Jasmine felt her pulse thump as Fallan closed the distance between the back door and the passing place where the Mondeo was parked. He moved on swift but soft feet, muting his steps, the lightness of his tread belying his build.

The gunman had disappeared from view. He had entered a short valley between horizontal spurs where he was temporarily out of sight from the

443

house and, crucially, the house was out of sight to him.

Fallan had already popped open the boot by remote control. He crouched down at the rear of the vehicle and reached beneath the flap covering the spare wheel. Then he eased the lid gently back into a closed position and took cover behind the oil tank.

The gunman re-emerged into view only seconds later, a lot closer horizontally than Jasmine had estimated. She ducked down out of sight, spooked momentarily by how near he was. There was no need for binoculars now. She had to see, though. She edged her head up, slowly, terrified that when he came into view again he'd be looking straight back.

He wasn't. He had one hand on the stock of the rifle, and with the other he was checking his phone, anticipating possible corrections to his course.

He didn't anticipate it ending only a few yards further on, at the edge of the garden, just past that oil tank.

Fallan emerged behind him, unseen, unheard, silent and steady, his automatic levelled in two hands. From the window, Jasmine saw his finger twitch and a shot rang out across the hillside. The gunman jumped in startlement and not a little pain, clutching a hand reflexively to where his right ear had been nicked. But before he could turn to look at his assailant, Fallan had already ordered him not to move.

'Eyes front. Drop the rifle. Slow and steady. Drop it *now*. It's over.'

The gunman complied, letting the rifle fall to the ground. He placed his hands behind his head

444

and dropped to his knees unbidden in a gesture of surrender.

Jasmine scanned his features for determination and deceit, but she saw only resignation and annoyance, a man who understood the game he was playing and knew when he had just lost.

'Good lad,' Fallan told him. 'No need for anything desperate. Cops will be a lot more interested in Sanquhar than they are in you, so you can cut a deal. Play it smart. Don't make me shoot you. It's a long wait for an ambulance out here.'

Then he called out to Tessa to find something they could restrain him with. She produced several lengths of high-strength climbing cord belonging to her son.

Fallan ordered the prisoner to lie face down on the grass, keeping the automatic trained on him at all times.

'These ladies here are going to pat you down for further weapons,' he told him, 'then they're going to tie you up like a spatchcock chicken. And just in case you are entertaining any thoughts of how you might turn this situation to your advantage, bear in mind that prison will be even less fun if I've had to put a bullet through your wanking hand.'

Cloistered Flight

His Range Rover cruised the westbound lanes of the M8 for what he knew must be the last time, smooth and effortless as always, traffic ever more sparse the further out he travelled. He passed landmarks he would never see again: the twin towers of Mackintosh's Scotland Street school; the exit at Tradeston that he always took for Pacific Quay; grey high-rises and brown warehouses taking on a new poignant aesthetic for being part of what he was leaving behind.

On he drove, out past Braehead, Hillington, Renfrew, until ahead of him loomed the bridge that spanned the river Cart and took the traffic back down to the exit for Glasgow Airport.

Holt hadn't called.

He said he'd phone at eight with a sit rep, but the call never came. By that time, Julian already knew it was over.

His brother-in-law had phoned at around seven: his sister's husband, David. He informed Julian that he believed it was his rifle that had been used to kill Hamish Queen, apropos telling him that the police had been back in touch to confirm this.

'They wanted to know whether you had been to the house recently,' David said. 'And they were asking what kind of car you drove. Probably just formalities, but I thought I'd better give you the nod in case somebody's stitching you up.'

They had the rifle, they had his connection to its owner and they must have had a vehicle sighting too. Who knew what else.

'I'll call you at eight,' Holt had said. 'By then, everything will be dealt with, and if it's not I'll give you a new ETA. Either way, I'll call. But understand this: there is no fallback position from here on in. In the extremely unlikely event that you don't hear from me, it's not because I'm running late or it slipped my mind. It means the worst-case scenario is in play. As a precaution, you may want to pack a bag, look out your passport and liquidate

446

whatever funds you can. The likelihood is about ninety-nine point nine per cent that you won't need them, but it just depends on your attitude to risk.'

Julian had made his preparations quietly, laid out the documents and got into the Range Rover. His wife was out for the evening, watching Scottish Ballet at the Theatre Royal, so he was spared the agonising deceit of kissing her goodbye.

The lights of the airport shone and glimmered below him to the north, traffic in front of him slowing as it approached the exit coming up on his left. Julian put his foot down harder on the accelerator and glided right.

That wasn't where he was leaving from.

Sniper Down

Catherine was sitting on the decking at the back of the house, the rays of the early evening sunshine warming the back of her neck and refracting little spectra on the wooden table through the liquid prism of her gin and tonic.

The boys were inside playing *Portal 2*, which had supplanted *Trail of the Sniper* as Duncan's obsession of choice, and thus been the recipient of his unspent report-card funds. In fact, you probably couldn't have sold Duncan *Trail of the Sniper* for a pound now, as it was already regarded as 'pure ancient' among the summer-club cognoscenti.

She had given up on her attempts to get them to come outside, away from the computer, and decided she and Drew should just make the most of the peace and quiet instead. Her G&T was going down nicely, the sun was still strong and there was a smell of barbecue on the breeze, whetting her appetite for the steaks Drew had marinated. It was pretty close to bliss.

But . . .

'You've got that face,' Drew said, not concerned, but somewhere between solicitous and mildly taking the piss. 'Like you're just not quite satisfied. Is it because you didn't get to clap him in irons?'

'Can't help but feel that meant it lacked a certain closure,' she admitted.

'Pretty closed for him, right enough.'

Julian Sanquhar had killed himself before they could question him. He'd stopped his Range Rover halfway across the Erskine Bridge and thrown himself off. His body was found the following day, washed up near Dumbarton Rock.

Before leaving the house that night he had written a confession and left it on his desk. In it he admitted to the murder of a young actress called Tessa Garrion at Hamish Queen's family home of Kildrachan House, Balnavon, in 1981. The letter contained a hand-drawn map showing the location of the old well where he'd disposed of her remains. Excavations were ongoing, but even without a body they knew it was true. Records showed the local police had investigated reports of a suspicious incident at the time, but the case had been dropped. There had been question marks over the reliability of the witness who made the initial reports, and he later withdrew the statement anyway. Sanquhar had got away with it.

Nobody reported Tessa Garrion missing, not until her estranged sister hired Jasmine Sharp to find her three decades later.

Jasmine bloody Sharp.

Sanquhar also confessed to the accidental killing of Hamish Queen at Cragruthes Castle, confirming Catherine's deduction that the intended victim was Veejay Khan. Veronica Simpson, as she was then, had been making her way home from Kildrachan House on the night of the murder when she bumped into Sanquhar on the path through the woods. She claimed that was all she saw, but Sanquhar assumed otherwise, possibly labouring under this fear for decades. So when Jasmine Sharp began looking for the woman he'd killed, a woman nobody previously knew was even missing, he had tried to silence the only possible witness to his secret crime: first by trying to shoot her himself, then by hiring a mercenary he'd met in Afghanistan.

'Two murders solved for the price of one,' she acknowledged. 'High-profile killing gets wrapped up with a high-profile perp. Brass are delighted. Influence and privilege no impediment to justice, blah blah, blah. Big result. *Big* result. But something about it . . . I just don't know.'

'You never like getting anything handed to you on a plate,' Drew observed.

'That's because I don't like the possibility that the plate's been very carefully arranged before being handed to me. It's difficult to feel satisfied with my investigation, having discovered that the whole time I was three steps behind Jasmine Sharp. There's just something about that girl I don't trust.'

Catherine had questioned her in depth the morning after Sanquhar's suicide and the arrest, a few hours before that, of Len Holt. She'd wanted to strong-arm her a little about withholding information but they both knew Jasmine had done Catherine's job for her, so it would have just looked like she was over-compensating, not to mention graceless.

Everything Jasmine gave her was useful, it all added up. So why were Catherine's alarm bells going off the whole time?'

'Maybe it's the company she keeps,' suggested Drew, an insight born of familiarity with how just the mention of Fallan's name could set Catherine's teeth on edge.

He was right. Perhaps it was merely the presence of Fallan in this scenario that was raising her suspicions, affecting the readings on her bullshit detector like the proximity of a magnet affected a compass.

'I suspect you've nailed it,' she said. 'The girl's only known him a year, but already I can see a lot of Glen Fallan in her.'

Delivered

Mrs Petrie said nothing on the drive north. They had traded brief formalities at the airport, but after getting into Jasmine's car she didn't utter a word throughout the hundred and thirty miles to Ardnamurchan. She simply sat and stared, though Jasmine guessed her mind was far away from what she was seeing through the windows of the hired Renault Laguna.

Jasmine had actually ordered a brand new S-type Honda Civic, but she wouldn't be taking delivery of it for another tantalising few days. It was a good bit

450

over the budget she'd been considering, but she'd received a substantial payout in compensation for the damage to her mum's car, and not from the insurance company. (Her problems there looked like being resolved, due to her recently being able to call upon some more sympathetic policing involvement, but it hadn't been insured for much.)

Sanquhar's hitman, Len Holt, had turned out to be driving a black BMW X6. It was a four-wheeled grotesquerie, in whose case the acronym SUV ought to stand for Singularly Unnecessary Vehicle, but most significantly it wasn't a silver Volkswagen Passat, leaving the outstanding question of who had petrol-bombed her car.

Laura Geddes had got Traffic to look back at the CCTV images from the camera on Nitshill Road closest to the junction leading to her office. They found the Passat leaving, at speed, at the precise time and date Jasmine had specified. They got a plate and from there furnished Jasmine with a name and address, but this only confirmed what Fallan had already coaxed her to remember.

'You said you were spooked the first time you saw this vehicle, but I'm guessing it *wasn't* the first time you'd seen it. You had seen it before, and so when you became aware of it outside your office, something subconscious said "threat". On some previous occasion you briefly saw someone driving it, or getting in or out of it, and thought about the danger he represented. If somebody had asked you ten minutes later what this guy drove, you probably wouldn't remember. At the time you were focused on the person, but your subconscious registered the car he was in too.'

They went to his address, a small modern semi

in Baillieston, where the Passat sat outside in the driveway. Jasmine stood behind Fallan, keeping her head down and her face out of sight, and let him do the talking.

'We're here about the advert,' Fallan said, holding up a copy of that week's *Autotrader*, hot off the press.

'Advert?' he replied testily. 'I'm not selling my car.'

'Oh, I think you'll find that you are, Liam,' Fallan told him, at which point Jasmine stepped into view of the lecherous ODA whose career she had recently ended.

Liam tried to close the front door but Fallan was way too quick. He got an arm up his back and frogmarched him into his tip of a living room, Jasmine following them inside, reflecting that it would be quite an understatement to say the place needed a woman's touch.

'We know you petrol-bombed my colleague's Honda,' Fallan told him, plonking him down in a horrible armchair. 'There's CCTV footage of you driving away from the scene.'

Fallan opened the magazine at the appropriate page and dropped it in O'Hara's lap.

'At two years old that model goes for up to twelve grand. You're advertising at ten for a quick sale. You get the money to Jasmine within seven days and we don't take it any further.'

Liam looked up with a scowl.

'CCTV footage proves nothing. It would take more than that to convince the polis I had anything to do with it.'

Fallan gave a quiet little laugh. It sounded like knuckles cracking.

452

'I'm not worried about whether it convinces the polis. It's enough to convince me. Jasmine, would you give us a minute? I just need to explain some of the complexities to Liam here.'

Jasmine went outside to the Land Rover and Fallan followed a minute or so later. She didn't know what he did or said, but five days later O'Hara turned up at the office and handed her an envelope containing ten thousand pounds in cash.

Shoppiness ensued.

She toured a few showrooms, even did some test drives on other makes and models, but she always knew what she'd be buying.

Another few days and it would be hers.

The Laguna was a smooth ride, ideal for a long trip such as this one. She put on some music, soft and low, something to cover the silence. It was plain before they'd even made it to Erskine that there wasn't going to be any conversation.

As they crossed the great span of the bridge Jasmine glanced at the plunging forty-metre drop to the Clyde and wondered about Julian Sanquhar's final moments. By that time Mrs Petrie was already in another place, alone with her thoughts.

How did you prepare yourself for something like this?

Jasmine and Fallan had joked about how they might break it to her.

'Well, Mrs Petrie, the bad news is, you're going to have to attend your sister's funeral. The good news is, it won't be your sister you're burying.'

Ah, yes.

Sharp Investigations: conspiring to pervert the course of justice since . . .

It was Sanquhar's suicide that made it possible,

together with the confession he left behind. Otherwise the real Tessa Garrion would be going to jail, belatedly punished for the desperate acts of a frightened young woman in the aftermath of being raped.

'Why would he say he killed you and not Saffron?' Jasmine had asked her.

'Looking at his career knowing what I do now,' Tessa said, 'I think Julian spent his whole life trying to compensate for what he had done. He was at his best, probably at his happiest, when he was making things happen for other people: selfless and pragmatic. Perhaps this was his last chance to do that.'

'A final act of decency and yet a final act of deceit.'

'Yes. He's given me the only reparation he could, but it means there will never be any justice for poor Saffron.'

'There is no justice for the dead,' said Fallan. 'Sometimes that troubles us, but the truth is I've yet to hear one of them complain about it. In this case, all that truly matters is what's best for those who are still alive.'

Jasmine could see Tessa already waiting in the back garden as the Laguna crested the final spur, the small figures of three children buzzing around her like electrons as she stood and watched the road. From the rear of the house it was possible to spot a vehicle's approach from quite some distance, but Jasmine doubted she would have been able to see this one coming a few short weeks ago.

At the sight of the car making its final approach an attractive young woman came out and ushered the children indoors: Tessa's daughter-in-law,

454

Fiona. She entered the house just as Jaffir Khan left it, striding out to stand next to his wife for support.

Jasmine pulled into the driveway behind three other vehicles and climbed out of the Laguna. She was about to walk around and open the passenger-side door for her client, but Mrs Petrie was already out and walking towards her sister.

The last time Jasmine arrived at this garden, Tessa Garrion had collapsed under the weight of revelation. This time it was Mrs Petrie who stumbled, breaking down in tears as she fell against Tessa and threw her arms around her.

'My wee girl,' Alice Petrie said, sobbing, clinging, eyes shut tight. 'My wee girl. My wee girl.'

Jasmine felt the world freeze-frame for a moment. All of the evidence had been before her from the start, but only now did she understand.

The age difference of sixteen years. The resentment of the freedoms encouraged in Tessa but denied to her. The bitterness, born of harsh consequence, towards Tessa's confidence and ambition, her 'passion and impulse'. The easeful temptation of gradually losing touch and pretending as though she'd never existed.

And then the desperate, aching need to make this right while there was still time.

Tessa wasn't her sister.